More praise for
A CALCULATED RISK

"Ms. Neville makes it all the more plausible because of her intimate knowledge of how international banking works. She plots well and takes the reader through the intrigues and backbiting of immense corporations."

—*The New York Times Book Review*

"The author keeps her plot twisting and turning and manages to build up a fine degree of tension."

—*Los Angeles Times*

"Love and money; San Francisco, New York, the Greek islands; wheeling, dealing, and stealing from corrupt bankers and financiers: A CALCULATED RISK seems sure to generate substantial reader interest."

—*Booklist*

"Brimming with adventure and romance."

—*Milwaukee Journal*

By Katherine Neville
Published by The Random House Publishing Group:

THE EIGHT
A CALCULATED RISK
THE MAGIC CIRCLE
THE FIRE

A CALCULATED RISK

Katherine Neville

BALLANTINE BOOKS • NEW YORK

A Ballantine Book
Published by The Random House Publishing Group

Published in the United States by Ballantine Books, an imprint of The Random House Publishing Group, a division of Random House, Inc., New York, and simultaneously in Canada by Random House of Canada Limited, Toronto.

www.ballantinebooks.com

Printed in the United States of America

ISBN 978-0-345-38682-3

First Hardcover Edition: November 1992
First Mass Market Edition: April 1994

21

"If you give me time, I'll make my fortune."

—Jay Gould

"I shall be rich."

—Jay Cooke

"I'm bound to be rich! BOUND TO BE RICH!"

—John D. Rockefeller

"Oh, I'm rich! I'm rich!"

—Andrew Carnegie

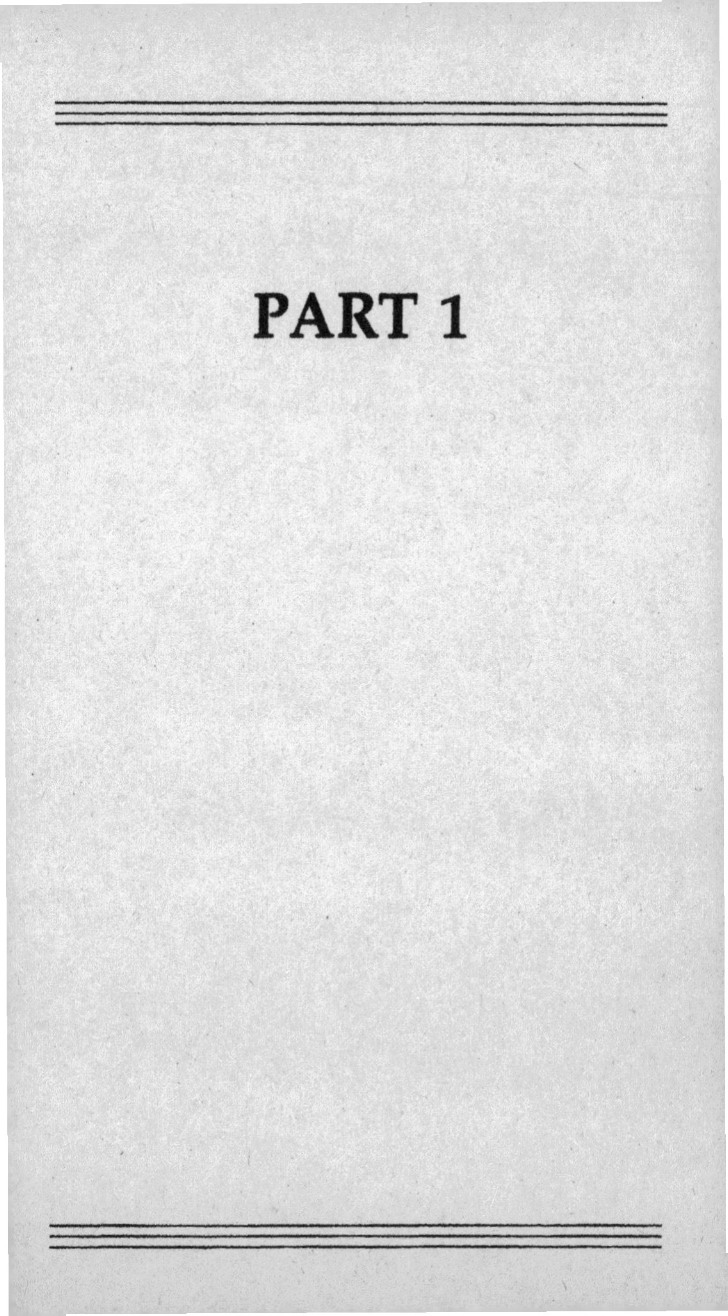

PART 1

Frankfurt, Germany
June 1815

IN A SHABBY OFFICE OVERLOOKING THE JUDENGASSE, A pale young man sat alone, watching the sun rise. He had been awake all night, and stacked before him were many cups containing the thick residue of bitter Turkish coffee. The ashes of a fire lay cold in the grate, but to light another fire seemed to him an unwarranted expense. He was a thrifty man.

The room was painfully bare, containing only a few chairs and a splintered desk. Against one wall was the small hearth, and opposite it a dirty window overlooking the street. Near the window stood a wooden structure that nearly covered the wall. It resembled a bookcase, but was divided into large cubbyholes, each with a doorlike flap of woven straw. All these doors stood open.

The only objects of value in the room were the rich chartreuse Moroccan-leather chair in which the man was seated, and the gold pocket watch that lay open before him on the desk. Both were well-worn. They, and the house in the Judengasse, were his father's bequest, and he would keep them always.

The Judengasse was the street where Jews were permitted to live and to eke out an existence as best they could. For many, that meant their changing and lending money. At this hour of the morning the street was still quiet, for the hawkers were not yet abroad. Soon the moneylenders would bring tables out into the street, and over the doors of their houses they would string up the brightly colored banners that proclaimed their business. In a few hours, the street would be filled with color and with the clamor of men trading gold.

The young man sat in silence, and as the sun rose he leaned forward to light his thin Turkish cigarette with a tallow candle. A small gray dove alighted on the ledge outside the open window. The bird cocked its head from side to side, adjusting its vision to the dim light. The man sat without moving, but in his blue eyes there was a strange gleam, as if a dark coal were being blown alive. It was a frightening look, one which many had cause to wish to forget.

The bird paused only a moment, then fluttered to one of the cubbyholes in the large structure near the window. It hopped through the opening, and the straw flap snapped shut behind it.

The man finished his cigarette and drained the dregs of his coffee. He picked up the gold watch. It was five-seventeen. He crossed the room and opened the door of the cage. Placing his hand carefully inside, he gently stroked the bird until it was calm; then, closing his hand over the creature, he took it from the cage.

Around the bird's leg was a small oiled-paper band that he carefully removed. On the paper, a single word was printed: Ghent.

■

GHENT WAS A WEEK'S HARD RIDE FROM FRANKFURT, and the countryside between was littered with the remnants of armies searching for one another through the forests of the Ardennes. But five days after he departed Frankfurt, the pale young man, weary and mud-spattered, hitched his horse to a polished brass ring outside a house in Ghent.

The house was dark, and he let himself in with a key

so as not to disturb the household. An old woman appeared on the landing in nightclothes, a candle in one hand. He spoke to her in German.

"Have Fritz take my horse around to the stable. After that, I wish to see him in the study."

Moonlight poured through the expansive mullioned windows of the study. Cut-glass decanters filled with liquor gleamed dully on the mahogany sideboard. Bunches of fresh-cut hollyhocks and gladiolus were arranged in deep vases, adorning the hand-rubbed marquetry tables placed about the room. A massive, carved pendulum clock stood beside the entry, and velvet-covered sofas were clustered near the marble fireplace. This room—so unlike the one he'd recently departed in Frankfurt—was kept immaculately, in constant anticipation of the owner's possible arrival.

He crossed to the windows, from which he had a perfect view of the townhouse opposite his own. The two houses were separated only by a small grape arbor. Both the parlor and drawing room of his neighbor faced the study where he stood, and he could clearly observe any activity there. He had taken this fully appointed house three months ago for that very reason.

He turned away and poured himself a cognac from the sideboard. He was weary, but he could not sleep—not yet. After nearly half an hour, the study doors opened and a large-boned man in rough clothing entered.

"Sire," he announced himself in thickly accented German, and paused for a response.

"Fritz, I am very tired." The voice was almost a whisper. "I must be certain that I know—I must know at once—if a messenger comes to that house. Is that clear?"

"Have no fear, sire, I shall remain here and watch. Any disturbance and I shall awaken you."

"There must be no mistake," the master said. "It is of the utmost importance."

Fritz waited by the windows throughout the night, but the house across the way lay silent in the moonlight. In the morning, the master arose, bathed and dressed, and came down to replace Fritz at his post in the study.

Their vigil continued for three days. The rains came and turned the countryside into pools of mud, making the roads nearly impassable. At the end of the third day, around suppertime, the old woman was just laying out a tray of food for the master when Fritz came in.

"Excuse, sire, but a man approaches—alone—by the eastern road from Bruxelles."

The other nodded, put back his napkin on the tray, and with a wave of his hand dismissed the two servants. Extinguishing the candle, he strode to the window and hid himself behind the damask draperies.

Within the neighboring house there was commotion. Several men bustled from room to room, lighting chandeliers and wall sconces with long blazing tapers. Soon the rooms glittered brilliantly, and through the dusk the watcher scanned the interior details: crystal that shimmered from the high-domed ceilings and dripped like diamonds from scalloped alcoves in the walls, furniture and draperies of richly embroidered tapestries in red and gold, mirrored walls and tables encrusted in gold leaf.

The pale young man tensed as he saw a single rider appear from the mist in the warm, wet twilight down the eastern road and approach the house opposite. The doors were thrown open and he was shown in at once, in his muddy cape and boots. The rider waited uncomfortably at the center of the room, turning his hat in his hands and gazing at the floor.

At last the inner doors burst open and a tall, heavyset man entered, surrounded by men and women who dropped back when they beheld the soiled and muddy horseman. The tall man paused expectantly, and the messenger bowed.

The observer at the window was scarcely breathing. He saw the messenger take two swift strides to the tall man and kneel as if in obeisance to a reigning monarch. The tall man stood in the center of the room, his head bowed, as one by one each person in the room came before him and knelt in the same fashion.

The pale young man closed his eyes. He stood for several minutes looking at nothing except his own inner vision. Then he turned and walked swiftly to the door.

Fritz was waiting outside, seated in a large chair in the foyer. He stood at once to attention.

"My horse," said the master softly, turning at once to ascend the broad staircase and gather his belongings.

He would not return to Ghent; his mission here had been accomplished.

■

HE DID NOT KNOW HOW MANY DAYS OR NIGHTS HE RODE through the rain-battered countryside. The land was like a marsh, and against the driving rain he could not tell where the sky ended and the ground began. His horse stumbled more than once, sucked down by the slimy mud that seemed to have no bottom. Although his body ached with weariness, still he drove on and on—he could not stop. He was headed to Ostend and the sea.

It was the evening of the second day when, wiping his eyes against the leaden sweep of rain, he made out the lights of Ostend flickering through the thick mist. As he approached he saw boats lashed down against the piers, great white waves smashing against the quay. All the town, it seemed, had gone indoors, and every house was shuttered against the weather.

Along the quay he found an inn that seemed likely to have seamen stopping there. The innkeeper kindly came out and took his horse to shelter. He went inside, drenched and weary, and ordered a brandy that he downed quickly as he sat beside the fire.

The sailors there were drinking hard whiskey and muttering sourly about the weather, for they were losing work and money each day the rains continued. The room was filled with the sweetish-sour smell of their tobacco. A few men turned away from their talk, idly interested in the newcomer who had broken the monotony of their long indoor confinement.

"Where do you come from in this godless weather, friend?" asked one.

"I come from Ghent, and I am bound for London," he replied. He used the French word *Londres*, for he observed that although they spoke in Flemish, most were French, and he wished to win those over. Romance mixed with pecuniary interest lay in every Frenchman's soul, while practicality alone made up the heart of the Flamand.

He held up three fingers sideways to the barman, to show he'd have more brandy and it should be poured that deep.

"It's been a week we've been stranded here," said another sailor. "Our goods are rotting on the docks and in the bellies of our ships. Yesterday, two whole piers were torn away and washed into the sea. Many boats have been lifted up and smashed upon the quay. You may be waiting here a good long while before the weather will permit you safe passage."

"I must pass to London—safely or not—and I must go tonight," he replied. "Which is man enough among you to bear me across the channel?"

The sailors laughed and slapped one another on the back and pinched each other's arms. This was a wonderful joke; they'd never seen so great a fool as the young man who stood before them.

The oldest of the seafarers was sitting near the fire. His face was as gnarled and brown as a walnut, and the others had cleared a space for him respectfully. The young man surmised he was a captain—perhaps the owner of his own ship.

"You'll not get a man at Ostend to bear you across the channel tonight, lad," the elder said sternly. "The sea is the mistress of a sailor, and tonight she's wilder than a jilted woman. You'll not find a man at Ostend who'd put his head on her bosom, with the mood she's in tonight!"

The others laughed at that, and someone had a pitcher of brew sent around. Each man took a healthy drink from it, as if to wash away the thought of putting out to sea in such weather. But as they laughed and drank, the captain looked with a clear eye upon the stranger, and thought he might hear more.

"What business is it that takes you to London?" he asked.

"It's a matter of gravest urgency," the young man replied, sensing he'd found an attentive ear. "I must cross the channel tonight. It will take none but a man of soul, spirit, and courage to get me there."

He looked at each man in the room until his eyes rested again upon the old captain.

"But heed the danger—"

"I must cross the channel tonight."

"You will surely die—a boat cannot get off the dock with waves such as these."

"I must cross the channel tonight," he said again, in a voice so soft and steady that the sailors stopped their laughter and, one by one, turned to stare at the mud-caked stranger in their midst. No one had ever seen a man so calmly announce his own death.

"Look here," said the captain at last, "if you must, then it's a thing worth more than life to you, for the sea will rise up and kill you, as sure as sure."

The young man stood there, his pale hair and skin transparent against the firelight, his eyes—not leaving those of the old man for a moment—as colorless and cold as the winter sea.

"Ah—it is the evil eye!" whispered the old man, and spat upon the floor to ward it off.

The rain smashed against the shuttered windows and doors. A piece of wood cracked and leaped off the hearth, and a few of the men jumped. They glanced about nervously as if a ghost had entered; but no one spoke.

The stranger broke the silence. His voice was soft and low, but each man in the room heard precisely what he said.

"I am prepared to pay five thousand French *livres*—in gold, and now—to the man who will bear me across the channel tonight."

A shock ran through the room; there wasn't a ship lashed to the piers outside that was worth so great a sum, unless fully laden with the finest goods. The price he'd stated might buy two ships outright.

The seamen tamped their pipes and looked into their tankards. He knew they were thinking of their families, how rich their wives and children would be with so much money, more than any man among them could earn in a lifetime. They were thinking it through, and he gave them time to do it. They were casting the odds—reviewing how their luck had been running of late and calculating the risk, whether any man might run the channel tonight and make it across alive.

"I tell you"—the captain cut the silence, his voice a bit too loud—"that if any man goes out in the channel on a night like this, it's suicide. Only the devil would tempt a Christian seafaring man this way—and no Christian would sell his soul to the devil for five thousand *livres*!"

The pale young man placed his brandy glass upon the mantelpiece and walked to the large oak table at the center of the room, where all could see him clearly.

"Then what of ten thousand?" he said softly.

He tossed a bag upon the table, and it broke open. The sailors watched in silence as the coins spilled across the table and clattered to the floor.

■

IN LONDON, A LIGHT MIST WAS FALLING.

When the doors of the stock exchange opened and its members filed in to take their places for the day's trading, a pale young man with cold blue eyes was among them. He removed his cape and left it and his gold-handled walking stick with the porter. Shaking hands with a few fellow members, he took his place.

Trading was erratic as British consols—war bonds—were being offered at large discounts. News of the war was bad. It was said that Blücher had been cut from his horse—his army had fallen to the French at Ligny—and that Arthur Wellesley, Duke of Wellington, was holed up in a miserable rain at Quatre-Bras, unable to pull his heavy artillery from the mud.

Things looked bad for the allies—for if the British under Wellesley fell as quickly as the Prussians had, Napoleon would be firmly entrenched in Europe again, just three short months after his escape from Elba. And the British consols that had again been drafted to finance a costly war would not be worth the paper they were printed on.

But one man in the room had fresher news. The pale young man stood quietly at his post and bought all the consols he could lay his hands upon. If his judgment proved wrong, he and his family would be ruined. But his judgment was based upon information, and information was power.

At Ghent, he had watched the messenger arrive from the battlefield at Waterloo and kneel before a tall, heavyset man as if he were regent. That simple gesture signified that the outcome of the war was in the hands of the British—not the French as everyone supposed. For the name of the tall man at Ghent was Louis Stanislaus Xavier, Comte de Provence. He was known to all Europe as Louis XVIII—King of France—deposed by the usurper Napoleon Bonaparte one hundred days earlier.

But such information was power only if used quickly and effectively. Braving ruin and fear of death in the channel, the young man had arrived here, at the London Stock Exchange, only hours before the news of the French defeat at Waterloo. But by the end of several hours' trading, he'd bought so many devalued consols that he'd attracted much attention.

"I say—what is the Jew up to today, buying all these consols?" one exchange member commented to another. "Has he not heard the news of Blücher's defeat at Ligny? Do you suppose he thinks a war can be won with half an army?"

"You might do well to follow him in the bidding, as I have," replied his acquaintance coolly. "It's been my experience, he is usually right."

When at last the news of Waterloo reached London,

it was soon learned that the young man had indeed cornered the market on consols—at less than ten percent of the face value.

The man who'd questioned his reasoning found his young colleague entering the exchange alone one morning.

"I say, Rothschild," he said, clapping him heartily on the shoulder, "you've done quite well in these consols of yours. It's said you've made over a million pounds in profits in less than a day!"

"Is it?" said the other.

"It's always said that you Jews have a talent for sniffing out opportunities for money, and that's why you have such large noses!" The man, whose bulbous red nose was larger by far than that of his companion, laughed. "But what I must know—from the horse's mouth as they say—is just this: Was it really Jewish intuition? Or did you know before all of London that Wellington had the battle in hand?"

"I knew," said Rothschild with a cold smile.

"You knew! But how the devil . . . did a little bird tell you?"

"That is precisely correct," Rothschild replied.

A NIGHT AT THE OPERA

Rheingold! Rarest gold!
O, might only thy purest magic
  waken again in the waves!
What is of value can only dwell in the waters!
Base and vile are those enthroned above!

—The Lament of the Rhein Maidens,
Richard Wagner,
DAS RHEINGOLD, Act I.

San Francisco

MORE MUSIC HAS BEEN WRITTEN ABOUT MONEY THAN about love—and often, with a happier ending and a catchier tune. Poverty might cause some to sing the blues, but wealth and greed seem to call for something on a larger scale: grand opera.

I knew well to what heights the souls of men were inspired by the theme of money. I was a banker. But to use the appropriate gender, I should call myself a "bankette"—a computer jock, and the highest-priced woman executive at the all-powerful Bank of the World.

If I hadn't been making so much money, I couldn't have afforded my box seat at the San Francisco Opera. And if I hadn't been sitting in that opera box that dreary night in November, I would never have come up with the idea. The idea was how to make more.

Grand opera is the last refuge of the wild capitalist. Nobody crazy enough to pay for it would dream of missing it. It's the only form of entertainment where so much money can be spent to see so much money being spent on so little entertainment.

It was a month before Christmas in the winter of the great rains; the rains washed even the fog away, and brought down mountains of mud, clogging the roads and bridges. Only fools would have ventured forth in weather like that. Naturally, the opera house was packed when I arrived.

I was dripping, literally, in velvet and pearls. There was no parking near the opera, so I'd had to slosh through water holes like a guerrilla in combat training. I was late and I was mad as a wet hen; neither condition had to do with the foul weather.

I'd just had a run-in with my boss. As usual, he'd shot me down—this time, in a way I was unlikely to forget. I was still trying to swallow my anger as I raced up the marble steps. The third bell was sounding as the white-gloved usher unlocked the door to my box.

Though I'd had the same seat for three seasons, I came and left so quickly I had time only for a nodding acquaintance with the others who shared the box. They were the sort who yelled *bravi* instead of *bravo*. They'd memorized every libretto and they always brought their own icer of champagne. If only I'd had time for that sort of commitment to anything at all but bloody banking.

I'm sure they thought it curious that I often arrived late and always alone. But as soon as I'd arrived at the bank ten years earlier, I'd learned that neither social life nor romance fared well in the pressure-cooker world of high finance. A bankette had to keep her eye on the bottom line.

I made my way to the front seat just as the lights were dimming, and sank into the upholstered chair. In the darkness, someone had the kindness to pass me a glass of champagne. I sipped the bubbly and hiked at my décolletage, which was drooping soggily as the curtain was rising.

The opera that evening was entirely appropriate to my mood: *Das Rheingold*, one of my favorites—the first of Wagner's massive, overwritten works in the *Ring of the Nibelungenlied.* It begins with the theft of precious gold from the depths of the Rhein. But the entire, four-opera *Ring* elaborates the ageless tale of corruption among the gods—who are so greedy they're willing to sacrifice their own immortality for a choice piece of real estate called Valhalla. At the end of the *Ring*, the gods are destroyed, and the palatial Valhalla goes up in a burst of flame.

I looked out over the glittering footlights into the murky blue depths of the Rhein. The dwarf Alberich had just stolen the gold, and the foolish Rhein maidens were splashing after him, trying to get it back. I gazed down over the audience: ghostly in jewels and satins and velvet, they seemed to float through cavernous treasure vaults deep beneath the river's floor. Actually, I realized, the San Francisco opera house itself strongly resembled an enormous bank vault—and that was precisely when the idea struck me: *I* knew as much about stealing as that wretched dwarf did! After all, I was a banker. And after today's events, I had plenty of motivation to do so.

As the dark waters of the Rhein vaporized into thin blue mist and the golden sun rose over the gods awakening on Valhalla, my mind clicked away like a calculator; I became obsessed with the idea. I was sure I knew how to steal a great deal of money, and I wanted to test it out at once.

Though there are no intermissions in *Das Rheingold*, when you have an opera box, you can, like royalty, come and go as you please. I had only to pop across the street to my office at the bank data center. I threw my soggy cape around my soggy gown and dripped my way down the marble steps and out into the Wagnerian night.

The streets were still shiny and wet, and the macadam looked like licorice. The lights of the passing cars reflected from the pavement's surface and, through the mist, gave me the eerie impression that they were driving upside down underwater.

I felt as if I were drowning, too. My spirits had been given a thorough soaking; I was sinking into the cesspool of my own career, going down for the third time. My manager was the dark cloud churning the waters.

Earlier that evening, when I'd dropped by my office

after a long day of harrowing meetings—ready now to head off to the opera—I'd found the lights turned off, the draperies drawn, and my boss sitting in darkness behind my desk. He was wearing sunglasses.

My boss was a senior vice-president of the Bank of the World—you can't get much higher than that. His name was Kislick Willingly III. And though my staff had created many imaginative names to call him behind his back, to his face most people called him Kiwi.

Kiwi had come from the heartland of America, the part I think of as the Interior, and he'd planned to be an engineer. A slide rule always hung from his belt, and he wore short-sleeved shirts with a plastic "pocket-saver" full of pens. He kept a mechanical drafting pencil there, in case he was called upon to draft something, and a gold fountain pen, in case he was called upon to sign something. He also carried colored markers so that when an idea struck him, he could dash into the nearest office and illustrate his thoughts on a wax board.

Kiwi was normally a cheerful and enthusiastic person, and he'd acquired his elevated position and salary by cheerfully and enthusiastically stabbing a great number of his colleagues in the back. In the banking business, this combination of enthusiasm and treachery is called "political savvy."

Kiwi had been on his high-school football team, and he still had the capacity to consume large quantities of beer; his stomach had expanded accordingly, so his shirttail often hung out of his pants as he barreled down the halls, off to sign something important.

His mother had insisted he give up football, beer, and the fantasy of becoming an engineer, and pursue a career in accounting—so he became a CPA. But he was unhappy as an accountant, which, I believe, brought out his dark side.

That dark side was something to be reckoned with, for Kiwi truly descended into states of darkness when he was thwarted or felt he couldn't have his own way. He'd take to wearing tinted sunglasses in the office and mirrored sunglasses on the street. He'd draw the draperies and turn out all the lights, conducting meetings in blackout mode. People like me can feel quite uncomfortable when forced to converse with a disembodied voice.

When such moods came over Kiwi, he'd slip into other people's offices, where he'd turn out the lights and sit in silence, in what he called a "state of incognito." It was in such a state that I'd found him in my own office earlier that evening.

"Don't turn on the lights, Banks," he muttered in the dark. "No one knows I'm here—I'm incognito."

"Okay," I said. And since his voice came from the chair behind my desk, I fumbled about for a seat across the room. "What's up, Kiwi?"

"You tell me," he replied petulantly, holding something aloft, large and rectangular, that I could just make out in the gloom. He tapped it with his finger. "This proposal, I believe, is your work?"

Kiwi could be unpleasant if he felt an employee had overstepped his bounds—especially if it meant the employee might get a share of the limelight Kiwi himself liked to bask in. I had, in fact, sent out a proposal to all of senior management only that morning, suggesting we beef up security on all computer systems that handled money and requesting the funds to do it.

I hadn't consulted Kiwi, since I knew he would reject any idea that wasn't his own. And the idea of security would never ignite his limited imagination; it wasn't glitzy or glamorous enough to advance his career—it was just good business. So I had end-run Kiwi by sending out the proposal without telling him first, and now he knew it. But I knew something he didn't, which made me smile secretly in the darkness—that was that any day, soon now, I would no longer be under his thumb.

Except for the formality of a background check and a written offer, I'd been technically accepted as director of security investigations for the Federal Reserve Bank—the insurance provider for every federally chartered financial institution in America. In a few weeks, I'd be assuming that responsibility—a job that would give me more clout over the financial industry than any female banker in America, perhaps in the world. And naturally, the first task I would set myself in that position would be to ensure that major money-center banks like the Bank of the World had adequate security to protect their investors' deposits.

The proposal I'd sent out today was just to get the ball rolling. And once I was at the Fed, Kiwi could hardly turn down my suggestions, as he had with every improvement I'd proposed in the past.

"The proposal *is* mine, sir," I admitted, still smiling to myself in the darkness. "I know that security is a subject very close to your heart." So were gas pains, I thought.

"Quite true." His voice in the dusk had a tone I didn't care for. "Which explains my surprise when I learned you'd put together a proposal without consulting me. I might have helped; after all, it's a manager's job to grease the wheels for his staff."

Translated, this meant that *I* worked for *him*, not the other way around, and that he knew more important people at the bank than I, whose wheels he could grease. But not for long—as I tried to remind myself while he ranted on. I was gloating so, that I nearly missed it when the hammer fell.

"I'm not the only one, Banks, who thinks you're your own worst enemy. The head of marketing has read your proposal, too. How's he supposed to *advertise* the fact that the bank needs to improve its security? What will our clients think if we say that? They'll pull their money out and cross the street to another institution! We can't waste funds on new systems like this, on things that won't attract a new and expanded client base. This lack of concern for the *business* side of banking has forced me to explain to the Fed that you're not the right candidate—"

"Pardon me?" I snapped to attention. There was a cold, icy lump forming in the pit of my stomach. I was hoping I hadn't heard correctly.

"They phoned this afternoon," he was saying as I

gripped the arms of my swivel chair. "I'd had no idea you were being considered for a position like that, Banks. You Indians should really keep your chief more informed. But of course, after this proposal fiasco, I had to tell them the truth—that you're just not ready . . . ."

Ready. *Ready?* What *was* I—a goddamned whistling teapot? Who was *he* to decide what I was ready for? I was so numb with shock, I could barely breathe—let alone speak.

"You're a brilliant technician, Banks," he was saying, in his let-me-rub-salt-in-those-wounds-for-you voice. "With proper guidance and a little patience, you could learn to be a halfway decent manager. But as long as you insist upon favoring sophistry over our grass-roots business needs, I'm afraid I can't give you the backing you'd like."

I heard him shredding my proposal—slowly, deliberately—in the gloom. I was speechless with fury. I felt my hands shaking, and was grateful he couldn't see them. Ten years, I'd worked toward this goal, and he'd crushed it all with a single phone chat. I counted to ten, and rose to leave; I'd never needed fresh air so badly in my life. I thought briefly of coshing his head with the bronze desk plate near my hand, but I wasn't sure I could find him in the suffocating darkness—I might miss, and I'd already had enough disappointments for one day.

As I reached the door he added, "I've bailed you out this time, Banks, and I've assured everyone you won't lose your head again by churning out foolish proposals. Besides, our security doesn't need improvement—our ship is as watertight as any in the industry."

So was the *Titanic*, I thought as I made my way to the executive powder room to change for the opera. I yanked the pearls out of my attaché case and tossed them on, staring all the while in the mirror at my drawn, white face.

I was still fuming now, more than an hour later, as I pushed my way back through the glass doors of the bank data center and stalked across the polished granite lobby. The guards were standing and chatting behind the massive control panel that ran the mantraps and electronic cameras all over the building. I suppose they took me for a bedraggled drunk who'd careened in off the streets, because one of them started toward me in alarm.

"Oh, that's all right," said the other, touching him on the arm. "That's Miss Banks; she lives here, don't you, ma'am?"

I agreed that I did indeed live in a goddamned data center.

That's what was wrong with me, I thought as I squished across the lobby to the elevator bays: I had the social life of an adding machine. I'd spent every waking hour in the last ten years eating, drinking, breathing, and sweating high finance—cutting out of my life everyone and everything that might interfere with my obsession and my goals.

But banking was in my blood; it was, after all, the family business. When my parents died, my grandfather—"Bibi"—had raised his granddaughter to be the first woman executive vice-president of a major financial institution. And now, in the space of a few short hours—during a self-elected opera entr'acte—I was likely, instead, to become the first female white-collar worker to knock over a world-class, money-center bank.

Of course, I thought as the elevator doors swished shut and I ascended to the thirteenth floor, I wasn't really planning on *stealing* any money. Not only do people question sudden wealth among bankers—because of my lofty position, for example, my own accounts were audited quarterly—but also, since I'd spent my life around it, money didn't mean all that much to me. Because I moved so much cash each day, I'd developed an esoteric awareness of the transitory nature of money.

It might sound odd to a nonbanker, but there are two big mistakes most people make about the nature and well-being of money. The first is to assume that money has some kind of intrinsic (or at least established) value. It hasn't. The second is that money can be physically protected by putting it in a bank vault or someplace for safekeeping. It can't.

To understand why not, you have to accept that money is nothing more than a symbol. The more money you move, and the faster you move it, the more symbolic it becomes: the harder it is to control its absolute value—or even its whereabouts. If big enough sums move from one place to another, and they move fast enough, they practically disappear.

Then, too, only the methods change in theft—not the concepts or the motives. People have been stealing since long before money was invented. But the more *portable* wealth becomes, the easier it is to steal; when cows were the medium of exchange, thieves had a real problem. With the advent of computers, however, cash has become so portable it barely exists, except as an electronic blip. I think of our age in high-tech banking as the Dawn of Fiduciary Symbolism—the era when money has become nothing more than tiny dots of light bouncing off satellites in space.

I should know how it worked; I was head of a group at the bank called Electronic Funds Transfer—or EFT. Our job was to move money, and there was a group like mine at every bank on earth that had a telex or a telephone. I knew what all these groups did, when they did it, and *how* they did it. I thought now that such knowledge might come in handy.

Naturally, you can't squeeze physical money through a phone line. The wire transfers we handled were just memos from one bank, authorizing another bank to take money out of the first bank's "correspondent account"—like writing a check. Most banks keep such accounts with other banks they regularly do business with; but if they don't, they must handle these transfers through a third bank where both hold accounts.

In the United States alone, about three hundred trillion dollars a year are moved through the wire transfer systems in this fashion—more than the total assets of all the banks in the country added together. Those banks have no idea how much cash they've paid out until they close at the end of each day and add up the total wires they've received.

There are also many countries whose governments are uneasy that money can fly across the border without passing the customs officials for taxes to be levied. Who knows whether some Iranian is moving money from Salzburg to San Jose a dozen times a day—and how can something be regulated that's happening with the confidentiality of a gentlemen's handshake in a private club? The rules governing banking have been around for aeons; the rules about wire transfers fill a three-by-five note card. If any banking activity needed better security, this was it. That's what I was banking on.

But like any banker with black ink in her veins, I never rushed blindly into new ventures. My grandfather, Benjamin Biddle Banks—Bibi—had taught me the rules of the game when I was four years old. "Always calculate the risk," he'd said. Too bad he hadn't followed his own advice. Bibi had owned a small chain of California banks he'd built from nothing. Though he was hardly in the same class as Wells Fargo, the Bank of America, or the Bank of the World, his little banks filled a need that no one else had met. Just after the great depression, when California was flooded with Hispanic migrant workers, Russian and Armenian immigrants, all looking for jobs, Bibi—through clever financing and unshakable principles—helped those people get on their feet, buy small plots of land for farms or ranches, and become the economic backbone that saved California from the fate suffered for decades by the rest of the civilized world.

In the 1960s, when conglomeration became a household word and my grandfather's chain went public, a group of midwestern businessmen quietly bought up his stock and—not so quietly—forced Bibi into a nonvoting, advisory job on his own board, where he could watch the blatant pillaging of the institution he'd spent a lifetime to build. He died within the year. That was the day I decided—bloodlines or no—that banking wasn't the career for me. I went to New York, studied data processing instead, and became a high-priced Manhattan technocrat.

It was the cruelest trick of a not-so-benevolent fate that the second company I worked for was bought in *another* leveraged buyout, just like the one that destroyed Bibi—but this time, by none other than the Bank of the World. I stayed for the transfer to San Francisco, because they made me an offer I couldn't refuse: money and power and the highest position ever held by a female executive—or any twenty-two-year-old—in the entire history of the bank. I was so impressed that I'd stayed ten years.

But they still treated me as if I needed a teacher's pass and an escort to go to the powder room. I'd sold my soul, and my grandfather's hopes and dreams, for a lifetime of reflected glory and a bronze plaque with a title on my desk. Instead of reading "Verity Banks, Vice-President," it should have read "The Whore of Banking," I thought. But it was never too late to change the cards fate had dealt you. Bibi had told me that, too, and I thought he was right.

Furthermore, I now had the right cards up my sleeve.

■

MY PLAN WAS TO BREAK THROUGH THE AUTOMATED security systems, get into the wire transfer system, and move some money to a place where no one could find it—then blow the whistle and point out to everyone how easy it had been.

A banker's first responsibility is to safeguard the money that others entrust to him. If I could cut through bank security like a hot knife through butter, and get my hands on actual dough, it would not only freeze the sneer on Kiwi's face—it would prove that the very problem existed that the Fed had wanted to hire me to solve. But to do it, I was going to need some help.

I had a friend in New York who knew more about stealing money than most bankers know about managing it—someone who had access to all the FBI criminal records, interstate police dossiers, and even some Interpol files. His name was Charles, and I'd known him for twelve years. Whether this surly prima donna would share his data with me—especially when he learned how I planned to use it—was another question.

Though it was nearly midnight New York time, I knew he'd still be up. Charles owed me more than one favor: I'd once saved his job and maybe even saved his life. Now the time had come to call in the debt. He ought to be grateful, I thought as I crossed the dimly lit floor of the data center from the elevators to my office.

But gratitude was not a word in Charles's vocabulary.

"This idea stinks," he told me with his usual reticence, when I explained what I had in mind. "The probability of your success is 1.157 percent greater than that of a snowball in hell."

My idea, in a nutshell, was to "kite" wire transfers. Most people, at one time or another, have kited a check—usually without realizing that what they're doing is illegal. You go to the supermarket on Saturday and cash a check for twenty dollars, though you don't have the funds in your account to cover it. On Monday, before the check clears your bank, you cash *another* check—perhaps for thirty dollars this time—using twenty of it to cover the *first* check. And so on.

The only thing that prevents more people from playing this kind of roulette is that merchants these days can cash checks faster than we check-kiters can get to the bank to cover them. To stay ahead of the game and build up a whopping big sum, you need to keep track of exactly how long it takes for each bad check to reach your bank account so you can get there first. Conveniently—when it came to the wire transfer systems at the Bank of the World—such information was not only managed by computer, but the systems that managed it were mine.

I didn't need Charles to tell me whether he liked my idea or not. I wanted him to tell me the probability of my success, using information he already had at his fingertips. For instance, how many "dummy" bank accounts should I set up to stash the dough? How many wire transfers should I "borrow" and return at any given time? How much money could I juggle in the air, without fear it would all come crashing down? And finally—how long could I get away with this game without getting caught?

To get the answers to these questions, I was willing to wait all night, regardless what sort of games Charles might choose to play. I sat, waiting for him to work his way into the right frame of mind, and I tapped my fingers on my government-issue, wood-veneer desk as I let my eyes wander around my office.

I had to admit that for a place where I spent, on average, a good twelve hours a day, it didn't look lived in. At night, as now, under the fluorescent light, it seemed ghastly—a mausoleum. There was nothing at all on the built-in shelves; the single window looked out on the concrete wall of the opposite building. My only decor was the pile of books on the floor that I'd never bothered to shelve in the three years I'd been in this space. It was what one might call austere; I resolved to get a plant.

Charles broke in on my observations, to share a few of his own.

"Statistically," he informed me, "women are more successful thieves than men. You commit more white-collar crimes—but fewer of you get caught."

"Misogynist," I said.

"Does not compute," Charles replied. "I only report the facts as I see them. I don't make value judgments."

I was about to retort in kind, when he added petulantly, "I've run the risk factors you asked me for. Shall I give them to you—or do you want me to analyze them, too?"

I glanced at the wall clock; it was after ten, which meant after one A.M. in New York. I hated to offend Charles, but he was slow as molasses—I doubted he could analyze his belly button in the time we had left.

As if my thoughts had been overheard by Divine Providence, a message was tapping itself out on my console:

"WE'RE TAKING HIM DOWN IN FIVE—PLEASE CLEAN UP."

It was well past Charles's bedtime, and his machine operators back in New York seemed to be shutting him down, as they did each night, for preventive maintenance.

"I NEED TEN," I typed in impatiently. "HOLD YOUR HORSES."

"MAINTENANCE WAS SCHEDULED AT 0100. WE NEED SLEEP TOO MADEMOISELLE. BUT BONNIE CHARLIE MISSES YOU. TAKE TEN, FRISCO. BEST REGARDS—BOBBSEY TWINS."

Frisco indeed, I thought, as I "saved off" as fast as I could the work Charles had calculated for me. Charles might only be a million-dollar chunk of hardware, but sometimes computers have more valuable insights than people. I slipped the diskette into my sequined evening bag.

As I was about to log off the system, I remembered to print out my computer "mail messages" for the day, which my earlier chat with Kiwi had made me forget. Just before I shut down, Charles's operators added a cheery last note on my screen:

"INTERESTING INQUIRY, FRISCO. PURELY THEORETICAL OF COURSE?"

"NO TIME TO CHAT—AND THOSE IN THE KNOW CALL IT SAN FRANCISCO," I typed back. "I HAVE A NIGHT AT THE OPERA. TA-TA FOR NOW."

"A NIGHT AT THE OPERA—A DAY AT THE BANK? T.T.F.N.," they replied, and a blank screen came up.

I went out into the cold, wet night and headed back to the opera. The champagne was lousy at the opera, but the Irish coffee was terrific. I ordered one before I went back to my box, and was sipping the whipped cream off the top as I watched the gods walk over the rainbow bridge and enter Valhalla. The golden strains of music wafted over me and the whiskey warmed my bones. I mellowed so much that I nearly forgot about

Kiwi, my aborted job, my ruined career, my failed life—my idiotic idea of retribution by showing up the entire banking system. Who was I kidding? But that was before I looked at the note.

The crescendos of music were rolling over the footlights in waves as I glanced at the crumpled wet piece of paper containing those mail messages I'd printed off just as I'd left my office. There were the usual—my tailor, my caterer, my dentist, a few from my staff—and one that, the time stamp indicated, had come in just *after* I'd finished talking with Charles in New York. I could feel the slow, heavy throb in my ears as I read the last message:

If you want to discuss your project, do call.

—As always,
Alan Turing.

This was disturbing on two counts. First, Alan Turing was a pretty famous fellow—a computer wizard and a mathematician—and he didn't know me from Adam. Second, he'd been dead for close to forty years.

A DAY AT THE BANK

An organized money market has many advantages. But it is not a school of social ethics or political responsibility.

—*R. H. Tawney*

IT CAME TO ME IN A FLASH THAT NEXT MORNING AFTER my night at the opera—as I stood drinking orange juice under a scalding shower—who Alan Turing, the phantom phone caller, really was.

Turing—the real one—was a math whiz from Cambridge who went on to develop some of the earliest digital computers. In his short life, only forty-one years, he became one of the leading figures in British data processing, and was widely regarded as the father of artificial intelligence.

Most computer types had read his works at some time or another—but I knew someone who was such an expert, he'd lectured on them. He was one of the foremost computer gurus in the United States—a technocrat of the first water.

He'd been my mentor twelve years earlier, when I'd first gone to New York. He was the most reclusive person I'd met—a man of a thousand faces and as many accomplishments. I might know more about him than anyone else did, but what I knew could barely fill a page. Though I hadn't seen him in years, and heard from him only rarely, he'd been the most important influence in my career and—other than Bibi—the largest in my life. His name was Dr. Zoltan Tor.

Everyone in computers knew the name: Tor was the father of networking, and had written the classic texts on communications theory. So famous was he, that younger people, reading the classics he'd written, imagined him to be long dead. Though he was not yet forty, and in strapping good health.

But now that he'd phoned—after all these years—how long was *my* health going to last? Whenever Tor decided to involve himself in my life, I got into trouble. Perhaps trouble was not the right word, I thought as I stepped from the shower. The word was danger.

Among Tor's many accomplishments was his mastery of cryptography. He'd written a work about it that was committed to memory by all research associates of the FBI. That's why I was nervous, because the book covered every aspect of the art of cracking computer codes, "hacking," stealing information—and it told how such thefts might be prevented.

Why was Tor/Turing phoning now? How could he have learned so quickly what sort of "research" I'd been up to last night? It was almost as if he could read my mind over three thousand miles, and already knew what I was thinking of doing. I decided I'd better find out—and quickly—what he thought about what I'd been thinking.

But first I had to find him. Not simple, given a chap who didn't believe in phones or mailing addresses, or in leaving messages under his own name.

Tor owned a company through which he handled financial transactions; it was called Delphic Group, after the oracle, no doubt, but its number wasn't listed in the Manhattan phone directory. That was okay because I had the number.

Tor never visited his office, however, and when you called there, you got a strange response. I gave it a try.

"Delphic," the receptionist snapped, not lavish with information.

"I'm trying to reach Dr. Tor—Dr. Zoltan Tor. Is he there?" Fat chance.

"Sorry," she said, not sounding it, "you've dialed the wrong number. Check your listing, please." It was like the goddamned CIA.

"Well, if you hear from someone whose name *sounds*

like that, will you give him the message?" I said impatiently.

"What message are you referring to?"

"Tell him Verity Banks phoned," I snapped, and slammed the phone down before she could ask me to spell or repeat it.

The veil of secrecy that shrouded Tor's life—more impenetrable than the security systems of the world banking community—was as annoying to me as, ten years ago, his constant interference in my life had been.

Meanwhile, I had a job to do. It was nine o'clock by the time I'd dressed, gone downstairs, pulled my battered BMW out into the thick soup of San Francisco fog, and headed to work—keeping bankers' hours. I made it a practice always to rise at the crack of dawn; but in winter, dawn doesn't crack until eight-thirty. I had the oddest feeling that—late start or no—it was going to be a very long day.

■

THE BANKING PROFESSION WAS RIDDLED WITH CONSULtants as a leper was riddled with sores. At the Bank of the World, we had efficiency experts to tell us how to manage our time, industrial engineers who told us how to manage our work, and industrial psychologists who helped us manage our environment. I never paid attention to any of them.

I wasn't interested, for example, in those studies showing that bankers derived an aura of power from wearing gray flannel suits. I preferred to dress as if I owned the bank, and had only dropped in to see how my dividends were doing.

I arrived at the office that morning wearing enough yards of midnight-blue silk to upholster a sofa. The garment looked like a simple tunic, but I'd been assured that the best minds of Milan had labored to exhaustion over it. So much for the dress code.

My staff didn't take such things seriously, either. As I stepped onto the thirteenth floor they were flying about in jeans and sneakers, wearing T-shirts that said things like "Good Thruput" and "Cold-Started."

I thought of the thirteenth floor as the trading floor. It was a rats' maze of modular units supposedly designed to induce an "atmosphere of problem sharing"—all done in "tranquilizing" blue . . . against a backdrop of "exhilarating" electric-orange carpeting. As far as I could tell, the combination produced schizophrenia—but then, computer types aren't all that normal, anyway.

I had learned the way through the maze to my office, and I went in and closed the door until my secretary, Pavel, could bring me a cup of coffee. Pavel was tall, dark, and handsome, with the manners of a diplomatic aide. He might have been a movie star, and was, in fact, studying by night to be an actor. He claimed that his job at the bank gave him exposure to life in its most primitive emotional state.

Everyone I worked with knew about the "two-cup rule": that I could not be communicated with until after two cups of coffee, or ten o'clock in the morning—whichever came first. Until then, I could receive, but could not transmit.

Pavel tiptoed in with the coffee and closed the door softly behind him. He placed the cup before me on the desk.

"Lukewarm, just the way you like it," he promised me. "You have three meetings today. I put them on your calendar. And do you still want the small conference room reserved for four o'clock? You can just nod if it's okay."

"Cancel the meetings," I told him as he looked at me with wide eyes. "I've already had enough coffee this morning to float a kidney. Kiwi canceled my proposal last night." Since no one knew about my job at the Fed, I thought it prudent not to mention that part.

"I figured as much," Pavel said in a breathless whisper, pushing back the rolled-up sleeves of his silk sweater. "I saw the shredded version in your trash basket this morning when I came in." He took a seat opposite me. He looked so worried, leaning forward with his chin cupped in his hands, that I smiled. "What are you going to do?" he asked.

"A new proposal," I said. "Bring me the red-tape file; I want every boring rule book at the bank."

Pavel grinned widely, and headed for the door, pausing only to raise his fist aloft.

"Power to the plebeians," he said. "Hoist them with their own horseshit."

■

KNOWING THE RULES—IN BANKING AS IN CRICKET—was the name of the game. *Playing* by the rules was something else again.

Some people say that rules are made to be broken, but I've never thought so. Rules are like flagpoles in a slalom race: you observe their presence religiously, skirt around them as closely as possible, and never let them cut your speed.

The Bank of the World was a very big bank—perhaps, as its name suggested, the biggest bank in the world. Because of its size, the bank had plenty of rules—so many that no one had time to read them all, much less to follow them.

There were whole departments whose sole function was to churn out new rules, and often they quarreled with each other over whose rules were the "official" ones. My desk was buried each week under new standards and procedures from groups I'd never heard of. The documents were duly filed by Pavel in the red-tape file, and promptly forgotten. I knew I'd find, amid all those reams of bureaucratic bullshit, something suitable to my purpose. After all, if there were so many conflicting rules governing the *managing* of money, there must be one that would enable me to *steal* some and prove Kiwi to be the irresponsible fool I knew he was.

It took the better half of the day before I found it: a packet of brand-new procedures from Wholesale Information Planning Systems, or "WHIPS," as they liked to call themselves. I knew the WHIPS group well; they were the most prolific policy setters at the bank. They'd set a record for producing useless paper. In this case, however, I felt sure there'd be an excellent use for their freshly hatched policy. It took a bit of imagination, but fantasy was always my strong suit. The first words that caught my eye were: "This methodology was used with great success at United Trust, to test their security systems."

How convenient.

It was a method known as Theory Z. I already knew plenty about it; it made me want to vomit. It was an import from Japan, and when it had first been touted in the business journals as the latest management vogue, I'd thought it was the most ruthless attack by the Japanese since Pearl Harbor. But now that I was a theoretical thief, Theory Z took on a whole new color. The color was rose.

The general idea was that managers were wholly unnecessary; everything in Japan, we were told, was carried out by little faceless teams called quality circles. They did everything required to make a product—designed it, built it, tested it—and all decisions were made by mutual consent: management by committee. The banking community loved it, they embraced it, they practically *enshrined* it. But they weren't really sure exactly what to *do* with it.

I thought I could tell them.

I buzzed Pavel and asked him to get United Trust on the phone, pronto, and connect me with their head of security systems. He'd only have to say, in his golden voice, that the Bank of the World was calling, and they'd jump to. Money talks—and the bank was as rich as Croesus, even in a bear market.

Pavel buzzed me back with the news that the security head was on the line. "He's a veep, and the guy's name—I swear—is Mr. Peacock."

"Yes, Ms. Banks," Peacock's voice bounded exuberantly over the line. (New York bankers always address you as "Ms."—they're really with it in New York.) "We *do* use Theory Z here; we use a quality circle to test *all* our systems. We put our best and brightest in this group.''

According to Mr. Peacock, his quality circle was trying to break through security and fiddle about with the money—trying to trick the security and control systems, to see if they were smart enough to catch them. The reports of his findings must have been pretty hot stuff.

''For security testing, the name of our quality circle is the SADO team,'' he told me. ''It stands for Search and Destroy On-line!'' He bellowed with laughter. (A trait in our industry is to turn everything into an acronym. I refer to this as the BOME—the Bane of My Existence.)

''So far,'' he went on, ''we've managed to crack our confidential customer password files, we've pulled off two active taps, and we planted a logic bomb only last week—we're still waiting for the explosion! Ha-ha.''

These things were far from mysterious; an active tap means you tap into a phone line while data (read ''money'') is being moved, and alter the transaction—change the amount, or make it payable to your account—as opposed to a passive tap, where you ''borrow'' someone's bank account number and password and take his money.

A logic bomb is more interesting, but you must have access to the computer to do it; you fix the system so that at a certain moment in the future it will suddenly do something it's never done before—like depositing money in your account, as a random example.

I was glad Mr. Peacock was so eager to share his experience with a total stranger. But I'd learned what I needed to know, and it had little to do with the success of his work.

I'd be sending out a new proposal tonight. A new idea deserved a new audience—and this one was a dilly: the Managing Committee, the group of big cheeses who decided how budgets would be spent at the bank. Their authority transcended all departments—including Kiwi's—and though *he* didn't sit on the committee, his *boss* was its chairman.

Using the information Charles had provided me the night before, I built my case. Were they concerned about the defenseless position of our systems? They should be, I told them—even a six-year-old kid could crack our files! But *known* computer crimes were only the tip of the iceberg; how many crimes had gone unreported? Bankers ought to know the answer to that better than anyone, I thought. *They* were the ones who didn't report the crimes. Depositors wouldn't like to learn that the cash they thought was behind twelve feet of concrete and steel was in fact being shot around the world on telephone wires, with all the security of a transatlantic call.

Once I'd whipped up their fears, I hit high gear: we had the technique, right here at the bank, to solve this dire problem—Theory Z, that wonderful method used so successfully by the Japanese!—a technique that was now *official policy*, with rave reviews, at major New York banks like United Trust. If the Managing Committee would approve my funding, I'd personally pick the experts and break into our own security, just like that. After all—how else was I going to do it?

I felt wonderful as I handed the proposal to Pavel in an envelope and asked him to stamp every copy urgent and confidential, and to get them out that night. I was confident no one on the committee would oppose it—it found use for a new theory and solved an old problem. Opposing it would be like putting the squelch on mothers and apple pie. Far from being victimized or suspected as a potential thief, I might actually be awarded laurels for ripping off the money and then handing it back with a flourish: Verity Banks, electronic bankette.

■

I'D AVOIDED KIWI BY STAYING LOCKED IN MY OFFICE all day. At eight P.M., I pulled on my trench coat, stuffed my work in my shoulder bag, and took the elevator down to the garage. It was dark and deserted, but I knew there were seeing-eye cameras everywhere, so if someone mugged me, the guys upstairs at the security desk could watch it in comfort. I drove up the ramp, popped my badge in the scanner, waited for the big steel gates to swing open, then drove through the fog-thick streets toward home.

When I pulled up before my building, the black streets were still wet with rain. It took quite a while to find a parking slot, but at last I got inside the lighted marble foyer and took the elevator to the penthouse.

I never turned on the lights when I came home. I loved to see the silhouettes of my myriad orchids against the distant lights of the city. Almost everything in my apartment was white—the plumpy sofas, the thick carpets, the lacquered étagères. The tables were thick wedges of glass, and on them were big glass bowls floating white gardenias.

Entering the apartment, one had the feeling of falling through space. The city glittered and shimmered in perpetual mist through the walls of glass, and the white orchids tumbled everywhere, like a jungle climbing up through a cloud.

As much as I loved it, I rarely brought others here. My apartment got mixed reviews and I knew many thought it was a mausoleum or museum to my own isolation. The white womb. And in a way, that's exactly what it was. I'd worked my ass off for everything I'd earned. And I spent it on what I valued—peace and solitude. A city mountaintop.

After dinner, I spent the time needed with Charles, to finish calculating the risk. I already knew I was talking about enormous sums of money. Billions a day moved through the bank's wire systems, and though it couldn't all disappear at once without being missed, I knew I could juggle a big chunk of that money for extended periods. The question was, how big a chunk? And how should I spread it around to best conceal my activities?

I also wanted to see how much the risk increased, from the perspective of international crime apprehension—which was why I'd gone to Charles in the first place. He could give me data about the number of crimes per year, audits per year, and the kinds of crimes disclosed through audit or by other means. After jotting some notes from last night's chat with Charles, I was ready to begin:

"GIVE ME THE SPREAD ON DOMESTIC ELECTRONIC MISAPPROPRIATIONS ON A FIVE-YEAR PLOT," I tapped in.

"YOU MAY SPEAK IN ENGLISH," said Charles. "I'M A USER-FRIENDLY MACHINE."

"HOW MUCH MONEY HAS BEEN STOLEN IN THE LAST FIVE YEARS USING COMPUTERS?"

"STOLEN FROM WHERE?" asked Charles. My patience was beginning to wear thin.

"DOMESTIC," I repeated, banging my fingers down on the keys.

"YOU WANT TO KNOW HOW MUCH MONEY'S BEEN STOLEN FROM PEOPLE'S *HOMES?*" he asked innocuously. Wise-ass.

"WITHIN THE CONTINENTAL UNITED STATES OF AMERICA," I said. "DON'T PLAY GAMES."

"I AM TRAINED TO SCAN FOR LOGIC—NOT FOR HIDDEN MEANING," Charles pointed out.

He went off to tax his brain—a rather rusty one, I had to admit. He was a computer of ancient but rare vintage, and despite his personality, I couldn't help hoping he'd still be in service a dozen years hence. I knew exactly how old Charles was; I'd known him most of his life. In fact, if it weren't for me, he wouldn't be alive today.

When I'd finished school twelve years earlier, my first job had been with the gigantic New York computer company Monolith Corp. Like most programmers, I was always searching for an all-night data center where I could get time on the big machines; and one day I found one as I was flipping through our massive *Data Center Guide to Manhattan.* It was called the Scientific Data Center—and judging by the address, no one in his right mind would go up there at night.

That evening, I took a cab to the small, grimy office building sandwiched between dark and foreboding warehouses, not far from the waterfront at East End. There was no night guard—not even a door buzzer—only a hand-pulled elevator that I found off the alleyway at the rear. Hoisting myself to the sixth floor, where the center was allegedly located, I found the sorry little room.

The space was barely large enough to squeeze in all the computers—you had to climb over them to get at the drives—and bunches of cable were hanging everywhere, even from the ceiling. There was an inch deep of soot over all; it looked like a cross between a car repair shop and a spaghetti factory. How could machines keep running in all that filth and disorder?

The night operators—two Brits, both named Harris—were amazed and thrilled to see me there. No one had visited this center in years, and they spent each lonely night playing chess, Go, and mah-jongg with the computers.

The center itself, as I learned, was actually an archive for the United States government—its only client—and had been accumulating data, year after year, through some forgotten regulation requiring off-site backup of historical government records.

That was the night I first met Charles—Charles the bonny, Charles the fair, Charles whose wonderful, earth-shattering repository of knowledge would keep me dazzled for years. And no one knew that he was there at all—or what his existence was worth—but me!

Over the years, Charles's data on transportation, banking, and a half-dozen other government-regulated industries had helped me with a myriad of jobs. My clients thought I was a genius when I pulled from thin air those impressive figures that should have called for years of research.

When Charles "came down" each night at one o'clock, the Harrises would leave and take a meal with me at a shabby Italian restaurant down the street, whose neon sign provided the only light on the dismal block.

Through a chicken-wire fence beside the table, we watched old men playing bocci for bottles of cheap Chianti; we ate pasta and veal parmigiana, and sang old Neapolitan street songs. And it was there—nearly a year later—that the Harrises told me in hushed whispers that Charles's life was about to end.

Machines do not grow old as people do—with their loved ones and lawyers clustered about their bedside awaiting the last gasp. Charles's model number had come up on the official "obsolescence list"—which meant that one day soon, with little fanfare, he'd be picked up, thrown in the back of a truck, and hauled off to a company that would "reclaim" the precious metals in his wiring and sell off the rest of him for scrap. It seemed a sorry fate for a computer as wonderful as Charles. And not only that; if Charles were scrapped, a *new* machine would be installed in his place, and someone might learn what a gold mine of data he had tucked away in his little core banks.

So, one morning, I went into the contracts department at Monolith Corp., pulled all the paperwork on Charles, and stamped it sold to the U.S. government. Voilà! Charles disappeared from the list of corporate fixed assets. I predated his "sale" to the previous year so that no one would notice it during this year's audit. The government would still pay for operating the center—a monthly rate, with the cost of Charles built into the price of the service. And Monolith Corp. would still maintain the facility—thinking the government now owned Charles, and was continuing to pay them only for service and premises.

Looking back, I found that the acquisition of Charles was my first illegal act. He'd been reborn, thanks to me, into a life of crime, so it wasn't surprising that now he was helping me to plot another.

■

BUT AS VALUABLE AS HIS DATA MIGHT BE, SPEED WAS scarcely Charles's middle name. It was well past his bedtime by the time he'd finished chunking out the one-page bits of graphs I'd requested, and I *still* had to paste them together by hand to see what they said:

Of $25 million in known computer thefts that had taken place over the last five years, only $5 million had been recovered. Across the top of my chart I'd printed a schedule in weeks—fifty-two—for one year. Down the side of the chart were bank accounts, by thousands, from one to fifty. The numbers Charles had printed across the page showed how much money (per week) I could deposit in each block of one thousand accounts. Over the top of all this—in little red X's—Charles had printed the graph that showed risk, by weeks and by dollar volume. The graph went off the page when I hit $10 million—not bad for a few months' work.

I poured myself a cognac and sat in darkness, watching the lights of a small boat as it sailed back from Tiburon to the San Francisco harbor. The fog had thinned, but I couldn't see the stars. It was altogether a lovely night to be alive, and in San Francisco. At such a moment, it was impossible even to imagine the brink of the decision upon which my life was now suspended. I chose not to think of it at all.

Suddenly, the phone rang, jiggling a few blossoms off the cymbidium on the glass table. I spilled a drop of brandy and wiped it away with my finger—then picked up the phone.

"Hello," said the old familiar voice. "You called?"

It was a soft, gentle voice, with the edge of a knife in it—the kind that makes chills in your spine, even if you think you're impervious.

"Why, Mr. Turing!" I said. "Just imagine hearing from you after all these years; I thought you'd passed away in 1953!"

"Old technocrats never die," said Tor, "nor do we fade away. Not when we have little protégées like *thou*, to keep us on our toes!"

"Protégée," I pointed out, "means someone who's sheltered—protected. That's hardly been the case with you and me."

"Protecting you from *yourself* is more like it," he admitted cheerfully.

"Isn't it a bit late to be calling for a chat?" I said. "Have you any idea what time it is?"

"The birds are chirping in the trees here, my dear, I've been trying to reach you all night. It seems your phone was tied up."

"What exactly is it that's so important it can't wait?"

"Don't try to deny anything. I get my information from a firsthand source: Charles Babbage, I believe he calls himself. You know quite well that I'm on a first-name basis with every computer in the country."

I knew quite well that this was the image Tor liked to project—but it didn't explain how he'd learned about Charles. I felt the throbbing behind my eyes and took another slug of brandy.

"How could you possibly know about Charles?" I asked. "He doesn't even *exist* on paper."

"That's certainly true, my dear," he agreed. "You pulled his dossier years ago, *didn't* you? And you've been using him ever since—"

"Have you any proof of these accusations?" I said, knowing the answer already.

"My dearest girl, does the pope ski in Gstaad?" he said charmingly. "If you were in my place, could you think of any reason that someone would—in the course of a few short hours—wish to review the Federal Reserve security standards, the American national standards for money transfer, *all* the historical archives on *all* the international wire transfer services—*and* the FBI criminal records archives on interstate wiretap convictions. . . ?"

"I'm a banker—it's my job to be interested in the security of financial systems," I said, rallying with the sort of indignation that can be mustered only by the genuinely guilty. "It might look suspicious, I admit—"

"Suspicious! Premeditated, is what it looks like! You falsified the records of that computer over ten years ago!

Breaking into confidential files with a stolen computer—''

"No one *makes* them dump their silly files there, do they?"

"Does he," Tor corrected. "My dear young woman—I'm afraid I know you far too well to write off your actions to idle curiosity. You could carry out that foolish job you have with both hands tied, and blindfolded. These attempts at girlish naïveté, I'm afraid, have left me quite unmoved. Now, I'd like to ask you a simple question—and receive a sincere answer—after which you may go to bed."

"Shoot," I said.

"Are you planning to knock over the Federal Reserve Bank?"

I had no idea how to reply. Though he'd picked the wrong bank, what I'd planned to do now seemed—in the cold, harsh light of reality—no more than the petulant whim of a child. What in God's name was I thinking of? There was silence on the phone; I couldn't hear even the sound of breathing.

"I wasn't planning on stealing any of their money," I muttered at last.

"No?"

"No." I paused. "I was only going to borrow some of it for a while."

"The Federal Reserve Bank does not lend money—except to other banks," he said. "Are you a bank?"

"I wasn't planning to take out a loan," I admitted. My lips were against the mouthpiece of the phone, my head pressed against the windowpane. I closed my eyes and took another big swig of brandy.

"I see," said Tor at last. "Well, perhaps we should discuss this further in the morning—when we're all a little fresher."

"Are you upset? Are you morally indignant?" I asked.

"No. I am not upset—nor morally indignant," he assured me.

"Well, what are you, then?"

After a pause, he said in a strange, detached voice, "I am curious."

"Curious? About what? I've told you what I'm doing," I said.

"Yes, you certainly have," he agreed. "But I want to see your plan."

"My plan? What on earth for?" I was truly alarmed.

"I'm an old hand, my dear. Who knows? Perhaps I might improve upon it. With that—good night."

And we hung up.

I lit a cigarette, and stared out at the city for a very long time. Then I crushed it out and made my way through the maze of orchids toward the bedroom. The emotions I was wrestling with were completely unfamiliar to me—I couldn't have even named them.

But I would go to New York that weekend. Of that, I was certain.

THE MOTIVE

It is a matter of indifference to the man of large affairs whether the disturbances which his transactions set up in the industrial system help or hinder the system at large, except in so far as he has ulterior ends to serve. But most of the captains of modern industry have such ulterior ends.

—*Thorstein Veblen,*
The Machine Age

I never desired wealth for its own account, but for the accomplishment of some ulterior purpose.

—*Thomas Mellon*

I NEVER WONDERED WHAT THE OUTCOME MIGHT HAVE been had Tor not phoned that night. From the moment he'd entered my life, I'd felt myself losing control. He wanted it to seem that *I* was the one who'd brought about those changes—that he was a mere observer—but I knew computers weren't enough for him; he wanted to change reality. *My* reality. That's what bothered me.

The first change had taken place by the very next morning, when I stood in the steamy bathroom and looked at myself in the mirror. I always squeezed fresh juice and ground some coffee beans so I could have a strong citrus-java infusion before facing myself in the mirror. The older you get, the wiser it is to take such precautions. But this morning, the face that looked back at me from the clear space I'd wiped in the mirror told me what a liar I'd been. It was the face of a born adventuress.

How cleverly I'd concealed this from myself. After ten years of frustration and bitterness—of battling with the System until I was blue in the face, just to do a decent day's job—I suddenly *looked forward* to going to work! I felt cheerful, and ten years younger, and I knew why: if Tor would really help me, as last night he'd said he would, I could pull off this setup of my hypocritical fellow bankers in style. I whistled a few bars of the "Ride of the Valkyries," threw on my clothes, and headed for the office.

■

I MUST CONFESS THAT ALTHOUGH MY BOSS, KIWI, HAD a reputation for cheerful treachery and obdurate ladder climbing, my own reputation in some circles was worse. The rumor that I ran my department like a galley ship was a great exaggeration; it was only that *I* knew what motivated computer people. And what happened that morning proved my point.

Individuals who work with computers are not ordinary human beings. Psychologists haven't scratched the surface of the breed—nor could they—because they start from the premise that everyone has basic primal needs like sleep, food, and human warmth. The sort of individual I'm describing does not have such needs. He's known within the industry as a teckie.

The teckie relates to computers more closely than to people. He does his best work at night, when all but nocturnal beasts of prey have gone to sleep. He eats little, subsisting essentially on junk food. He never sees daylight or breathes air, flourishing instead in artificial lighting and climate control. Should he marry and breed—which is rare—he classifies his children by whether they are analog or digital. He can be arrogant, unruly, ungovernable, and antisocial. I knew all about teckies, because I was one myself. And I considered teckie traits—from the evolutionary standpoint—to be assets, rather than liabilities.

Every teckie at the bank knew of my reputation; they came to me from far and wide, because they knew I'd pay them fairly and work them to death. They hankered after tight schedules, long hours, and problems so tough they'd make Einstein grow pale and God scratch his head. Since I always tried to deliver this sort of environment to them, it was rumored that I had balls—a colloquial teckie expression signifying moxie.

That morning, my reputation paid off: I arrived to find a large packet on my desk from the personnel director. The packet was full of résumés from technicians throughout the bank, with a cheerful little note from the director himself:

> Dear Verity—I hadn't realized you were recruiting. The personnel director is always the last to know.

The personnel director might be the last to know, but the grapevine was always the first. I hadn't posted any open positions—my proposal had only been printed and mailed last night—and there were résumés in this packet from some of the most heavy-duty teckies at the bank, all applying for my new project: the quality circle to implement Theory Z. This meant, of course, that the grapevine knew something I didn't—until just now: that the Managing Committee had read my proposal, and they'd liked it. They were going to bite.

■

SOMEONE ELSE WAS ON THE VERGE OF BITING: KIWI had been frothing at the mouth outside my office as Pavel held him at bay. I'd been locked up all day, interviewing applicants for the quality circle as soon as I got my official approval, and I'd already hired Tavish—one of the top technicians at the bank—over his boss's heated objections. But before I confronted Kiwi on the subject of going over his head, there was something else I needed to deal with: my forthcoming trip to New York.

First thing that morning, I'd sent Kiwi the papers he had to sign, hoping that without noticing, he'd approve my travel plans. I had my own budget for such trips, and it was usually just a formality for him to initial one. Ordinarily, Kiwi loved nothing better than to pack me off so he could run around supervising my staff. He had few "direct reports" of his own—just a handful of managers who knew their jobs and considered him an unnecessary obstacle to doing them. When I was gone, my own staff hid out in the latrines to avoid him.

"What did Mr. Willingly want?" I asked Pavel as I peeked out of my office. "Were those my plane tickets he was waving around out here? Has he signed them yet?"

"Who ever *knows* what he wants?" Pavel moaned. "He doesn't even know, *himself.* He doesn't have enough to keep him busy; you should learn to delegate upward, and keep him off our backs. 'Kiss-it Willingly the Turd'—that's what we call him in the secretarial lounge. Everyone empathizes with you, having to work—"

"Pavel, I asked you a question," I said, my voice unusually brittle. Pavel glanced up at me in surprise. He rearranged the pencils on his desk.

"His Majesty wants to see you in his office at once," he told me. "Now. Yesterday. The day before yesterday. Something about Tavish—that guy you just interviewed—and his boss, that fish person."

The boss over whose objections I had just hired Tavish was a pompous Prussian named Peter-Paul Karp. I decided I'd better deal with this, and left Pavel sulking at his desk.

Kiwi's office, across the floor from mine, was reached by threading the maze. His secretary waved me in without looking up from her typing. I was braced for the worst—but I was in for a surprise.

"Ah, Banks!" he greeted me, breathing deeply, as if he'd just come from a brisk walk in a large meadow. My defenses went up at once. "Good news! Good news! But first—let me give you your paperwork—I've signed everything. So you're off to New York at the weekend, are you? And about to launch a new project as well—so I hear." He handed me the travel file.

"As a matter of fact, I was just on my way to discuss it with you—"

"And a high-visibility project, too, so they tell me. I want you to know I'm here to help, Banks, my door is always open. As Ben Franklin said—'We must all hang together or we'll all hang separately.' And Ben Franklin was right." He shot me a glance.

Yep, that Ben Franklin sure was some fellow.

What this meant was that I'd been right to jump the gun. The Managing Committee had approved and funded an even larger proposal than the one Kiwi had shot down. His traitorous kibosh of my Fed job had gotten him nowhere. He couldn't cancel *this* project and rap my knuckles. Nor could he take credit for it, since I'd made sure he didn't even have a copy of it to read. So he was going to try to stick his nose into it—but I could field those attempts, as I had with others in the past.

Before I could pat myself on the back for a game well played, he added, "So you can imagine my surprise, when you didn't share with me the *recruitment* problems you've been having, before your project is even off first base." Recruitment problems? "Our friend Karp, down in foreign exchange systems, just rang me up. Seems he doesn't want this"—he consulted his desk pad—"this 'Tavish' to come across the fence. That right?"

"As a matter of fact," I said, silently cursing Karp for getting Kiwi into the problem, "it only happened a moment ago. Karp's been unreasonably obstinate about it all."

"So you told him he could call Lawrence if he didn't like it—that right?"

I nodded glumly. Lawrence was Kiwi's boss—one of the highest-level executives at the Bank of the World, and head of the Managing Committee. I'd tried that ploy only because I knew Karp would never do it. Nobody ever called Lawrence—he called *you*. And if he did, you usually wished he'd never found a reason to look up your number.

"We seem to be getting off on the wrong foot with this project," Kiwi was saying. "We don't want to upset Lawrence with our petty little staffing squabbles, do we? I told Karp we'd talk turkey, you and I, and find some solution. If this chap Tavish is so indispensable to Karp's work down there, do we need to pry him away? Besides, Karp claims Tavish owes him a favor."

This put me in a real bind. The biggest problem with Theory Z was that, by definition, a quality circle functioned *without* a manager. I could select members for the team, but once established, they would operate behind closed doors—without my involvement. Therefore, I needed an ally within the group—one who was strong enough technically to garner respect from the others, but still do things my way. Tavish was the only one I could think of who'd do all that *and* keep Kiwi's hands out of the cookie jar. I could hardly use that as a justification to Kiwi, however.

But something was bothering me about Kiwi's attitude. He was being too reasonable—not to mention cheerful. It seemed to me that this Karp business was a red herring. I decided to find out what lay beneath the surface.

"What was the good news you were talking about, when I first came in?" I asked.

"Well—I'm not supposed to tell anyone . . ." he said, grinning from ear to ear.

Bingo. I went over to close the door, then took a seat opposite him. "You don't have to tell me," I said, leaning forward, "but you know I *can* keep a secret."

"This is strictly between us," he said, glancing about as if the walls were bugged. "Guess where I'm dining tonight?"

I rattled off the name of every posh restaurant I could think of in town. Each time he shook his head in the negative, his grin grew broader. The light was beginning to dawn, though I hoped I was mistaken.

"It's more exclusive than those; a private club," he said.

I sat there, numb, as the anger inside began to build to rage. Kiwi was so excited, he'd forgotten what he had done to me only two nights before, by knocking the pins out of *my* career advancement. I tried to prepare an expression that would fall somewhere between amazement and enthusiasm, but I felt my true feelings setting like plaster across my face.

"The Vagabond Club!" he whispered, his voice trembling with hysterical joy. "Lawrence is taking me!"

The Vagabond Club was Kiwi's most cherished fantasy, as everyone knew. He would have slashed his wrists if he thought that, in the hereafter, such a sacrifice would gain him entry to the hallowed halls of the Vagabond Club.

In San Francisco, a city that boasted more private, male-only clubs than any other in America, the Vagabond Club was a luminary. It was neither the oldest men's club in the city nor the most exclusive. But more high-powered deals were cut within the ivy-covered walls of the Vagabond Club than in all the boardrooms of all the banks in America put together. It infuriated me that when women had finally gotten the vote, a paycheck, and a seat at the round table, they'd moved the whole game behind closed doors. In fact, the bank *paid* for executive membership in such clubs, whose policy was to treat other executives (myself, for instance) like scullery maids to the stars. And they were using shareholders' money to do it! At the Vagabond Club, there were guards posted outside the door, to ensure that no *woman* was permitted to enter and sully the conversation—or grab a piece of the pie. Mother Nature still called the shots. Brains were not the right equipment to join this coven.

I complimented Kiwi on his luck, which was due to an inarguable asset: he was a man.

"Since Lawrence is recommending me for *membership*," Kiwi was gushing on, breathless as a schoolgirl, "I *can't* very well upset him. Couldn't you throw Karp some sort of bone till this blows over? If you *must* have this Tavish, then find Karp another body that will do as well. I leave it to you, Banks; you're a good man—woman, that is. I'll phone and tell him we've found a mystery candidate. Someone wonderful. I leave it to you to ferret out who it will be."

I left Kiwi's office clutching my papers for New York.

I felt fortunate to have come out as well as I had. After all, I'd be able to hang on to Tavish for at least another day—till I came up with a plan to keep him—and by Friday I'd be in the Big Apple. Once I had Tor on my side, there wasn't much that could stop me. And tossing around a few million dollars, even if only for a short time, would assuage the complaints of any disgruntled employee.

At least, so I thought at the time.

■

I'D INVITED TAVISH TO DINE WITH ME THAT NIGHT AT my *own* club—Le Club, my favorite restaurant in San Francisco. If I were leaving for New York by the weekend, I wanted the quality circle in full operation before then. And I knew exactly what they had to do.

Tavish—an honorable, forthright teckie—might be squeamish about a few things I had in mind. On the other hand, if I didn't give him *some* guidelines, they'd still be looking under the wrong rocks when I returned. I was only trying to be helpful. After all, they'd be breaking into the very systems *I* had managed for the last ten years.

When I pulled up before the restaurant, I saw Tavish loitering under the dark green canopy. He was wearing a suit, necktie, and sneakers. His shoulder-length blond hair had been freshly trimmed, making him look nearly as old as his twenty-two years.

"Gee, I hope you didn't buy that suit just for dinner tonight," I told him when I'd parked and come down the block. "Where's your T-shirt? I thought it was your only uniform."

"I'm wearing it beneath my dress shirt, like Superman," he told me. "I feel it gives me a sort of closet panache."

Though Tavish might have seemed boyish and ingenuous, he'd cut his teckie teeth on some impressive number crunchers.

The oddity of the data-processing business is that many teckies, regardless of their age, earn more than most powerful executives do. According to the figures in Tavish's file, he had exceeded *my* current income when he was barely eighteen. So impressive were his credentials that I wondered why he was here at the bank working for a bozo like Karp; he could write his own ticket thirty miles away, down in Silicon Valley. I wanted to know more about what *did* motivate Tavish; that's why I'd asked him to dinner. And I didn't wait all five courses to get to the point.

"I like this place," Tavish said half an hour later, surveying the warm, cozy room where we were seated in a deep green velvet banquette. The waiters were delivering a beautifully prepared meal and replenishing our champagne in unobtrusive silence. "And I'm happy to have the chance to thank you, for getting me out of the clutches of Karp."

"I'm afraid you're not quite out yet," I told him, following my blanquette de veau with some terrific pouilly-fuissé. "Your pal Peter-Paul phoned Kiwi today—just after I thought I'd hired you—and said the deal's off. In a sense, I thought this might be your farewell dinner; he seems to think you'll see things *his* way. Says you owe him some sort of favor."

"I owe him, all right," Tavish said grimly, "but not what he thinks. It's no secret, at least not with you. I've worked with Karp before, you see, down in the peninsula. He hired me to develop copyrighted software that his firm would market. I'd get fifty percent of the royalties—or so he claimed—and something else that I wanted even more."

"And what was that?"

"He said he'd sponsor my green card: a permanent resident visa. Without it, as a foreigner, I can't work in this country, unless it's under the table. But Karp's business went belly-up, owing me half a million in royalties. All *my* profits went up his nose, but I couldn't turn him in, since he was my official sponsor."

"You mean cocaine?" I said, surprised.

"He's got a hundred-thousand-dollar-a-year habit he can't support, even on his inflated salary," Tavish told me. "So he's using his staff and the bank's computer systems to churn out software that he sells on the open market. Though I can't prove it, I believe his whole staff is moonlighting—that he pays them kickbacks. He's asked me to do the same, or he'll turn me over to Immigration."

"But you aren't here illegally," I said, "you're on temporary visa—trying to get your green card. I saw your file only this morning."

"He no longer has a right to sponsor me. The firm he owned is technicaliy defunct. In that sense, I'm at the bank under false pretenses as well. He supplied my references here, you see. If I were deported back to the U.K., I'd be fortunate to make a small percent of what I make over here for my technical skills. I'm not an 'old schoolboy,' you see—I'm just a working-class chap."

"You realize this puts me in a real bind," I lied. (What an astounding miracle of good fortune this dinner had turned out to be.) "I can't blow the whistle on Karp if we have no proof of his illegal activities—and if I tried, you might get deported, or terminated at the very least, for coming to the bank under false pretenses. But if I could buy some time by finding someone else to work for him—someone he couldn't refuse—then we could work out the details later about getting you out of this jam."

"I've been thinking of nothing but that all day. I felt utterly sure he'd put up a fuss like this," Tavish told me, "and I thought of the perfect person at last—someone who's been wanting to get into that department forever."

"You know someone who *wants* to work for Karp?" I said, amazed. "Whoever he is, he must be firing on two cylinders."

"It's a she," he explained. "Her name's Pearl Lorraine, and she manages foreign exchange for the bank. She's an econometrician—a client of mine, since I'm supporting her systems. She's brilliant—and black. He'd have to come up with some pretty good reasons to refuse her."

"Pearl Lorraine? From Martinique? She knows the exchange business far better than Karp, and has some computer background, too. But what does *she* think of the idea?" From what I knew of Pearl Lorraine, she wouldn't make such a move without plenty of motive; she was widely regarded as the most militant career opportunist at the bank.

"She says Karp is a bit of a Nazi, among other things; it seems he refers to his black employees as jungle bunnies, and brags that he hires only black female secretaries, because they have nicer derrieres."

"Good Lord," I said, "if all that's true, what makes you think she'd work for a guy like that?"

"Simple," said Tavish with a grin. "She's *better* at foreign exchange than he is—she wants his job. And if you want to hit a home run, you have to be next up to bat when someone strikes out."

I agreed with Tavish that under our pressed circumstances, Pearl afforded the perfect solution. I decided when the cheese and fruit arrived that it was time to move on to the *real* topic of tonight's dinner.

"I'll be leaving for New York at the end of this week," I told Tavish. "The quality circle will all be on board by then—six of you—and there are a few things I'd like us to discuss before I go."

Tavish regarded me seriously over his silver fork, and nodded for me to continue.

"First, I want you to crack the file that holds customer and correspondent bank account data—and then to hit the electronic funds transfer system."

"Wire transfers? Your own system?" said Tavish. "That must be the hardest system at the bank; you'd have to get in from at least two places—"

"You need the test keys," I agreed, "to get at the wire transfers themselves—and you'd need to know the customer account numbers and secret passwords to get money out of specific bank accounts."

"You mean, we should steal one test key for one day—just to illustrate it can be done?"

"All those banks out there *can't* change their keys daily," I said. "There must be a program in the system that deciphers *all* the keys, and can somehow determine their validity even if they change without notice."

"Astounding," said Tavish, "and impossible to believe. If there *were* such a sort of 'decryption' program, you could take money from any account you liked, and move it anywhere—assuming you had the account numbers."

I smiled, picked up a cocktail napkin, and drew a little diagram:

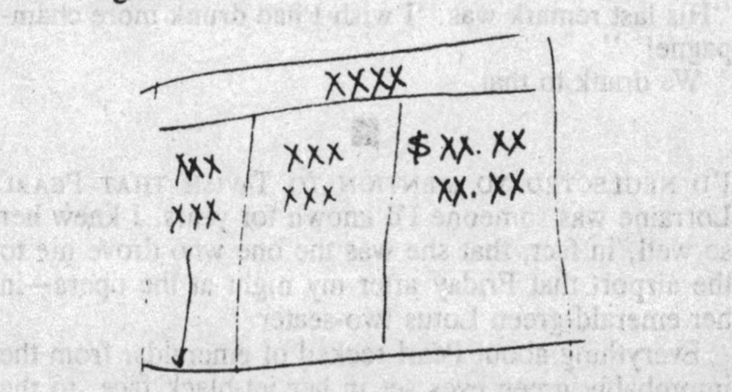

"Each bank branch keeps a card like this. The number at the top is the location number; it tells us which branch is making the transfer. This first column has a special code for the current month, the second column shows the current day, and the third column is the dollar amount of the wire transfer. These four numbers—location number, month code, today's date, and dollar amount—*are* the test key! Each key changes as the day and dollar amount change—that's it!"

"You're joking," said Tavish. "I work in foreign exchange systems; I don't know anything about the bank's branch operations. But if it's as simple as all that, anybody could break into the system and rip off funds!"

"Perhaps they have," I said, sipping my champagne.

"That's what you're supposed to find out. But of course, it may be more difficult than I've imagined; I myself haven't seen the systems that decode these keys."

"How complex could it be, given input like this?" said Tavish, waving the napkin in excitement. "After all, they're only programs in there, aren't they? But if you are right about this being the way it really works, it's bound to be a security horror beyond all imagining!"

"Any regrets about signing on for this project?" I asked.

"Lord Maynard Keynes was asked, on his deathbed, whether *he* had any regrets about his life," said Tavish. "His last remark was, 'I wish I had drunk more champagne!' "

We drank to that.

■

I'D NEGLECTED TO MENTION TO TAVISH THAT PEARL Lorraine was someone I'd known for years. I knew her so well, in fact, that she was the one who drove me to the airport that Friday after my night at the opera—in her emerald-green Lotus two-seater.

Everything about Pearl reeked of emeralds, from the improbably green eyes set in her jet-black face, to the skintight emerald suede pants she was wearing, to the *real* emerald pendant dangling in the cleavage exposed by her extremely low-cut sweater.

Pearl was a racy lady but, to my taste, a bit too fast behind the wheel. Now I was wondering if she was trying to break the sound barrier as she whizzed past a blur of eucalyptus, shot into a gear I didn't know existed, and took the freeway ramp on two wheels.

"Gee, I'd have had you *drive* me to New York, if I'd known we could get there faster than by air," I told her, gripping the door with my fingernails.

"Sugar, don't buy a fast car if you can't drive one," she said, then hit her horn and sucked some paint off a taxi that was crawling along at eighty. "Besides—I took off work early so we could take some time, sit down, have a drink, shoot the breeze. You've become such a hermit, I never see you anymore."

"I think we'll have plenty of time for all that," I assured her. "We've just passed the international date line. Looks like they don't have remedial drivers' ed in Martinique."

"When the world loves a wise-ass, sweetheart, you're going to be on top," she informed me blithely as we screeched up before the gate. Pearl leaped out as the dust was still settling, tossed her keys and a ten-dollar bill to the astonished porter, and gave him her dazzling smile. "We'll get the bags." She bustled me inside.

"They have valet parking?" I asked.

"Don't look a gift horse in the mouth," said Pearl, maneuvering me into the lounge—a nightmare of Polynesian bric-a-brac that looked as if it had been designed by a team of Mormon architects from Guam.

Pearl had ordered Bloody Marys and was already munching her celery stick when I returned from checking my bags.

"Thanks for getting me into the job with Karp—that wet fish," she said between crunches. "Anytime you want a return favor . . ."

"Let's wait till you've been there a few weeks; you may want to pay me back differently," I told her as I tentatively took a sip of watery tomato juice. "Tavish told me you *wanted* to work there—to take over Karp's job—though I can't imagine why. I heard he was a bigot. This isn't some sort of vendetta? But that hardly seems your style. . . ."

"Sue him for discrimination, you mean?" Pearl laughed, and flagged down the waitress for another round. "Of course not; I hate that stuff—mingling with lawyers and all. I've always thought there must be some reason why the French words for 'attorney' and 'avocado' were the same. No, I don't give a fig about Karp. It's power—reins, sweetheart—that's the name of the game. I have a master's in economics—and that means I can add up the digits on my paycheck. Karp earns *twice* as much as I do, but all *he* produces is trouble.

Before I'm done, I'll put his ass in a Singapore sling and shoot it into outer space."

When I'd first met Pearl in New York ten years earlier, her father had been a top broker of African and Oceanic art, a field just entering its golden era as museums clamored for the goods he'd collected over the past forty years. He'd started from nothing as a runner—some say smuggler—and he died when Pearl, only twenty, was an economics major at NYU. There she'd acquired her taste for salty Yankee slang, fast cars, hard-driving feminism, and the color green, which she said reminded her of money. Papa had left her plenty of green. That had helped, more than all her education, to break down the doors in her ever-upward quest for power.

Though Pearl was more aggressive than I, we had this much in common: money was far from what we were after.

As if she'd read my mind, she said: "It's not the money, it's the principle. I mean the ethical kind—not the kind that earns interest. What difference does it make if I'm rich and don't need the job? No one at the bank except you knows that anyway. I *deserve* that job, and Karp doesn't. I've been running foreign exchange for years, and made millions for the bank. If I were only after money, I should have retired when I stepped off that boat from Fort-de-France; I'd have saved myself ten years of hassles."

"Sure, but how do you plan to get his job by going to work for *him*, when before, *he* had to keep *you* happy by providing systems for you?" I wanted to know.

"He'll slip up eventually," Pearl said with a mysterious grin as our second round of tomato-flavored water arrived, "but I always keep a banana peel in my back pocket, just for such contingencies. Now, let's get off this topic; I want to know how long you'll be in the Big Apple, and what you're going to do. After all, it's practically our old hometown!"

"A week is all I have time for," I told her.

"Get real," said Pearl, crinkling her nose. "Why

don't you take time off—hang loose? Everyone knows you're a slave driver, but why drive *yourself* this way? Hit the theaters, buy some exotic rags, meet new faces, eat designer food—get *laid*—you know what I mean?''

''Don't you think this conversation is rather personal?'' I said.

''We've known each other ten years,'' Pearl informed me, ''and besides, I'm not known for my discretion. I wasn't born in a gray flannel suit—with a pencil between my teeth, and my legs cemented together—as you were. I may be fucking men *over* at the office, but I assure you, I find better uses for them after the five o'clock whistle blows. *You*, on the other hand, are starting to resemble a Buddhist monk!''

''I'm going to New York on business,'' I said flatly.

''Bah—this quality circle stuff is hardly business. Why did you set it up in the first place, when you've got a five-million-dollar division under your thumb? I know all about it—you've pissed off every manager at the bank.''

''I have an excellent reason,'' I told her calmly. ''I'm going to knock over the bank.''

''My ass,'' said Pearl, sipping her drink with aplomb. ''I'll eat this emerald first.'' She studied me, tapping a long red fingernail on the table. ''By God, if I didn't know you better, I'd think you meant it,'' she added.

I let her stew awhile before I said quietly, ''I *do* mean it.''

''You can't be serious,'' said Pearl. ''*You*, the quintessential banker—'Woman of the Year,' 'Girl of the Golden West'—you're going to toss away everything your granddaddy ever wanted—''

She stopped in her tracks and gave that a little thought.

''By God, maybe you *do* mean it,'' she said in amazement. ''Making up for lost time and past injustice . . . But what on *earth* could drive an ice cube of virtue like *you* over the brink—that's what I want to know.''

Just then, they called my plane over the intercom. I rose and tossed some money down for the drinks.

"Did you ever wonder, Pearl, why banks have so many educated, qualified, dedicated, ethical, and relatively underpaid middle managers like us—when at the very top, there's a bunch of ignorant, greedy, boorish, self-congratulatory snobs, who are only concerned for their own well-being?"

It was the longest admission I'd ever made to Pearl—or anyone else—of how I felt, and she looked at me with wide eyes before she replied.

"Okay—why?" she said.

"Shit floats," I told her.

Then I left to catch my plane.

THE MACHINE AGE

The machine discipline cuts away that ground of law and order on which business enterprise is founded.

What can be done to save civilized mankind from the vulgarization and disintegration wrought by the machine industry?

—*Thorstein Veblen,*
The Machine Age

It was nice to fly on the bank's credit card, because I always flew first class, but on most airlines, even first-class food was enough to gag me. So I usually brought a picnic basket packed by my local trattoria, Vivande.

This time, the lifted napkin revealed a treasure trove of culinaria: cold caviar and white bean salad, a wedge of pancetta layered with crushed figs, a bitterly lemon tart, and a split of Verdicchio to wash it all down. I sat back, plugged into the Mozart track on my headset, and tried to erase all thoughts—but my mind kept moving back to my newly hatched scheme. And to what would happen with Tor.

Though I'd launched the quality circle with fanfare, piqued Pearl's interest, and was now en route to Manhattan to initiate my mission, I knew it was still not too late to kick everyone off the bandwagon if I decided to get cold feet. At least, it wasn't too late *now.* After I'd met with Tor, it might be.

Many years ago, he'd pulled me out of some sticky situations. But I'd known him long enough to realize that, even then, it had been *his* involvement that had stuck me there in the first place! Asking for Tor's assistance with a computer problem was like getting Leonardo's help in sketching: it seemed invaluable—until you got the bill.

And I knew that Tor believed in collecting his accounts receivable. For the first time in the many years since I'd last seen him, I had the sick and giddy feeling that I was standing with one foot perched atop the "debts called due" spindle, and the other on a roulette wheel. Not the favorite position of one who likes to remain in control.

■

WHEN I'D MET ZOLTAN TOR TWELVE YEARS AGO, I HAD been a computer bunny of twenty, fresh in my new job at Monolith Corp., one of the largest computer vendors in the world. Knowing nothing at all of the DP business (I thought IBM was the name of a clock and Honeywell that of a thermostat), I instantly received from my firm an impressive title, and was sent—as a "technical expert"—to install large-scale mainframe systems.

Naturally, it was quite a scramble to bone up on the myriad subjects my clients believed I already knew. Running at a hectic pace, I took prolific notes at each account, raced back to my office to find experts who'd help, and returned to the clients the next morning with the answers. I was always terrified of being unmasked, but for several months this routine seemed to be working. Then the rug was yanked.

One Monday, I arrived at my office to find my boss, Alfie, a flabby, whining fellow who disliked me, standing at my desk with lips pursed and hands on hips.

I'd been hired by someone higher up than Alfie and thrust on him as a trainee. He hated nothing more than training people he thought had better connections than he had; so instead of training me, he expended all his efforts trying to show up my incompetence. The more often I performed to the letter those assignments he threw at me, the more infuriated he became.

"Verity, I'd like to see you at once in my office," he said in a sneering tone, looking around the suddenly silent floor to be sure everyone was noting my discomfort.

Alfie's glass-walled cubicle at the rear of the floor afforded him an overseer's view of the galley ship of desks, ranged in long, straight rows across the floor. From behind, he could make sure that each programmer was hard at work. If he ever caught us whispering to one another, he tapped a bell on his desk; and he counted the lines of code each of us pumped out every month, tacking those statistics to the bulletin board at the entrance, with little gold, red, and green stars affixed—it was just like kindergarten. Each hour of the day, like clockwork, a shopping cart moved around the floor; as it passed we were to drop our coding sheets and punched cards to be sent for processing. We had two potty breaks a day and a half hour for lunch; any other absences resulted in docked pay.

Because I worked mostly in the field with clients, I managed to avoid much of that Dickensian atmosphere.

"Verity," Alfie said when we were seated behind his glass wall, "I'm going to ask you to take on some new accounts." He pulled out a lengthy list and passed it to me. I ran my eyes over it.

"But sir, I already have more clients than anyone else," I said. "And some of these firms use different hardware and programming languages than the ones I'm familiar with. It may take some time—"

"There is no time," he informed me, with what suspiciously resembled a trace of glee. "If you didn't want to work hard, you shouldn't have come to Monolith; there's no place for idlers on our payroll. Half your colleagues out front would give anything to be in your place—and I'll put them there, if you botch up. That will be all."

I was over my head now—and I knew it. I had twice as many accounts to service as anyone in the office. Many of these were the most sophisticated of "users" as well as those with the heaviest back list of work to be done. They'd find me out in under a month.

By the end of that week, I was exhausted from working dawn till the wee hours; my desk was piled with things to take home and work on over the weekend. It was well after quitting time on Friday, when Alfie showed up with a forbidding pile of manuals. He dropped the load with a thud on my desk.

"Louis is going to bestow a great honor on you," he informed me. Louis Findstone was Alfie's boss—the division manager. "On Monday morning, crack of dawn, you'll be presented to the board of directors of Transpacific Railroad—our largest client—as their new representative. You won't be asked to say anything at the meeting, but I thought you might want to read up on Transpacific over the weekend, just in case you're asked any questions."

It certainly was a great honor, as I knew. Teckies were never brought out in public before a lofty group like that. But how on earth could I read all those books, and also get my other catching-up done?

As if he'd read my mind, Alfie added, "Frankly, I don't agree with the choice of *you* for this assignment; you're still wet behind the ears, and it seems to me you've been treading water, just trying to stay afloat with your daily work. But I leave it to Louis's judgment." And with that, he departed.

So I remained there that night, after everyone had left for the weekend, trying to wade through the books Alfie had left—too many and too heavy to carry home on the subway, since I certainly couldn't afford a cab.

It didn't take me long to understand that I was in real trouble; these books were like witches' brew. The terms might have meant something to a person schooled in business, but I was a math major—I couldn't even read a financial statement!

I decided to wander through the building, on the off chance that someone might have stayed late on Friday night. But as the elevator doors opened upon floor after floor of empty darkness, my hopes waned.

I went downstairs to the all-night data center, packing with me a heavy tome, thinking one of the night machine operators might be able to explain it.

"Looks like mumbo jumbo to me," said the one I found there. "All the others are out having dinner, and I think the rest of the building's shut down for the night—but let's have a look."

He went over to the building control panel and searched the floors. "Hmm—some juice is still running on twelve—maybe somebody who's burning the midnight oil like you. I'd give it a try."

When the elevator doors slid open on the twelfth floor, a few corridor lights were on—but the rest of the floor lay in complete darkness. I walked down the glassed-in corridors to each corner of the building, but indeed, all the offices were dark and empty.

"May I help you, little girl?" The soft voice was just behind me.

I nearly jumped out of my skin; I felt my lip trembling from the sudden fright as I swallowed and turned.

There stood the most amazing-looking man I'd ever seen. He was tall—perhaps five or six inches over six feet—and he stood bent forward with one ear cocked, as if accustomed to dealing with people far smaller than himself. He was as thin as he was tall, with pale skin, close-set intense eyes above a hawklike nose and a narrow mouth. His hair was precisely the color of copper. Though his manner suggested he was older, he could not have been more than thirty. Something about him put me at ease at once; I later learned he did not have that disarming effect upon everyone.

There was something else about him, too—more difficult to explain, but still vivid in my memory after all these years. There was a sort of volatile energy, like a harnessed atom kept under control only through great restraint. Having seen this trait in just a few others during my lifetime, I've come to believe that it is, purely and simply, intelligence—but intelligence of such enormous quantity that it's hard to imagine how it might all be used. Those who possess this rare quality seem to contain a huge explosive, whose trigger mechanism might go off with the slightest jar. Such people speak softly, move slowly, and seem to bear with infinite patience the traffic they must have with the outside world. But inside are seas and mountains of upheaval.

I stood there for a long time in silence, before I realized he was watching me with a bemused expression—almost as if he, too, were seeing something for the first time. I hadn't a clue what that was, but I had the uncomfortable feeling he could observe the cogs moving inside my head, an impression I was to have on many subsequent occasions. At the time—in the dim corridor light—I didn't register the color of his eyes.

"My name is Tor—Zoltan Tor," he said, speaking gingerly, as if unused to having to introduce himself. "Have you lost your way? Perhaps I could help you out."

The way he said it—he pronounced each word as if cutting it with a knife to make it more precise—made me pause in replying. Though he'd only asked whether he could help me out of the building, it seemed as if he'd asked whether he could help me out with my life.

"I don't think so," I told him sadly. "I need a technical expert, I'm afraid." And he certainly didn't look like one, in his three-piece custom-cut suit. Perhaps a diplomat would wear a silk shirt and gold cuff links like those, but no teckie would dress that way.

"Why not tell me your problem?" he said with a smile. "I only dabble in technology, for my own amusement. But sometimes, what I have to say amuses others as well."

I wasn't sure what that meant, but I was so distraught—and relieved at his offer of help—that I rattled off everything nonstop while standing there in the hallway.

When I got to the part about the great opportunity I'd been offered only that evening, he stopped me with a hand on my arm.

"One moment, one moment," he said quickly. "You say you work for a man named Alfie? That's Findstone's division—transportation systems—isn't it?"

When I nodded yes, a slow smile spread across his face.

"So, Alfie and Louis are giving you this great opportunity, are they? I find that quite interesting—really I do." He paused for a moment, not looking at me, and seemed to arrive at some private conclusion. Then he said, "But you don't believe what they've told you." It was more an observation than a question.

"No, I don't," I admitted—though I'd only just realized it as I said it.

Tor scrutinized my face closely, as if looking for truth in a crystal ball. "What you *do* believe is that you'll be called upon to make some sort of presentation before the client—and that you'll appear a fool. In fact, even before this situation arose, you'd been concerned about just such a possibility."

"I don't understand all I should," I admitted, "but I think you're wrong about Alfie and Louis; it wouldn't make sense. Why would the very people I work for wish to set me up that way—in front of their own clients?"

"I've long ago ceased trying to comprehend the motives of the ignorant and ineffectual," he told me. "It's a poor use of time that might be better spent learning something of value. How long have you, before this momentous debut?"

"Early Monday morning," I told him.

"Though you're young, it's clear you're wise enough to know that preparation never harmed anyone. The worst result will see you a bit wiser than before. How would you like to understand—by Monday morning—exactly how computers work, and what makes companies run?"

"I'd love it! I have some more books like this one," I told him, offering the fat one Alfie had given me; I'd stood there with it still jammed under my arm.

"You won't need them," he said, not glancing at the volume. "They're probably worthless anyway. I know everything necessary about the Transpacific Railroad. The chairman is a chap named Ben Jackson, I believe?"

"That's right," I said, flushed with excitement.

At least I'd learned *something* poring through those books.

"Come to my office," said Tor. He seemed satisfied about something, but wasn't giving out any information. "You've got hard work ahead; I hope you haven't made plans for the weekend. I'm quite free myself, and happy to be of service."

I couldn't believe my luck. It never occurred to me to wonder why this perfect stranger would take his own time, be so helpful, to someone with credentials as unimpressive as mine.

"I promise to take good notes," I told him cheerfully as I trotted beside him down the hall.

"You needn't bother; I want everything *carved* into that eager little brain. You have to begin to *think* as a computer does. Those who cannot keep pace with the revolution in technology will find, in a year or two, that they themselves are obsolete."

So began the most important weekend of my life—a weekend when I entered the cocoon as a computer ignoramus, and emerged as a full-blown technocrat. We spent nearly the whole time in Tor's office, though I was allowed to go home each night to catch a few winks, bathe, change clothes, and return at dawn. What began as a painful ordeal turned into purest pleasure—like climbing a mountain—worth all the agony, once you reached the top.

I soon discovered that Tor had a remarkable gift: the skill to explain complex subjects and make them crystal clear. Grasping all he told me was as easy as swallowing honey.

By the end of that first night, I knew enough about each computer, operating system, and programming language to teach a course myself on the subject. After Saturday night, I knew as much about the products of all the competitor firms, and how their products compared with ours. By Sunday, I could explain how each machine on the market was used in major businesses and industries. The details were an adventure story;

Tor's every word stuck in my mind—without notes—as he'd promised.

But one glimpse of his office had told me more about the man himself than the three days I spent at close quarters.

I'd assumed his office would be like all the others in our standardized building: glass walls, regulation metal desk, files and bookcases. Instead he had led me to the building core—where elevators and fire doors were located—and marched me into a broom closet!

When we switched on the light, there were mops and pails, and rows of metal shelves holding supplies—punched cards, pens and paper, technical manuals—all covered with a thin veneer of dust.

"The space behind the elevator bays was designed for storage," he told me as he pulled a key from his waistcoat and unlocked a heavy metal door hidden behind the last row of shelves. "But I found a better use. I hate working in that fishbowl out there, so I partitioned the stockroom with soundproof walls. I have the only key. Privacy—like eating and breathing—is one of life's basic requirements."

We entered an enormous, oblong room with parquet floors, walls paneled from top to bottom with books: many were leather-bound, and a glance informed me that few, if any, dealt with computers.

Fine Persian rugs were scattered about, as well as worn leather chairs, greenish-blue Tiffany lamps that looked like the real thing. A Spode tea service was displayed on an étagère, and an old copper samovar with three spigots rested on a table in the corner. At the center of the room was a large, round, leather-topped table, inset with thick green baize. Arrayed on it were dozens of small figurines in metal, enamel, ivory, wood. I went over to examine them, and Tor picked one up, handing it to me. I noticed the carved-out base.

"These are signets," he told me. "Do you know anything about them?"

"Only that in the old days they were used to seal the wax on letters," I said.

"The old days—yes," he agreed, laughing. "With that, modern man sums up everything that has occurred in the last five thousand years. Yes, signets were used to seal documents—but more than that: they were the first encryption. The intaglio imprints were used as a sort of code, depending upon where they were placed on a document, or in what combination."

"You've made a study of encryption?" I asked.

"I'm a most avid student of the entire art of secrecy—for it *is* an art," he told me. "Secrecy is the only liberty still afforded us, in this 'best of all possible worlds.' "

Perhaps I imagined it, but he sounded somewhat embittered.

"Are you quoting Dr. Pangloss?" I asked. "Or his creator, who said, 'I laugh only to keep from hanging myself'?"

"Why, that's it!" he said, neatly avoiding my question. "It's Candide you remind me of: that same naive impressionability one loses so quickly by encountering the real world. But you must take care, and see it always works to your advantage—*revealing truth*, as the child did in the story of the emperor's new clothes—not ending in cynicism and isolation, as in Candide's case. Just now, your mind's like a piece of fresh, hot wax, in which no print has yet been left—"

"So you plan to stamp your intaglio in me?" I asked.

Tor, who'd been arranging the signets on the table, glanced up sharply. Now I noticed the color of his eyes. They were strangely disconcerting—an intense, coppery flame burning in the depths—so at odds with his aloof and formal manner. It was as though he could penetrate like a laser—stripping away those layers of veneer with which we all protect ourselves—cutting to the very bone. Then he squinted, and the impression vanished.

"You're a strange child," he said, still studying me. "You have the ability to see truth without really understanding what it means. A mixed gift, and a dangerous one, if you always blurt things out tactlessly like that."

I wasn't sure how I'd been either truthful or tactless, so I simply smiled.

"I've studied this art of secrecy so long," he went on, "encryption, decoding, intelligence, espionage . . . but in the end, I've been left with one great fact: nothing can be hidden from X-ray vision, regardless how things are concealed. Truth has divine properties, and the ability to see it is a gift that's given, not acquired."

"What makes you think *I* have it?" I asked, for I knew that was what he meant.

"Never mind; it's enough that I recognize a gift when I see it. All my life, I've searched for challenges—only to learn in the end that the greatest challenge was in finding a challenge at all. How sad, that when I met it at last, it should arrive in the guise of a fourteen-year-old child."

"I'm twenty," I pointed out.

"You look fourteen, and so you behave," he said with a sigh, coming over to set both hands on my shoulders. "Believe me, my dear, when I say that I've never been accused of being an altruist. In some languages, there's no way to express, as there is in English, the concept of time as a commodity—of wasting, spending, or killing it. When I use *my* time for something, I expect commensurate value. If I pluck a waif from the halls and offer to improve her through my tutelage, I assure you that my goal isn't to improve the lot of beleaguered mankind."

"Then why?" I asked, meeting his gaze.

He smiled, perhaps the most intriguing smile I'd ever seen.

"I'm Pygmalion," he told me. "When I'm through with you—you're going to be a masterpiece."

■

BY MONDAY MORNING, I FELT I *WAS* A MASTERPIECE—though I didn't look much like one. My hair was disheveled, and dark rings circled my eyes.

But my head was jam-packed with knowledge, and just as Tor had predicted, I hadn't lost a stitch. For the first time in my life, I felt that calm confidence that comes with being truly knowledgeable on a subject—completely prepared. I felt I'd taken a long dip in a refreshing pool.

I'd wanted to give Tor the good news at once. But the meeting, and what came after, had taken longer than I'd thought. I passed through his floor several times during the day, but even the dingy stockroom was locked.

I was just about to leave for the day when I received a note at my desk:

Come to the supply room when you have a chance.

When I rapped at the door, Tor opened it at once. He was standing there in evening clothes, looking elegant. As he ushered me into the room I saw a large silver bucket sitting where the samovar had been, and before it, two crystal glasses.

"Champagne, madame?" he asked, folding a linen towel over his arm. "I hear you've scored quite a success today."

"I'm sorry—I don't drink," I told him.

"Champagne isn't drinking—it's celebrating," he told me, and filled the glasses with dangerous-looking bubbles. "Incidentally, do you own a dress?"

"Of course I do."

"I'd like you to go home and put it on," he said. "I want to escort someone to dinner who has legs. I've been meaning to discuss the subject with you, anyway. Stop trying to look like a boy; you're fooling no one, no matter how you try."

"You're taking me out?" I was flabbergasted.

"This compulsive innocence is unbecoming," he told me. "Drink your champagne."

I took a slug, but the bubbles went up my nose and burned my throat and I coughed. I started to hand back the glass.

"Don't guzzle that down like a horse at the trough," he chastened me. "Champagne is meant to be sipped slowly." He replenished the glass.

"It tickles my nose."

"Well then, take your nose out of it. Now, tell me about your success this afternoon. Then I'll take you home to change into something more presentable—if that is possible."

So I told Tor that Alfie, as expected, had used the meeting to try to humiliate me in front of the client. He'd introduced me as an expert in everything, then turned over the entire meeting to me, to let me prove it. And Louis—who hadn't been aware of this plan—had started chewing stomach pills and throwing black glances at Alfie. He was a wimp who was about to lose the account, and had trusted Alfie to bail him out, not to sabotage him. But things had not turned out as either of them had planned.

Thanks to Tor's tutorials, I knew enough about the transportation industry, and our role in it, to knock their socks off. Before we left the boardroom, the client—who'd been about to bid our firm farewell—had decided to place a big equipment order instead. The chairman of the board, Ben Jackson, even complimented Louis and Alfie for bringing me to his account.

"While you were achieving star status," said Tor, "what were Louis and Alfie doing—picking their noses?" He was pouring me some more wine, though my toes were already tingling.

"I'm getting drunk," I told him.

"I'll be the judge of that," he said, nodding for me to proceed.

"They interrogated me all the way back in the cab," I said, "to learn how it was I'd learned all this stuff so fast. I hope you don't mind—I told them I'd been working with *you*. At first they didn't believe me, but when they did, they spent an hour discussing how they might use this to their own advantage."

"And how was that?" Tor asked, smiling at me.

"It seems that you failed to inform me what you really do around here,'' I told him. ''You're our firm's secret weapon—the one-man think tank of Monolith Corp.'' Tor winced, but I went on. ''Louis thinks that if you could be induced to spend a few hours here and there with selected clients, the way you have with *me*, it would be worth millions to his division alone.''

''Quite true,'' Tor agreed, ''but it's more fun to spend them with *you*. That's the sort of thing Louis could never comprehend; he's got a soul made of cardboard.''

He leaned over and turned the empty bottle upside down in the icer, then stood up.

''They actually believed they could use me as a 'lever,' '' I went on. ''That you'd be willing to go on spending your time with me like that forever. I've risen considerably in Louis's esteem—and Alfie pretends to feel the same—though neither of them can figure out why you did it.''

''They're perfectly right,'' Tor said, offering me his hand and escorting me to the door. ''I *am* going to—and I can't figure out why, either. But while we ponder this weighty question I suggest we go to dinner.''

■

TOR HAD A DARK GREEN STINGRAY, AND HE DROVE IT very fast. He dropped me at my apartment house near the East River, and waited in the lobby.

I changed into a dress: black velvet, and very short. When I returned to the lobby, I found him seated in a large chair, looking gloomily at the ceiling. When he saw me, he squinted his eyes as I crossed the space between us, then stood up and took my arm.

''What a lovely spot you've chosen,'' he said, motioning to the lobby. ''Replica of Bluebeard's castle, isn't it? Good location, though.''

He didn't speak again till we were ensconced in the car and pulling away from the curb.

''I compliment you,'' he said then, studying the road as if I weren't there. ''It seems you *do* have legs, after all. I applaud your decision not to show them often;

Manhattan has enough traffic congestion as it is. Tell me—do you like to eat at Lutece?"

"I've never been there—but I know it's horribly expensive," I told him. "I can't understand French menus, and I'm not a big eater, so it seems—"

"Never fear. The portions are small, and I'll order for you. Children shouldn't be permitted to select their own meals."

Tor was well known at Lutece; everyone kept calling him "doctor" and making quite a fuss until we were settled. After he'd ordered, I broached the subject I'd been wondering about.

"You greeted me with uncorked champagne. How is it you knew—before you saw me—that there would be something to celebrate?" I wanted to know.

"Let's say that a little bird told me," he replied, studying the wine list as if committing it to memory. Finally, he looked up. "A friend of mine phoned—name of Marcus."

"Marcus? Marcus *Sellars*?"

Marcus Sellars was the chairman of the board of Monolith Corp. I'd known Tor was important—but not that he was *that* important.

"Marcus had received a call from Ben Jackson—your new client—asking whether Ben could get on the waiting list for some of this new equipment he'd heard we were about to release. Since he was talking about hardware that hadn't been announced yet—even internally—Marcus felt he should inquire about how *you* had gotten that information. A trace of my style showed through, it seems—and Marcus is nobody's fool."

"You mean, you had me present a lot of equipment that hasn't even been *built* yet?" I said in alarm. "What did Marcus do?"

"Presumably, he pulled out his pen and took the order. Then he picked up the phone and called me. He was pleased to see I was taking an active interest in the business again. Marcus thinks I need some stimulation. I've not visited many of our paying customers lately. He says they miss me."

"And what do *you* think?"

"I think I'd rather discuss wine," said Tor. "Which one do you prefer?"

"I've heard of one called Lancers. . . ."

"I'll order the wine," he said, motioning slightly.

A wine steward materialized beside the table, and after brief consultation, Tor picked a wine with a long, complicated name. When the steward had brought it and Tor had tasted and poured, he turned to me.

"You know, it's amusing—what you said about Louis and Alfie planning to use you as their instrument. I should think we might turn this situation to your advantage—don't you think?"

"To *my* advantage? I'm actually in a predicament because of this," I pointed out. "They'll expect me to get all the information from you that they might want, or ever dream up. Alfie will use it as a weapon against me if I refuse."

Tor pressed his fingertips together and rested his chin on them.

"And what do you need Alfie for?" he asked.

"What do you mean? He's my boss!"

"Aha—but *why* is he your boss? Because you *let* him be!"

"He pays my salary," I said. It was entirely unclear to me what Tor was talking about.

"The firm pays your salary—never forget that," he pointed out. "And they'll stop paying it the moment you stop making money for them. Now I repeat: what do you need Alfie for?"

I thought about that, and felt a cloud clearing from my mind. In perspective, I had to admit that Alfie had never done anything but thwart my attempts to do a decent job. This morning, through his shenanigans, he might have lost a client altogether.

"I guess I might do a lot better without him," I admitted; perhaps it was the champagne talking. But I chose not to dwell on that possibility, and took a sip of the new wine, too.

"Well then, it's settled. Get rid of him," said Tor,

leaning back as if the rest were obvious. "Simply tell Louis that you no longer need Alfie; he'll get the picture."

I couldn't believe it was all as easy as that. Just then, the waiter appeared with our first course.

"Here are your oysters," Tor said, "widely regarded as the food of love. Don't munch them; they're supposed to be eaten from the shell at a gulp. That's it—let it slide down your— What in heaven's *name* is that wretched sound you're making?"

"They're raw!" I told him.

"Of course they're raw. What on earth am I going to do with you?"

"Don't worry—I'm going to eat them *all*," I announced. "My mother told me that people who were afraid to try new foods shouldn't be permitted into restaurants."

"A wise woman, your mother. Would that she were here now; I've no experience at wet-nursing children."

"I'm not a child," I said.

"Oh, yes you are, my dear. You've the emotions of a three-year-old and the brains of a sage of ninety, the grace of an adolescent boy, and the body of a prepubescent nymph—ah yes, don't look at me like that. Eat your oysters. I'd like to be there one day, when all those parts come together into a grown woman. It might be quite a treat."

"I'd rather be a man," I said, suddenly realizing that was true.

"I'm well aware of that," he told me with a smile, "but you're not—and you never will be. Accept that you're a woman, and I assure you it'll work tremendously to your advantage. It already has."

■

THE STEWARDESS WAS ASKING US TO CHECK OUR SEAT belts for the descent into Kennedy. Idly, I wondered how much richer than I was today I'd be if I'd invented the seat belt and earned a dollar for every one that had been checked by every passenger since the dawn of commercial flight. I liked doing such calculations in my head—but this one was depressing.

Despite all those advantages Tor had assured me I had just by being a woman, he'd overlooked one or two drawbacks. In fact, only a few months after he'd pitted me against Alfie, my boss, Tor himself had *left* Monolith Corp. to start his own company—abandoning me in the lurch.

"*You* know what to do," he'd told me, patting me on the back. "Just tie up the loose ends."

I'd finally succeeded in giving Alfie the coup de grace, though it wasn't easy. And little good it did me: I was never promoted to management at Monolith Corp. According to senior management, male technicians would never be able to bring themselves to work for a female boss; I suppose they'd all have quit the firm, or drunk hemlock or something, first. But when I pointed out things like that to Tor—that the payoff was hardly worth the pain—he only laughed.

"In order for women to have equal rights, they have to give up a few," he said.

But no one seemed to grasp that "rights" weren't what I wanted. It seemed my special curse to care for people who tried to hand me life on a silver platter—a platter with plenty of strings attached. Ten years ago, my decision to break with Tor and make it on my own had cost me plenty—and I don't mean financially.

Now, as my plane circled in the famous Kennedy holding pattern, I wondered just how much this next rendezvous with Tor was going to cost me.

THE CONTRACT

> If a man gives to another silver, gold, or anything else to safeguard, whatsoever he gives he shall show to witnesses, and he shall arrange the contracts before he makes the deposits.
>
> —*The Code of Hammurabi*

MOST AMERICANS LOATHE NEW YORK CITY AT FIRST encounter. The filth and squalor, the graffiti and noise, the hysteria and violence, the decadence and outrageous expense—these impressions smite the sensibilities of visitors from the more orderly and well-tended cities of the west. But it's all clever camouflage—designed to keep out the fainthearted—as any New Yorker knows. If you *must* live in a city, New York is the only city in the world.

"You from New York, lady?" my taxi driver asked through the speaker box in the bullet-proof partition that separated us.

"I've been gone a long time," I told him.

"You ain't missed nuttin'—it's old, it's new, it's all the same. The more they change, the less they change; same old dump, but I call it home, ya know?"

I knew . . . *plus ça change.* That very quality of permanent change—that constant, violent, atom-splitting atmosphere of upheaval—produced an energy I really thrived on. Long before we reached the hotel, my biorhythms were in synch with the heart-pumping beat of the Big Apple.

I checked into the Sherry, saw my luggage to the suite, and went down to the restaurant for a late-night snack and cocktail. Sipping sherry at the Sherry Netherland was my own private tradition—it reminded me of Christmas in New York.

Sitting there alone, gazing through the frosty windows overlooking Fifth Avenue, I could see people laden with stacks of holiday packages, promenading through the snow. As I sat, warm and cozy, sipping the light, nut-flavored wine, I wondered again about Tor.

New York might be timeless, but people change. Since I'd last seen Tor, he'd become rich, famous, and exponentially more reclusive—while *I* had become a bankette. I wondered how he had changed, whether he'd gained a midriff bulge or lost his hair. And what would I seem like to him after all those years—years when I'd thought of Tor, oddly, more often as his calls slowly trickled off . . .

I looked at my reflection in the window—tall and skinny, all eyes and mouth and cheekbones. I still looked, as he'd said, like a fourteen-year-old boy playing hooky to go fishing.

I finished my snack and drink and then, about ten o'clock, went out to the front desk and picked up my room key. The clerk handed me a note with the key:

Your favorite restaurant. Noon.

There was no name, but I recognized the style. I folded the note, slipped it into my pocket, and went upstairs to bed.

■

MY FAVORITE RESTAURANT IN NEW YORK IS CAFÉ DES Artistes—across the park from the Sherry.

Like a fool, I decided to walk through the bitterly cold snow; I regretted the decision long before I'd reached the middle of Central Park South. Bracing myself against the cruel wind, I shoved my fists in my pockets and occupied myself for the rest of the miserable hike by recalling the glittering sunlight on San Francisco Bay, my winter orchids, those little white sailboats gliding across blue-green waters—and I soon found myself getting cold feet about everything to do with the luncheon I was about to attend.

Somewhere deep in my subconscious, I knew the problem wasn't only concern over jeopardizing my already dead-end career, breaking the rules or the law by perpetrating what was essentially an honorable crime, or dragging my colleagues along with me into a scheme that might blow up in our faces. What made me nervous was being here in New York again—with Tor—though I couldn't imagine why.

But one step inside the door of Café des Artistes brought me back to reality—what New York was all about. The café was built in the twenties, and it still resembled something from Paris during the expatriation of the literati. It was originally a watering hole for painters, whose upstairs ateliers were later converted into expensive private apartments. The restaurant walls were plastered with murals of jungles filled with parrots, paintings of Spanish conquistadors stepping from galleons, monkeys, wild flora, and nude coquettes with golden limbs, unexpectedly peeping from the dense foliage—all done in a mishmash style combining Watteau, Gibson Girl, and Douanier Rousseau—real Big Apple kitsch.

Today, a brass cart stood at center, groaning with fruits, floral bouquets, patisserie, and baskets of freshly baked breads. The rabbit pâté and decorated salmon mousse were also on display.

A few steps up to the left, where the bar angled off like a hallway, I found Tor in a private booth along the walls. If he hadn't flagged me down first, I mightn't have recognized him, he'd changed so much. His coppery hair now tumbled in ringlets to his collar, his skin seemed paler, his eyes more intense. Instead of the elegant three-piece suits that had been his trademark, he wore a casual fringed leather shirt with beadwork, and thin chamois trousers that revealed the taut muscles of his legs. He looked virile and healthy and ten years younger—but his wry smile remained the same.

"Did you *walk* here from San Francisco?" he asked sarcastically as he rose to greet me. "You're thirty minutes late, and your nose looks like a maraschino cherry.''

''Gee, that's a nice thing to say after ten years,'' I replied, sliding into the booth opposite him. ''I was just about to remark that *you* looked wonderful in that outrageous getup.''

I reached out and flipped the beaded fringes, and he smiled his dazzling smile—the one that set off warning signals in my brain.

''Thank you,'' he said with no small amount of charm. ''You're not looking bad yourself—at least, if you'd stop dripping all over the tablecloth. Here, take my handkerchief, and try to make appropriate use of it.''

I took it, and blew my nose.

''The sound of a nightingale, the manners of a queen,'' he told me.

''Why don't we get down to business?'' I suggested. ''I haven't come all this way to chat about my table manners.''

''You've been gone a long time,'' he told me. ''You've forgotten, we don't do things that way here. First, the aperitif—the fish, the fowl, the salad, the sweets, perhaps the cheese—but business is discussed over the demitasse. Not before.''

''I'll be happy to watch you stuff your face, if that's the custom. But I can't pack away food like that.''

''Fine—then leave it all to me,'' he said, and at a slight flick of his hand, the waiter materialized beside the table, with a bucket of wine already on ice.

''I've meant to ask—how do you *do* that?'' I said, gesturing toward the disappearing waiter.

''Restaurant ESP—mind control,'' he said blithely. ''It works every time. With two powerful transmission devices, a copper wire is unnecessary to complete a successful link. How do you think I found your friend Charles Babbage—or got in touch with *you*?''

I stared at him across the table as he filled my glass.

''So you tapped into our wavelengths. Terrific—I'm having lunch with Nostradamus. You can't control my mind, and you never could. I can't believe I'm sitting in a restaurant at the heart of Manhattan, seriously discussing mental telepathy."

"Fine. If you'd prefer, we'll discuss robbing banks—since that seems more sensible to you."

I glanced around quickly to be sure no one had overheard. It had taken Tor no time at all to get my dander up. How could he put me on the defensive like that? It *was* rather as though he could read my mind, and knew what would get to me quickest.

"Let's discuss the menu instead," I suggested coolly.

"I've already ordered," he informed me, twirling the bottle in the ice. "As I've always said, children should never be—"

"I'm thirty-two, and a bank vice-president," I informed him, trying not to sound huffy, "and I've chosen a few meals on my own. I'm a full-grown woman now—not your little protégée—so you can stop the *sage philosophe* routine."

I couldn't understand what it was about Tor that raised such irritation in me. I'd known again—the moment I saw him rising to greet me—that *he* was the reason I'd left New York ten years ago, not some tempting offer from the Bank of the World. Like my grandfather, Tor was the quintessential artisan in search of a lump of clay; he'd said as much, hadn't he? Was it *my* fault that I wanted to be the sculptor of my own fate?

But after that little diatribe of mine, he was watching me with a strange expression; I couldn't read it.

"So I see," he said cryptically. "Quite right, you *are* a grown woman. So that's what's changed—it had never occurred to me." He paused for a moment. "I see I shall have to revise my plans."

What plans? I wanted to ask—but I bit my tongue as the lemon sole arrived. I made idle chitchat through the rest of the meal, trying to come to terms with my mixed and indefinable feelings. The fish course was followed by veal chops with tiny vegetables, a salad of soft buttery lettuce, and finally, fresh strawberries—a luxury at this time of year—with thick Devonshire cream.

Tor had been strangely silent throughout the meal. I felt like a blimp, since despite my demurral I'd held up my end of the table—and I turned away when Tor tried to poke a strawberry, dripping with cream, into my mouth.

"I don't need to be force-fed," I protested. "I'm not a plant—nor a child, either. . . ."

"We've established that," he said curtly, pouring some coffee from a small silver pot. "Since we're here on business, now's the time. Why don't you show me your scheme?"

I pulled the thick folder from my bag, and handed it to him. One by one, he unfurled the pastiched charts Charles had produced for me. He ran his fingers over the crude lines that depicted risk against stolen dollars.

"Good Lord, what did you run these on—a dinosaur?" he asked, glancing up at me.

He pulled from his pocket a tiny machine, smaller than a calculator—a pocket microcomputer of the type they'd mentioned in the press; they weren't yet on the market. Tapping in a few numbers, he studied the results closely.

As he was so embroiled, scratching numbers on a scrap of paper and glancing back and forth between the machine and my charts, I flagged a passing waiter and ordered a crème caramel with extra burnt sugar.

Tor glanced up at me briefly in disgust.

"I thought you couldn't eat another bite," he said.

"It is woman's prerogative to change her mind," I pointed out.

But when the dessert arrived, without looking up from the charts, he stuck out a spoon and helped himself to some of the gooey custard. He glanced up with a naughty expression.

"I've always been secretly amused by your desire to have everything your own way," he admitted.

He tapped his pencil on the charts before him.

"According to these figures, you must pull off this theft of yours within a limited window of two months—no more. And the *maximum* you could hope to steal would be around ten million." He picked up his cup and sipped the coffee.

"I suppose you think *you* can do better?" I said sarcastically.

"My dear young woman," Tor said with a smile. "Did Strauss know how to waltz? It seems you've forgotten all you once learned under the baton of the master."

He leaned forward until his face was close to mine, and looked me straight in the eye.

"I can steal a billion dollars in two weeks," he said.

The waiter was hovering around, refreshing our coffee and swishing crumbs from the tablecloth with a flourish. Tor asked for the check, and paid it on the spot, as I fumed in silence.

"You told me you wanted to help me—not try to up the ante!" I hissed as soon as the waiter had left. "You said if I showed you my plan, you might improve on it; that's why I'm here!"

"And I *have* improved upon it," he said, still smiling his catlike smile. "There are many problems with this plan of yours. So I've developed one of my own—a superior model, if I may say so. I've always believed, you see, that it's easier to steal *really* large sums of money without using a computer at *all*!"

"Oh no—you're not suckering me into this one," I told him, gathering my charts together. "If you think I'm crazy enough to steal a billion dollars *without* using a computer, you're out of your mind."

"Don't be absurd," said Tor, putting one hand over mine on the table, to temper my haste. "Of course I don't think so; I wasn't suggesting you do anything of the sort! Naturally, I was speaking of *myself*."

I froze, and looked at him—his eyes dark fires, his nostrils flared, like a pawing Thoroughbred before the starting gun. I should have been warned—I should have known that look—it had cost me plenty in the past. But I couldn't resist my curiosity.

"What do you mean, *yourself*?" I said cautiously.

"I'd like to propose a little wager," he said. "We

each steal the same amount of money—you, *with* a computer, and I, without. In effect, I'll be like John Henry with his little hammer, and you'll be the great steel-driving engine—a timeless test of man against machine, soul against steel!"

"Very poetic," I admitted. "But not too bloody practical."

"John Henry *won* his bet, as I recall," Tor said smugly.

"But he died doing it," I pointed out.

"We all die sooner or later; it's simply a question of timing," Tor explained. "Better to have one *big* death than many little ones—wouldn't you agree?"

"Just because I'm mortal doesn't mean I want to choose my burial plot this afternoon," I told him. "This started as a little caper to prove the bank's security doesn't work. You said you'd help me, but it seems you want to turn it all into an international financial scam. A billion dollars? I think you've flipped your lid."

"Do you imagine that those bankers you work with are the *only* ones who aren't nice people?" he said seriously. "I deal almost daily with the SEC, with the commodities, mercantile, and securities exchanges. I know things about their behavior that would make your blood run cold. The best help I can give you, my lovely soubrette, is to expand your horizons—as I intend to do right now."

He stood up unexpectedly, and held out his hand to me.

"Where are we going?" I asked as we put on our coats and headed toward the door.

"To have a look at my etchings," he said mysteriously. "It seems you're a girl who needs to be seduced into action."

■

WITHIN THE WARMTH OF THE TAXI, HEADING DOWNTOWN, Tor turned to me.

"I want to show you my part of the wager," he said, "so you'll see just how serious I am."

"I'm giving the money back, you know," I told him. "Not even taking it—just moving it around where it can't be found for a while. All I want is to see their faces when they can't find it. So, even if I agreed to this ridiculous bet of yours, what would be in it for you?"

"What's in it for me, as you so charmingly put it, is quite the same as for you—and something more. Not only do I want to see their faces, I want them to clean up their act."

"Who's 'they'?" I asked, with sarcasm. "You haven't mentioned where this billion of yours would be coming from."

"Haven't I?" said Tor with a smile. "Why, let me correct that, then, my dear: I thought I'd hit the Big Board—the New York Stock Exchange and the American as well."

■

THEY ALWAYS SAY THERE'S A THIN LINE BETWEEN GEnius and insanity—and I thought Tor had crossed it. But then, taken in perspective, my own little scheme was hardly the product of a mind spilling over with sober judgment. It seemed I was getting in deeper by the hour.

We were dropped off in lower Manhattan, in the maze of the financial district, where shimmering mist from the nearby river hung suspended in the narrow canyons, between buildings that seemed to touch the sky. Before us was a glass and concrete edifice that loomed forty stories above Water Street, with the number "55" in bold letters on the front.

"Inside this building are my etchings," Tor said with a smile as he rubbed his hands together against the cold. "Or perhaps I should say 'engravings'—this structure houses the majority of stocks and bonds traded on all the major exchanges over the last thirty years.

"The concept dates back to the 1960s, when the brokerage houses around the world were becoming overloaded with paper. There was so much work required to transfer stocks and bonds from one hand to another, they decided to put it all to a stop. Securities are kept in 'street name'--the name of the brokerage firm that last traded them. Ownership is monitored by the same firm, and the physical instruments themselves are now put here. This is the most important financial building in New York; it's called the Depository Trust."

"*All* the securities traded in the United States are in this one building?" I said.

"No one knows exactly what percent is stored here—as compared with those stocks and bonds still in the hands of brokers, banks, or private individuals—but the effort has been to move them all here, for the sake of efficiency."

"I can see why it's a big risk; what if someone dropped a bomb here, for instance?"

"It's a bit more complex than that," he assured me as we walked around the side of the gigantic structure to have a better look. He brushed the first snowflake from my face, tossed his arm casually over my shoulder, and went on.

"I attended a meeting only last week, at the SEC. They'd gathered executives from large brokerage firms and money-center banks. The purpose of the meeting was to get these bankers and brokers to use a new computer system developed by the SEC that will track the physical location of securities."

"Securities aren't tracked by computer?" I said, amazed.

"The trading, yes—but not the physical location," Tor informed me. "The SEC believes that five to ten percent of all the stocks out there in bank vaults, attic trunks—even inside the Depository Trust—are either fraudulent or stolen. If they could put them all on computer, they'd find out which were duplicates or otherwise fakes. They want a physical inventory—and they want it now."

"Sounds like a great chance for everyone to clean house," I agreed.

"Does it?" Tor said with raised eyebrow, looking at me in the darkening light. "Then perhaps you can explain why every single institution—without exception—turned it down."

Of course, it didn't take a genius to figure that one out. The SEC didn't own the banks and couldn't force them to conduct an inventory, even if they provided the system. And none of these institutions wanted it known how many of their *own* securities were worthless! So long as they pretended they were real, they could keep trading them, or use them as collateral for other things. Once they were proven fakes—bingo—they'd be holding an empty bag. I realized suddenly the extent of dastardly behavior rampant in the entire financial industry—just as Tor had said. And it really made me see red.

But I realized something else, too: I'd underestimated Tor by quite a margin, and I felt dreadful about it. Why did I have to be so bloody self-righteous, assuming that *I* was the only one on earth with principles, and the desire to carry them through? He was right when he'd said I needed to expand my horizons. Now I knew what I had to do.

I glanced up and caught him watching me as we stood there in the mist that had turned to lightly falling snow. He was smiling his old wry smile, and for just an instant, I felt suspicious again—as if he'd mapped out the cogs in my brain beforehand, and had known precisely how many revolutions it would require to get me to this point.

"So you accept the wager, then?" he said.

"Not so fast," I told him. "If it's a *wager*, and not just a double-whammy theft—shouldn't there be some stakes?"

"I hadn't thought of that," he admitted, unsettled for a moment. "But you're right. If we're going through all these pains, I suppose there should be."

He thought awhile as we walked arm in arm back up the empty street in search of a cab. At last, he turned to me and put both hands on my shoulders, looking down with an expression I couldn't fathom.

"I have it," he said with a mischievous grin I didn't

care for at all. "Whoever loses will have to grant the winner's fondest wish."

"A wish?" I said. "That sounds like a fairy tale. Besides—maybe the loser would be in no position to grant such a wish."

"Perhaps not," he said, still smiling. "I only know that *you'd* be in a position to grant *mine*."

THE LIMITED PARTNERSHIP

Men of thin skin with a conscience all the time full of prickles, are out of place in business dickerings. A prickly conscience would be like a silk apron on a blacksmith.

It isn't how you get your money, but what you do with it that counts.

—*Bouck White,*
The Book of Daniel Drew

I was certainly relieved I'd had the chance to hike on Wall Street after lunch. Even so, I could barely put away a quarter of the dinner Tor ordered at the Plaza dining room that night—saumon en papillote, duck à l'orange, soufflé Grand Marnier, to scratch the surface—as we finished ironing out the kinks in our bet.

Tor was unwilling to reveal what his wish might be, should he win the wager. And so, based upon prior experience with him, I thought it best to come up with more substantial terms for our stakes. The ensuing negotiation began over the salmon, not the coffee. It took hours; and afterward, although my head ached long before the cognac was served, I couldn't remember the last time I'd had such fun.

Tor had always been able to explain anything with amazing clarity, but his mind itself was baroque. He was a master of complexity and intrigue, and loved to examine an issue from every possible viewpoint. I knew he'd dreamed up this wager as much out of boredom as moral indignation. As usual, life itself just wasn't enough of a challenge.

"It's far too simple," he said off the bat, "just to walk off with a billion dollars; any hacker can do that.

To make it *really* interesting, I think we should leave undefined the specific amount of the theft.''

''How can we tell who's won, then?'' I wanted to know.

''We'll put a time limit on it—three months or so—perhaps a bit extra to plan the details. Then we take the money we've 'borrowed' . . . and *invest* it! This throws in the added challenge of speculation. So the issue is not who steals the most money, but who makes best use of it. We'll target a reasonable sum. Whoever reaps the agreed-upon amount first will win.''

''Stealing a billion isn't tough enough,'' I commented, not expecting an answer.

But Tor was tapping away at his small machine. ''Thirty million dollars!'' he announced, looking up. ''That's how much you can make, with a decent return on a billion, in three months' time.''

Without waiting to hear from me, he pulled out a pocket calendar. ''Today is November twenty-eighth—nearly December,'' he went on. ''It should take me two weeks, as I said, for the actual theft, then the three months for the investment. With a few extra weeks to set up and prepare, I should be able to finish by . . . April first!''

''April Fools' Day?'' I laughed. ''That seems more than appropriate. But what about me? Charles said I could steal only ten million. How can I invest *that* to make thirty?''

''I'd never disparage Charles,'' he said with that smile. ''But I looked at your charts. As it happens, you asked him the wrong question—how many *domestic* wire transfers you could steal—a drop in the bucket! What about money from *outside* the United States?''

Good Lord, he was right! It was double the volume or more—but I hadn't included those transfers in my study. Though I didn't control systems like CHIPS or SWIFT—the government's huge wire transfer networks—I certainly interfaced with them, and that money still moved in and out of our bank.

''I'm beginning to feel grateful to you,'' I admitted,

sipping my cognac with a smile. "It's a deal, if we can agree on the stakes. I know what *I* want—I've thought this through all day. I want to be head of security at the Fed; I had the job, anyway, until my boss told them not to hire me. I know, with your contacts, you could get me the job back. But I won't ask you to—unless I win, fair and square."

"Very well," he agreed with a grimace. "But my dear, as I told you twelve years ago, you don't belong in a financial institution. Those people don't know red from black—they think loans are assets and deposits are liabilities. You belong to me; I've invested too many years in you to watch you pumping out columned ledgers for bankers—a bunch of ignoramuses who can't appreciate what they've got."

"My grandfather was a banker," I said with injured pride.

"Not really; he lost his shirt to men like these. Believe me, I know the story. What was he lacking—have you asked yourself? I doubt very much that intelligence or integrity is the answer."

He motioned for the check as he continued, somewhat irritably.

"Very well—you'll have what you want. But if I win—as I shall—I feel no compunction about collecting what *I* want: you'll come to work for me, as you should have done long ago."

"As what—Galatea, your flawless creation?" I said with a laugh, though I didn't find it so awfully amusing. I'd escaped from this ten years ago; now again, I found myself staring it in the face. But even if I lost, I wasn't going to be a patsy to Tor's hubris for the rest of my life.

"For how long?" I asked him. "You couldn't expect it to be forever?"

He thought about that for a moment.

"For a year and a day," he said cryptically, not looking at me.

" 'The Owl and the Pussycat'!" I exclaimed. "I remember that poem: 'They took some honey and plenty of money . . .' "

" 'Wrapped up in a five-pound note,' " Tor said, looking up pleasantly surprised.

" 'And they sailed away for a year and a day, 'neath the light of the silvery moon,' " I finished.

"It would seem—mature and seasoned banker that you are—you still recall your fables, my dear little pussycat," said Tor with a smile. "Who knows—perhaps you'd enjoy losing this wager to me far more than winning it."

"I wouldn't bank on it," I said.

■

THERE WAS ONLY ONE THING THAT MADE TOR UNCOMFORTABLE about the wager he'd dragged me into. In order to carry out *his* part of the bet, he needed an accomplice. Though he knew everything there was to know about computers, there was one necessary skill he himself did not possess.

"I need a photographer," he told me, "and a good one."

By coincidence, I happened to know one of the best photographers in New York. I agreed to take Tor over there the very next morning.

"Tell me about this friend of yours," he said as we taxied uptown on Sunday. "Is he trustworthy? Can we tell him the truth about our plans?"

"*He* is a *she*, and her name is Georgian Daimlisch," I said. "She's my best friend, though I haven't seen her in years. I can assure you, she's totally trustworthy—but don't believe a word she says."

"I see," he said. "The picture you paint is much clearer—we're about to meet a reliable schizophrenic. Does she know what we're coming to see her about?"

"I'm not sure she knows we're coming at all."

"Didn't you tell me you spoke with the mother?" Tor said.

"Lelia? Yes, of course—but that doesn't mean anything."

Tor was silent the rest of the trip.

It had always been hard to describe Georgian, though she'd been my best friend for more years than she'd permit me to reveal. When she lived anywhere, it was at her mother's apartment on upper Park Avenue. But Georgian never settled anywhere for long; she was a butterfly of a rare breed, and wildly independent.

Georgian wasn't independent financially—or, I should say, no one knew exactly how much she had. As a photographer, she traveled around the world, stopping at châteaus and palaces that were far beyond ordinary means. On the other hand, she usually dressed in tattered jeans and T-shirts, and wore so many gold rings she seemed to be sporting brass knuckles.

Most of her acquaintances thought she was frivolous, sex-crazed, extravagant, and more than slightly batty; I found her serious, reclusive, and a brilliant business manager with a mind like a steel trap. How could one person engender such diverse impressions in the minds of so many? Simple—she was unique, her own creation. She'd become a photographer to fashion her own universe, and then live in it.

I saw her rarely, because when I did, she expected *me* to do likewise.

As soon as I'd agreed to introduce Tor to Georgian, I began to have reservations. They had a lot in common: both were highly possessive of me and thought they could fix whatever was wrong with me—but their ideas of how to achieve that fix were incompatible. Tor wanted to introduce me to reality; Georgian wanted to strike the word from my vocabulary. I feared they'd hate each other on sight.

The lobby of Lelia and Georgian's building looked like a fancy auto showroom; it lacked only the Cadillacs scattered about the floor. Enormous chandeliers hung from the ceilings like bunches of frosted grapes; a number of deep red, flocked-velvet divans were scattered across the floor, and brass cuspidors were, for some reason, placed beside each. There were forests of marble pillars—more than at Pompeii—and plastered on each wall, white fenestrations lavish with gold. Enormous black funerary urns were stuffed with rainbows of silk flowers, and over the elevator bay a plaster cornucopia spilled over with fruits that tumbled down to lodge with festive abandon between the doors.

"Whatever happened to good taste?" Tor mumbled, wincing as we crossed the vast floor.

"Wait till you get a load of *Lelia's* place," I said. "Her tastes run to French Decadent."

"But you said she was Russian," Tor said as we reached the elevators.

"White Russian—raised in France," I explained. "Lelia can't speak her native tongue too well—or any other, for that matter. She's sort of a lingual potluck."

"Goodness, if it isn't Miss Banks!" said Francis, the elevator operator. "How many years has it been? The baroness will be delighted, ma'am—does she know you're in town?"

This was Francis's discreet way of saying he should phone upstairs to announce us. I told him to go ahead.

On the twenty-seventh floor, Francis unlocked the elevator doors with a key and we stepped into the large marble foyer, where the maid greeted us with a little curtsy and ushered us through another set of doors into the great hall—a vast marble corridor mirrored like Versailles at either side.

When she went off to find our hostess, Tor turned to me and whispered, "Who's the baroness?"

"That's Lelia," I said. "I think it's an affectation—like being a Romanoff: who's to say whether you *are* one or not?"

As we waited there in the hall sounds reached us from several rooms away—a good deal of female shrieking, and doors banging shut. At last, a door was slammed with finality, making the crystal wall sconces tinkle.

One of the mirrored French doors flew open, and Lelia popped out wearing a long teal satin kimono with tendrils of marabou wisping about as she moved.

Though it was nearly noon, her honey-blond hair was tousled as if she'd just rolled out of bed.

Clutching me, she pressed her face against mine once at either side, in the French manner, then gave me a big Russian bear hug, her marabou tickling my nose.

"Darlink! Happy happy happy! Too bad you must do the waiting, but Georgian is *très mauvaise* today."

To compound the confusion of Lelia's borscht-bouillabaisse lingo, she often forgot in midsentence what she'd been talking about, replying to something you'd asked on a different occasion. When she said Georgian's name, it came out "Zhorzhione," causing many to think she was describing an Italian dessert.

"I've brought my friend Dr. Tor to meet her," I said, by way of introduction.

"Ce qu'il est charmant!" cried Lelia with sparkling eyes, appraising Tor.

She extended her hand to him, and damn if he didn't kiss it!

"This beautiful man you are bringing—like a statue of gold he is. *Vi nye ochin nrahveetis*—and his costume, *très chic*—the finest Italian cut!" She touched his sport coat delicately, as if admiring a piece of art. "Always I am despairing for you, my darlink; you are working so hard—no time for the young men—but now you are bringing this handsome—"

"Stop despairing, Lelia," I told her. Though Georgian might be difficult, I'd forgotten that Lelia was downright dangerous when it came to comments about my private life—not a subject I was eager to broadcast. Not that I *had*, in her terms, a private life. "Dr. Tor is a *colleague*," I hastened to add as she accompanied us along the hallway.

"Quel dommage," Lelia commented sadly, glancing at him like a trout that had gotten away.

"We've business to discuss with Georgian," I explained, peeping into a few rooms where the mirrored doors were ajar. "What's keeping her?"

"That one!" huffed Lelia. "Impossible! She dress like for driving the truck—but to change for the guests?

Quel enfant terrible. What should a mother do? You go sit; I will make something nice to eat. Zhorzhione, she comes soon."

Lelia settled us behind the louvered doors of the Blue Room—her favorite color—thus indicating that Tor had met with her complete approval. Lelia classified everyone by color. She kissed me, patted my hair, took one more approving look at Tor, and departed.

A few moments later, the beribboned maid reappeared bearing a little tray with a decanter of vodka and two crystal shot glasses. Tor poured us each a glass, but I motioned mine away. He downed his own in one gulp.

"Stolichnaya," he said, licking his lips.

"Some judge *you* are," I told him. "That's Lelia's home brew—it's two million proof. You'll be out cold if you do another like that."

"It's the correct way to drink vodka," he assured me. "And it's highly inhospitable to refuse a drink in a Russian home."

When the maid returned to tell us that "Mademoiselle" would see us, Tor quickly polished off the vodka in my glass, too—no doubt so our hostess would not take offense—and accompanied us to the "Plum Room," at the end of the hall.

The Plum Room had been a music room, and the walls were mirrored above the wainscoting. Everything else I remembered had been changed.

The old Bösendorfer piano was shoved into a corner across the room, all the upholstered chairs around it were draped with sheets, and the peach, mauve, and gray Aubussons, which had once graced the travertine floors, were now rolled up, tipped on end, and standing like pillars against the far wall.

Now the floor was spread with dark green tarpaulin, and scaffolding spanned the vast space like a huge jungle gym. Beneath the structure stood three angular mannequins draped in satin, sequins, and sprays of white feather; they were frozen in their poses and scarcely breathing.

High above, sprawled over the scaffold like a spider in a web, was Georgian, cameras hanging from her neck and others mounted on the bars all around her. Big klieg lights glittered everywhere, beacons in the otherwise darkened room.

"Hip," Georgian said. A model moved her pelvis forward a few inches. "Naomi, I can't see your thigh—good, that's it. Birgit, your nose is in the feathers—chin up, right angle—stop." *Click.* "Phoebe—shoulder back, right foot out." *Click.* "Shoulder down—lift those feathers, there's a shadow. Good." *Click.*

Tor watched everything intently in the darkness: the placement of lights, Georgian's position on the scaffolding, the trajectory from her cameras to the models, who moved like automatons below the twelve tons of steel and equipment. Finally, he looked down at me with a smile.

"She's very good," he said softly.

"Silence on the set!" snapped Georgian, then went on with: "Head down, lift arm, good." *Click.*

After nearly half an hour of this mystical staccato code between Georgian and her prey, she pulled her head up from the steel matrix, hung her cameras and loose lenses by their straps over the scaffold pegs, and swung herself down from the ceiling like a monkey.

"Lights," she called as from somewhere the draperies were pulled back to let the harsh glare of cold winter light flood the room. The models looked suddenly strange and grotesque, disrobing right there—stripping down to their panty hose and rubbing cold cream on their faces, as if no one else were present.

"Good Lord! You've come back!" cried Georgian, rushing to me across the room, and ignoring Tor and the others.

She planted a big, wet kiss on my mouth, then hooked her arm through mine, and glanced briefly at Tor. "Don't mind us—we'll be right back," she told him, bustling me through the doors.

"Where on earth did you find *him*?" she whispered

just outside. "For a girl that doesn't get about much—I'm amazed—he's sex on a stick!"

"Dr. Tor is a colleague—my mentor, in fact," I explained, somewhat stiffly. Georgian and Lelia were carrying on as if he were a Greek god.

"I'd like to have a few colleagues like *that*," Georgian assured me. "All of mine are the type that stick their pinkie out when they talk to you. Has Mother seen him yet?"

"You bet; he kissed her hand," I told her.

"She's probably out in the kitchen right now—baking strudel. She doesn't miss a trick. As opposed to *you*," she added, touching my many-layered yardage of clothing as if it were diseased. "You look like a panzer tank in drag. Have I taught you nothing in all these years? Drama—that's what you're missing. Introducing him as 'doctor' indeed. Doesn't he have a first name? Philolaus or Mstislav—something sexy, I bet. Or Thor! Thor Tor!"

"It's Zoltan," I told her.

"I knew it—I'll bet she's making piroshki, too."

"Who is?"

"My mother, who else?" said Georgian. "Come with me; I've got something I need to do."

She dragged me off through the maze of rooms to her suite at the back, muttering all the way.

Everything about Georgian was dramatic. Her sculptor's hands with those long, graceful bones—her huge blue-green eyes and wide cheekbones, that chameleon-like face—funny or tragic—flickering with her moods, and her wide, expressive, sensual mouth with rows of straight, white teeth. "With teeth like that," her mother used to say, "I could have eaten up half of Europe."

Back in Georgian's boudoir—a room that seemed designed by a six-year-old, all gingham and ruffles and porcelain—she plopped me down before the dressing table and started brushing my hair and pulling out the pins that had held it in place.

"You've got a lot of nerve, criticizing *my* clothing,"

I said, looking at her torn T-shirt. Those holes seemed placed for maximum effect.

"I've got plenty of panache—for a deadbeat." She laughed.

She was glossing my lips and brushing strange things on my face, from the messy assortment of bottles that littered her table. "If you had *my* style, you'd have them all eating out of your hand."

"Somehow, I don't think gold lamé and sparkly pumps would go over at the Bank of the World," I pointed out. "I'm an executive, not a jet-setter like you, and I simply cannot comport myself—"

"Comport? To hell with that goddamned bank," she said. "Do they send spies around, to monitor your attire? You come in here, dragging that gorgeous golden hunk—everyone faints on the floor in a sexual frenzy—and you keep calling him your *colleague*! Your *mentor*! He wasn't looking at you just now as if he wanted to teach you all about corporate profit margins, I can tell you that, but you just refuse to see it. Be honest, when was the last time you leaped out of bed, threw open the window, and said, 'Thank God I'm alive! This is the most glorious day, and today I'm going to do something so fabulous it will change my *entire life*'?"

"You mean . . . before coffee?" I said, laughing.

"You're insane!" cried Georgian, ruffling my hair and pulling me to my feet. "You know I love you. It's just that I want you to stop *thinking* your way through life—and start *feeling*."

"What's the difference?" I asked her.

"That's the point—precisely," she told me, pursing her lips.

She went to the closet, pulled off her T-shirt, and pulled a fluffy pink sweater over her close-cropped, silvery blond hair.

"Can you honestly say you're not attracted to him?" she asked seriously.

That question was one I'd avoided even asking myself. Tor *was* my mentor, even my Pygmalion—but no one ever told the story from Galatea's point of view!

What happened inside *her*, after she—Pygmalion's perfect creation—turned from stone to living flesh? With all the problems I already had in my career and my life, I wasn't ready to solve that one—not by a long shot.

"If you're not interested, my friend," Georgian was saying, "I'd be happy to take him off your hands."

"Be my guest," I shot back at once, wondering why my voice sounded brittle even to me.

"Ha-*ha*!" cried Georgian with a devilish grin. "Rather quick on the trigger, wouldn't you say?"

Suddenly, I deeply regretted having brought Tor here at all. Whenever Georgian got that *look* of hers, it meant something terrible was about to happen. I didn't even want to imagine the possibilities.

"I want you to control yourself," I told her sternly. "He *is* my colleague, and you're not to turn this project into your usual three-ring circus."

"I've got a project of my own now," she said cryptically, "and I know wherein my duty lies. As usual, you've been lying to yourself, but this is very stimulating to me: correcting people's impressions of themselves happens to be my forte."

She tossed her arm across my shoulders and walked me back through the maze, humming a cheerful tune, as I cringed inwardly. When we reached the wide hall, we could hear the murmur of voices from the Blue Room.

"Are these pictures of your family?" Tor was asking as we came in.

"*Nyet*," said Lelia. "My family, they are all dead. These are my dear friends: Pauline, who made the costumes, how you say couturière—Pauline Trigère. And this is Schiap, another costume maker, dead also. And this is the Contessa di—"

"What are you boring our guest with, Mother?" asked Georgian, coming up to take her arm.

"Who's this old fellow?" asked Tor. "He looks familiar."

"Ah . . . that is Claude, my very dear *ami*. He was so sweet, how he loved all his flowers. But unhappily he was, how you say, hard of seeing. I would go to his gardens at Giverny, and explain how the flowers were looking to me—and then he would paint them on his canvas. He says I am his young eyes.''

''Giverny? This was Claude Monet?'' Tor glanced at Lelia and then at us.

''*Da*—Monet.'' Lelia looked at the photo wistfully. ''He was very old and I was very young. There was one flower that I loved so much—you remember it, Zhorzhione? He made me a little watercolor of it. What was the name of this flower?''

''Water lilies?'' suggested Georgian.

Lelia shook her head. ''It was a very *long* flower—*poorpoorniyi*—the color of raisins, what you call grapes. Purple—is that a word?''

''Long and purple like grapes?'' I said. ''Maybe lilacs?''

''No matter,'' Lelia dismissed us. ''It will come on me later.''

''Mother,'' Georgian interrupted impatiently, ''I haven't met True's friend yet.''

''Of course not!'' snapped Lelia. ''Because you leave the guests always in the foyer; they could die there! And no *au revoir* for the mannequins, either—they have to leave through the service door, like the *femme de ménage*! Be thankful to *le bon Dieu* that you have a mother to look after all the little bad habits.''

''Yes, I thank God every day for that,'' Georgian said dryly.

''Georgian, may I present Dr. Zoltan Tor,'' I said formally. ''He's nearly as old a friend of mine as *you* are.''

''And just what is *that* supposed to mean?'' she said sweetly.

''True?'' said Tor. ''That's very nice.''

''It means the same as Verity, doesn't it? And it's so much less prissy-bankerly—'Verity-in-lending'—and all.'' Turning to Lelia, she added, ''Mother, True wants me to discuss business with her friend here—so why don't you run off and see that we're not disturbed?''

Lelia looked crestfallen, but Georgian put her arm around her, and physically ushered her from the room. There were a few sharp whispers in French outside the door, and Georgian returned alone.

"Mother likes to participate in everything," she explained.

"I find her charming," Tor said with a smile. "Tell me, did she really know Claude Monet?"

"Oh, Mother knows everyone," said Georgian, adding loudly, "but only because she's such a dreadful *snoop*."

We heard the clatter of little feathered shoes outside, scurrying off down the corridor. Georgian smiled and shrugged, plopping herself down on an ottoman.

"I'm sorry I ran off with True before," she explained as Tor and I took seats, "but I haven't seen her in so long. She comes to New York all the time, but never calls me—not when she's in 'business mode.' She has two *completely* different personalities, you know."

She batted her eyes innocently. I felt it coming on—the desire to strangle her—though I knew she had only begun.

"Two personalities? I'm afraid I've only seen one of them," said Tor, reproachfully.

"Perhaps so—since she says you're only a 'colleague'—but she isn't *anything* like how she appears at that bank-of-whatever-it-is. All that's a total sham." She waved her hand nonchalantly.

"I'd always suspected there was another Verity," Tor agreed.

"Then you don't know about our exploits?" Georgian raised her brows. "Living in the harem at Riyad? The *kama sutra* odyssey in Tibet? Being sold into white slavery in the Cameroons? The cattle crossing to Morocco?"

"Georgian—" My teeth were gritted, but Tor cut in.

"Please continue," he told Georgian, and turning to me with admirable composure, he added, "It seems there are a few things you've concealed from me. I feel

I've a right to examine your background—before entering with you into any further business dealings."

My background, my ass, I thought. But Georgian was carrying on.

"Exactly. She's lovable—but a hypocrite. Now, as to our first adventure—True and I were very young—"

"How young *were* we?" I asked maliciously.

She shot me a look, but it didn't break her stride.

"Not long ago—we were very poor, no money at all—but we longed to go to Morocco. We lacked talent to pay our way, no bankers or photographers were needed. The only ship where we could secure passage was a dreadful old cattle boat, absolutely *crawling* with vermin—flies in the cowshit, that sort of thing. We had to travel in steerage."

"No pun intended?" Tor interjected.

"Literally—we slept with the bovines—a real nightmare. But True was more fortunate: the captain took a liking to her. One night he came down and saw her sleeping amidst the dung, and cried out, *'Ach! Das ist ein voman!'*—or something to that effect."

"He was a German then, this captain," Tor deduced with a smile I didn't care for.

"Tall, blond, and gorgeous," Georgian agreed. "Come to think of it—he looked a bit like *you.*"

"Did he indeed?" said Tor, leaning back with his arms folded. I noticed he didn't look at me now.

"He swept her into his arms, carried her to his cabin, and seduced her without a word. She was held there three days—without food or water—but when she was released, she was hardly upset as she might have been. To the contrary, she loved the experience. But do you know what *I* was doing all this time?" she added. "I was shoveling cowshit the entire trip! While *she* paid our entire passage to Morocco by lavishing sexual favors on the handsome golden captain and his crew of young Adonises—"

"The crew as well," echoed Tor, raising an eyebrow.

"There wasn't one that was over twenty." Georgian raced on, hardly pausing for air. "She swam in the buff, cavorting like a dolphin with the lithe young junior officers as they fed each other papaya with their fingers—"

"This was Morocco—not Tahiti," I pointed out, tapping my foot in impatience.

"—it was like something from *Mutiny on the Bounty.*"

"Page three-twenty-seven, to be precise," I said, wondering if the torture would ever end.

"But it was the captain she really fell for," said Georgian. "A woman like True needs to be *mastered;* she admired him for having the audacity to take the upper hand. . . ."

"There's a lesson in this, is there?" said Tor, still trying to suppress his smile.

"I've no doubt that she hoity-toitys around with *you*—calling you her colleague, and *comporting* herself, and such. But don't be misled by her cool demeanor and tentlike attire!"

She stood up and went behind my chair, where she dug her hands into my mess of already disheveled hair, and messed it further.

"While *inside* is this seething, writhing, insatiable mass of unfulfilled *passion*!"

"It's lucky you've torn the veils from my eyes," said Tor as I spat hair from my mouth in fury. "My dear Verity—now that I've seen this other side—"

"What *side*?" I stormed. "There is no side! Can we please get down to work?"

"Naturally," said Tor, looking warmly at Georgian. "Now that things are more aboveboard, may I add that I think this is the beginning of a most productive relationship?"

Though Georgian was still behind me, I swear that what passed between them was a conspiratorial wink.

■

I'VE NEGLECTED TO MENTION THAT THE BLUE ROOM was one of the seven wonders of the world. It appeared small, but I'd measureu the dimensions once while helping Lelia install the pink quartz *faux* mantel, carved with dimpled cherubim, entwined with eglantine and wild swans.

That room embraced no fewer than seventeen chairs, sofas, ottomans, *fauteuils*, and recamiers—all upholstered in ice blue with white lacquer trim—and ranging in style from Louis XII through XVI. The tables, ranging in height, were heaped with piles of Lalique, cloisonné, and porcelain—so overburdened that it seemed they'd topple over from the sheer weight of bric-a-brac. The walls were decorated in trompe l'oeil lattices, through which one caught tantalizing glimpses of so many vistas that walking around the room gave the dizzying impression of completing a world tour by merry-go-round.

As an added touch—if anything else were needed—Lelia's exhaustive collection of photos and miniatures was scattered wherever space afforded. Many of these memorabilia were affixed to the lattices, so it seemed hundreds of eyes were watching as the viewer tried to bring into focus the dizzying landscape beyond.

That Georgian, Tor, and I sat there for four hours was a testimonial to our stamina. Perhaps the vodka helped. But by the end of the third hour we were sprawled on the floor, singing "Troika"—I playing the part of the sleigh bells, as I knew no Russian. We were interrupted by the maid, who entered with great decorum, daintily stepping over our bodies and bearing a tray of food.

"What did I tell you?" asked Georgian, looking up from her daze. "Piroshki!"

"And clear borscht!" added Tor, sniffing the air like a bird dog. "With real Russian curds!"

He staggered to his feet as the maid departed, and with great ceremony spooned food into plates and bowls, spilling a bit here and there. I hadn't realized how hungry I was until I smelled Lelia's cooking.

"This borscht is delicious," Tor said between slurps.

"Don't eat too much; you'll encourage her," said Georgian from the floor. "Then the food will come marching in like *The Sorcerer's Apprentice*—we'll be buried in mountains of food—we'll have to throw ourselves against the door to keep it out."

"I'd gladly die this way." Tor sighed, inhaling the aroma of the piroshki. He reached for the nearest one and wolfed it down. "But now, since the singing's done, I may as well tell you why we're here."

"My God—back to business?" said Georgian, rolling over and putting a pillow over her head.

"Verity and I have made a little wager," he informed the pillow. He paused, resumed spooning down borscht as if it were lifeblood. "And, if *she* loses this wager—she'll have to grant my fondest wish."

Georgian's head came out of the pillows. She sat up and looked at me.

"A wish? Give me a bowl of that soup. What kind of bet is that?"

"One that I think you might enjoy being party to," said Tor with a smile, dishing up the soup. "To beat her, you see, I'm going to need an ally—a very good photographer."

Georgian was now fully alert.

"What does each of you get, if you win?" she asked Tor.

"If Verity—True—wins, she gets a job at an even more boring financial institution than the one she's imprisoned in now," he said as Georgian wrinkled her nose and grimaced at me. "But if *I* win—she'll have to come to New York and work for me—be my slave, if you will—for a year and a day. You see, your little story had a moral, after all."

Georgian looked at him as over her face spread a beatific, and dangerous, smile. She held out her hand, and Tor took it.

"Do you mind if I call you Thor?" she asked.

"Thor?" He looked at me with curiosity.

"I think it's Old Nordic for 'death by conspiracy,' " I said.

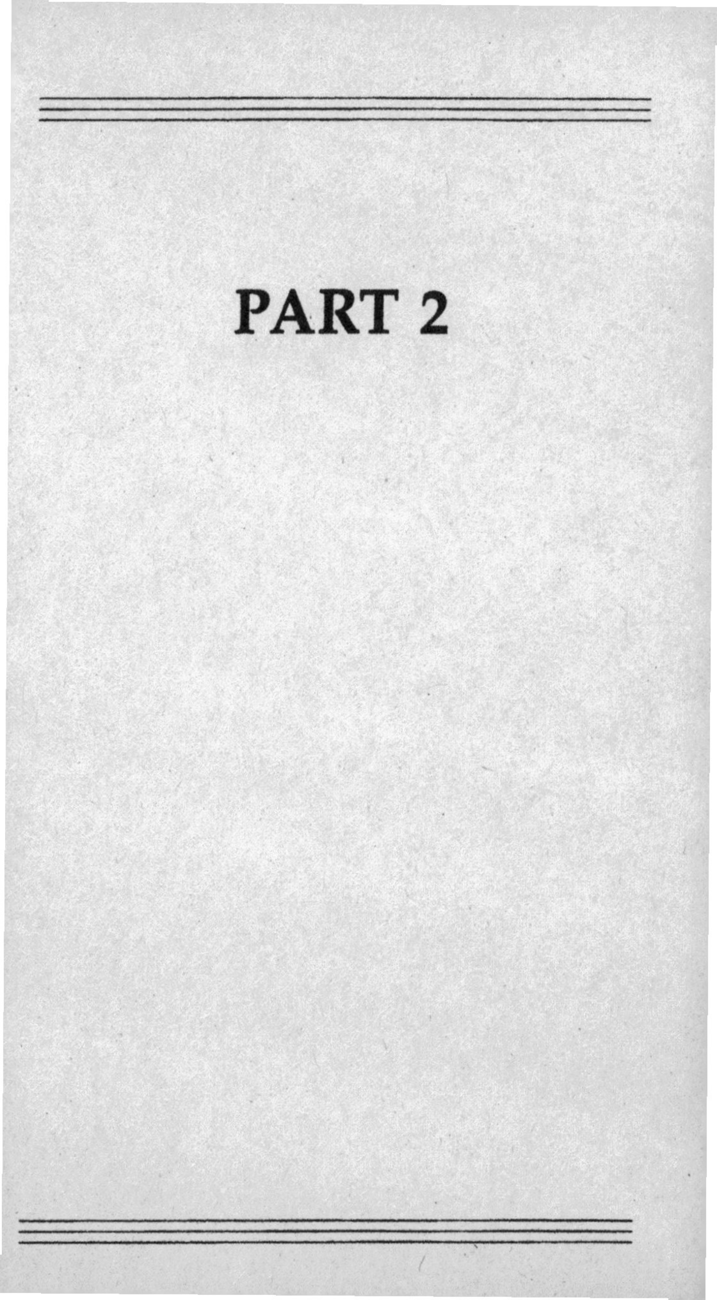

PART 2

Frankfurt, Germany
Autumn 1785

THIRTY YEARS BEFORE THE MORNING NATHAN ROTHSchild had waited for a bird to arrive at the small room in Frankfurt's Judengasse, two men sat in a drafty castle outside the city, playing chess. They did not know that this particular chess game would mark the first move in the Rothschild banking dynasty—which was to take root that very night.

"So, have you taken my advice, Landgrave?" the general asked, sipping his cognac.

"Knight to E seven," said the Landgrave, his face red and sweaty from the effort of thought. He, too, took a swig of cognac. Leaning back, his eyes still on the board, he said, "Yes, I sent the message this morning. They have permission to bring the Jew from the compound tonight; it's perfectly all right. But they close and seal the gates at sunset—we must keep him here until morning."

"It's a shame they have to lock them up like that," the general said thoughtfully. "Knight to G five."

"It's for their own protection," commented the Landgrave. "You know what bloodbaths we used to have when these Jews were permitted to run about on the loose; it's better this way. Would you care for more cognac? It's quite good, isn't it? I have it brought from France and age it myself. Give me your glass."

"Thank you," said the general. "But still, it seems a shame. Take this fellow Meyer Amschel, for example—a very brilliant fellow."

"Oh, they're all bright, I've no doubt of that—but only when it comes to the common sort of thing. Barter. Trade. They've no culture, these people. You know that as well as I, von Estorff."

"I think you'll be surprised at this particular chap, Landgrave. But you needn't take my word for it; see for yourself."

"Here, have a taste of this," said the Landgrave, passing von Estorff his replenished glass. "If you get drunk, perhaps I'll win a game of you."

"Only with God's intervention." The general laughed. "In twenty-five years, you've never done so yet! But it's your move."

"Knight takes bishop," said the Landgrave. "I don't like placing my affairs in the hands of Jews, however, von Estorff—so please don't expect it of me. I'm willing to give the man my ear. If I find his ideas plausible and they make money, he certainly won't go unrewarded."

"That's all anyone could ask," agreed the general, "though I should point out he's a great expert in numismatics, your favorite interest! Knight takes pawn at F seven."

"Damn—why did you have to make that move?" the Landgrave cried, looking up in irritation as a page entered the room. "What the hell do you want?" he snapped. "Can't you see that we are engaged?"

"A thousand pardons, sire. But a Jew is at the door, claiming he was bidden here to see you. Though I explained it is after the curfew and that you were occupied, he insists—"

"Yes, yes. Well, show the fellow in."

"As you wish, sire." The page bowed and departed. A few moments later he reappeared, and clicked his heels. "Meyer Amschel, the Jew!" he announced, then bowed again and left the room.

The Landgrave did not look up from the chessboard. He sat, a scowl on his face, studying the pieces carefully. After a moment, he noticed a shadow cast upon the board. He glanced up to see the intruder leaning over the board, rapt in concentration.

"What's this fellow's name?" the Landgrave demanded of the room at large.

"Meyer Amschel," the general replied.

"Excuse me, sire," Meyer Amschel corrected him, "but I go by the name of 'Red-shield.' "

"Ah yes—I'd forgotten," apologized the general. "He's adopted the name of Red-shield, after the color of the weapons shield hanging before his place of business in the Judengasse."

"A coat of arms?" said the Landgrave with raised eyebrow. "Where will it end, von Estorff? Well, Rothschildt—the 'beknighted' Jew—have a seat over there till we've finished; you're blocking my view."

"Excuse me, sire—but I prefer to stand, if you don't mind."

"You see how it goes, von Estorff." The Landgrave sadly shook his head. "First Jews have coats of arms—then they have preferences. Look here, Herr Coat of Arms, you've no right to a weapons shield unless you've been knighted. And you've no right to be out of compound after the curfew. Sit down at once, or I'll have you arrested for arrogance and insubordination!"

"Excuse me, sire—but is it your move?" asked Rothschild.

"I beg your pardon?" said the Landgrave in total astonishment.

"Yes, Meyer," the general replied with a gleam in his eye, "it is the Landgrave's move—and he's playing the black pieces."

"In that case, Landgrave," said Meyer Amschel, "may I point out that you're assured of a victory in eleven moves?"

"What!" cried the Landgrave, outraged. "How dare you presume to advise me in how to play chess?"

"William, William," said the general, laughing as

he put his hand on the other's arm, "let's see what he has in mind. I'm intrigued—and we can always play another game if he is wrong."

"Von Estorff, are you completely mad? Imagine if it's said of me about Frankfurt that I've taken to playing chess with Jews! My chess playing is already a laughing matter in some quarters."

"But we won't be playing chess with him, we'll merely be listening to his advice. And that's why you brought him here, isn't it? What difference whether the advice is about chess or money?"

"If you want me to believe that a Jew can understand a complex matter like chess, von Estorff—then why not have my Borzoi in here, and he can bark out the paternoster in Latin?" When he saw the grim set of his friend's disapproving features, the Landgrave added, "Very well—I know what a bleeding heart you are. But keep in mind, Herr Coat of Arms, that I'll be judging your capabilities in more crucial matters, through your performance in this."

During this exchange, Meyer Amschel had been as unobtrusive as if he were a piece of the wainscoting on the wall. Now he folded his hands behind his back, his face expressionless.

"Simply castle," he said.

"But my God, man! That leaves my queen within reach of his cavalry!"

"Queens have fallen into the hands of the cavalry in the past, William," said the general, greatly amused, "and a few have even survived!"

The Landgrave did as he'd been asked, shaking his head and muttering. General von Estorff smiled all the while, as if participating in a classroom exercise.

"Now, Meyer," he said, "what move do you wish *me* to make?"

"It really makes no matter," he replied, "for the Landgrave has won the game."

The Landgrave could not contain the look of disgust that crossed his face. Taking a big swig of brandy, he turned away from the board.

The general hesitated for a moment, watching the Landgrave's profile—then picked up his knight and took the Landgrave's queen.

"My God! My God! I told you! He's taken my queen!" cried the Landgrave, his face flushed and beaded with moisture, as he gripped the edge of the table.

"Be advised, sire," Meyer said calmly, "that a queen is not a game. It is the king, of course, that should be the object of your never-wavering attention!"

The Landgrave's face had taken on the purplish hue of apoplexy—his breath came in quick, dry rasps as his hands, gripping the table, began to shake. Von Estorff, in alarm, rushed to the sideboard for water and poured a goblet full, handed it to his friend to drink, then turned aside to Meyer Amschel.

"Are you certain we should . . . ?"

"Perfectly. Let us proceed," the other replied.

The Landgrave choked on the water, pushed the glass away, and threw down another mouthful of brandy instead.

"What is it the great chess master asks me to sacrifice next"—he sneered—"for the sake of *winning* the game?"

"Nothing," said Meyer politely. "You may now place his king in check."

Both men's eyes widened as they stared at the board.

"Aha!" cried the Landgrave at last, picking up his bishop and moving it down. "Check!" he cried, leaning back with a gloating expression.

"Be advised," Meyer commented calmly, "that a check is not a mate, although it's true that for each action he takes, you now have an appropriate counter. The laws of chess are as beautiful as those governing the universe—and as deadly."

As the two men made their moves under the guidance of Meyer Amschel, the Landgrave became progressively more cheerful. At last, the general himself leaned back with a smile of approval—though he saw he had lost the game.

"My dear Red-shield," he said to Meyer, "this is the most refreshing game of chess I've ever played—and the most enlightening. I confess, though I play every day of my life, your mind seems ten moves ahead of mine. I'd find it most enlightening if you'd conduct a postmortem analysis of our game so I might learn what I might have played to bring about a different result."

So Meyer Amschel remained at the board until the wee hours, instructing the two older men on the variety of moves—which he called combinations—that each might have played at each juncture in their game.

Only when the sun was rising over the river Main did the three men rise wearily from the board and make their way to bed. The Landgrave paused on the stairway to place his beefy hand on the shoulder of the little chess master.

"Rothschild," he said, "if you can maneuver money as well as those little ivory pieces, I predict you'll make me a very rich man."

"The Landgrave is already a rich man," Meyer Amschel pointed out.

"An accident of fate. But you are born with another kind of wealth—a quality the world will recognize a hundred years from now. I'm not a clever man, but I'm clever enough to recognize someone who knows more than I—and to make use of him."

"With such a recommendation, sire," said Meyer Amschel, "perhaps it will not require a hundred years."

THE ZEN OF MONEY

Money, which represents the prose of life, and which is hardly spoken of in the parlors without an apology, is in its effects and laws as beautiful as roses.

—Ralph Waldo Emerson

Monday, November 30

AT EIGHT A.M., TOR WALKED INTO THE NEW YORK Public Library and asked for directions to the business section. The woman who gave him instructions looked after him with a sigh as he headed toward the marble steps. Men of his appearance rarely came to the information desk of the public library.

Tor bounded up the steps, dressed in a charcoal suit of Italian gabardine. His pale gray pin-striped tie with a tiny touch of mauve was held in place by a gold stickpin that precisely matched the design of his cuff links. Several heads turned as he swung down the corridor into the business section. Inside, he asked the librarian where he could find the *Standard and Poor's* and the *Moody's* directories. She pointed to the appropriate shelves.

In the back of the stacks, Tor lifted the heavy volume of *Moody's* from the shelf and flipped through to the more recent issues, which had already been bound. Turning to municipal bonds, he thumbed through several pages until he found what he'd been seeking.

Glancing quickly about, he turned back to the book, pulled a sharp penknife from his pocket, and cut the page from the volume. He folded the page carefully and slipped it back into his pocket along with the folded knife. Then he returned the book to the shelf, thanked the librarian, who was still staring at him, and left the library.

■

LESS THAN AN HOUR LATER, TOR ENTERED THE OFFICES of Louis Straub discount brokers, on Maiden Lane. As he swung through the glass door he saw a room filled with brokers leaning over their phones, their ties loosened, jackets tossed casually over the backs of chairs. Secretaries and clerks ran from desk to desk, dropping papers into file baskets and leaving off phone messages. The floor was pandemonium.

The girl at the front desk was chewing gum and painting her nails while carrying on a busy telephone conversation. She interrupted her activities to ask Tor impatiently if there were anything she could do for him.

"I'd like to open a new account," he told her with a wry smile. "That is—if you're not too busy."

She blushed, and put the caller on hold, then pushed her intercom button.

"Mr. Ludwig," she said into the intercom as her voice echoed across the floor. "New account at the front desk. Please pick up."

"He'll be here in a minute," she told Tor, returning to her phone conversation. Tor glanced over the floor.

Louis Straub was the largest discount broker in the nation. The firm handled enormous volumes of securities for those who didn't need help in planning their portfolios or estates.

Five years earlier, a young man named Louis Straub had seen a need in the United States for a brokerage house that handled stocks and bonds as if it were a supermarket—where clients could pick out what they liked themselves, and the brokers would simply ring up the sale. They didn't give coffee or personal attention to their clients. The whole transaction at Louis Straub was so quick and clean that often a broker could not even remember his clients' faces. That was why Tor had come here.

Mr. Ludwig, a small, balding man, came through the swinging gate and shook Tor's proffered hand almost without looking at him.

"You'd like to open an account, Mister . . ."

"Dantes. Edmund Dantes," Tor said. "Yes. Actually, it's open and shut. I'd like to buy some bonds as Christmas gifts for my nieces. I've made a list of what I want."

"So will it be a cash transaction? We take credit cards or personal checks, if you have two forms of ID." He was leading Tor across the floor to a small messy desk at the back of the room.

"I'll give you a cash deposit, we'll choose the bonds, then after you tally it up, I'll bring you a cashiers' check in about half an hour."

"We can't purchase anything until we have the money or a line of credit established, you understand," said Ludwig.

Tor nodded, and handed him the torn page of *Moody's*, with a collection of bonds circled on it.

"You have a lot of nieces," said Ludwig, looking at Tor with a faint smile.

"I do this every Christmas," Tor replied. "Usually, my broker handles it for me, but it's late in the season and he's just gone on vacation. They're very sweet girls; I'd hate to miss Christmas."

Ludwig looked at Tor as if he were wondering just how old these girls were—and how closely related. But he bent his head to the sheet and began tapping numbers into his calculator.

"Without checking our computer, I can't tell you exactly what's available or what the buy-in rate will be," he told Tor. "But it looks as if you're talking about fifty thousand dollars, max, for these bonds, Mister . . . ah . . ."

"Dantes," Tor repeated. "Fine. My office is at Thirty Park Avenue—the Cristo Corporation—if you need to reach me. Why don't you start working on the list, and I'll be back with a check for fifty thousand at ten-thirty. If there's any variance in price, you can credit me or give me a check for the difference."

"Okay," Ludwig agreed. "Do you mind my asking a question? It seems you've picked one of *each* type of bond here—you've got dozens of different types. I mean, why not just give your nieces one each of a *few* different kinds? It'd make things much faster and simpler if I could buy blocks of multiples at a time. You could still give them separate certificates."

"I just don't think that Susie would like to have the same bonds as Mary Louise," Tor said.

Besides—he could hardly give the real reason why he needed to buy an individual bond of each type. He was already on his feet to head for the door.

"See you within the hour," he said.

He crossed the floor, swung through the gate without a nod at the chatting receptionist, and headed for a restaurant near his bank. The bank wouldn't open until ten, but it didn't take long to draw up a cashiers' check. And then they'd be in business.

■

WHILE TOR WAS SIPPING A COFFEE IN A SMALL CAFÉ off Wall Street and waiting for the bank to open, Georgian was getting out of a taxi in front of a massive concrete building in the Bronx.

The building was surrounded by high mesh fences with barbed wire at the top, and there was a guard gate. About every hundred feet along the perimeter of the fence, a guard stood watch with a German shepherd. All the guards wore guns in hip holsters, and they all looked up attentively as Georgian approached the guard station.

She was wearing a dress that left little to the imagination: electric-red suede, and extremely short. She wore high black patent-leather boots, and over one shoulder was draped a slinky black wool cape.

"Hi," Georgian greeted the guard. "I hope I'm not late for the ten o'clock tour. I took the subway as far as I could, but then I had to take a taxi. I'm almost completely broke, and I'm frozen to pieces."

"That's okay—the tour hasn't started yet," the guard told her. "It starts over there at the main entrance. You can step in here to warm up if you'd like, and I'll have the cart come pick you up. They always expect a few stragglers at the gate."

"Oh, thank you *so* much," said Georgian, stepping into the tiny booth as the guard picked up the phone.

She pulled off her mittens with the Santa Claus faces on the backs, and rubbed her hands together as the guard spoke a few words into the phone. She observed through the glass walls of the booth that the other guards posted around the fence were glancing at each other with grins and nodding toward the booth. Her guard turned back to her.

"So how come a girl like you is interested in touring a printing plant on a gloomy day like this?" he asked.

"I had no idea how bad the weather would be," Georgian replied, looking out at the overcast skies, heavy with the promise of snow. "I'm a student at the Art Students' League, and I've wanted to come here on tour for ever so long. All my classmates told me you have the finest master engravers here on the entire East Coast."

"Oh, that's certainly true," agreed the guard. "U.S. Banknote is the oldest security printer in the country. We get lots of commercial engravers, and students like yourself, on tour here. When you go on the tour, you should introduce yourself to the engravers; they'd be happy to talk with you and show you what they're doing. Whoops! Here comes the cart already, and I didn't ask you to sign in. Just put your name and address on this log, if you don't mind." He handed her a clipboard with a sheet full of signatures.

Georgian printed her name carefully: "Georgette Heyer." Next to it, in the column that read "Company Name," she printed: "Art Students' League." She was happy she didn't have time to talk further with the guard;

Georgian wasn't even sure where the Art Students' League was located.

Waving her hand to the guard, she ran from the little glass booth, hopped into the small electric cart that was sitting before the gate, and rode away.

■

"I HAD NO IDEA," GEORGIAN SAID AS SHE SIPPED THE foam from her mug of beer and peered through the gloom of the darkened bar, "that U.S. Banknote printed so many different *kinds* of things! I'm so glad I went on the tour and had the opportunity to meet all of you wonderful gentlemen."

Around the brick-red Formica table sat five of the master engravers from U.S. Banknote, with large smelly sausage sandwiches half-devoured on the plates before them, and half-full steins of beer. They were all ogling Georgian with avid scientific curiosity, as if she were a new form of engraving tool.

"Just think," she ran on, "food stamps and postage stamps and travelers' cheques and stocks and bonds—and even leather-bound books! But don't you have to *specialize* in something? I mean, is each of you an expert in everything, or are some better at . . . intaglio printing, and others better at roto . . . roto . . ."

"Gravure," said one of the men, and the others laughed.

Georgian looked flustered, and let her gaze, wide-eyed with admiration for all of them, wander around the table.

"We all have specialties," another engraver admitted. "We're always happy to have you students come on these tours. Who knows but that some of you may become apprentices? The students of today are the master engravers of tomorrow."

They all nodded in agreement and ate their sandwiches and drank their beer.

"But the field I'm really *most* interested in," said Georgian, blowing on the foam of her beer, "is *photo*engraving. I'm studying photography, and what I'd like to do is turn one of my photographs into a really superb engraving. Do you do any photoengraving here?''

''Not much,'' one of the engravers admitted. ''The people doing the best work in that field are the Japanese; their color lithography and engraving are incredible. They do the kind of thing you're talking about. You ought to go to some of the museums in Manhattan and see what they're turning out.''

''We don't do much of that here at the plant,'' added another, ''because we deal primarily with security instruments—things that have cash value, like travelers' cheques, where all the engraving plates have to be hand-etched. The printing has to be very sophisticated, so the instruments we produce will be hard to counterfeit. Sometimes, this takes as many as thirty colors on a single document. Surely you wouldn't need to do anything that complex to engrave a photograph?''

''I'd like to know how,'' said Georgian. ''Is there anyone you know who could show me?''

''Actually,'' said one of the men, ''there is that Japanese photoengraver over on Staten Island. He works out of his own home. He does sophisticated stuff—some of it commercial, but mostly artistic. Do you recall his name, Bob? Remember—he was the guy who made that plate of a one-dollar bill a few years ago, and showed the bills in a gallery. The plates were such good counterfeits that the FBI came to his house and broke them! What was that guy's name?''

''Oh yeah,'' said the other. ''I remember—it was Seigei Kawabata.''

Tuesday, December 1

IT WAS EARLY AFTERNOON WHEN GEORGIAN, COMpletely enveloped in her bohemian black cape, got off the Staten Island ferry and hiked up the landing plank through the falling snow. She hailed the first taxi she saw, and gave the driver the address.

She paid the driver and disembarked before an old gingerbread house on a tree-lined street. It didn't seem the sort of spot where one would find a famous engraver; she'd expected something a bit more high-tech.

Georgian went up the icy front walk, climbed the steps to the front porch, and rang the bell. After a few moments, she heard the sound of footsteps shuffling to the door. The door creaked open and a wrinkled little face peered out.

"Mr. Kawabata?" said Georgian. The old man nodded, watching her carefully, but not opening the door any wider. "I'm Georgette Heyer; I telephoned you from the city. From the Art Students' League."

Georgian smiled at him as sweetly as she could, but privately cursed him for keeping the damned door half-shut; she was freezing.

"Ah yes," said Mr. Kawabata at last, opening the door and ushering her inside. "The Art Students' League—I lecture there myself quite often. Who are your instructors there? I'm certain I would know them. Would you care for some tea?"

■

GEORGIAN WAS FORCED TO ADMIT TO MR. KAWABATA, over tea and cookies, that she was not a student from the Art Students' League. She was in fact a commercial photographer who was thinking of going into photoengraving—but she did not want any of her competitors to know she was branching out into a new field. Even to her, this excuse sounded flimsy, but Mr. Kawabata accepted it.

"Mr. Kawabata, the engravers at U.S. Banknote told me you'd done a perfect engraving of a dollar bill. Is that true?" she asked as Kawabata was leading her through his maze of high-ceilinged Victorian rooms.

Each room was immaculately clean, with hand-painted paper screens covering the tall windows, and beautiful pastel pots of paintbrushes clustered like art objects on the pale lacquered tables.

"Yes," replied Kawabata. "The government was very angry with me for that. After my gallery opening, they came to my house and conducted a thorough search, looking for other plates. They thought I was a professional counterfeiter, but I explained that I was merely attempting to show the state my art has achieved in the Western world. If you like, I will show you a print from that series that they did not confiscate."

Georgian agreed that she'd like that very much. Kawabata led her into a room overlooking a small Oriental garden—the only room whose windows were not covered with paper. The garden was beautiful, with its small pool and smooth black stones paving the walks between beds of carefully trained bonsai trees. The floor of the room was covered with willow matting, and hand-painted cushions were placed about the periphery.

On one wall was a small engraving about one foot in diameter. The background was a dark plummy gray, beautifully textured. At the center of the engraving was a small apple on a table, and beside it, propped up on end to face the viewer, a perfect dollar bill. It looked as if it had been pasted, in collage, into the picture; the color was perfect, the lines were flawless.

"This is magnificent," murmured Georgian. She took a dollar bill from her handbag and compared it with the one in the print.

"That is a photoengraving," Kawabata replied in his soft-spoken voice. "I actually photographed the bill separately from the apple and the table, then I overlaid the two photographs. I did the plates separately. If you are interested, I will show you how it's done."

He conducted Georgian into a room that contained several small printing presses and a larger one. The hand presses sat on hard wooden tables at one side of the room; the large press was against the far wall. The floor was protected by heavy tarpaulin. At center, a large-format camera was suspended from heavy exposed beams where the ceiling had been removed. Beneath the camera stood an enormous table with a broad, smooth surface covered in clean white paper. Everything was immaculate. Georgian thought this was the cleanest print shop she had ever seen.

"Shall we do a sample print?" asked Kawabata. He pushed a button on the camera mounting; the camera lowered with a whir. "If you wish to do excellent engravings, you must use a large-format camera in order to secure a very high resolution print. The larger the negative, the more detail you will be able to achieve—just as in photographic printing. Such order of detail requires great patience and great perception. Take this photographic loup, and look at your dollar bill again."

Georgian took the small glass cube he handed her, and looked through it at the dollar bill. In magnification, it seemed to leap to life. What had appeared a sea of sage-green embellishments now appeared as a myriad array of complicated dots, swirls, dashes, and carefully textured blackish-green shadows.

"When you observe the left half of the Great Seal, the one with the pyramid of Egypt," Kawabata was saying, "you will notice that the Masonic mystic eye suspended above it is surrounded by age lines! It is that kind of precision we must aim for."

Georgian looked up from the loup. "What shall we print?" she asked.

"Why not your dollar bill?" asked Kawabata, smiling and picking it up from beneath the loup. "But let's make it interesting. As this is merely an exercise, let's pretend the dollar comes in many colors, as other countries' currencies do."

With a felt-tipped pen, Kawabata carefully colored in the mystic eye in red, so that it looked as if it had spent a rough night over the pyramid.

"This way, I can show you some more sophisticated engraving techniques. Young people nowadays are often in a great hurry to get somewhere, without really knowing where they are going. But engraving cannot be rushed. Engraving is like the tea ceremony; it must be done one step at a time, and each in its turn. Then it unfolds its secrets to you, like a flower."

Kawabata took her to the darkroom beside his studio and there showed her the painstaking, step-by-step processes required to mask the photo plates, coat the engraving plates with photosensitive emulsion, prepare the acid baths, and carefully time each part of the operation. It was similar to the film development and printing process, but Kawabata stressed the importance of taking extreme care in each precise detail—well beyond the level of cleanliness and care required to produce an excellent photograph.

"To mix a color," said Kawabata when they'd rinsed the last plate and carefully dried it, "even if the color is only black, it must be the *right* black. You must feel it in your soul. Now we must go to my study to meditate."

"Meditate?" said Georgian, confused.

"A master engraver must always meditate before he prepares the color," said Kawabata, "in order that he may bring his soul's vibrations into harmony with the universe."

■

GEORGIAN DID NOT REALIZE HOW LATE IT WAS WHEN they'd finished the printing. She and Kawabata were seated in the large living room where they'd had tea earlier. She sipped her warm plum sake and held the perfect red-and-green dollar bill between her fingers. She felt as if she'd just graduated from a ten-year course as a master engraver.

"Mr. Kawabata," she said, dreamy from the exhaustion of the work and the effects of the hot sake, "I can't tell you what this afternoon has meant to me. I'm going to go right home and start practicing everything you've taught me."

"Do you have a press to work on?"

"No—but I imagine I can buy one. There must be presses listed for sale in the papers?"

"These new presses all have automatic color mixers

on them. They are quite sophisticated, if you wish to do assembly-line printing. But for an artist such as yourself, I think it would be preferable to use an older style of press, where everything can still be controlled by hand. Then you can mix your color to perfection. You will not destroy the delicate nuances of your engraving."

"Where would I find a press like that?" asked Georgian.

"I have one here, which I can lend or sell to you, Miss Heyer. It is quite old, but in extremely good order. How will you be going home? It's possible that we could squeeze it into a very large taxi. And I believe two people could carry it down the steps to the walk. If you do not have to go up five flights at the other end . . ."

■

THE PHONE WAS RINGING, AND LELIA WAS TURNING over piles of cushions on the sofa trying to find it. At last, she dug it out and answered breathlessly.

"*Allo? Allo?*" she cried into the receiver. Then, after a moment, she said, "Oh no! Oh *merde! Oui*—he is here. Yes, I will make him to come at once. But you are *complètement fou*, my *chérie*."

"What I can't figure out," said Tor, coming in from the kitchen with floury dough all over his hands, "is how you always get the raisins to puff up in the strudel if you're putting them between two layers of dough—What's wrong?"

Lelia was standing there, regarding him with stricken face.

"It is Zhorzhione," she said, replacing the phone in its cradle with a sigh. "You must to go and fetch her."

"Where the hell is she?" he said, wiping his hands on the cloth tied around his waist. "It's nearly five o'clock—she was due back at noon. Has something gone wrong?"

"*Oui.* She is waiting at the Staten Island ferry for you to fetch her."

"Why doesn't she take the subway uptown?" he asked.

"She is at the ferry landing *on* Staten Island," said Lelia.

"Then why doesn't she take the ferry and *then* take the subway?"

"Because, *mon cher ami*, there was no one to help her on and off of the ferry with her printing press."

MERGERS

Money in itself cannot grow.

—Aristotle

Friday, December 4

I DIDN'T SEE GEORGIAN OR TOR FOR THE REST OF THE week. They'd been so mysterious and secretive about their plot—but they assured me they would reveal all at dinner on Friday night, before I returned to San Francisco. Meanwhile, I had work of my own to do.

New York was full of banks, and my secretary. Pavel—who loved making long-distance calls—had apparently phoned every one of them to put on my itinerary. Though my visits to these security divisions had been set up to camouflage my jaunt to see Tor, now that he was my competitor in a wager—no longer my adviser—the rules had changed as well as the stakes. Since I was here in New York anyway, a bit of boning up on security might not hurt at all.

Mr. Peacock at United Trust was near the end of my list, but he had nothing new to tell me, so I managed to weasel out of my luncheon date with him. I needed some time alone to think. But when I went to my last planned appointment, I was in for a big surprise.

There must be a hundred thousand people in New York named Harris, so I was taken by surprise when I found that the Harris in charge of Citibank security was one of my old pals—the Bobbsey Twins!

Ten years earlier—the last time I'd seen him—he'd

been slightly overweight, with unkempt hair, loose shirttails, and cigarette ashes sprinkled over his belly. Time and money had clearly worked in his behalf.

As he rose from behind his elegant rosewood desk to greet me, I noted his well-trimmed silver sideburns, his cashmere blazer and rep tie, and the rack of expensive foreign pipes gracing his bureau.

''Harris!'' I cried as he came around to embrace me warmly. ''What on earth are you doing working *here*? When I spoke with Charles last week, you were at the data center uptown—''

Harris put a finger to his lips and glanced through the window in his office door.

''Rather bad show, if they got wind of it,'' he told me. ''I'm regarded as something of the high official. I say—have you any luncheon plans? Perhaps we could get away and have a chat.''

So Harris grabbed his camel overcoat and a fringed silk scarf and we headed off to the Four Seasons—a slight upgrade from the bocci court where we'd dined in days of yore.

■

THE BUILDING THAT HOUSED THE SCIENTIFIC DATA Center hadn't changed much in the past ten years, as I learned when we taxied up there after lunch. It was charred as if it had been gutted by fire. The copper wires in Charles's core banks must be green by now, I thought, if they were still keeping the windows ajar to ''cool him down'' with Queens factory fumes.

Brits like the Bobbsey Twins always addressed one another by surname; a bit confusing, since their names were the same. As teckies, they'd resolved this problem by calling each other by subscripts: Harris Sub One and Harris Sub Two. And so I still thought of them.

When we entered the data center, Harris-$_1$ was standing, his back to us, embroiled with a machine that had many moving parts and seemed to be folding and stuffing envelopes. The noise was deafening.

The room itself seemed slightly cleaner than in the

past. Charles Babbage sat at center, squat and happy as a pasha surveying his harem. He'd been painted a cheerful sky blue, and was sporting an old Brooklyn Dodgers baseball cap, perched atop his console. Even in this disguise, he was easy to recognize.

"Blimey, if it isn't Verity Banks!" Harris-$_1$ cried, when he turned to catch sight of me. "Charles, look up, lad—your mother's here!"

"Turn off that infernal racket!" yelled Harris-$_2$. "I can't hear myself think."

Harris-$_1$ switched off the envelope stuffer and came over to us, beaming. He, too, looked remarkably well, in his tweedy jacket with leather elbow patches and a heathery turtleneck sweater. He'd grown a salt-and-pepper beard, and seemed every inch the country gent.

"You've both done well, I see," I told them. "You're looking fine, and if I'm not mistaken, there's even more hardware here than ten years ago!"

"Actually, we've gone into the mail-order business," Harris-$_2$ explained. "Charles Babbage is the president of our corporation, and we're the vice-presidents. There was plenty of machine time unused here, and going to waste for many years. We were endlessly bored, sitting about each night—that's why Harris-$_2$ took that daytime job at the bank. We found we could manage *this* place, even with one of us working outside. Then we got a bit more creative and opened a business. We've made quite a bundle—the three of us—these past few years."

"Sounds wonderful, if slightly illegal," I told them. "After all, you don't own this data center."

"You've been using Charles Babbage yourself, for the past ten years," Harris-$_2$ pointed out. "We *do* read the logs, you know! But we've said, many times, that if you hadn't saved his life as you did, we'd never have amounted to much ourselves. Charles has somehow given us the inspiration we needed to become entrepreneurs."

I was flipping through some of the listings in Charles's print basket as we spoke.

"What *is* this stuff?" I asked them.

"That's an inventory of a mailing we do for our largest client," Harris-$_{2}$ explained, "a consortium of East Coast universities. They've combined their alumni mailing lists so they can cull the cream of the crop—the really wealthy alums—and solicit special types of joint endowments."

"We've refined the data," chimed in Harris-$_{1}$, "by adding information from Dun and Bradstreet, the Social Register, and even real estate holdings, along posher sections of the seaboard. If we chose to sell this mailing list, it *alone* might go for half a million."

As I listened I studied the list more closely. Not only did it include name, rank, and serial number—but family statistics, political affiliations, business connections, club memberships, property holdings, and tax-free donations made to various institutions. It was gold, and I knew it. That list might be worth half a mill to the Bobbseys, but it was worth far more to me.

I smiled. Once again, Charles Babbage had come to my aid, without even knowing it. I had to set up thousands of dummy accounts when I got back to San Francisco, didn't I? Accounts where I could put all that dough while I invested it, without anyone getting suspicious over the size of the deposits passing through. I could hardly think of better names than those on the list before me. And now I wouldn't even have to invent social security numbers or credit status; it was all spelled out right here.

But the clincher, of course—from my point of view—was that many of the muckete-mucks on that list were *also* members of the Vagabond Club! Maybe there was some justice in this world.

■

I WHISTLED ALL THE WAY BACK TO MY HOTEL. FIFTH Avenue was strung with lights like a Christmas tree. The scent of winter was in the air, and the crowds moved at a brisk pace up the glittering thoroughfare. It was nearly dark when I swept through the glass revolving doors of the Sherry.

When I got to my room to change for dinner, I saw the red phone light flashing, so I rang up the desk to collect the messages. There'd been two calls—one from Pearl, one from Tavish, in San Francisco. I glanced at my watch: seven-thirty here meant four-thirty in California, not yet quitting time at the bank.

I decided I had time for a shower first. I phoned room service for a bottle of sherry and went off to make my ablutions. When I came out of the steamy bathroom fifteen minutes later, my hair wrapped in a towel, the tray with glasses was set up in the living room. I poured myself a drink and picked up the phone.

"Miss Lorraine isn't at this number any longer," the bank secretary told me. "She works for Mr. Karp now. Please hold, and I'll transfer you."

After a minute, Pearl came on the line.

"Hello, sweetheart," said Pearl. "I'm glad you called back. I thought I should let you know that a few things are going on here. Our pal Karp and your boss Kiwi have been plotting something dire in your absence. I have the office next to Karp's—if you can call this dump an office—and I can hear everything they say through the walls. I foresee a long ocean voyage in your future."

"What do you mean? They're trying to get me fired?"

"Worse than that, sugarplum," she said glumly. "They've somehow learned that your little quality team is looking with maximum scrutiny at *their* systems. The latest plan is to get you transferred to Frankfurt for the winter—a charming place this time of year. With no one here to stop them, they could make your project vanish, get rid of *me* with impunity, and Karp could do with Tavish as he wished. By the way, it's Frankfurt, *Germany*—not Kentucky—and it's *not* considered a promotion!"

"A lateral arabesque," I agreed. "Well, I'll be home tomorrow—we'll discuss it when you pick me up. If you can bring Tavish to the airport with you, do. It's time I shared some other news, as well."

"Since we're alone, I'd better ask now—seen any action in Manhattan?"

"I've hardly spent my time dashing around trying to 'get laid'—if that's what you mean," I told her curtly.

"Use it or lose it," Pearl said with a sigh.

"Thanks for the sage advice," I replied, and hung up.

Tavish wasn't at his desk, I assumed, when I heard the phone roll over to another location. Someone picked up at last, and while I waited I could hear the squeak of disk drives in the background, and the open whir of the climate control systems, before Tavish came on the line.

"Where are you—the machine room?" I said. "Can you talk?"

"Not just at present," he told me in hushed voice. "But *you-know-who* is taking a very active interest in our work. He's asking for status day by day—hour by hour."

"You mean Kiwi," I said. "What have you told him?"

"I don't work for him; I work for you," Tavish said. "But he's curried favor with the others on the team, each and every one. I'm pleased to report they're not traitors—not yet. But it's only a question of time before he completely loses control—whatever small measure he possessed to begin with. When will you be back?"

"Tomorrow. Pearl Lorraine's giving me a ride; can she pick you up on her way to the airport in the morning?"

"Delighted. I hadn't realized you knew her so well. By the way, she and I have done a bit of politicking in your absence, to try to protect what we could—"

"I've just spoken with Pearl," I told him. "Tell me—have you cracked any files yet?"

"Afraid not, but we're working on it," said Tavish. "Perhaps by tomorrow there'll be better news."

I was disappointed that Tavish had not been able to decipher the test keys or get into the customer accounts file. Without entry to the latter, I couldn't even establish accounts for those prestigious names I'd garnered from the Bobbsey Twins' list.

On the other hand, this might be fortunate. If the quality circle *had* cracked any files or codes, Kiwi might have learned of it somehow and reported it to management. So *he* could get the kudos. *And* take charge of "fixing the problem"—me.

I knew by now it had been a mistake to start up the quality team in my absence, and an even larger error in judgment to let Tavish operate in the dark. He needed to know my real plans, if I wanted to count on him for help. It's dangerous to have a cog in your wheel that doesn't know what its job is supposed to be.

But the biggest of all my mistakes had been to turn my back on Kiwi—even for a week. If he succeeded in shipping me off to Germany, my plans were wrecked and my wager lost, before either got off the ground. It was lucky I'd be back tomorrow. Perhaps there was still time for a quick fix.

I splashed myself with powder, brushed my hair, threw on my evening clothes, and headed out to Fifth Avenue for a cab to Lelia's—to find out how the other half of our wager had progressed.

■

IN HONOR OF CHRISTMAS, THE LOBBY OF LELIA'S building had been decorated with a giant pink foil tree, and garish red lights obscured the plaster fruit basket and chandeliers. It looked like a design scheme dreamed up by Mary Magdalene, prior to her conversion.

"Pink champagne for the guests," said Francis the elevator operator, holding out a plastic glass of the bubbly for me.

The maid was in Lelia's entrance hall, bobbing and bouncing, a little holly wreath circling her brow. She ladled me a crystal cupful from the punch bowl on the entry table. I dumped my plastic champagne, helped myself to some cookies from the big silver platter, and went into the hall. The doors to the Red Room, halfway down, were open.

"We're dining in half an hour," Tor informed me as soon as he saw my fistful of cookies.

"Let her eat! She must be fatter!" cried Lelia.

She was ensconced in a red silk chair, her feet propped on an embossed leather ottoman. Tor, standing beside her holding his own cup of grog, was wearing a burgundy velvet dinner jacket with peach silk ascot. His coppery ringlets shone in the firelight. He looked dashing, like someone from another era. I was certain Lelia had had a hand in his attire.

Lelia was even more radiant, sitting there before the thick tree whose branches were laden with crimson satin bows and fat tallow candles. That brocaded, dark red caftan beautifully displayed the two-ton dog collar of canary diamonds that plastered her throat. Her tawny, disheveled mane was pulled back to reveal enormous crystal cabochon earrings, surrounded by cut diamonds, which dangled nearly to her shoulders. When I bent down to kiss her, she smelled of vanilla and cloves.

"You both look great. Where's Georgian?" I said.

"She prepare the excitement for you," said Lelia. "She want very much that you will look surprised when you see all the work she has made this week."

Then she pursed her lips and regarded me sternly. "My darling—again you are wearing the black—but why? No one is dying here; there is no need to arrive in mourning. When I was your age, the young men stopped as I walked on the Champs-Elysées. They brought me flowers and jewels, and kissed my hand, and they suffered if I was forgetting to notice them."

"Times have changed, Lelia," I said. "These days, women want more than flowers and jewels."

"What?" she said, raising her eyebrows. "What more *is* there? These make the romance. You do not understand—that is clear. You must have a great *manque* in your life, which causes you to act in this fashion."

"What—pray tell—is a *manque*?" Tor asked with a smile.

"A loss . . . a hole . . . an absence of something," I translated.

"Quel sangfroid," said Lelia. "She has always been *très difficile*, this one."

"I should say," agreed Tor. "She's *très difficile* in French, English, or any other language. She isn't wearing black for grieving, you see. Black is widely regarded as the color of power—and power is what she wants."

"What is power?" cried Lelia. "Charm is everything. *You*, for example, are a charming man—*très gentil. . . .*"

"Well-mannered, polite," I told Tor with a smile.

"This charming man—he has only one thought in his mind," Lelia told me, "and that is to make love with *you*. But you are so much a fool, you do not see it—and talk of power and being the man, instead!"

Tor wasn't smiling.

"Indeed?" he told Lelia coolly. "I'd hardly jump to conclusions about my interest in black-clad fiscal wizards. They're not quite as appealing as some might think. I believe I'll go see what's holding things up with Georgian." And he departed without so much as a glance at me.

"Lelia, you've embarrassed Dr. Tor," I said sternly. "All this continental wisdom of yours is amusing only up to a point."

"He loves you, I say," she hissed under her breath. "You say I'm a foolish old woman, but often it takes *la folle* to speak the truth, out in the air where everyone can hear. The blindness of Monet, I could help—I could see the flowers *for* him—but there is no help for the blindness which comes from the heart."

Just then, Georgian arrived in a tiny dress no longer than a shirt, coated in salmon-colored paillettes that glittered when she moved.

"Thor's on his way to the Plum Room," she announced. "Come—come! We have it all set up!"

In the Plum Room, the big printing press was at center, the tarp spread out on the floor beneath. There were tables with boxes of supplies and, mounted on the scaffold, a photo enlarger and a huge camera, both trained down upon the surface of the large table.

Georgian stood before it, twisting one leg around the other like a child, and looking at us with great round eyes.

Tor was mucking about, moving levers and switches as the equipment shifted up and down with whirring and clicking sounds. He didn't look up when we arrived.

I wondered just how much Lelia had picked up about our little wager. She was standing—all ears—just at the door.

"Isn't it fabulous?" asked Georgian, barely able to contain her excitement.

"It is impressive," I agreed. "But what are you going to do with all this stuff?"

"We're going to counterfeit securities," said Tor, still screwing with the levers, "just as I told you before."

"You never said that," I told him. "I thought you were going to rob that place—the Depository Trust—to prove how easy it was."

"Not quite," he replied with a smile, looking up for the first time with that penetrating gaze. "I see no reason to *steal* securities. Not if you can arrange it so that they never get there in the first place. Why would I need a photographer, if I only planned to rob a vault?"

At last it all made sense. They would copy the stocks and bonds—keeping the *real* ones—and they'd put the *fake* ones into the vault! Why hadn't I seen that before? But even so, I realized, there were a few unanswered questions.

"If you're not going to break into a vault, how will you substitute the fake for the real?" I wanted to know. "It seems you'd have to swap them *before* they got there."

"Precisely," Tor agreed, with a smile.

"Let me explain," Georgian chimed in.

She plucked a document from the table and handed it to me. It had a blue border and wavy, complex lettering. I ran my fingers over it and felt the irregular surface.

"Thor's gotten copies of many kinds of bonds that are being traded heavily this month," she said. "These are the likeliest to be transported to the Depository Trust just now. We've made multiple copies of each kind—this is an example."

"*You* printed this?" I asked, and when she nodded proudly, I added, "but don't securities have serial numbers?"

"Yes, and other identifying information, too," Tor agreed. "We won't know the unique identifiers for each bond we'll be copying—not until we actually see the physical instrument itself. And we won't see it until it's being sent by a brokerage or bank to the Depository's vault."

"We'll only have a brief time to engrave those unique numbers onto the security," Georgian added. "That's what I'm most concerned about—the drying time for the ink. Fast-drying ink crumbles and slow-drying ink smears. But we have to have a flawless copy."

"This one looks pretty good," I admitted. "Is there someone, an expert, you could ask?"

"Not unless you'd care to phone the Treasury Department and request *their* opinion," Tor said dryly, leaning against the wall with folded arms.

I had so many questions, but they stood there making it all sound so simple.

"How do you plan to get your hands on these securities—knock over a Brinks truck?" I asked. "And what about watermarks? All negotiable instruments have those—even cash—"

"Ah, but we must retain *some* secrets," Tor cut in with a smile. "After all—you're the enemy!"

"That's right!" agreed Georgian. "This is a competition! Our lips are sealed from now on."

"I think you're overlooking the value of my contribution," I told them, feeling suddenly very much left out. "After all, I'm a banker. For instance—I bet you haven't thought of the registration!"

"What registration?" Georgian wanted to know.

"When stocks are purchased by someone, they print the purchaser's name on them. Or even if they're registered in 'street name,' the title company keeps track of who the owner is. Tor's certainly aware of *that*—he told me so himself."

"Is this true?" Georgian demanded.

"Absolutely," said Tor with that cryptic smile, "which is why we are *not* going to counterfeit stocks, my little feathered chickadee. We're going to counterfeit bearer bonds instead. And bearer bonds are gold!"

■

DURING OUR CONVERSATION, LELIA HAD SLIPPED AWAY, and had not yet returned when the maid came to announce that dinner would soon be served. So we three headed back up the hallway.

"Just how involved is Lelia in all of this?" I asked Georgian.

"Oh, you know Mother. You can't keep her nose out of anything. She's volunteered her help in every imaginable way. I'm not sure she understands that it's not just a game, though. In fact, I'm not sure I believe it myself. We're actually doing something illegal—regardless of the purity of our motives. If we're caught *before* we give the money back, we'll wind up in jail!"

"All the more reason to keep Lelia out of it," I agreed. "You know how she is."

Tor was dawdling behind us, examining the paintings that hung between every set of mirrored, louvered doors.

"You don't have to do this at all, you know," I told Georgian. "In fact—though the whole thing was my idea—I feel over my head myself. It was Tor who turned this into a circus. He loves doing that to me—that's why I've avoided him like the plague all these years. Though I'm not always smart enough to remember it."

"If you want my opinion," she informed me, "he's the best thing that ever happened to you. You haven't done anything even close to adventurous in years."

"You haven't *seen* me in years," I pointed out.

But I had to agree. If Tor hadn't gotten himself involved, it was unlikely I'd have gone through with a scheme as foolhardy as the one I was about to launch. That was what worried me so.

He caught up to us as we reached the dining room, but Lelia still wasn't there. The rich, dark table had been rubbed with oil till it shone, the charming arrangement of white narcissus and holly was reflected in its surface. Multitiered candelabra stood at each side, and the tall champagne icers at either end. A wonderful glow was all about us; it smelled of Christmas.

We were about to be seated when Lelia dashed into the room.

"I made the solution!" she bubbled brightly.

With a complicitous smile, she drew her hands from behind her back and held out a large, revolver-shaped hair dryer. We stared at it in silence.

"Mother—you're a genius!" cried Georgian at last. "I should have thought of that myself."

"It is as plain as the hairs of your head," agreed Lelia, quite pleased. "I shall make the little stand to hold it in place while you are drying the papers for the great crime. Then I shall be important, no?"

"Then you'll be important—yes," Tor agreed, giving her a hug.

As usual at Lelia's dinners, the food was wonderful: cold carrot vichyssoise, aspic with baby vegetables and black truffles—arranged within the jelly, like a *giardiniera*—roast pheasant with gooseberry sauce and chestnut puree. When we could eat no more, the sweets and coffee arrived.

Lelia passed Tor a box of cigars and took one herself, clipping the ends and lighting each with a long taper. Tor was mellow and, as he puffed, in the mood to talk. Lelia solicitously poured him a balloon of cognac.

"You know," Tor told me, "I've been thinking about this problem at the Depository for years. But if you hadn't surfaced with that cockeyed idea of yours, I'd probably never have done a thing about it."

"I don't see why you need *my* involvement—or this bet," I pointed out. "You'd have caught their attention just by grabbing a few million dollars and mailing it in."

"It would hardly take a billion to prove my point about security," he agreed. "But there's another lesson—of vital importance—that needs to be taught. *That's* why I wanted our wager. I've seen far too much rampant corruption and greed in the world financial community. Though they are entrusted with safeguarding other people's money, bankers and investors—in time—often come to regard those assets as their own. They play fast and loose, taking risks, employing neither forethought nor hindsight. Whole civilizations have been destroyed through this kind of mad roulette."

"I see," I said wryly, hearing this pretty speech. "You're Crusader Rabbit—setting the world economy on its ear. I thought you were the sort who never did anything for altruistic motives."

But I knew he was right; something had to be done and soon. Banks were folding right and left, with none of it caused by men of particular honor or integrity. The "mistakes" that had been made in my own bank ranged from criminal incompetence to outright theft, but nobody blew the whistle—or even slapped a wrist. Kiwi's intransigence over security seemed the slightest offense of the lot, when you thought of it.

"Tell me," I asked, "how does our little bet fit into the grand design?"

"Believe it or not, it does," he assured me, sipping his brandy. "The way I plan to *invest* our money will certainly drive home the point. But it's only a gleam in my eye just now; I'll explain later, in detail."

"I can hardly wait," I told him, meaning it. I was dying to know what Tor really had up his sleeve.

"If high finance were practiced as it once was—in the days of the Rothschilds, for example—" said Tor, "things might be different now. They were clever—perhaps even ruthless—but not corrupt. The Rothschilds almost single-handedly created the arena of international banking we know today. They stabilized currencies across state lines—built a world economy, where only warring special-interest groups had existed before—"

"So boring a story," Lelia cut in. "They have to make marriage *avec leur propre famille*, to be accepted. That old one . . . he was a real *cafard*!"

"A cockroach," I translated for Tor, who'd been as surprised at her outburst as I. "The Rothschilds had to marry into their own family, in order to inherit, or so I gather."

"*Quel cochon*," Lelia muttered.

"What a pig," I explained.

"Mother—that's quite enough," said Georgian. "We've been over that all before."

"If the truth is not spoken, these things come like the *ronde d'histoire*," Lelia went on, oblivious. "Your papa, he would rise up in his *tombeau* . . . he was murdered in his . . . *comment dit-on âme*, my darlink?"

"His soul," I said. "If we don't discuss these things, history will be repeated. Your father's soul was killed, he'd rise up in his grave, if—"

"*I* know what she's saying! She's *my* goddamned mother!" snapped Georgian.

"Maybe I shouldn't have brought this up—" Tor began. But Lelia cut in again.

"Wisteria," she said.

"Beg pardon?" Tor looked at her, confused.

"Wisteria—that is the name," Lelia elaborated.

"Wisteria—it's the name of the flower Lelia used to admire," I explained to Tor. When he made no reply, I added, "In Monet's garden at Giverny."

"I see," said Tor.

"A previous conversation," I pointed out.

"Quite so," said Tor.

■

"I'D LIKE TO SHOW YOU SOMETHING," TOR INFORMED me as he pulled his car out of Lelia's underground garage and headed down Park Avenue.

"Now? Good Lord, it's nearly midnight! I have a flight tomorrow morning—can't this wait?"

"Never fear, it won't take long," he assured me. "It's something I've bought. I want to know whether you think it's a good investment."

"If you've already bought it—what difference does it make what I think? This isn't the sort of investment that can be viewed only from the recesses of a sofa, is it?"

"Far be it from me—at this late date—to sully your impeccable virtue." He laughed. "Believe me, *this* investment requires hundreds of yards of open space to be fully appreciated."

"It's outside? You must be joking—tonight? Where are we going? This is the way to the bridge!"

"Precisely; we're going to Long Island, where no civilized person sets foot this time of year. But then, you and I were never all that civilized, were we?" He ruffled my hair with one hand and swung up the ramp to the bridge.

I awakened, what seemed like hours later, with my head in Tor's lap. His coat had been removed and tucked in around me, and he was absentmindedly stroking my hair.

I sat up and peered through the frosty windows. Before us, the moon reflected from the glossy black surface of the ocean. At least, it looked like the ocean. But then I saw it was some sort of pond or lake, and the expanse I'd thought was water was in fact black ice. Embedded in the ice were dozens of boats.

"How can people leave those boats out there?" I asked. "Don't they get hurt if they freeze up like that?"

"Yes, they would—if they were ordinary boats," he agreed. "But these are magical boats: iceboats. And the one out there with the tall red mast is mine."

"An iceboat—that's your investment?" I said.

"Come. I'll show you."

We got out in our evening clothes, and crossed the crunchy snow. The air was colder than I'd imagined, and the wind lifted the snow—moving it back and forth across the surface of the ice. It gave the lake a mystical appearance. I thought of the story of the Snow Queen, guiding her sled across the skies—sending splinters of ice to earth to freeze childrens' hearts.

"You see," he was explaining as he helped me up to the dock where the wind seemed stronger, "this boat is extremely lightweight, with a sail to catch the wind. It has two runners—"

"Like Hans Brinker's racing skates," I said.

He unlocked a trapdoor in the deck, pulled out the yards of folded sail, and began to lay it out.

"This works much as a sailboat would; the propulsion is afforded by the wind. But because we skate on the surface, which is slick and offers no resistance, it's much faster than a water boat and requires less wind."

"Why are you rigging it?" I asked. "You're not planning to take it out *now*?"

"Sit down," Tor told me, shoving me into a seat. "Use that strap and buckle."

I attached the harness as he whipped the sail around with expert-looking movements. The beautiful black ice seemed suddenly menacing. I could picture with amazing immediacy what it would feel like to be cast out, sliding across the surface out of control, as the sharp, jagged teeth of ice shredded me to ribbons—or to fall through a thin place and get trapped beneath the sinister surface in subarctic waters.

"You'll enjoy this tremendously," Tor assured me, smiling as he yanked down a rope and looped it around a cleat.

The sail whipped out sharply against the wind—my head snapped back, and the boat shot forward onto the lake. We picked up speed so swiftly and silently that it took me several seconds to realize how fast we were moving.

When I turned to face into the wind, it cut at my eyelids. Needles of snow from the surface were hurled against my face, burning my skin. I kept my eyes shut as I felt the cold slash against me. When I tried to speak, ice dragged through my lungs like grappling hooks.

"How do you *turn* this thing?" I yelled against the whine of wind.

"I shift my weight or the sails," Tor said as the clatter of ice against the hull increased. "Or I can move the rudders slightly with this lever." He sounded so calm and tranquil, I tried to feel assured.

We were flying over the ice so quickly now, I feared we'd soon be airborne. The lump of fear in my stomach was starting to burn like cold, icy metal as it turned to terror. My eyes were streaming with water from the needles of sleet; I wondered how Tor could see without using goggles.

When I let go of the seat to wipe my eyes, we were shifting our course ever so slightly. My heart leaped into my mouth as I saw we were now rushing headlong toward the far shore. As the line of frozen grasses and rocks and trees whizzed toward us at breakneck speed, it felt as though we'd jumped into high gear.

The land was rushing up so fast, I couldn't believe Tor saw what was happening—I felt like screaming aloud. Pieces of ice were clattering against the hull like machine-gun fire, and a blanket of snow obscured my sight as we went faster and faster. Now I caught glimpses of trees and rocks that seemed to jump toward us across the ice—and I recognized, with sudden hysteria, that it was too late to turn!

I could feel my choked, burning throat, the blood throbbing—no, thudding—deep in my eye sockets. I gripped the side of the boat as if I were riveted in place, forcing myself to watch as we hurtled wildly—utterly out of control—into the deadly black line of shore. The bottom of my stomach wrenched sickeningly just as the impact came.

But we were cast sideways as Tor shifted his weight, and the boat moved into a clean, tight, sweeping curve, elegantly tracing the edge of shoreline. Time seemed to stop, and in that instant I could hear the heavy beating of my heart.

As we pulled out of the curve the adrenaline flooded

through me in a hot gush, pumping blood back to my heart and lungs.

"Did you like that?" Tor inquired cheerfully, not seeming to notice I was at all ruffled.

My legs and spine were spaghetti. I'd never before felt fear like that. I was furious—and I wondered if it would be possible to murder him, and still get back to land in one piece.

"Now that we've warmed up, let's try something *really* exciting—shall we?" he suggested.

I felt certain my heart wouldn't take much more excitement. But I was so dazed and shaken, I couldn't speak. Furthermore, I suspected that any sign of weakness on my part would only prolong the agony. Tor loved to test my nerves.

Without waiting for my response, he hooked the sail into the wind again, and began picking up speed. Soon, we were moving so fast that the shore beside us was only a blur in the corner of my eye. But as long as we hugged the land, it seemed cozy and safe. When he suddenly whipped out onto the lake, the vast black expanse seemed to unfold before me, like the dark, wide, open jaws of death.

"These boats can do well over a hundred knots," he said casually, pitching his voice beneath the monotonous whine of wind.

"How much is a knot?" I forced myself to ask—not really wanting to know. I felt if only I could keep him talking, he might forget his idea to "try something really exciting."

"A nautical mile," he said, "well over a hundred land miles per hour. We've picked up to seventy already."

"How thrilling," I said, but my voice betrayed my feelings.

Tor glanced at me sideways. "You're not frightened?" he asked.

"Don't be ridiculous," I replied as the hot blood came up behind my eyes. I was sure I was going to faint.

"Great! Then we'll open her up—and really *fly*!" he said with glee.

My God, I'm going to die, I thought.

The sails seemed stretched to the breaking point—the snow crossing the bow was so thick it formed a tunnel of insulation that blocked all view. We were inside a pillowcase of silent snow as I strained my eyes and ears to make things out. The silence and blindness were more terrifying than what they obscured.

Suddenly, the snow vanished—and my heart stopped. We were nearly on top of the dock! Ships loomed before us, surrounding us like horrible leering monsters! As we hurtled into them Tor dropped the iceboat on its side. If I hadn't been lashed in, I'd have fallen out on my head. The turn was so tight I was sure the blades would slide from beneath us, and we'd crash into the dock. For one awful instant, my head nearly touched the ice as gravity pulled us down and down. Then we sheered sharply the opposite way, and headed around in a smooth, sure circle toward the dock.

I was literally gasping—gulping down air—so I wouldn't black out. Tor was slaloming gracefully back and forth, in smoothly widening arcs. At the instant we reached shore, he dropped the sail, slid the boat into the slip in an unexpected diagonal slash, and leaped from the deck to tie her up.

I was frozen—immobile with fear—so shaken, I could barely stand. When he reached for my hand, I wasn't sure I could move at all. But when I stumbled to my feet and Tor helped me onto the dock, I was amazed suddenly by a rush of warmth—a powerful, glowing energy far beyond excitement or hysteria. It took me a moment to understand what it was. It was euphoria.

"I loved that," I said aloud, surprising myself.

"Yes, I rather thought you would," he said. "Can you tell me why?"

"I think it was the fear," I blurted out, wondering why that should be.

"Precisely—the fear of death is the affirmation of life," he explained. "Men know that. But women—

almost never. I saw it in you that first night—standing there in the hallway like a lost child. You were so afraid, you actually jumped when I spoke. You were afraid of what was about to happen in your job as well—but your fears didn't stop you. I held out my hand, and you took it. You went up against them all, and all alone."

He smiled, and lifted me off the dock. He held me a moment too long, the warmth of his body penetrating my heavy coat, his face in my hair. I felt suddenly frightened—panicky—though I couldn't say why.

"That's why I chose you," he told me at last.

"Chose me?" I asked, pulling away to look at him. "What on earth do you mean?"

"You know perfectly well what I mean," he replied.

He looked a bit shaken himself. The dim moonlight turned his pale skin and hair to silver. He put his hands on my shoulders and bent toward me. I'd never seen this expression before.

"Perhaps I'm too jaded," he told me. "I've always been bored with the people around me. Life holds no challenges for a mind like mine any longer. I've missed you, my dear. I'm happy you're back at last."

"I'm not *back*," I said, feeling the pounding in my chest. Surely the throbbing in my brain was caused by the rush of the iceboat. "Besides, I thought *I* was the one with jaded emotions—or so you've always said."

"Your emotions aren't jaded—they're repressed," he told me coldly. "How can something be worn-out, when it's never been used?"

He turned on his heel and headed for the car. I stumbled after him in my ridiculously inadequate evening shoes. It was astonishing they'd stayed on my feet through the maelstrom.

"My emotions have been used," I called after him. I saw he was opening the door, and I raced ahead through the drifts.

"I have an emotion myself, that's about to be used," he told me, shoving me into the car. "It's the emotion of anger—and you evoke this emotion in me so frequently, I wonder that I haven't taken a bullwhip to you yet!'' He slammed the door.

He got in on his side, yanking his gloves on. I was silent as he started the engine and waited for the car to warm. I could see my breath fogging the windows. I didn't know what to say.

''I think it's a good investment,'' I told him at last.

''You think what's a good investment—for me to lose my temper? Or are you suggesting I purchase a bullwhip?''

''No, the iceboat,'' I said. ''I think it's a good—why are you laughing like that? Isn't that what you brought me out here for?''

He was wiping the tears from his eyes.

''Fine—the iceboat is an excellent investment. The banker of the year has given her seal of approval. I'm glad you like it, my dear—feel free to use it whenever you wish.''

''Don't be silly,'' I told him, lighting a cigarette to distance myself from the way I felt. ''I can't use an iceboat—I live in San Francisco. And that's where I plan to stay.''

''You live in your fantasies,'' he snapped, in a tone of voice I'd never heard him use.

He threw the car into gear savagely, and pulled out onto the road, kicking up snow clouds.

I watched his grim profile, outlined in the dim green lights from the dashboard. It was a while before I could bring myself to speak.

''I don't understand you,'' I told him at last. ''I never have. You say you want to help me—but you *seem* to want to own me. You keep making me over, into some image in your mind, but I don't know why. I never know why.''

''Neither do I,'' he admitted quietly. Then he whispered, as if to himself, ''Neither do I.''

We went on in silence for quite some time. At long length, I saw him smile.

''I suppose I think of you just as you think of that

iceboat,'' he admitted. He looked over at me in the gloom and smiled.

''Perhaps you're a good investment,'' he said.

NEGOTIATIONS

A very good device, I found, was first to haggle with the farmer over the price, and beat him down to the lowest penny. For, strange as this might sound, this inclines the farmer to trust you.

I had learned good and early that if you haven't got honey in the crock, you must have it in the mouth.

—*Bouck White,*
The Book of Daniel Drew

When my plane circled San Francisco, the air was still glittering with sunshine, the bay was still blue, the little houses on the hillsides were still pastel-colored, and the eucalyptus trees still fluttered in the balmy breezes. The torrential rains in the past weeks had washed everything cleaner than before.

Pearl and Tavish were waiting outside in the green bomber, wearing matching T-shirts that said "Quality Inspected." But I hadn't thought of the problem of fitting three people and luggage into a car designed to be entered with a can opener.

"We'll let Bobby figure this one out," Pearl said, jumping out to hug me. "Men are better at these menial chores."

"In Scotland," Tavish muttered, picking up my bags, "the *women* do the hod carrying while we blokes retire to the nearest pub—to deliberate upon the role of labor in society."

But it proved to be a team effort, with the bags tucked into every available space and Tavish installed precariously over the stick shift between us.

"There's something I have to tell you both," I admitted as Pearl shot onto the freeway, setting a new sound barrier record for surface traffic. "I didn't set up the quality circle just to test security and prove Kiwi and everyone wrong. I actually plan to rob the bank."

"So you said." Pearl smiled wryly. "But nobody believes you're going to toss your career down the toilet, sweetie, just to prove a point. Why not write a book about it instead?"

"Things have gotten a bit more complex than before," I told her. "I'm not just proving a point—I've made a bet that I can *do* it."

"Curioser and curioser," Tavish said in a muffled voice, sandwiched between us. "*You've* wagered you can rob the bank with impunity, and *I* wager we'll all wind up in jail, without—as you Americans say—passing Go! You must be off yer bloomin' bean, madame."

"Oh shit," said Pearl, casting an uneasy glance in her side mirror. "We're about to get some company."

She pulled off the freeway, threw open her door, and jumped out, pulling down her T-shirt and adjusting her "quality inspected" merchandise.

I craned over my shoulder and Tavish's knees to get a better look at the big, handsome—and very young—patrolman who was ambling our way, ticket book in hand.

"I've been behind you since the airport, ma'am," he told Pearl as he came up. He peered in at Tavish and me—twin anchovies. "You've got too many passengers in here for safety—I'm going to have to cite you for that. Weaving in traffic, speeding, reckless driving—you were running on the shoulder of the freeway for a while—no seat belts installed in vehicle . . ." He flipped his book open, shaking his head.

"My . . . *what* an attractive uniform, officer!" said Pearl, rubbing the fabric of his jacket between her fingers. "Are these a new design?"

The officer dropped his book, and she picked it up quickly and handed it to him with a smile. I thought he blushed, but I couldn't be sure. I'd never seen a cop who was any match for Pearl.

"Yes, ma'am," he was saying. "Now, if I could just see your license and registration . . ."

"They fit so *nicely*. Do you have yours tailored?" We'd be lucky if she didn't get arrested for soliciting. "Officer, I really must apologize—but to tell the truth, I was having trouble with my car. It's so hard for me to control all that power. Sometimes, things with so much power just seem to get out of hand, if you see what I mean."

"This *is* a high-performance vehicle," he agreed. "I know it's a Lotus, but I've never seen one like it before."

"You must know a lot about cars," Pearl said with admiration. "I belong to the Lotus Club—this is a limited edition—there are only fifty cars like this one in the world. Not many people would have recognized that."

"I worked as a mechanic in the army," he admitted modestly.

"Oh, you were in the *armed forces*," said Pearl. "You look too young to have had all that active duty! But maybe you can tell me what to ask for when I get my next servicing—so the car won't get away from me like that again?"

"Would you like me to take a look under your hood?" he inquired politely, slipping his ticket book away.

Tavish and I glanced at each other and smiled.

"I can't *tell* you how much I'd appreciate that," Pearl said, and led him up to listen to her engine run.

■

WE HAD LUNCH AMID THE FEATHERY PALMS AND UNder the vaulted glass roof of the Palace's Palm Court—eggs Benedict and Ramos fizzes and lots of dark, rich coffee. When the waiters had stopped replenishing our water glasses, we were alone.

"It seems you've chosen the right friend to help you with your crime," commented Tavish. "We've just seen Mademoiselle Lorraine violate with impunity half of the state highway regulations—*and* try to bribe a police officer. With her body!"

"He was a highway patrolman," Pearl corrected him. "California has the cutest highway patrolmen of any state in the country, and believe me, I'm a seasoned judge. I love it when they pull me over like that."

The restaurant was nearly empty, the sea of peach-and-gold carpeting, marble pillars, and crisp white tablecloths restored to impeccable elegance after the luncheon crush. The time had come.

"I want to talk turkey with both of you," I told them. "As of last week, I had a very important job lined up with the Federal Reserve Bank: director of security. I've been working all my life toward remedying the deplorable way banks are run—at least, in my own small way. But I'm at a dead end; I can't get any higher where I am, and I know it. There are no women executive vice-presidents at the bank, no women on the board. It's unlikely I'll live long enough to realize any of my goals. But I could have, at the Fed."

"What happened?" asked Tavish.

"What do you think? Kiwi sabotaged the job for me—and guess why?"

"You'd be breathing down his neck to get him to do all the things he's refused to do so far," said Tavish. "Like spend fifty cents on control of any sort."

"So it's a vendetta," said Pearl with a smile. "You want us to help you rob his systems, to prove he's an ignorant boob."

"I think it began that way," I admitted. "But I've learned a few things since then. Kiwi's the tip of the iceberg—there are plenty more like him. I want to nail them all, but I need your help."

"Let me get this straight," said Tavish, sipping his café. "We're going to expose every nefarious banker on earth—force the world banking community to behave like gentlemen all with one blow—just by proving we can break into one little system here at the Bank of the World?"

He was cynical—but I did notice he'd said "we." I smiled.

"I have to agree with the surly Scot," said Pearl. "I

think you've been carried away—but it's not too late to stop all this. I'm sorry; I should have told you on the phone that Tavish and I have done something in your absence which might change a few of these plans."

"We had to do it," he chimed in. "We didn't realize you were serious about this mad idea of theft. We were only afraid you'd be sent to Frankfurt in the dead of winter—and *we'd* wind up working for the likes of Kiwi and Karp, without any leverage at all."

"Oh no," I said, my heart sinking. "You'd better tell me what you've done."

"We sent an official report to the Managing Committee," said Pearl. "We recommended the quality circle be taken away from your control. . . ."

■

I WAS BLIND WITH FURY; THEY HAD TO CALM ME DOWN and order another drink. After all my machinations and planning—in one fell swoop—they'd lost both the quality team *and* my wager for me. I certainly couldn't whip up another scheme like that one, not on such short notice—and after this one had failed. If I couldn't see my way out of this, in a month I'd be working for Tor in New York.

They were filled with apologies, but kept pointing out the wisdom of their deed. At last, I was calm enough for them to explain precisely what they'd done.

"We didn't exactly say that the quality team should not work for *you*," Pearl assured me. "We knew Kiwi was planning to seize the group for himself—turn it over to Karp, perhaps—but he needed to make sure that our thrust did not affect any of his own systems. You would have been gone—in Frankfurt. There was nothing we could do about that."

"So we told them," said Tavish, "that the quality team—due to the sensitive nature of our work—should not report to *any* managers in charge of cash-clearing systems. After all, those are the systems we're supposed to be hitting, right?"

"We thought if they moved the team from your control, Kiwi wouldn't be so hot to send you away,'' said Pearl. ''I guess we blew it?''

''Maybe not,'' I told her, feeling drained but no longer angry; after all, their intentions had been the best. ''Do you know where they're going to put the team? They can't give it to Karp—he has money systems, too.''

But when I thought of it, I knew there wasn't one banker there who would accept responsibility for a group like mine, without diluting its task beyond all recognition. It would be like advertising your colleagues' dirty-laundry lists.

''Our proposal says we should report to *no* one,'' said Tavish. ''At least—not an official line manager. We're supposed to be above all that.''

''They have to put you somewhere,'' I told him. ''You're not like a roving wolf pack—you have an official mission statement, blessed by the highest steering committee at the bank.''

But of course, that's when I understood. No ruling had been passed yet—perhaps it was still not too late.

''What if I joined the quality circle myself—as coordinator?'' I suggested. They stared at me.

''Sweetie,'' said Pearl, putting her hand over mine, ''you'd be expected to give up your whole division to do that. You'd be down at the bottom of the barrel, floating around with the pickles. Do you know how long it might take to crawl out of there again?''

''You'd do all that,'' said Tavish, ''just to prove you could rob the bank? You really must be mad.''

''I told you, I've made a bet,'' I said, smiling again as I thought of it. ''And in this case, perhaps there's more honor among thieves than among bankers. The gentleman I'm talking about has wagered that he's a better thief than I am. I can't let him get away with that.''

''Perhaps the whole world has gone mad,'' Tavish philosophized. ''And to think that only last week, I thought Karp was the biggest problem in my life.'' He looked at me, and brushed back a lock of blond hair.

"So, who *is* this friend of yours, who thinks he can—and should—steal more money than you?"

"Have you heard of Dr. Zoltan Tor?" I asked.

They were both silent a moment.

"You're joking," said Tavish, his eyes boggling. "Is he still alive?"

"I dined with him last night in New York," I assured him. "We've known each other a dozen years."

"I've read all Dr. Tor's books," Tavish told Pearl with excitement. "He's a genius—a wizard. He's the reason I got into computers, when I was no more than a child. Good Lord, how I'd love to meet a man like that! But he must be in his dotage by now."

"Doddering along at thirty-nine, and looking rather well," I agreed with a smile. "You asked who made the bet with me. I'm afraid this is the sort of game Tor loves best."

I filled them in on what had transpired, and they sat there in silence through it all. When I'd finished, Tavish was beaming. Pearl rubbed her hands over her face.

"Sweetie, you really take the cake," she told me. "Here I've been abusing you all these years for being a stick-in-the-mud. I take it back; you're not just a gray flannel banker, if you're willing to throw it all away on a dare."

"It's not just a dare," Tavish said in my defense. "It's a principle—and frankly, I think she's right. Now I'm sorry we sent that letter, and I hope we haven't messed things up too badly. I'd like to help win your bet."

"Perhaps you were right to do it," I told him. "Anyway, now there's nothing for it but to make it work. Are we a team?"

They both put their hands over mine on the table.

"Then let's go get a copy of that letter so I can see it. By Monday, we have to have our scrimmage straight."

■

MONDAY, DECEMBER 7, WAS THE BEGINNING OF THE third week after my night at the opera. It seemed an eternity.

Pavel was standing at my office door, coffee cup in hand. I gave him the gift I'd brought from New York, in its sky-blue Tiffany box. He exchanged the cup for the box, and followed me into my office, untying the silky white ribbon.

"*The divine Sarah!*" he exclaimed, when he saw the old photo of Sarah Bernhardt Lelia had given me, in its silver art deco frame. "This is from Oscar Wilde's *Salome*, just before she makes love to the Baptist's severed head! I love it—it will go on my dresser at home. But speaking of severed heads, I hope you know what's about to happen to *yours*! Lord Willingly's spent the week in a real snit—hibernating, dark sunglasses like a movie star, curtains drawn, Do Not Disturb sign on the door—wants to see you first thing. It seems your little quality circle has gone over his head. I keep my ear to the wall, you know."

"I'm not in yet," I told him, sucking down my tepid transfusion.

"I'm afraid you are," he informed me with a grimace. "There's a worse problem. Lawrence rang up this morning, nearly at dawn—I'd just walked in the door. Said you're to be sent up to see him first thing. Seems the lions *do* squabble, when there's only one Christian to be dished up."

Lawrence's suite of offices was on the top floor—a cluster of glass-walled spaces that sat like a feudal fortress overlooking the city.

In the banking business, power is measured in yards of carpeting, and Lawrence had cornered the market on gray broadloom. It took ten minutes to navigate the distance from his office door to his desk; but I'd been there before, so I knew the pitfalls of the crossing. If you extended your hand too early in the traverse, you looked like a goose trying to get off the lake in a strong wind—mired in pile before reaching the goal.

Of the many executives at the Bank of the World, Lawrence was the one who never dabbled in politics and intrigue—no locker-room gossip for him. Lawrence believed not in plotting against others, but in gaining complete mastery of them. He was king of the total mind fuck—a banking term designating Do Unto Others Before They Do Unto You.

His office was the key weapon in this game. He liked to conduct meetings there, whenever possible. When you entered this no-man's-land, the absence of color enveloped you like a battlefield shrouded in mist. Everything was neutral—shades of gray and taupe—so you knew you were losing ground, without knowing where the ground really was.

There were none of the usual amenities—no papers littering the desk, no diplomas or paintings on the wall, no snapshots of the wife and kids on the credenza—nothing your eye could cling to for refuge. The effect was like a neutralizing gun applied to your psyche, everything so understated it practically vanished. Everything but Lawrence.

Against this voidlike background, his persona burned like a hard, cold flame—a man with no ties, no attachments, no silly emotions to clutter up his decision-making prowess. He was forty, slender, handsome, and lethal.

When I entered his office, he was wearing a gray suit and gold-rimmed glasses. His ash-blond hair, silver at the temples, glinted in the sunlight streaming through the walls of glass. He rose, watching me expressionlessly as I crossed—as a spider might watch an insect entering its web, indifferent whether it arrived in time for lunch or dinner. Lawrence was a born predator, but not the usual species. He was the kind that killed by instinct, not for survival: it was simply rote mechanism with him.

"Verity, I'm sorry I called you here at such short notice. I'm glad you could make the time to get away."

Lawrence liked to call you by your first name at once so you'd feel at home, though his tone suggested that without his goodwill, you'd find no other home on this planet.

There's a protocol associated with power. Take the seating arrangements of the power wielder versus the wieldee. Lawrence's expansive ash desk placed him at least twelve feet away from his prey, and the seat he motioned for me to take would place his head a foot higher than mine.

"Let's sit over here so we can talk," I suggested, indicating a seating area near the far windows, where there'd be no desk between us.

Lawrence made the best of the situation by choosing a chair where the reflections of buildings across the street would form squares on the surface of his gold-rimmed glasses. Seeing this, I did something that was likely unprecedented: I moved my chair so I could look him right in the eye.

Looking Lawrence in the eye was not a pleasant experience; he had the unique knack of seeming to snap his pupils shut—as a cat does—when he didn't want to reveal what he was thinking.

"I understand you've just come back from New York?" he began when we were seated. "Ah—I envy you. My first ten years at the bank were in the Manhattan bureau. Tell me how you passed the time—did you go to the theater?"

This preliminary camaraderie was not to be confused with idle banter. Predators have been known to make friends with their food—toy with it for hours—before they eat it.

"I didn't have time for that, sir," I told him. "But I went to many excellent restaurants—as you'll see when you get my expense report!"

"Ha-ha. I can see that you've quite a sense of humor, Verity."

He was the only person I'd ever met who could laugh without smiling.

"You're perhaps aware, Verity, that in your absence I received a report from the quality circle you manage?"

"It was sent to you upon my advice, sir," I told him—as Pearl, Tavish, and I had agreed I should.

"Are you aware, Verity, that this document proposes to remove the quality circle from the hands of those who control production systems? Most specifically, those who direct on-line systems handling financial resources of the bank?"

"I've read the report," I said.

Now, if Lawrence wondered how in hell I could have read a fifty-page memo—when I'd just this moment set foot in the bank after a week's absence—he didn't show it; he never missed a beat.

"Then you propose that this quality team—whose activities you yourself initiated—be withdrawn at once from your control?"

I looked directly into Lawrence's eyes; it was like having an ice pack slapped on my stomach. "It seems to me that's not the only alternative afforded by this proposal—sir," I said.

His pupils narrowed briefly, for a flicker. "Indeed? Perhaps you interpreted it differently than I."

"It says simply that auditors should be separated from what they're auditing," I pointed out. "Have you an objection to that?"

His pupils tightened considerably, and I congratulated myself on my choice of seating. But I knew I wasn't playing the part of the "huntee"—giving no quarter, showing no fear, don't let them pick up the scent.

"Let's see if I understand," he said, inching his way across the crevasse. Lawrence was nobody's fool; he knew a setup when he saw one. "You mean to say you're *not* recommending I take this quality team out of your hands? Perhaps we should review the case so far. You initiate a group to take a hard look at bank security. You approach the Managing Committee for funding—without first obtaining the support of your own management. . . ."

Hitting below the belt, but I let it pass.

"You travel to New York to garner support from the banking community— Are we tracking so far?"

"We are."

"In your absence, a report is sent to me—under your auspices, you say—claiming that managers like you, controlling mainframe money systems, should be removed from all involvement in this group's activities."

"Correct."

"Because of possible conflict of interest: to be certain that this group will have no vested interest in examining one system more than others. Or less than others. And yet you're claiming now that this doesn't mean you should wash your hands of the quality circle?"

"That's not the *only* possibility afforded, sir."

"You seem to be a person who's aware of many possibilities," he said calmly. "The only other path I see is for you to abandon your role as head of money systems altogether."

"That seems to be it," I agreed.

He sat there for a moment. I couldn't be sure, but I thought I recognized a look that approached respect—though it quickly turned to something more like calculation. Then he hit me with the left hook.

"Would you recommend that I endorse this proposition, Verity?"

Shit. I should have seen it coming. If I said yes—with no commitments up front—I was screwed. If I said no, I looked like a damned fool, since I was supposedly the one who'd sponsored the proposal.

If I couldn't get Lawrence to commit, up front, to move me and the team to his department—beyond Kiwi's control—I'd be at the mercy of whatever prevailing winds might blow. I had to get the ball back in Lawrence's court—get him to make a serious offer.

"Sir," I hedged, "what would be your interest in *declining* this proposal?"

He stared at me. His pupils snapped shut, then opened wide.

"Banks, do you play chess?" he asked, not looking at me.

"Yes, sir—I play a little," I admitted.

"I would have said you played a lot. Tell me what you want."

"Pardon me?"

"What do you want out of all this—*you*—Verity Banks?" He turned and looked at me. "What were your expectations when you came up here? What did you hope to gain for yourself, from this little interview?"

"You invited me here, sir," I pointed out.

"I'm aware of that," he said impatiently. "But you expected some decision from me, or you wouldn't have sent that damned letter. Now, what will it be—the quality circle, or money transfers? You can't have it both ways."

But he still hadn't said whether the circle would report directly to him!

"Sir, I wouldn't presume—"

"You needn't presume anything—I'm telling you. Obviously, your letter's placed me in an untenable position. If I don't break off this quality circle from all production groups, I'll be having auditors for breakfast, lunch, and dinner. So the quality circle reports directly to me—as of today. Do you come with it—or stay in money transfers with Willingly? Willingly, incidentally, is not a nice chap to work for when his toes have been stepped on—which you've managed to do several times this last month."

Perhaps it was my expression that caused him to laugh.

"I suppose you're thinking I'm not much of an improvement over Willingly in that respect," he added. "But if you do come here—I hope you won't find your bridges burned behind you."

"With all due respect," I told him, "some bridges fall down all by themselves, anyway. I'll take my chances with you."

I stood up, and he walked me to the door.

"Banks, I must say that you, for a woman, have got more balls than anyone I've ever met. I only hope you don't trip over them—it can be a painful experience. I haven't time to fool with these things just now, but I'll clear out some offices on the west wall for your group. Have premises bring your things up here today. And by the way, try to avoid Willingly for an hour or so, until I can explain to him how things stand."

He extended his hand for me to leave. I took it, but didn't leave at once.

"With all respect, sir . . ."

"Yes?" He raised an eyebrow.

"The *east* wall has a view of the bay."

■

ON THE WAY BACK DOWN IN THE ELEVATOR, I CONgratulated myself again—for having made sure that Pearl and Tavish had sent copies of that innuendo-riddled report both to the WHIPS group and to internal audit.

I was whistling the "Sword Theme of Nothung", feeling invincible, as I crossed the floor to my office. Which explains why I didn't see Pavel—frantically waving his arms at me—until it was too late. He cringed as Kiwi's voice bellowed from within.

"Buzz me in two minutes, with an urgent call," I whispered to Pavel.

He nodded resignedly as I slid by him. Inside, Kiwi was installed behind my desk, wearing *mirrored* sunglasses. More than a decade ago, Tor had taught me how to deal with managers I no longer needed. I had only to play for time.

"Hi, Kiwi!" I said cheerfully, pulling open the draperies so light flooded the room. "What's up?"

"*You're* up! Up to no good!" he informed me, in a voice I didn't care for at all.

I started going through my "in" basket and opening the mail as if he weren't there.

"Perhaps you could clue me in," I said nonchalantly. "I've been in New York for a week—"

"And plotting against me all the while, there *and* here!" he cried. "Don't try to be Little Mary Sunshine with *me!*"

Though this time his paranoia had some basis in reality, it annoyed me nonetheless.

"Don't you think you're being a bit extreme?" I asked him. "Why don't you say what's bothering you—so we can stop playing these games?"

"You're the one who should tell me," he said, his voice wavering out of control. "If you're so blameless, why haven't you mentioned that you've just been to Lawrence's office—how about that? What were you doing there, half the morning?"

Jesus Christ—Kiwi had spies everywhere. Just then, my intercom buzzed.

"Urgent call, Miss Banks," Pavel's voice came through. "Pick up on line six, please."

"Excuse me," I told Kiwi politely.

He had to dislodge his carcass from my chair so I could get behind the desk to answer the phone. He moved to a chair opposite, and glared at me as I picked it up.

"Hello, my friend—guess what *we're* doing?" Georgian's husky voice came through the line. Good Lord, it was a real phone call!

"What are you doing?"

I glanced up at Kiwi. Even through those sunglasses, I could feel the heat of his anger. It seemed he was staying.

"You sound preoccupied," said Georgian. "Should I call back later?"

"In situations like this, I think matters should be handled very differently," I told her.

"What the hell are you talking about?" she said. "Is someone there with you right now?"

"My point precisely," I told her. "I'm glad you've perceived the problems we're having on *our* end."

"Someone is there—but you don't want me to hang up," she said. "So what should I do?"

"Take your time—explain carefully what you've accomplished so far," I told her. "I need the facts so I can present the situation to my boss—who happens to be sitting right here."

Though Kiwi was soon to be my ex-boss, I had to play for time until Lawrence could inform him of the fact. I raised my eyebrows meaningfully at him, as though something really critical were going on at the other end of the line.

"Your boss? You're not in any trouble, I hope?" said Georgian. "Gosh, I feel like a heavy-duty espionage agent or something. Are you sure he can't hear me?"

"I think we should take every precaution to make sure nothing like that will occur," I told her.

Even at a whisper, Georgian sounded like Tallulah Bankhead playing Radio City Music Hall.

"Thor's been here all week," she told me, "hovering over me and my printing or out cooking in the kitchen with Mother—his potato latkes are divine."

"Get to the point," I said, knowing Kiwi wouldn't hold forever. "How is your project going?"

"Last night I made a breakthrough," she said. "I got the idea to *print* watermarks on the paper, using a glycerine-type oil. When you hold it to the light, it's translucent, just like a real watermark. You could only detect it through X ray, I think. They surely don't inspect them that carefully. . . ."

Kiwi had picked up a magazine and was leafing through it in irritation, crossing and uncrossing his legs as if he could hardly contain his impatience.

"And Thor's been moving my equipment around—industrial engineering, he calls it—so we now can get eight certificates on a single photo plate. If we print hundred-thousand-dollar bonds, that's nearly a million bucks per photo! Not bad, compared with fashion layouts, I'd say."

I was doodling on my desk pad, keeping one eye on Kiwi, as she rattled on about expenses and complexities. I found it hard to concentrate, when Kiwi was about to blow.

He stood up, tossed down the magazine, and started pacing back and forth, coming a little closer to the phone each time. I tried to muffle the receiver in my shoulder, and began reducing my replies to monosyllabic grunts—but he was nearly breathing down my neck.

"So—what's the bottom line?" I interrupted, to shut her up. "Are you going to meet the schedule? Are you ready for the next phase?"

"We'll be ready next week—maybe earlier," she assured me.

Shit, and I hadn't even cracked one file.

"But, Verity, now that we're close, I'm really getting panicky, you know? I mean—it's illegal if we get caught before we're through. Do I really want to do this? How do you feel?"

"Me too," I said.

"I mean, we're not keeping the money. My only excuse is, we're doing something honorable."

"Me too."

"Of course—there *is* the aspect of adventure. When Zoltan told me about the bet, I said what the hell. I think your life could certainly use some improvement."

"Me too."

"On the other hand, if we did get caught, I think we should give all the profits to Mother Teresa—it would make me feel happier about going to prison, maybe."

"Me too."

Kiwi skidded to a halt before me, breathing in my face. He yanked off the sunglasses and glared at me.

"Me too, me too, me too!" he exploded. "What kind of conversation *is* this?"

"Excuse me," I told Georgian, "an emergency has just arisen in my office." Turning to Kiwi, I said, "I am speaking on the telephone. Perhaps we could schedule an appointment to continue this chat when it's a little more convenient?"

"We're talking, and we're talking *now*, Banks," he said, his face black with rage. "Neither wild horses nor God himself could drag me from here—I'm rooted to the spot. Now wind up this conversation of yours, and quickly."

"Excuse me, Mr. Willingly," Pavel said to Kiwi from the doorway. "I have Mrs. Harbinger on the phone. She says her boss would like to see you in his office—at once.''

Mrs. Harbinger was Lawrence's secretary. I smiled sweetly as Kiwi stood there indecisive, rooted to the spot.

''Tell her I'll be there shortly,'' Kiwi muttered.

''Perhaps you'd better speak with her yourself then, sir,'' Pavel told him. ''She's on my line—she says they've tried to reach you all morning, but you weren't in your office.''

''Mr. Willingly has been in *my* office all morning,'' I said casually.

Kiwi glared at me.

''Yes, they finally tried him here. It really seems quite important, sir,'' Pavel said.

''All right, all right,'' Kiwi muttered, stomping to the door. ''But you'd better be here when I return, Banks. I want your ass in your office—in that chair—when I come back.''

He departed, cold with rage, as Pavel and I smiled at one another across the open space.

''What's going on?'' asked Georgian over the line.

''Some wild horses and God himself just came into my office and dragged my boss away,'' I explained.

''Sounds like life in the banking business isn't as dull as I'd always pictured it.''

''It's a laugh a minute,'' I assured her. ''Let's finish up—because I have to phone the building people in a minute to move my stuff. My ass will be in the same chair—in my office—when he returns. But my office will be on the thirtieth floor, not the thirteenth.''

''What are you talking about?''

''Just mumbling to myself,'' I told her. ''Tell me now—exactly how far are you?''

''I've printed blank copies of every bond Thor gave me,'' she said. ''All I need is my first real security so I can print in the serial numbers and such. It should start any day now—any moment, in fact. Thor's out looking for a job.''

"A job? What for? He owns his own company," I said.

"I think he'll need *this* job," she assured me. "Let me tell you how it works. . . ."

TAKING STOCK

I was young. But that's the time to start in. Early sow, early mow. During those days I was always on the go—never was one of your lazybones; better to wear out shoes than sheets, was my motto.

The early cow gets the dew.

—Bouck White,
THE BOOK OF DANIEL DREW

Tuesday, December 8

DUKE JIMMY UNBUTTONED THE FLY OF HIS TROUSERS and took a nice warm pee in his favorite doorway on Third Avenue. Fastening up his pants again, he pulled down the soft old cashmere sweater that had been mended and given him by the St. Mark's Rescue League. The sweater was a very pretty shade of burgundy, and looked nice with the tweedy, patched jacket he'd gotten from the Divine Light Mission.

He ambled on over toward Union Square, where he thought he could pick up his usual morning handout. A building near there had a nice hot-air grate he liked to sit near while he drank his breakfast. But the morning was colder than he'd realized. By the time he got to Union Square, his hands were cold and were shoved in his threadbare pockets, and he could feel the wetness of the snow working its way through the newspapers lining his shoes.

While he was sitting near the grate with one shoe off, he noticed the man standing there watching him. Duke Jimmy glanced up; there was something odd about the chap. Then he realized it was the color of his eyes—Jimmy had never seen eyes like that except on an alley cat.

"Top of the morning to you, sir," said Jimmy pleasantly.

"Hello," said Tor. "It's a much colder morning than the weatherman reported. You must be chilly in that outfit."

"Right you are," said Jimmy. "I was just thinking to myself that a nice bottle of red wine would warm my old bones."

"I wonder," said Tor, "if you would mind standing up for a moment?"

"I hope you're not planning to rob me," said Jimmy, putting on his shoe and standing up before Tor. "If so, you've certainly picked the wrong chappie."

Tor walked slowly around the old bum, looking him up and down.

"I think you'll do," he said. "How would you like to make some money?"

"That depends," said Duke Jimmy cautiously.

"You seem to be about the same size as I. How would you like to sell me those clothes you're wearing? Just the toppers—I'm not interested in the undergarments," Tor added quickly. He'd gotten a good whiff of the old wino, and wondered how much disinfectant it would take to rid the clothes of lice.

"How much are you talking about?" asked Jimmy. "These clothes are practically family heirlooms, you know. They don't go cheap."

"Fifty dollars," said Tor.

"Sounds fair to me," Jimmy agreed. "But what am I going to wear if I sell my last suit of clothes?"

Tor hadn't thought of that. Nor did he want to get into a shopping expedition to outfit the fellow.

"How about that suit *you're* wearing?" Jimmy suggested. "If my clothes fit you, your clothes ought to fit me."

"This suit is rather expensive," said Tor.

"That's fine with me," replied Jimmy. "That's why they call me Duke Jimmy—because I knows quality when I sees it."

■

THE COURIER OFFICE IN MIDTOWN MANHATTAN WAS crowded with sweaty bodies. The steady buzz of voices, like the droning of a fan, would cease for a moment each time someone's number was called by the clerk up front.

Tor rose from the back of the room when his number came up. He was conscious of the strong smell of dry-cleaning fluid and disinfectant that accompanied him as he moved through the room, and an aroma beneath it that seemed slightly stronger. But no one seemed to notice.

He followed the clerk into a large back room with many desks.

"Mr. Duke?" said the interviewer, who barely glanced up as Tor entered the cubicle.

"Yes—Jimmy Duke," said Tor, suppressing a small smile.

"I'll just put James down here—shall I? Is that your given name?"

"People call me Jimmy," said Tor.

"Fine," said the interviewer, printing James in the blank space. "May I see the questionnaire you've completed?" When Tor handed it to him, he asked, "Have you ever done work like this before?"

"I've delivered for grocery stores," said Tor.

"Ah yes, so I see," said the interviewer. "All right, let me explain the job. We get a call from a brokerage firm, or perhaps from the stock exchange. If you're called, you go to the address indicated. The securities will be held there for you in a satchel. You pick up the securities and check them to make certain they're all there, then you initial for them and give the brokerage a receipt. Get them to sign your pink slip so we can bill them properly."

"Then what do I do?" asked Tor.

"Take them to the Depository Trust, where they'll be logged in. They'll check all the forms against the securities and give you a receipt. We charge them ten dollars for a delivery, and you get paid eight dollars an hour. Most deliveries will take you very little time, since the offices are almost all in the financial district. We supply the bicycle. That's all there is to it."

"Fine," said Tor. "When do I start?"

"It'll take about two weeks to get you bonded. But I see here on your form that you don't have any arrests or a criminal record, and we're short of staff just now—so you can begin at once. We'll send you your papers when your bonding comes through in a few weeks. Report to the courier office on Broad Street tomorrow morning at eight."

"Fine," said Tor, taking his departure.

He wouldn't have to wait for his bonding papers. In two weeks, the entire theft would be completed.

Wednesday, December 9

AT NINE O'CLOCK THE MORNING OF DECEMBER 9, A man in a frayed tweed jacket and burgundy sweater entered the doors of Merrill Lynch. He was wearing mud-spattered sneakers with bicycle clips around the calves of his trousers, and carrying a clipboard with sheets of scribbled paper attached. He went up to the receptionist's desk.

"Pickup for Depository," he said.

"Are you a courier?" she asked, and Tor nodded. "Next floor up," she told him.

Tor came off the elevator on the next floor. There was a long hallway with a door at the end that said DELIVERY. He went down and pushed the buzzer, and the door unlocked with a click.

"Pickup for Depository?" Tor said to the man at the window.

"Okay, he's here!" yelled the man over his shoulder. "Come on, step on it—we haven't got all day. Anything else for A through G? I haven't got H through M yet. S through Zed, you're okay. . . ."

He was glancing through the piles on his desk as he ticked off securities on a ticket before him.

"Okay, I guess that's it," he told Tor.

They both went through the securities and checked off the numbers. Tor dropped the securities into the canvas satchel the man handed him. He gave the man a receipt and the man initialed his clipboard. Tor picked up the satchel.

"You handle these securities alphabetically?" asked Tor.

"Yeah, what's it to you?" said the man behind the window.

"If I have to drop some off here, should I bring them to you?"

"Nope. Those go to receiving—next floor up."

"Thanks," said Tor. As he turned to leave he added to himself, "The left hand knoweth not what the right hand doeth."

"What's that?" said the man, already preoccupied.

"A biblical quotation," said Tor as the door clicked shut behind him.

Without biblical aid, they had no way to reconcile the daily arrivals and departures of securities like these he held in his bag, he thought as he went back down the hall. If things were handled and filed in so many places, it would be hard enough just to reconcile the gross dollars that moved in and out the door. Tor smiled.

The streets outside were slushy and dirty with snow. Tor walked over to the bicycle and threw the canvas satchel into one of the pannier-type baskets slung over the back of the frame. He unlocked the bicycle from the rack and rode away through the steel-and-concrete canyons of Wall Street.

An hour later, covered with mud and laden with many such canvas satchels, the bicycle moved laboriously through heavy traffic to the subway entrance at Wall Street.

Tor pedaled wearily to the rack at the east entrance, locked his bicycle to the rack, and hoisted the panniers over his shoulder. Groaning a little beneath the weight, he descended the steps into the subway.

■

LELIA FLEW DOWN THE CORRIDOR AS SOON AS THE MAID threw open the double entry doors.

"Mein Gott in Himmel!" she cried. "Mud! Mud! *Qu'est qu'il fait?* Do not let him enter—he will ruin my floors! What does he want?"

"Lelia, my charming one, what hospitality," said Tor, wiping dirt from his eyelids to clear white patches that looked like goggles.

"Oh, *mon cher*," said Lelia. "What have they done with you? You are dragged in the gutters, so dirty. Where have you come by these clothings?"

"This seems to be the appropriate attire in the courier business," he assured her. "I've made a study of it. The transfer agents would have taken alarm if I'd arrived in a Brioni suit. It seems they prefer couriers who are more on the seamy side."

"You must take off these things, and we will have Nana make you a nice bubble bath," she told him, turning up her nose slightly at Tor's aroma.

"No time for bubbles, my dear," he replied. "Where's Georgian? It's time for her to go to work."

Georgian was in the Plum Room, setting up papers and cleaning equipment. Tor and Lelia lugged the bags down the corridor, opened them one by one, and examined the contents, listing what they'd taken from each bag and placing those securities they'd selected in a small pile on the floor.

Lelia kept a running tab of the face value of each bond they extracted for printing.

"You'd better go wash your hands before you touch those anymore," Georgian told Tor. "Or let Mother do it—you're making a real mess here."

"If you do your job right," he said, grinning with white teeth against his black face, "these won't be going back at all."

Georgian stared at him.

"My God, this is it—this is really it, isn't it?" she said.

"I don't know what you mean by 'it.' But these are certainly negotiable securities, and we're going to take the dollar values and certificate numbers from them and engrave them on our blank certificates. Don't tell me you're having second thoughts at *this* late date?"

Georgian stood dumbfounded.

"Allons, allons!" said Lelia all at once. *"Mach schnell! Dépêchez-vous!* We have all this work to do, and you are making the reveries. You begin the photos—and I will make some *potage* for the poor Zoltan. He will need the food, to restore the good health."

"Mother, my God, do you never think of anything but food?"

"It makes strength for successful criminals," said Lelia, standing up.

Tor was looking down at the pile of securities they'd out-sorted, flipping through them with his thumb. He glanced up grimly.

"We have only twenty," he said.

"Twenty what?" asked Georgian.

"Twenty certificates—out of all those satchels—that we can actually use. They have to be types we've already prepared engravings for. And if all the securities we get are like these—only five thousand dollars apiece—we'll be making engraving plates for months, just to plug in the numbers."

"It did take most of the weekend to make the plates for those bond samples you bought," Georgian agreed. "It might take all day just to engrave the numbers on these few."

"We don't *have* all day," snapped Tor. He bent over quickly and retallied the amount of the pile. "Less than ten million," he said irritably.

"What's wrong with that?" asked Georgian. "Your bet with True is whoever can steal thirty million first! We're well on our way, with our very first haul!"

Tor sighed and stood up.

"Not *steal* thirty million—*earn* thirty million," he

explained patiently. "That calls for a billion in collateral."

"So borrow bigger certificates for me to copy, then," said Georgian with her own brand of logic.

"I am doing my best," said Tor, biting off each word. "Considering that I have to take what the houses feel like transferring, and that you've become the Zen master of printing—perfection or nothing—I should say we'd wind up this little caper by sometime next June!"

"You don't understand," said Georgian tearfully. "I have to make a completely new plate—take the photo, develop the film, do the acid etching, the works—for every damned bond you drag in the door. There are too many steps for each one. Besides," she added, picking up a bond and waving it at him, "half the numbers on these stupid things aren't even engraved—they're just slapped on with a printing press. So I don't see why I have to go through so much effort—"

"What did you say?" cried Tor, snatching the bond from her fingers and staring at it.

He smiled slowly, and looked up at Georgian.

"My little featherbrained genius," he said wryly. "I believe you've just saved all our necks."

■

TOR WAS WOLFING DOWN HIS SECOND BOWL OF LELIA'S delicious minestrone as he finished explaining the face of the bond to Georgian.

"Just as before, we can engrave almost everything up front, before we get our hands on the actual bond we want to copy. The border design, the issuer's name and number—these never change, regardless of the amount or series of the bond."

"Right," agreed Georgian. "Everything else can just be photographed and printed right from the photo, without making engraving plates. That is, everything but the denomination of the bond—its 'face value.' That seems to be engraved rather than printed on every kind of bond."

"But run your fingers over that number," said Tor.

"It may be engraved, but the ink is just a bit thicker than the parts of the bond that are only printed. Furthermore, the denomination is located in the *center* of the certificate. If the border *around* it's engraved—and that's what you'd be most likely to touch when you're thumbing through a pile of securities—you'd hardly notice whether some flowery number in the middle was engraved or printed."

"It would certainly cut down on time," Georgian admitted. "I can get eight securities on one photo negative, and print right from that. A lot easier than taking the photo and then making eight engraving plates before printing."

"I'm willing to take this risk if you are," Tor told her. "After all, I'm the one who has to deliver these fakes to the Depository Trust. I'll be the one caught with his pants down, if these don't pass inspection."

"I'd like to get a photo of *that*." Georgian laughed. But she looked really worried. "I'm so nervous when the least little thing goes wrong," she explained. "I feel like we've walked into a nightmare. . . ."

"No time for the nightmares—or the reveries, either," said Lelia, coming to remove the soup bowls. "You must not put off until tomorrow what you can do the day after."

"All right, Mother." Georgian laughed. "Get the hair dryer—it looks like we're in business."

■

IT WAS TWO-THIRTY WHEN LELIA ENTERED THE ANcient, fishy-smelling foyer of the South End Yacht Club below Whitehall on East River Drive, a large envelope tucked beneath her arm containing the twenty completed certificates.

"Excuse me, ma'am"—the porter stopped her—"but you can't enter unless accompanied by a member."

"But Dr. Tor is expecting me—on a matter of *grave urgence*," she explained.

"Perhaps he's been detained," said the porter. "He hasn't come in today."

Lelia was about to protest, when the porter looked up toward the door in alarm. Tor was bounding up the steps, covered with mud, in his frayed tweed and faded pants, the pannier baskets swinging from his shoulder.

"I'm glad you waited, darling," he said, taking Lelia gingerly by the sleeve of her fur coat. "George—this is Baroness Daimlisch. We'll be having tea in the private dining room, it's reserved. And send up a bottle of that thirty-two claret, will you?"

The astounded porter tried not to look at Tor's costume, but reached into the closet behind him and brought out a necktie printed with the tiny block insignia of the club. This he handed to Tor, who draped it around the neck of his burgundy sweater and made a knot.

Then he offered Lelia his arm and headed for the room.

"Oh, and George," he called over his shoulder, "keep an eye on my bicycle, will you? It's just out front."

"Certainly, sir," George replied.

■

"THIS IS EXCELLENT CLARET," LELIA SAID AS SHE SAT beside the fireplace in the dimly lit, paneled private club room.

"And these are exquisite engravings," Tor replied, thumbing through them carefully. "Now we'll put them back into the right satchels for delivery. I've picked up some more while you and Georgian were working on these. It's a quarter to three now; do you think you can get back uptown, copy them, and return by five so I can get them into the Depository?"

"It will be *difficile*," Lelia admitted. "But she has completed this last printing in less than one hour. It was the time required for me to get here from the subway that makes it so long. Though this is faster than the taxi."

"Perhaps I can meet you at the subway, then?" he suggested. "And no more stopping for lunch or cocktails, after today. Time's of the essence, so I'm happy you're willing to be our runner. I hope you understand, though, you're taking a risk."

"What is life, if one is afraid to take the chances?" asked Lelia.

Tor nodded and looked down at one of the fake securities they'd done. He ran his fingers over the scalloped number at center, which read: "$5,000 and no/100"—a number that had been printed rather than engraved. Only an expert would notice the difference. It was the sentence six lines below it that bothered him. Not because of the way it looked, but because of what it said: "Subject to prior redemption, as provided herein."

They'd printed a callable bond—a security that could be "called in" like a note if the issuer wanted to pay it off early—why hadn't he noticed that earlier?

Oh well, he thought, it couldn't be helped. The likelihood was slim that anything would happen. And, as Lelia said, what was life if one was afraid to take the chances?

Tor slipped the bond into the satchel for the Depository Trust.

■

THE DEPOSITORY TRUST'S FORTY STORIES OF CONCRETE and glass concealed a vaultlike inner construction where hundreds of thousands of securities, like those in Tor's bag, were stored.

Most standard deliveries were made through the front entrance, which housed the Chemical Bank. But the deliveries that counted—the constant traffic in securities—were made through the rear of the building.

At the back of 55 Water Street was a pair of nondescript doors made of twelve-inch steel. Beyond the steel doors was a series of double-door "mantraps." Through them passed, all day long, unkempt messengers in faded jeans and sneakers, delivering satchels and suitcases packed with corporate and municipal bonds, common and preferred stocks.

The vaults where the securities were stored were located in labyrinthine, multilevel subbasements of the building. But the messengers never entered these hallowed halls, nor did they enter the offices scattered throughout the upper stories. Everything beyond the steel doors was controlled by security camera, security badge, and guard station.

At precisely four-fifty on the evening of December 9, a man in faded tweed jacket, burgundy sweater, and muddy sneakers entered the Depository Trust Company. Slung over his shoulder was a double-pannier basket containing mud-spattered satchels of securities. He pushed through the steel doors and cleared the maze of succeeding doors, past cameras and guards, and entered the small room where drop-offs were made. Standing in line behind another messenger, he waited at the Dutch door until his turn came.

One by one, he hefted onto the counter his satchels and their accompanying clipsheets. The clerk behind the counter opened every satchel in turn, and briefly inspected the securities to be sure that everything on the list was present.

She removed and initialed the four-part form attached to the satchel, then sent one part of the form off with the securities to the vault. She filed the second part of the form—and returned the last two parts to the messenger as evidence that the deposit had been completed. The messenger would return one of these copies to the owner of the securities.

He picked up his receipts and passed out through the steel doors. Transaction completed.

Tor looked at his watch when he got outside. It was barely five, but the sky was completely black. He walked wearily back around to the front of the building, where he'd left his bicycle. He unlocked the bicycle and looked up at the building. The lights of the Chemical Bank glowed brightly, though the bank by now would be closed for the night.

Of the two runs and printings he'd made today, he had deposited close to $30 million in bearer bonds.

They would lie on the shelves of the Depository Trust Company from today until eternity.

And no one had even glanced at them—to see whether they were real.

Friday, December 18
Utrecht, Netherlands

It was the last Friday before Christmas holiday, and Vincent Veerboom sat in his office at Rabobank, scratching notes to his secretary and occasionally glancing up to look out the window.

The one dim window in his impregnable office overlooked the steaming, snow-covered city of Utrecht, the ugliness of its squat, gray buildings dissipated by the thin veil of crystalline snow trickling through the darkened sky.

He heard a soft tap on the door; his aide entered the room.

"Yes?" barked Veerboom, irritated by the disruption of his preholiday reverie.

"Sir, excuse please. I know you're preparing to depart for holiday—but the Baroness Daimlisch is outside. She wishes an audience with you."

"I'm not in," he said.

It was nearly time to go; the bank would be closed in a quarter hour, and he'd been thinking all afternoon of that moment and what would follow fast upon it. His wife and children had preceded him to their ski lodge in Zermatt, and he would not join them until the following day. As soon as he left the bank, he would spend a romantic evening enveloped in the billowy bosom of his mistress, Ullie, who was presumably warming up supper for him even now, in the little apartment he leased for her in the suburbs of Utrecht.

"Sir, the baroness claims it's a matter of utmost urgency. She wishes to make a sizable transaction today—before the bank closes.''

''On the eve of the Christmas holiday?'' snapped Veerboom. ''Certainly not—it's absurd! Let her come back when we're open.''

''The bank will be closed for a week,'' the aide pointed out, ''and the baroness leaves tonight for Baden-Baden.''

''Who is this Baroness Daimlisch, anyway? The name sounds familiar. . . .''

The aide crossed the room and whispered into Veerboom's ear as if someone were listening at the keyhole.

''Ah, I see,'' said Veerboom. ''Well then, show her in. Let's hope we can make it brief. I abhor doing business with these shrill, overbearing German women.''

''The baroness is Russian by birth,'' said the aide. ''An expatriate, you understand.''

''Yes yes, thank you. These things do slip one's mind at times. And what was the baroness's Christian name, Peter?''

''Lelia, sir. Her name is Lelia Maria von Daimlisch.''

The aide departed and a few moments later ushered Lelia into the office.

She was cloaked in white fur, shod in tall white lizard boots. As she entered she tossed back the cape, and the display of diamonds at her throat made Veerboom catch his breath. Recovering himself, he stepped forward and took her proffered hand in his.

''Lelia, how good it is to see you again,'' he said cordially. Veerboom had not become a successful Dutch banker by throwing charm out the window. ''You're more radiant than ever—still the young girl I remember. How long has it been? It seems years—but in some ways, less than a day.''

''For me,'' Lelia said, fluttering her eyelashes demurely, ''time is not relative.'' She'd never before seen this man; bankers were so pretentious.

''My sentiments exactly,'' he agreed warmly, motioning her to take a seat. He sat in a chair beside her and pressed a small bell for the valet.

"Perhaps my assistant has explained that I have a rather pressing business engagement this evening, which unfortunately limits the time I may give you. So perhaps we can go at once to the matter at hand. What brings you here to Rabobank with such urgency, on the eve of the Christmas holiday?"

"Money," said Lelia. "A bequest of my dear late husband. He left a large sum for the care of my only daughter. I wish to invest a portion of this in your bank—if that is possible?"

"Naturally. Of course. We shall be happy to play whatever role you wish. You'd like us, perhaps, to act as trustees on her behalf?"

"Not at all. My daughter is moving here to Europe, and I wish her to have as much as she needs. But I am giving you the . . . my own investments . . . which I do not wish to make into cash."

"I see," said Veerboom. "You've something to use as collateral, and you wish to borrow against it—is that it? In this way, you won't have to turn your investments to cash and lose the interest, but simply use them to secure a line of credit. And you wish this account in your daughter's name?"

"No—in my name only," said Lelia. "And I want to take the moneys from it as often as I wish—now, for example."

"Well, that is somewhat different, then," said Veerboom. "You want to establish not *only* a line of credit—but an opening balance, in the form of a loan, which naturally will involve interest payments. If I understand correctly, you'll give your daughter drafts as she requires from this initial amount—thus you will retain full control of the money. Quite sensible, if I may say so."

"Then this is possible for you?"

"But of course, nothing simpler, my dear lady. And how much did you wish as a loan, to establish the opening balance?"

"It is this reason that I wished only to speak directly

with you, Monsieur Veerboom. It is somewhat a large amount."

"And how large a sum are we dealing with, my dear baroness?" asked Veerboom, smiling politely.

"Twenty million dollars American, my dear Monsieur Veerboom."

Veerboom stared at her for a moment—then recovered his charm.

"Why, certainly. And what did you plan to use as collateral to secure this loan?"

"Will forty million be enough?" she asked sweetly.

"Forty million to secure an advance of twenty?" asked Veerboom, wondering whether his ears were working correctly. "This will be no problem whatever, my dear baroness. But perhaps—as it's a holiday, and the bank is closing now—I might ask you to sign a few papers today, and contact you in a week or so at Baden-Baden, where I understand you are—"

"This will not be possible," Lelia assured him. "I wish to take several millions with me now—today. Because of this need, I have brought the security—collateral—with me."

Lelia opened the large bag she carried, and pulled out the stack of genuine bearer bonds, copies of which were now sitting—gathering dust—within the vaults of the Depository Trust in New York. She fanned them out across the table as Veerboom tried not to gape.

Just then, the valet entered.

"Tea for madame," Veerboom told him; he was practically choking, his throat was so dry. "And would you bring me brandy? Bring a decanter, in fact. Madame, you would join me in some brandy, perhaps?"

Lelia nodded her assent, and smiled sweetly.

"Oh—and Hans," Veerboom added as an afterthought, "will you have Peter telephone my six o'clock appointment, and tell the gentleman that I shall be late? Thank you so much."

THE FINANCING

Under no economic system earlier than the advent of the machine industry does profit on investment seem to have been accounted a normal or unquestionably legitimate source of gain.

—*Thorstein Veblen*,
The Machine Age

SUNDAY, DECEMBER 20, WAS NEARLY ONE MONTH AFter my night at the opera. This day, for the matinee, the German gods had vacated in favor of that famous French fortune hunter *Manon*. It seemed a fitting tribute to that earlier, inspired evening.

I love the scene where Manon throws over her life as queen of Paris and—dripping in diamonds—rushes to Saint Sulpice, to seduce her former lover on the eve of his entry into the priesthood.

Manon is a girl who's torn between love of men and love of money. But as usual in opera, money wins out in the end. As she's dying, in poverty and exile, even the stars above her head remind her of those diamonds she used to wear when she was rolling in cash.

I went home somewhat cheered not only by the charm of the music; but by the fact that it was Manon who had taken the fall, not I.

The fog enveloped my apartment like a white sock. I went out to the terrace and clipped a few of my winter orchids to bring inside. From out there, the fog was so dense I couldn't even make out that phallic tower Lillie Coit had erected atop Telegraph Hill, as a tribute to those firemen she used to chase around town.

I was inside making myself some tea when the phone rang.

"Good evening, my dear," said the soft, familiar

voice. "I phoned because I thought you might want to wish me a happy birthday."

"Is today your birthday?" I asked. "I knew it was Beethoven's."

"Great minds are guided by the same planets," Tor agreed. "And it seems I've got plenty to celebrate today: we're right on schedule."

Damn. Did that mean he'd gotten all the bonds he needed in order to start phase two—the investment? And *I* wasn't even off first base. Since Tavish and the crew hadn't yet cracked a single code, I couldn't get my hands on a nickel. The entire idea of this bet suddenly began to depress me.

"So what have you three been doing to celebrate?" I asked him, to change the subject.

"Georgian and I are still working, of course," he told me. "We should be finished with the printing later this week. But Lelia's gone off to Europe to help us get a jump on the gun."

So there was good news and bad news. The good, of course, was that they weren't yet through—I still had a week to catch up. But the bad news . . . I thought I'd better find out.

"You sent Lelia to Europe all alone?" I asked. "I hope you understand what you're doing."

"She can't get into much trouble," he assured me. "She's taken those bonds—the genuine ones we replaced with our forgeries—and she's establishing lines of credit at various banks on the continent. No one would question a woman of her standing, in any country, with opening accounts of that size. But she's not actually taking out cash—just setting things up so the money's available when we're ready to draw on it."

"I hope this gun you're 'getting a jump on' won't backfire and blow your head off," I warned. "I've known Lelia longer than you have. She likes to handle things her own way."

"Let me worry about that," he said blithely. "Besides, someone had to start the ball rolling. By the time we've finished printing and substituting the bonds—by the end of the week—it will be too late to set up any accounts over there. It's nearly Christmas—and the banks in Europe will be closed for the holiday. We would have had to wait until after the first of the year."

Good Lord, he was right! That was something I hadn't considered myself—four days from now, on Christmas Eve, all of our test systems at the bank would shut down for year-end maintenance. If, by then, I hadn't put programs in place to grab off those wire transfers, I, too, would have to wait until after the first of the year. We'd be weeks behind Tor—and lose all that huge volume of year-end money to boot! How could I have been such a fool?

"And how is your own little theft coming along, my dear?" asked Tor, as if he'd read my mind.

"Just great," I lied, cursing myself for this dreadful oversight, and trying to figure out what the hell I could do.

The teapot began to whistle. I picked it up absently, and nearly splashed boiling water on my foot. When I jumped away, the phone crashed to the floor. I picked it up, and heard Tor laughing at the other end.

"Sounds as if you're doing splendidly." He chuckled. "So things are as bad as all that? I do think your attitude is wrong. You're going to quite enjoy living in New York again after all these years—and working with me as a technocrat, a destiny you were born for. Why don't you give in, and admit you've lost this bet?"

"Premature chicken counting," I told him, wiping the floor with the sock I'd pulled off my foot. "Don't you have to beat me, for me to lose?"

"I've always admired this determination of yours, in the face of complete disaster," he assured me. "You haven't cracked a single system yet, and you know it."

"I'd like to get the record straight," I told him, dragging the phone with me to the fog-encircled glass-walled living room. "Even if I did lose—and had to pay up by working for you—that's not my *destiny*; it's just a debt. You can't put me in a cage."

Tor was silent for several moments. Then he said quietly, "You've built so many walls around yourself, I'd never dream of replacing them with a cage. I only want to tear them down and set you free—please do me the service of believing that."

"That's why you lured me into this little wager, I suppose—to free me of the silly burden of my *chosen* career?"

"Whether or not you wish to admit it now," he said gently, "that's precisely the case. But in the unlikely chance you win, I intend to keep my part of the bet. As I expect you to keep yours." Then he said, with a bit more cheer, "Now, if you don't mind, I think I'll go uncork my birthday champagne."

When we hung up, I sat in the stark white room until darkness fell. Then, without bothering about dinner, I went off to bed. I knew now, no matter what happened, I had to win this bet. Though for the life of me, I couldn't imagine why it seemed so bloody critical to do so.

■

FIRST THING THE NEXT MORNING, TAVISH ENTERED MY new glass-walled office on the thirtieth floor. He was scratching his shaggy blond head, and sat across from me, teacup in hand.

"I've thought of something; let's see what you think," he told me. "If I were trying to get onto the production system—but the computer didn't recognize my password—after three attempts on my part to enter the system, I'd be locked out and my terminal shut down." He looked at me and waited.

"Right," I agreed. "That's the way security works, to keep unauthorized people from tampering with live systems—what's your point?"

"Well, if I *were* an authorized person, but I just happened to forget my password, what would they do?"

"They'd give you a new password," I told him. "But I don't see how that would solve our current problem. Any new password they gave you would only admit you to the parts of the system you have clearance to access.

It certainly wouldn't get you into the security systems—and that's what we need to crack."

"You're right," said Tavish with a grin. "But the password *would* let me in—if I were the person *in charge of security systems*!"

I stared at him.

"His name is Len Maise," said Tavish. "His terminal number is three-one-seven. It's located on the eleventh floor. And he left last Friday for Tahoe—he won't be back until after the holidays."

"How do you plan to get them to give *you* his new password?" I asked, though my heart was now fluttering.

"I try three times to log on to his terminal, the system shuts me down, I phone up—as Len Maise—and ask for a new password of my choosing so I can remember it this time. To put this new password on the system, they'll need a signed note—authorization from a vice-president. Since Len's boss, unfortunately, is away as well, I guess *you'll* have to be the one to write the note."

"Why don't you bring me a cup of whatever that is you're drinking?" I suggested. "And while you're out—pick up an authorization slip as well. It seems Len Maise, over in security, is going to need a new password."

■

THE END OF THE YEAR IS A HOT TIME IN THE BANKING business. The Bank of the World had a private motto: We never shut our doors while the money's pouring in. At least, that captures the general sentiment.

We extended our hours over Christmas, not only for the folks buying turkeys and gifts, but for wire transfers and all other services as well. It was year-end closing all over the world, which meant tax shelters and investments of all sorts couldn't be put off any longer. This crazed banking frenzy posed a double quandary for me.

The production systems, now up and running around

the clock, were clearing more cash than at any other time of year—money I'd be losing if I couldn't get inside the system to grab it. But on Christmas Eve the test system would be shut down. It was through the test system that all brand-new programs like mine got put into the production environment—where the cash was handled. I had to get in that door before it closed.

But on Wednesday, the day *before* Christmas Eve—though Tavish had broken into the security system by now—he still hadn't cracked the test key code, the little program that decoded all the wires flooding in, that unlocked the bank's cash clearings so we could deposit them in accounts.

Furthermore, I could hardly open up thirty thousand brand-new bank accounts, all with zero balances. It would look more than suspicious.

So I chewed my nails and went crazy, watching the dozen clocks beyond my glass wall, which showed the time ticking away for countries all over the world, as it was for me.

By Thursday morning—the day before Christmas—Tavish still had not cracked the codes. Pavel was already off, "avoiding the madness of the city," so when the phone rang, I answered it myself.

"Darlink," said Lelia's muffled voice, "this is the subject of *grave urgence*! Such unhappiness I am having—you must come now, today."

"Slow down, Lelia. Come where? I thought you were in Europe."

"*Da.* I am in Europe—but now I am here, in my bedchamber."

I'd forgot that in times of crisis, Lelia could only conjugate one verb tense.

"We'll take this step-by-step," I told her. "You *were* in Europe, but now you've come home. Where are Georgian and Tor? Is there someone there who can translate for me?"

"No, *bozemoi*, I am so *fatiguée*! Zhorzhione, she has gone to Europe instead—but Zoltan, he will not do the speaking with me. They are both very *fâchés avec moi.*"

"Why are they both angry with you?" I said, alarmed. "Why has Georgian gone to Europe in your place? Why didn't Tor phone me himself, if there's a problem?"

"There is no phone where he is being," Lelia assured me. Even in prison, they had telephones—where could he be?

"He's not where you are?" I asked.

"Là? Mais non! Je suis dans ma chambre!"

"I don't mean in your bedroom—I meant in New York."

"He is near, but it is not possible for him to be speaking with you. He want that you come here to New York—*tout de suite*—today. I send you a ticket at *l'aéroport—tu vas venir? Je m'explique* when you are arriving."

"When will you *explique*, Lelia?" I demanded. "I'm busy here—I can't go flying to New York during year-end closing! You tell Tor, if he wants to talk, he can phone me himself—I've had it with these little intrigues of his, and frankly I'm amazed he'd put you up to this."

"Tu me crèves le coeur!" cried Leila. "You are not having the trustingness in me! You come here—I make all the little explains when you arrive."

"I'll tell you what," I said with more than a little irritation, "I'll leave a message on Tor's answering service. If it's that important, he can call me back and explain it in English."

"You do not understand my *anglais*," Lelia moaned.

I'd had about enough of these games. I kissed her over the phone and hung up.

But my other line was flashing, and when I picked it up, I forgot about Lelia for the moment. The last thing I'd expected was a call from Peter-Paul Karp—Tavish's old boss and Pearl's current one. He was inviting me to lunch.

The prospect of spending an hour or more with Karp

was like a penance. I decided to accept—if only to learn what he had on what I loosely referred to as his mind.

We met at the restaurant of his choice: the Coût que Coût—which means "cost what it may" in French. I knew it well—it was the sort of place where the waiters, in timeless French tradition, saunter past your table at least once every two or three hours, to see if you're interested in eating yet. Karp arrived, fifteen minutes late, and made a point of schmoozing with the entire staff—including the chef, who came out from the back—before arriving at the table where I was waiting.

He refused to get right to the subject of our meeting. First he dawdled over the menu and wine list until I nearly screamed; when at last we'd ordered, he gave me a greasy smile.

"I've just returned from a visit to my homeland—Germany," he informed me. "I heard *you* were being considered for an assignment there, yourself."

"I know—thanks for the recommendation," I told him. He brushed it aside.

"It's a wonderful place, Banks. You shouldn't have been so hasty to throw away that opportunity. Of course, it's different for me—I speak the language fluently—and my family, of course, goes back for over a thousand years. . . ."

"Really? What a coincidence," I told him. "So does mine! We just can't remember who they are."

I got the glare I expected, but at least it dragged him back to the subject.

"I asked you here to warn you, Banks," he informed me, leaning on his elbow. "Just a friendly word from one colleague to another. The trouble you've made is hard to express—waves through the whole banking system. Last week I get a call from Willingly—he says it's very urgent. I go to see him. He says: 'Banks is not playing the game.' You know what game I mean? It is the game of men in business. Being that I'm German, I understand how women are different from us. You understand?"

"What's your point?" I asked, feeling I could skip this little course in biology.

"You know, he's very close to Lawrence—your boss, Willingly. Lawrence has even proposed him for membership in the Vagabond Club! Perhaps he'll be installed this very month."

"What should I do—burst into tears? It's certainly not my cup of tea. But Kiwi's happy, Lawrence is happy—everybody's happy."

"Everybody but me," he told me glumly. "I've told you all this, because now you owe me something."

"Let's get something straight, Karp. I owe you nothing but a free lunch sometime—that is, if you pay for this one. I already know about all this. Kiwi told me himself."

"Did you know, too, that Willingly's going to be promoted? To Lawrence's job. It shouldn't be long now. As soon as Lawrence is bumped to the top."

"Bumped to the top?" I repeated mindlessly.

I tried to be nonchalant, but I felt my jaw slackening. The top of what? Surely even the board members—limited though their imaginations might be—wouldn't be naive enough to make an unscrupulous SOB like Lawrence president of the bank! That was electing the fox to preside over the chicken coop.

"Now you *do* owe me a favor," he was saying smugly. "You can see that your days are numbered. You'll be back in Willingly's court again—and he will be offering the ball."

"Serving the ball," I corrected him, though he sure had his full court presses straight.

I was dead meat—finished—if Kiwi got his hands on me again. There was no use pretending with Karp; he probably knew more about my fate than *I* did at this point. With Kiwi in charge, I could kiss my theft, my bet, my job, and my ass good-bye.

"So just what is it you want?" I asked him. "You'd better ask now; it seems soon I won't be in a position to do many favors."

He leaned farther forward, and whispered in confidence, "You must get rid of her! She's trying to ruin me! She wants my job, and everyone knows it. I'll die of stomach ulcers if I have to wait until Willingly's there to get rid of her for me. But I know she'll listen to you. You can make her go."

"You mean Pearl?" I asked, trying to suppress a laugh.

"Yes—the *schwartze*," he hissed. "This is hardly a topic of amusement. She's really gone mad—makes me fill out forms all day long, all the red tape—she follows me to the latrine! You know as well as I that nobody follows all those rules, we'd have time for nothing else! But if I fail to do even one thing, she'll report me for it—she's told me as much. I think she's a spy!"

The veins on his nose were standing out now in excitement, and I recalled what Tavish had told me about the cocaine habit. But I remembered something else, too—his illicit traffic in computer systems.

"What could you possibly be doing that's interesting enough to spy on?" I asked him sweetly.

"Don't you think *I* know how you found out about Frankfurt in time to save yourself? How you ended up going to work directly for Lawrence? Don't you think Willingly and I both know what you're up to with that quality circle of yours? Trying to break into the passwords and test keys, too. You want to get at his wire transfer system—to prove his security's the worst at the bank!"

Luckily, Karp was giving away more than he was getting! But this was awful news. It meant Kiwi was right on my heels and knew everything we were up to, though hopefully not *why*. Karp couldn't have sniffed this out all by himself, not with all the coke he'd put up that nose of his.

I had to do something, at once.

"Peter-Paul," I said nicely, "I'm not as close to Pearl as you seem to think, but it's possible I might think of a way to entice her to leave your department. What would you say if I told you I knew a job she'd jump at in a minute?"

"I'd be forever grateful, Banks—your devoted slave."

"I'll do what I can," I assured him, wondering how the hell I was going to pull this one off. "But if I succeed, you'll have to stop plotting with Kiwi against me. Stop this war between our departments, at least until I finish this project. And you can't have Tavish back till then, either—is that understood?"

"Absolutely," he said with sincerity. "Tavish was the last thing on my mind."

Stuff it up your deviated septum, I thought. But aloud, I said, "I trust you."

■

RIGHT AFTER LUNCH, I HAULED TAVISH INTO MY OFFICE. He was looking rather glum.

"I want you to slap tracers on all passwords that are accessing any of our programs or files," I told him. "Somehow, Kiwi and Karp have learned what we're up to, and that Pearl's in on it, too. If they haven't bribed someone on the quality team, they may actually be tracking our activities on the system itself."

"At once," Tavish agreed, "but first you should know that Kiwi's been after me—he took me to lunch today."

I stopped in my tracks. "Divide and conquer, it seems," I told him. "I had lunch with your dear friend Karp. He wanted a favor—what did Kiwi want?"

"He offered me a job—offered is not the right word—he threatened me."

"Threatened you?" I was flabbergasted. "What do you mean by that?"

"The moment that we succeed in violating a single system or file, Lawrence expects us to make a formal report on all our activities—then our group will be disbanded at once. Kiwi says I can come to work for him. The alternative is to go back to Karp."

"Why not stay with me, on my next project?" I suggested, trying to calm him down.

"You aren't going to *have* a next project," he informed me. "They've really got their knickers in a twist; they plan to get rid of you for good this time—and Pearl along with you."

Great. Those two bozos actually expected me to hand Pearl over to them as a parting gift. And clearly, Lawrence was behind it, too—what sleaze. Why did being a bastard seem a prerequisite for banking?

"As a matter of fact," I told Tavish, "I do have another project up my sleeve. I told you about my wager with Dr. Zoltan Tor, but I never mentioned the stakes."

"I wish I'd never heard of that dreadful bet," said Tavish grimly, his hand on the door. "Who cares what the stakes are? They're far too high for me. I'll wind up in prison, or deported as an undesirable alien, and all because I tried to do something as noble and honorable as robbing a bank!"

"You can drop out of this anytime you like," I assured him. "But I still have a bet, which amounts to this: If Tor loses, he'll get me back that job at the Fed that Kiwi blackballed me for. But if *I* lose, I must work a year directly for Dr. Tor."

"Work for Dr. Tor?" Tavish brightened. "That'd hardly seem to *me* like losing a bet. If I could even meet him—shake his hand, talk to him awhile—I'd feel I'd died and gone to heaven. I've been wanting to ask, since you know him so well, whether one day that might be arranged."

"I can tell you the very day," I assured him. "It will be the day you get out there and crack that goddamned code."

■

AT FIVE, PEARL WAS IN MY OFFICE, PACING LIKE A PANther.

"So *then* what did he say?" she fumed.

"He asked me to get rid of you—find you another job."

"Where?"

"In Siberia—why should he care? He said you drove

him crazy filling out forms, that you even followed him to the men's room!"

"That's a blatant lie!" she cried. "Maybe I've waited *outside* the men's room once or twice. . . ."

"You have to lay off." I laughed. "I agreed to get you away from Karp, and I must. It's only for a little while, but I can't afford to risk Karp's hysteria—my time's running short. If we don't get into that system tonight, I've lost the bet, and Tor will guess it at once. Maybe I'd still be able to move some money around—show up a few Karps and Kiwis, as I'd first imagined. But the whole bank's breathing down my neck now. It won't take long for them to figure out the rest—and when they do, I'd better be able to trump their ace, or clean up and get out of town."

"Tonight?" said Pearl. "Honey, I can't believe this. It's been a few weeks—a month at most. Somehow, till this moment, it seemed like a game to me. But you're really going to do it—aren't you?"

"You bet," I told her, then winced at my choice of words.

It was this stupid, bloody bet that, in less than a month, had plunged me into the mess I was in now. How had Tor managed all this, in one short day in New York? A month ago, I was the highest woman executive at the biggest bank in the world. I'd spent a lifetime learning banking, I had a twelve-year track record in technology, and the promise of an even more successful career ahead.

By midnight tonight I'd either be robbing a bank or on a plane to New York to sign myself up for what seemed eternal bondage. All thanks to Tor, who'd fanned my spark of revenge into an international vendetta. Good Lord, didn't I ever learn?

Just then, there was a soft tap at my office door. The lights were off beyond the glass—as they had been since three, when the bank shut down for the holiday.

Pearl and I peered at the shadowy form hovering outside.

"What should we say I'm doing here, if it's Karp?" asked Pearl in hushed voice.

"We're discussing your new job," I whispered back.

She got up and opened the door. Tavish stood there, his arms filled with computer printout. He stalked across the room and spilled the massive pile onto my desk. Even looking at it from upside down, I knew what it was, and my heart skipped a beat.

"We've broken the test-key encryption, madame," he said. "We'll set up those bank accounts now. I believe we can expect some major deposits coming into them tonight."

"Kismet," I said with a grin as Pearl and I slapped hands.

I only hoped we weren't going to be too late.

■

I PHONED THE FLORIST AND ORDERED THE FLOWERS—all white—lilies, chrysanthemums, narcissus, baby's breath, white lilacs, and branches of cherry—a month's supply. The florist was floored.

I rarely asked people to my home, because it was my own escape, the cloudlike region where I went to decompress. But on this evening, I decided it would be comfier for Pearl and Tavish and me to be here than to stay in a darkened data center eating cold pizza—probably safer, too, from the standpoint of possible detection.

I called the liquor store, too, and ordered the chilled champagne—and the Szechuan deli, where I selected by phone all the specials on Mr. Hsu's daily list.

Arriving home, I saw that the doorman had already left the wine, in its crate of dry ice, outside my door. Mr. Hsu was sitting there beside the stacked flower boxes, on the top step.

"Madame True," he said, rising to greet me. "I bring these foods because I am on my way home just now."

"Mr. Hsu, will you stay for a glass of champagne?"

I asked, hauling the flowers inside as he followed with boxes of food.

"No, I must return home, my wife is expecting me. But I wish to know one thing before I depart—how many persons will you expect to dine with you this evening?"

"Two others. Why do you ask?"

"It is just as I told my wife: Madame True always orders for thirty—even if there are only three. My wife did not believe me, foolish woman. One day when you come to my restaurant, you must explain to her your philosophy. It is very American."

"You mean, better to have too much than too little?" I said.

"Yes. I like this American philosophy very much. One day, it will make me a very rich man."

I didn't explain to Mr. Hsu that all computer types are compulsive "leftover" junkies, but left him to bask in his capitalist dream. Mr. Hsu helped me carry the champagne crate inside, then took his leave.

I barely had time to open and arrange the flowers, put away the champagne, pop the food into dishes to warm in the oven, and bathe and change. I'd powdered and put on cologne and pulled on my floppy cashmere sweater just as the doorbell rang.

Pearl arrived in a flamingo-colored angora sweater that wrapped like a bathrobe, and Tavish in a T-shirt to match—surely picked out by Pearl. It read "Real Men Eat Beluga Caviar."

We broke out the champagne, settling the bottle in the silver icer beside the coffee table, and flopped down on cushions to feed and relax in preparation for the night's computer crunch.

"Sitting on top of the world like this, surrounded by flowers and champagne," Pearl commented, "it makes me feel everything else—the bank, my awful career, that creep Karp—they're all unreal."

"But thanks to modern technology," said Tavish, "they're only a phone call away."

That was the phone call that was going to change my life, I thought.

■

AT NINE, WE WERE GATHERED AROUND THE BIG LACquered table in my study, Tavish tapping away, a determined expression on his face. Pearl and I, weary with exhaustion and a bit too much champagne, were now drinking strong black coffee and checking his work from time to time.

"This computer—Charles Babbage, is it?—he has some personality." Tavish grinned from behind the terminal. "He's just told me he expects to be paid overtime for this job."

I'd worked out a deal with the Bobbsey Twins, to keep Charles up late tonight so we could "patch through" his mailing list to the bank's computer and set up our new customer accounts.

The bank got new customers every day, so establishing accounts like these was standard procedure, as long as we'd have a beginning balance to start them off.

And we'd have that money—from the wire transfer system—as soon as our "program changes" were moved from the test system into live operation in production. Since we didn't know until five o'clock that evening—when Bobby cracked the code—exactly what those new programs would do, it was a rush to get them written, and the authorized paperwork filled out to notify the data center these changes would be coming in tonight.

On the other hand, it was a convenient time of year to be asking for last-minute changes to production systems. There was always a huge queue of things to go into production on every system, just before year-end closing, and the wire transfer system was no exception. I just clumped our programs together with all the others before I left the office. I was sure that long before midnight, the codes would be inside the computer, catching wires and scattering that money through all our accounts.

But at ten o'clock, something went horribly wrong.

Pearl and I were out on the terrace in the late-night

fog, calming down from the crazed hysteria of the day. Tavish was inside, wrapping things up. He'd just finished copying the list from New York, and released Charles Babbage to go off to nightly maintenance.

Suddenly, we heard him yell: "Bloody hell! Oh, bloody hell!"

We ran inside, and saw Tavish staring at the terminal screen with wild eyes.

"What's happened?" I cried, dashing around the table to look at the screen.

Tavish's voice seemed to reverberate from the back of my brain as I looked hopelessly at the green letters glowing there:

BANK OF THE WORLD TESTING
HAS ENDED FOR THE DAY.
HAVE A VERY MERRY CHRISTMAS
AND A HAPPY HOLIDAY!

"They've brought the bloody test system down!" Tavish was nearly screaming. "My bloody programs are sitting out there in the queue—and they've brought down the bloody system—*two hours early*!"

"Shit," I said, staring numbly at the screen, wondering what in hell to do. I'd never felt so helpless in my life.

"And we were lolling around," said Pearl, "eating Chinese food and swilling champagne, as if there were nothing but time. What exactly does this mean? What happens now?"

" 'From where you are, you can hear their dreams,' " said Tavish. " 'The dismays and despairs and flight and fall and big seas of their dreams . . .' "

"What's that supposed to mean?" asked Pearl, looking at Tavish as if he'd really flipped.

"Dylan Thomas," said Tavish. "It means our dreams have died—our system has died—our project has died—*we* have died."

He rose, and drifted from the room in a vaporlike trance, without glancing at either of us.

"Is this it?" Pearl asked me. "Isn't there anything we can do?"

"I don't know," I told her, still staring at the screen. "I really have no idea."

■

IT WAS ELEVEN P.M., AND PEARL HAD JUST TOLD TAVISH she would dump her champagne over his head, if he said "If only we hadn't . . ." even one more time.

That was when I got the idea. I knew it was a long shot—a wild-assed piss into the wind was more like it—but I was ready to try *anything*, rather than staring at walls all night and cursing myself for the next week until I could get on that system again.

"Bobby, can you write object code?" I asked him.

"A little—but it's hardly a hobby of mine," he assured me.

"What's object code?" Pearl wanted to know.

"Machine language," Tavish told her. "It's what other programs are compiled into—bits and bytes—executable instructions, orders the machine can understand and carry out."

"What are you cooking up?" Pearl asked me, but I was still looking at Tavish.

"Could you take the object code from those programs you wrote, and put it right into the live production library—as if it were already compiled and ready to run?"

"Sure, I guess so," said Tavish with more than a trace of cynicism. "Of course, we'd have to get the operations department to bring down the wire transfer system—which is running right now twenty-four hours a day—and let me get on the machines to do it. But I'm sure they'd be delighted to halt production for us, if we explained we just had to get in there and rob the bank tonight."

"I didn't mean that," I said, knowing that what I *did* mean was even more farfetched. "What I meant was—if I could get you on the production system right now—

could you make the changes while the wire transfer system is still up and running?''

Tavish looked at me and started to laugh.

''You're joking, of course,'' he said.

''Translation please,'' said Pearl. ''Does this mean the gray flannel mind's come up with something outré?''

''She's bonkers, all right,'' agreed Tavish. ''Those are 'virtual' machines down there: they have hundreds of peripheral devices running on-line, all shooting data in and out like gangbusters—and hundreds of partitions open, paging and thrashing at nanosec speed—''

''Hold on,'' said Pearl. ''I meant a translation into people-friendly English.''

''Basically,'' he said with exasperation, ''it's like the Harlem Globetrotters from hell—juggling a million basketballs at once, and all at the speed of light. Going into a machine like that to make changes would be like trying to do brain surgery on a kangaroo while using a stopwatch.''

''A pretty fair description,'' I complimented him. ''Do you think you can do it, if I can get you on?''

Tavish shook his head, and looked at the floor.

''I'm crazy—but not that crazy,'' he told me quietly. ''Besides, there's no way to get on the system from a dial-up terminal like this.''

''I wasn't suggesting you phone in the changes,'' I said with a smile, ''I thought we'd install them in person.''

''You mean—inside the machine room itself?'' gasped Pearl.

Tavish leaped to his feet and tossed his napkin to the floor.

''No. No. No—and again no!'' he cried. ''It's completely impossible!'' He seemed slightly hysterical, and I could certainly see why.

If we made even the slightest error while a complex mass of machines like that was running, the entire system could come crashing down—with that sickening death rattle that gives computer types nightmares. Once you've heard it, even a flickering brownout in a supermarket makes you wince. In this case, it would be even worse than crashing a machine—since if we screwed up here, we'd bring down production for the entire worldwide processing of the Bank of the World.

But finally—if something like that happened while we were on premises—we'd be locked deep within the bowels of the data center, inside concentric circles of mantraps and guard posts. We'd be trapped for good and all, with no way out.

"You're right," I admitted glumly to Tavish. "I can't ask something that dangerous of you. I was mad to even think of doing it myself."

"You've been carried away with this wager of yours," he agreed, calming down a bit and taking a seat. "Of course, if your friend Dr. Tor were here, things might be different. He could certainly do what you've asked—he's written books on the subject."

Terrific—and I hadn't bothered to return his message at all. But Tor would hardly have been anxious to jet to the coast in my aid—even if I'd known what aid I was going to need. After all, we were competing, as he loved to point out.

Just then, the phone rang. And though I knew it would be stretching synchronicity too far, I had the oddest feeling who it might be as I nodded to Tavish to pick it up.

He put his hand over the mouthpiece. "Chap by the name of Lobachevski," he told me. "Says it's rather urgent."

I smiled with a grimace, went over and got the phone. It was all over but the shooting now. Tor had somehow sensed from three thousand miles away that he'd won the bet.

"Why, Nikolai Ivanovich," I said sweetly, "what a joy to hear from you. Haven't seen any treatises of yours on Euclidean math since—when was it—1850?"

"Eighteen thirty-two, to be precise," said Tor. "You never returned my call."

"I've been tied up," I assured him. "In knots—to be *precise*."

"If I send you an urgent message, I expect at least the courtesy of an inquiry into my situation. It's the very least I'd do for you."

"You didn't ask for an inquiry. You wanted me to hop on a plane—because you snapped your fingers—and fly to New York!" I protested hotly. "Have you forgotten I've a job to do? Not to mention a bet to win."

Tavish was looking at me with big eyes as he realized who it must be.

"As I say—it's the least I'd do for *you*," Tor repeated testily. "Now, may I get out of this blasted fog and come upstairs? Assuming, of course, that your guest or guests wouldn't mind."

I stopped breathing for an instant.

"Where *are* you?" I asked in hushed voice.

"At the newsstand down the block," he told me. "I'd never before seen this city of yours—and I still haven't. Are you sure there's a town around here? All the way from the airport it was socked in just as now—we were fortunate the plane could land at all."

I closed my eyes, put my hand over the mouthpiece, and whispered, "Thank you, God." Then I shot a wink at Tavish.

"What a coincidence," I told Tor over the phone. "We've just had one of those psychic transmissions of yours—so we've been expecting you."

■

I'D NEVER BEEN SO GLAD TO SEE ANYONE IN MY LIFE.

When I buzzed Tor into the building, and finally saw him ascending the last flight of steps from the elevator to the penthouse—bundled in his elegant cashmere overcoat, his coppery curls illuminated by the hall lamp—I wanted to rush out and embrace him. But that might have been ill-advised, considering what I wanted to ask of him the minute he walked in the door. So I took his coat instead.

After brief introductions—Tavish was quite stricken dumb by this first-time meeting with his idol—I settled them all in the living room so Pearl and Tavish could fill him in on our last eight hours of trauma; I went off to the kitchen to start the ball rolling.

"Charming place," Tor called after me. "Virginal white—reminds me of that chapter in *Moby Dick.* Quite appropriate to your personality, though."

Regardless of his cynical brand of humor—always at my expense—I knew that even if Tor hadn't been my mentor all these years, even if he hadn't suckered me into this bet, even if he didn't need a favor urgent enough to pry him from the bosom of his beloved New York, he'd still never leave me in a lurch like the one I was in tonight—most especially when he had the chance to flourish all that technological magic he alone could wield. And it *was* going to take magic, as Tavish and I understood only too well.

In the kitchen, I pulled the list of emergency numbers from the drawer, running my finger down until I found the home number of the VP of operations. Like mine, his number was there as a last resort, if a major production run aborted during the night.

I knew Chuck Gibbs, the VP of operations. We'd spent plenty of long, bleak nights in the past, down at the center, when production work had crashed. I also knew that Chuck had five little kids, and a wife who was getting tired of sleeping alone with cold feet. Tonight was Christmas Eve—when none of them would be delighted to hear the news I was about to spring on them.

"Chuck, this is Verity Banks from Electronic Funds Transfer," I said when he answered the phone. "I hate to disturb you tonight of all nights—but I'm afraid there's been a crisis in production."

I could hear tiny voices squealing in the background—and a woman's voice saying, "I don't believe it—on Christmas *Eve?*"

"Oh, that's okay," Chuck told me. "The pitfalls of the profession, I guess." He sounded as if I'd just track-cleated across his mother's grave, and he added hopefully, "Is it something maybe one of the operators could resolve?"

The operators were already there at the data center, while I knew that Chuck lived in Walnut Creek, across the bay—a good hour's drive away.

"I'm afraid not," I told him. "There seems to be a malfunctioning drive, but we can't bring down the system to replace it. You know it's year end—our peak time of the year. We might crash the system if we start switching off peripherals in the middle of production. If we accidentally crashed, we'd have to cold-start the system and do roll-forward recovery."

"That's bad," he admitted, verging on real depression.

Damned right it was—that's why I'd thought it up: it could take weeks, even longer, if we had to recover all those live transactions that were pouring in just now. If Chuck had to shut down production, the bank could lose tens of thousands of dollars—and the news wouldn't exactly be private. Even the press would hop on it, if a bank the size of ours went down over Christmas.

"I'm going to bring in a field engineer," I told Chuck, "just to be on the safe side." This would save Chuck's ass as well, if something went wrong. "But I feel that a high-level manager should be present to make a decision, if the situation is worse than we think."

"I agree," Chuck said, sounding absolutely miserable. I could hear his wife saying, "You're *not* driving the Bay Bridge on Christmas Eve—and that's final!"

"I'll tell you what"—I tossed the bone—"if you like, I can go over there in your place. I live only five minutes from the data center—and I don't have kiddies waiting for Santa to come down the chimney! If it's serious, I could call you—but it seems a shame for you to drive so far, if it turns out it's not absolutely necessary."

"Boy—that would be terrific!" Chuck said, nearly leaping through the phone to shake my hand. "You're sure you don't mind?"

"I know you'd do the same for me," I told him. "But

I'll need clearance, of course, to bring in the engineer."

"Done," Chuck said with enormous relief. "Martinelli's in charge of graveyard shift—you'll be cleared for entry in less than half an hour. And say, Banks, I can't tell you how much I appreciate your doing this."

"No problem," I told him. "We'll hope for the best."

I put down the phone and went out to the living room. Tor glanced up from his conversation with Tavish and Pearl, and smiled.

"I've just learned of your plight, my dear, from your colleagues here," he informed me, beaming broadly. "I gather I'm expected to lend a hand. I suppose it's the fate of genius to constantly prove itself, but I'm always happy to be of service. Just remember, my feathered chickadee—after tonight, you owe me one."

"Let's go then," I told him, wondering how it always happened this way. "We haven't much time—we've got a date with a machine."

■

IT WAS AMAZING THAT ONE SIMPLE PHONE CALL COULD enable us to melt through six layers of security and penetrate the inner sanctum without a flurry. We'd agreed to let Pearl and Tavish go home—that we'd call if we needed bail.

Tor strolled behind me, head bowed, carrying the briefcase containing Tavish's object code for the programs we needed to load, and wearing a battered trench coat we'd borrowed from Tavish. It had seemed more appropriately teckie, to suit his image as a field engineer.

"Boss says you've got a malfunctioning drive," said Martinelli, the night-shift supervisor, as we came into the brightly lit data center.

A chubby Italian in sweatshirt and jeans with a flattop military crew cut, Martinelli oversaw the functioning of millions of dollars of state-of-the-art hardware, spread over ten acres of floor space that covered three stories at the Bank of the World.

"We've checked all the drives," he added as Tor set down his briefcase with professional decorum, "but we can't find anything wrong at all."

"We're getting an error message when we try to write on drive seventy," I told Martinelli. "Perhaps you've overlooked something."

He bristled a bit, but checked his configuration list.

"There's no such drive 'genned onto this system," he assured me, which meant that the system refused to recognize a drive with that number, because it had never been told about it.

Of course, I was lying my brains out—flying by the seat of my pants. I just wanted to get Tor onto the goddamned system, in any way possible.

"That must be the problem, then," I told Martinelli. "Our system's trying to capture wire transfers—but somehow, the address of the drive where it wants to put them has disappeared. Have you guys been switching peripheral devices on us?"

"Nobody fucks with this system," Martinelli assured me, patting a nearby processor. "This here wire transfer system runs on the mainframes—the most reliable, quality-assured system we got."

"Unless somebody decided to switch a few plugs," I said condescendingly. "We're paying this engineer here—don't let him sit on his thumbs. Let's get the bug detector mounted, give him clearance to enter the supervisor, and maybe we can call it a night."

The bug detector was a diagnostic program that acted as a kind of computer physician—buzzing around inside the machine while other programs were running, examining them to see whether they were sick. If you permitted it to override the "supervisor"—which governed the entire system—it could go in and make changes to those "sick" programs, without anyone being the wiser. Tor had told me to set things up this way, and to let him do the rest.

Martinelli—muttering something about women and

ships—whipped a tape off a nearby rack and slapped it on a drive, flipping the leader around until the ribbon sucked down into the shaft. He let the glass door slide up, walked over to the console, and punched in a few things on the keyboard.

"You're on," he told Tor, and stepped away from the console.

"Do you have a butt I could bum?" I asked Martinelli, knowing that he loved smokes, and that he wasn't permitted to do so within that climate-controlled atmosphere. "Let's let this guy earn his exorbitant fee—shall we?" I gestured toward Tor.

Martinelli and I went down the loading ramp to the small coffee room beyond the data center's sliding glass doors. From the corner of my eye, I glimpsed Tor at the console, his long fingers caressing the keys. I preferred not to think what might happen if something went wrong and he made even one tiny slip.

I kept Martinelli out in the coffee room as long as possible, hanging on his every word about how his team was faring in the interbank bowling league. The graveyard-shift coffee was—if possible—even worse than what we got during the day.

When at last we returned to the machine room, Tor was still standing there, his back to us, tapping away.

"Well, Abelard?" I said, clapping him on the shoulder. "How's it going?"

"Just about finished—Héloise," he replied, shrugging me off with disdain. In profile, I noticed that his skin was even paler than usual, and that his brow was beaded with a thin, faint line of moisture. I hoped to God everything was going all right.

I glanced with concern at the listings before him, which Tavish had given him—listings he'd never seen before tonight. They were all in hexadecimal code—totally meaningless to me. But Tor had scribbled a few scratchy-looking notes in red ink in the margins. And though they were gibberish to most people, I knew my life and the fate of all of us depended upon their being a hundred percent accurate. Just one slip of the wrist, and we might as well both commit hara-kiri right here on the data-center floor.

"Did you find out what it was?" Martinelli asked Tor, crossing over with a few of the night-shift operators in tow. "We run a clean ship here—we never got no message of a problem. What did you do to fix it?"

"Elementary, my dear chap," said Tor, logging off the system, to my great relief. "I changed the device designation and let her rip."

"Impossible," said Martinelli. "You mean, *in* the program—while the program is running?"

"Really—it was nothing at all," Tor assured him. "Just give us a call anytime."

We moved through the last set of mantraps to the elevators. Down in the garage I could barely climb into the car, my legs were shaking so. I felt cold beads of sweat chilling my brow, and a clammy lump at the pit of my stomach. I expected alarms to go off at any moment, sealing us into the building when the computer at last encountered Tor's newly inserted code. But I drove up the ramp and we left without a flutter.

Tor had been strangely silent throughout our escape from the scene of the crime. I wondered what he was thinking, and whether he'd been as scared as I.

"I hope the goddamned system doesn't abort at three in the morning," I told him, wending my way in the dark through the blinding fog.

"What effusive gratitude," he said. "Remind me to fly three thousand miles in the dead of night to help you out again sometime."

"I'll buy you a brandy when we get back to my place," I said.

"We're not going to your place—that white death trap," he informed me. "If you're longing for a shroud, my dear, it seems to me you can stand out on any street corner in this entire ghastly white metropolis. You still belong in New York."

"I hope you're not planning to take me there tonight," I said, peering through the windows to try to find the street I was driving on.

"I certainly should do so—but sadly the last plane has left by now," he explained. "Keep going straight until you reach the bay—I've studied a map of this dreadful town while I was en route to you. We're going to a place called Fisherman's Wharf."

"Maybe you've studied a map," I told him, "but you didn't study the local customs. It's after one A.M.—everything in San Francisco's shut down by now."

"Disgusting primitives," muttered Tor, whose own town—like Las Vegas—never closed. "However, keep driving as I said. I've been assured that the place where I'm taking you will remain open as late as we like."

I didn't like—but I knew I owed Tor not only a favor, but my life. I doubted there were many folks on the planet who would or could have done for anyone what he'd done for me tonight, least of all on such short notice. If he wanted to see the bloody wharf, why not?

We pulled up near Fisherman's Wharf—there was plenty of parking available at this hour—and I locked up the car. If it weren't for the fog, I would've been scared out of my wits. But I figured anyone who wanted to mug me in all that soup would have to find me first.

Tor took my hand and guided me down the wharf, where the shops and bistros fell away and—down near the end—boats creaked and sloshed in the water between the ghosts of rickety, dilapidated buildings.

"This looks like the one," he said, pointing at a small motorboat I could barely make out in the gloom.

"You're taking me on a boat ride?" I said, slightly hysterical. "On the bay—at this time of night?"

But he climbed down without a word, and was fumbling about.

"Let's see, the key should be . . . here it is." I heard his voice in the fog. "Now, my dear girl," he added as his hand came up out of the fog for mine, "have I ever introduced you to any experience you didn't, in the long run, enjoy?"

"It seems this may be the first," I assured him. But there was little I could do about it—so I gave him my hand and climbed down into the boat.

We were out on the water before I knew it—cutting out into the bay. When we'd cleared the wharfs and were out far enough, the black waters glittered with light from the city beyond. The bay was clear but for patches of mist, and the tall buildings of San Francisco soared above their whipped-cream shroud of fog like lost Atlantis rising, dripping with foam, from the sea. The moon above was fat and full, and draped with scudding clouds. I'd never seen anything so magnificent.

"It's incredible," I whispered to Tor, though there was no one within miles to hear. "I've never been out on the bay at night."

"Just the first of many such experiences I see in your immediate future," he assured me.

"Where are you taking me? Or is this just a general excursion?" I wanted to know. After all, he'd said the place would be open.

"We're going to an island—our island," he said softly, as if to himself. "In the midst of the wine-dark sea . . ."

THE HOSTILE TAKEOVER

It is not from the benevolence of the brewer or the baker that we expect our dinner, but from their regard to their self-interest.

We address ourselves, not to their humanity, but to their self-love, and never talk to them of our necessities, but of their advantages.

—Adam Smith

TEN YEARS IN SAN FRANCISCO, AND THE ONLY ISLAND in the bay I'd heard of was Alcatraz, though I'd never been there. But Tor, who had only left New York that afternoon, had found another one. He loved to impress people with that sort of omnipotence. But I couldn't say I minded much. It was absolutely lovely.

It was small—perhaps one hundred yards—with a rocky coastline, and lawns still green after the winter rains. With the lights of Berkeley on one side and those of the city on the other, it seemed a refuge invisible from without—a lake isle in a womb of water—the gentle sloshing of waves eradicating the sounds of those real worlds on the farther shores.

"How did you ever find this place?" I asked Tor.

"The same way I found you," he told me, "by magic or intuition."

It made no difference—I loved it. We went hand in hand from the pier across the lawns. There was a little frame two-story house at the point, with cheery light inside. When we reached it, he fumbled in a pot of gardenias for the key, and unlocked the door.

"I'm very tired," he told me, opening the creaky door. "It's three hours later for me—nearly five A.M. If we were in Manhattan, I could hear the birds already chirping in the trees. I think I should call it a night."

A night?

"You surely don't plan to sleep here?" I said.

"You don't think I'd spend a night in that coffin you call home?" he said irritably. "I need space, and time to unwind. It's been quite a day for me—thanks largely to you. And it should be really lovely, waking here in the morning."

"Now look—" I began, but he cut me dead with a glance, took me by the hand, and led me to a soft, puffy sofa there in the living room. He shoved me down into the stuffing.

"No—*you* look," he said in anger. "I've known you twelve years, and in all that time, have I ever moved to put one finger upon you? There is no historical precedent for these fears you seem to be harboring."

"We've never stayed alone in a deserted farmhouse before," I pointed out.

"Do I possess the character traits of a traveling salesman?" he snorted, going over to the trunk near the fireplace, on which were stacked linens and towels. "There are nightshirts and blankets and quilts—and there are half a dozen bedrooms here—or so I've been assured. No man in his right mind, weary as I am, would trouble with all that complexity, to secure the holy temple of your person. Why don't you go choose the room you want so we can get some sleep?"

I was being ridiculous, of course. All that he said was true—but that wasn't what was bothering me. The fact is, I felt afraid—more than an hour ago, under the stark lights of the data center, when I'd had something genuine to be terrified about. The only danger here was . . . it was absurd even to think of it. There was absolutely nothing to be nervous about at all.

I plucked a nightgown from his arms without a word, and headed upstairs to find a room. Tor stayed below, rummaging about in the kitchen off the main room, and came upstairs at last with a bottle of brandy and two glasses.

He set one on the oak washstand near my bed, poured

me some, and said: "Drink your nightcap—you deserve it. I'll come back and tuck you in."

"You needn't bother," I told him quickly. "I've found everything—the bathroom and all—for myself."

He smiled and departed, softly closing the door.

I knew what was wrong, of course—I understood. I quickly disrobed and pulled the heavy flannel nightgown over my head. Tor made me feel weak, he drained my power. He had a way of sucking me into things way over my head, pulling me in deeper and deeper, as he laughed. I had been the most successful woman I knew—until this bank caper of his came along. But now I was in the quagmire neck-deep again, with no way out in sight.

But there was something else, far worse than this predilection for risking my neck. Other than my grandfather Bibi, Tor was the only one who could make me feel like a child that needed protection—not a feeling I'm especially fond of. He threw me into situations where I had no control—then raced to my rescue so I'd have to take his hand. He expected me to genuflect, like Tavish and all others, to his superior strength and intellect—to follow wherever he led. It really pissed me off. If I did what I knew he was thinking of tonight—he'd redouble his efforts, and try to steal my soul.

I poured water from the pitcher into the bowl on the washstand and splashed my face, looking at myself in the mirror. In those yards of cotton flannel, with that pinched face and mass of messy hair, I looked like a small boy dressed in a tent. Nobody would try to seduce someone who looked like that, I assured myself with a certain bravado. I scrunched up my nose in the mirror and stuck out my tongue.

Just then Tor came back into the room. He was wearing blue pajamas and had a pile of quilts in his arms.

"What are you doing running around like that in bare feet?" he said. "You'll catch your death of cold. Get into bed."

When I crawled between the cool, damp sheets, he tossed the quilts over me one by one. Then he lit the candle beside the bed and went over to flick the wall switch. The room was thrown into darkness, the candle glowing in a small circle. Golden fingers of light licked the walls, touching the oak armoire and brass bedstead. Beyond the lace-covered windows, the waves lapped the rocky shore.

Tor came over and sat on the edge of my bed, looking at me with those flame-colored eyes.

"Why are you sitting on my bed?" I asked him.

"I'm going to tell you a bedtime story," he said with a smile.

"I thought you were so exhausted you couldn't move."

"Not quite," he said. "This is something I've needed to do for a very long while." I hoped that didn't mean what it sounded like.

He leaned on the quilts, his hand resting over my belly. I could feel the warmth seeping through the thick goose down. I waited, without a word, for him to begin.

"Once upon a time, there was a little girl," he said. "She was a very bad little girl."

"In what way?" I asked.

"I think she wanted to be a little boy. She was very independent."

"What's so bad about that?" I said. "Sounds appropriately self-sufficient to me."

"Don't interrupt the storyteller, or you won't hear the end," he told me.

"Okay—what happened to her?"

"She got what she deserved," he said. His voice was very soft. I felt the chill I always did when he spoke that way.

"And what did she deserve?" I asked—not at all sure I wanted to know.

"She deserved to get exactly what she wanted. Do you know what that was?"

"No."

"I didn't think you did." He smiled.

"How on earth should *I* know what she wanted?" I asked.

"Because you're the little girl," he told me.

"Oh—then it isn't a story at all," I said.

"It is a story—it's your story—and only *you* know the ending. Perhaps I'm a character in it—but it's up to you to decide what part I'm going to play."

"What part do you want to play?" I asked—realizing all at once that I was skating on very thin ice, this time without an iceboat.

He continued to watch me in silence, his dark eyes and coppery hair burning like flame in the candlelight. I felt weak and strange, and knew I couldn't move. It seemed his eyes were searching a place in my depths—a place I'd never tried to seek myself—a place cut off from the world, as we were cut off, here on this island.

He closed the quilt slowly into his fist above my stomach, not looking at me. His voice was low—it seemed to cost him something to speak.

"I want to make love to you," he said. Then, so softly it seemed he was whispering to himself, he said, "Very, very much."

I could hear a clock ticking somewhere in the hallway, and the sound of the waves washing against the shore. I felt something falling inside of me—dropping away in pieces. I was scarcely breathing as Tor sat motionless, studying the flame of the candle as if he'd never spoken at all.

We remained there in silence for a very long time, neither of us moving an inch, his hand still gripping the quilt, as if it were a rock providing strength. After what seemed an eternity, I saw him close his eyes; he took a deep breath, and turned to me with an expression of irritation.

"Well?" he said impatiently.

"Well what?" I asked.

"I've just told you I want to make love to you."

"What am I supposed to say?" I said defensively. I was shaken, really shaken, my resolution completely shattered. I hadn't a clue what to do.

He stood up. "I've never before told a woman anything like that—and I may never do it again, when I'm met with such enthusiasm!''

''What do you want me to say? What do you want me to do?'' I asked, sitting up abruptly with the bedclothes spilling around me. I was completely at sea.

''My God, you're impossible!'' he said. He threw the covers aside and grasped me by the shoulders. He bounced me up and down in the pillows as if he'd throttle me—laughing all the while, as if he were unhinged. Then he dropped me in the quilts like a bag of potatoes and headed for the door.

''Where are you going?'' I cried in alarm.

''I'm getting something you need—stay there, I'll be right back.''

Maybe it's a shotgun, I thought as he disappeared into the hall.

My stomach felt like jelly and my legs were weak. I jumped out of bed and paced around the room. A dozen emotions were warring within me—all of them unfamiliar. What in God's name was I doing here? How could this be happening? I was so confused. What should I do?

Tor was gone what seemed an awfully long time. He returned at last, bearing a tray with cups.

''I thought I told you to stay in bed,'' he snapped, setting down the tray. ''Do you want to have pneumonia? It's damp outside.''

''You sound like my grandmother,'' I told him, crawling back into bed with some relief he'd returned.

''But I don't intend to behave as your grandmother would,'' he assured me. ''Shove over—I'm getting in there, too.''

''What's in the drink?'' I asked, trying to chattily hide my dismay at the fact we were now side by side under the covers.

''It's something good for your health and disposition—which could use some improvement, I might add.''

He handed me the cup, and I sipped.

"Say, this is wonderful, Granny. What is it?" I asked.

"Hot milk, honey, and brandy—an aphrodisiac. Wonderful for seducing young boys—I hope it works on you."

He plumped up the pillows behind my head as I drank, then settled in and said, "I've another story for you."

"Okay, what is it?" The milk was really wonderful and warm and sweet. I could feel its effects deep inside, like a soothing balm. It nearly calmed the hysteria that had been mounting.

"Once upon a time there was a little girl who preferred to act like a boy . . ."

"This story sounds familiar," I said between slurps.

"Only this time, it's *my* story—not yours. Shall I proceed?"

"Go on."

"She was wrong, you see. But though many had tried—no one had ever succeeded in showing her the advantages of being a woman."

"That's where *you* come in, I suppose?"

"Your feet are freezing," he told me. "I told you to stay in bed. And stop wriggling around like that—I'm not going to torture you. This isn't the Spanish Inquisition."

"Let's hear the end of the story," I said. He was looking at me with that smile again. I tried to concentrate.

"This little girl had a friend she'd known for many years. They'd always behaved with great propriety toward one another. But he never knew—and she never knew—that they wanted to make love with each other. Not until they found themselves alone one night in a deserted house on a remote island—"

"I haven't said I wanted to make love with you," I pointed out, as much to assure myself.

"Oh, yes you have, my dear—though perhaps not in words. I know all the little things—I know how that confused mass of cogs works in there, the myriad tiny wrinkles in your gray matter. And believe me, too, I know what you've been afraid of all these years."

I looked at him, there in the candlelight, and the fear came back at once in a hot gush. But I knew he'd only begun.

"You're afraid of losing control, you see," he said softly. "But control means nothing—even the control of one's own soul—not if you have to build a fortress to defend it. It's clear you've placed a value greater than gold on those walls of yours. Like it or not—they're coming down tonight."

I wanted to change the subject at once—I couldn't even think of this.

"So what's the end of the story?" I asked, my voice sounding falsely cheerful even to me. "How did the two friends wind up?"

"They made love—robbed a bank—and lived happily ever after," he said with a smile.

"That's not how my story would end," I told him.

But he was looking at me as if my time were up. He took away the cup I still clung to and set it aside. Then he leaned toward me—eyes glowing, his lips inches from mine.

"I want you," he said quietly.

"I'd have had a story with less sex and more action," I said softly.

"I want you," he repeated.

He turned my face to his, his hands buried in my hair. His warm breath, scented with milk and brandy, mingled with mine. He let my hair slide through his fingers, touching it as if it were watered silk.

"I want you," he whispered again.

Taking one hand from my hair, he pulled the ribbon loose from the eyelets at the throat of my gown.

"What are you doing?" I tried to say. My voice was barely audible.

"What I've assured you you might rely on me never to do," he replied with a wry smile. "I'm seducing you."

"My God," I murmured.

"Too late for faith," said Tor.

He swept the hair away from my throat and buried his face in my neck as I felt the shock run like cold pinpricks through my nerves. He bit me there, and sucked the place, and the pinpricks filled with heat. When he leaned back to unfasten the other lace, he slid his palm over my throat and shoulders where the fabric fell away. I quivered as I watched him hovering over me, his skin bronze in the candlelight, his hair glittering like dark gold. He was truly so beautiful, I couldn't bear it. All my resolve melted like ice in the sun.

I reached up, pushing his hand aside, and unfastened the top button of his pajamas, then one by one, the others in a row. He watched me without breathing, in a sort of trance, as he leaned on one elbow above me. His lips parted slightly, watching in silence, as I moved my hand over the hard chiseled muscles of his chest where his shirt had fallen away—the soft hair glinting gold in the dim light. Suddenly, he reached out and grasped my fingers and pressed them to his lips.

"You liar," he whispered. "You've wanted it as much as I have—haven't you?—from that very first night."

"It's woman's prerogative to veil her desires in mystery," I said, faintly smiling at my attempt at bravado.

He stared at me in astonishment—then his eyes narrowed for a flicker. "And it's man's prerogative," he said, sitting bolt upright, "to rip away the veil."

Grasping the throat of my flannel gown—with one vicious wrench, he slashed it apart to the waist. He bent over me, his mouth on mine; he bit my lips and my mouth was filled with the moisture of his. He pulled his fingers through my hair and moved his palms over my flesh until I trembled. Then, pulling the clothes away, he drew his body across mine. I could feel the impact of his flesh—the heat of his thighs as he pulsed against me.

I was taut and quivering like a rope about to snap; he was touching me in ways that made me ache inside—deep in places I hadn't known were there. I felt my control unraveling, and I fought against the force that was sucking me down. It was all happening so fast—I couldn't hold on. . . .

He seemed to know this, and pulled away to look at me. His hair was disheveled, candlelight flowed over him, his eyes glittered darkly. The heat of his passion filled me with an unbearable, aching longing. I wanted to drown in him. But still I could not let go.

Gently, he opened my fists I hadn't known were clenched, and kissed the palms with infinite tenderness.

"Release it—let it go—you must, my love," he said softly in my ear. Then drawing back to look at me again, he whispered: "Come into me."

"I'm afraid," I said in a small, choked voice. He nodded once, and smiled.

He folded his arms around me, and closed me into him. I felt the darkness swallowing me. I felt the dark blood beating in my veins.

■

I CRIED UNTIL I COULDN'T FEEL ANYTHING. I CRIED UP the years of boredom and anger, frustration and struggle and doubt. I cried up everything inside—and when I thought I could control it all, it burst like an unleashed dam once more. I cried up things I hadn't known were there. The hot tears came, burning my throat until I couldn't breathe and I gasped for air. I clutched at Tor, grasping his hair and shoulders as he held me—but still it went on and on.

It seemed forever before it all broke free, and the slow dragging sobs and the tears subsided. Tor held me and stroked me and rocked me, and twined his fingers in my hair, until at last the warmth washed through me, and I felt a sort of peace I'd never known. He kissed my head gently, and when I looked up, his face was streaked with tears—whether his or mine I couldn't say.

"A blend of both," he said softly, reading my mind.

I was somewhere in a void between sleep and languor, drifting on a quiet sea, lulled to the sound of the waves beyond the window.

"It's unbelievable," Tor told me, "but I still want you—not again, but still."

"I think I've been quenched," I admitted, with a smile.

"You?" He laughed, tugging my hair. "We've learned what a liar *you* are!" He pulled me up to him and kissed me as if drinking a draft that would never satisfy his thirst. "We must have been mad to have waited twelve years for this," he told me.

"You were the one who was pooping around," I assured him.

"I'm going to murder you for that," he said fiercely. Then he added, "Actually—it seems you've killed a little part of *me*."

"Which part? Not that one?" I said, touching him beneath the covers.

"No." He laughed. "That one seems very much alive."

"Which one, then?" I asked as he grasped the hand that touched him and kissed the palm.

"It's hard to explain," he said. "I've always believed that intellect and passion were a dangerous, volatile combination, hard to control. Passions can feed and grow like a hungry beast. The part you've killed in me, I'm afraid, is what kept the beast in check. One thing's certain—I no longer want to control what I feel for you."

"Why would you want to control your passion?" I asked.

Tor put his finger under my chin, and tilted my face up to his.

"You know, my dear—if you go on stroking me there, you'll be sprayed with a great deal of passion in a place where you're least expecting it."

"Will you spray it on my stomach?"

"What on earth am I going to do with you?" he said, laughing and ruffling my hair.

"I have a few suggestions along those lines. . . ." I began.

"Yes, I've a few of those of my own," he told me, his lips silencing any further talk.

■

I WAKENED TO THE SOUND OF THE SEABIRDS WHEELING and screeching outside my window. The sky was a flat, brilliant white, and I saw three pelicans drift through the fog beyond the lace curtains. Tor wasn't in bed, but I heard bumping and odd sounds in the hallway, as if a large object were being dragged along the stairs.

Lying there in the rumpled quilts, I tried to understand the mélange of feelings I'd had since the night before. But I smiled when I realized that no matter what changes would result from all this, last night might well be the best Christmas gift I'd ever had. Georgian and Tor had been right when they'd called me a liar and hypocrite—I saw now I'd been both. All the running I'd done had been from myself. I could never escape from my feeling for Tor—it was kismet.

Just then, Tor arrived. He smiled when he saw me sitting there in the torn remnants of my borrowed gown.

"You're awake," he said. "Get up—I've a surprise for you."

"What's that all over your pajamas?"

"Dirt," he said, looking down at the mess. "Get out of bed and take off your clothes."

"Before coffee?" I laughed.

"We're going for a swim," he informed me.

"Is there a heated pool on this rock?"

"Don't be absurd—we're on an island surrounded by water. We're going for a dip in the bay."

"Pardon me, but I've recently checked my almanac, and discovered it's Christmas Day. Maybe *you're* going for a dip in the bay—but I'm not about to die of overexposure!"

"You'll never feel more alive," he assured me. "I swim in the north Atlantic every Christmas morning. Even with all that fog of yours outside, this seems like a tropical paradise to me."

He yanked the covers away and pulled me out by the

feet, kicking and protesting. Tossing me over his shoulder, he sprinted out the door and downstairs, and jogged across the lawn to the pier where our boat was tied. He leaped off the end with me in his arms and we hit the water.

When the water enveloped me, I thought my entire system would crash. The shock of cold knocked the breath from me, filled my blood with ice, and drew my stomach into a knot. Tor was holding me in the lapping waves, to make sure I didn't sink.

"Breathe deeply—in and out very slowly," he counseled me. "Let your body relax—that's it. It seems a violent way to enter the water, but it's soon over and far more gentle. How do you feel now?"

"Sadist," I gasped, flopping over onto my belly in the waves. "Your mind is sick—this is the worst thing you've ever done to me." I felt I'd come down with lockjaw, my teeth were clenched so tightly.

"You're still too tense," he said. "Loosen up, and you'll love it."

"I hope you die of pneumonia," I croaked.

"If you'd swim a bit, you'd warm up faster," he said.

"Thanks for the advice. May your—" But he put his hand on my head and dunked me, so the cold seemed to penetrate even my brain. I came up sputtering, but at once realized that I felt suffused with warmth.

"Gee, what happened?" I asked. "I feel warm and glowing, all of a sudden."

"Hypothermia," he told me. "The first stage of shock—just before you freeze to death."

"Very funny."

"Truly—we mustn't stay long, and must swim a bit, or it might be so. This water's less than forty degrees."

We swam a lap around the little island. Then freezing all over—our wet nightclothes stuck to our bodies—we clambered up the rocky shore and fled across the lawn to the house.

"Come in here," said Tor, grabbing my arm as we went down the hall to the room. He dragged me through a door, and I then understood what all the racket had been about earlier.

It was another bedroom—larger than mine—with a seating area and a vast bed built into the window bay beyond. On the back wall, facing the windows, was a huge fireplace with a roaring fire already crackling away, a giant log at center. Tor must have been up at the break of dawn and used superhuman effort to drag that thing up the stairs.

He stripped off his dripping pajamas and threw them in a soggy pile on the floor. Then, picking me up in my tattered wet gown, he carried me to the bath, where a hot tub of bubbles was waiting, and lowered me in. My skin tingled and burned. Tor climbed in after me.

The tub was a deep enameled affair, with lion's claws for feet. The water went up to my nose when I sank down.

"Did you enjoy that?" he asked with a smile.

"I loved it," I admitted. I held my nose and dunked to rinse the rubble from my hair. When I surfaced, I said, "But now I'm starving."

"I'll make you some food—this place is fully stocked, as I arranged it to be when I phoned from New York. The owners offered to cook all our meals as part of the plan. But I was hoping to have some time alone with you to talk."

"I'm still recovering from last night's little chat," I told him with a grin.

"I'm serious," he assured me. "I was unprepared for the adventure you sprang on me the moment I walked in your door—and for what followed between us, too—though I confess *that's* crossed my mind more than once in the last twelve years. I came here, in truth, to ask for *your* help. Did Lelia tell you what she'd done?"

"She said you and Georgian were angry with her. She didn't say why," I replied.

"Then I'd better explain. She took the bonds to Europe—but she didn't establish the lines of credit I wanted—she took money out in the form of loans instead."

"It's nearly the same," I pointed out.

"Except for the interest," he agreed. "But we're not yet ready to invest the money, and thanks to Lelia we have to start making payments *now*. That's not all—she got lousy terms as well. With collateral worth two hundred cents on the dollar, we should have secured great rates. But Lelia signed contracts with prepayment penalties, too!"

It looked pretty bad, I had to admit. With this kind of deal, he couldn't give the money back and say it was all a mistake—nor could he repay the loans early, even if he wound up making a pile on his investments. If he tried to do either, he'd have hefty fines to pay.

"What I don't understand," he was saying as he lathered his chest with soap, "is why she did it. She wouldn't give me an answer. She kept saying 'That will show them, that will show them'—as if she were trying to prove a point."

"Oh," I said, blowing bubbles from my hand and sinking further down in the tub.

"Oh?" said Tor. "Please fill me in—I assure you, nothing would surprise me at this point."

"It's the Rothschilds, I think," I told him. "Remember how angry she got when you spoke of them that night? Not the Rothschilds themselves—but German bankers—*all* bankers, maybe. The Daimlisch family were German bankers, too, you know. That's how I knew them so well—through my grandfather. Lelia's husband was the black sheep, the one who wanted to break away and do something new and different with his life. . . ."

I paused as I realized this hit rather close to home. Tor was beaming broadly at this, my first hint that perhaps banking didn't run through my blood like a genetic trait.

"Daimlisch did well on his own," I went on, "but when he was ill and dying, they needed money. Lelia went to Germany—against her husband's advice and without his knowledge—and asked his family for a loan."

"They refused?" said Tor, surprised.

"He'd gone his own way—turned his back on the bank; they didn't give her beans. She hocked her jewelry—even today, I bet what she wears is mostly paste. She's never recovered. I knew how she and Georgian felt about banking—that's why I felt they'd leap into our bet!"

"So she wanted to be rich in her own name—if only for a day?" he said, raising his brow. "Perhaps that explains her cockeyed reasoning, but it doesn't solve my problem. I've got millions in bonds out there, securing loans in Leila's name. I'll have to watch them like a hawk now, until they're paid off—in the event any of them are called."

"Called?" I said. "What does that mean?"

"We were in a hurry during our printing," said Tor. "I made the mistake of letting us copy some callable bonds as collateral—bonds that can be recalled whenever the issuer chooses to pay them off. The bearer—or owner—then has a fixed number of days in which to redeem them at face value."

"You're afraid the real owners will take them from the vault to redeem them, and find out the ones *they* have are fakes," I said.

"That's not all," Tor told me. "So long as ours—the real bonds—are securing Lelia's loans, those banks in Europe will expect us to send them in for redemption—they might even do it *for* us. To avoid that, we'd have to pay off our loan at great penalty—as Lelia has helpfully arranged—or get other collateral to secure it. We have no other collateral, unless we want to rob a bank."

"Oh no, you don't," I said. "As long as I keep those wire transfers *inside* the bank—especially in fake accounts under other people's names—I'm not technically doing anything illegal. At least, they'd have great trouble tracing anything to me. But to move my hard-earned 'musical money' outside of the bank in order to pay off real loans in another country—that's a federal penitentiary rap!"

"Your hard-earned money?" he said, raising his brow with a naughty smile. "It seems you've forgotten our little tryst at the data center last night. Who was it that saved *your* charming, dimpled bottom, my dear?"

"I'm at your knees in gratitude," I assured him, kissing a knee that had surfaced from the water, "and I'm also turning into a prune in this tub. I'll take the list of your endangered securities and track them by computer, but I'll have to clear it with my support crew—you met them last night—to see if *they* want to stick their necks out to actually cover your loans. By the way—what are you planning to use all that money for, if I may ask?"

"I'm starting a tax haven—a place like Monaco or the Bahamas—where those who wish to engage in tax-free business transactions will be sheltered from such a burden. Our profit will be made by their having to deal in our currency and within the terms of our fiscal laws."

"What country will let you set up your own laws and currencies and operate as a tax haven?" I wanted to know.

"None of them," he said with a smile, getting out of the tub and toweling off. "So I suppose I must simply start my own country."

I wanted to ask a good deal more—but Tor said we'd discuss it later, and left the room. I turned on the shower as the tub drained, and shampooed all that bay dirt from my hair. Then I dried, wrapped myself in a fluffy towel, and went out to dry my hair beside the fire.

Tor had been downstairs, and had set out coffee and steaming muffins with honey and butter, which smelled delicious. He was standing there, not wearing a stitch, stirring the fire as I came in from the bath.

"I feel like a drowned rat," I said, rubbing my hair.

He turned and stared at me, wrapped in my towel, but he didn't speak.

"Granny—what big eyes you have." I laughed.

He set down the poker and came over to me. He peeled the towel away, and it dropped to the floor.

"The better to see you with, my dear," he murmured. He ran his hands over my body slowly, as if committing every inch to memory.

"Granny, what big hands you have," I said, feeling more than a little weak.

"The better to feel you with, my dear," he whispered, then he swept me into his arms like a bundle, and headed for the bed. "Aren't you concerned about what comes next?" he asked naughtily.

"Don't flatter yourself—it's not that big."

"Big enough." He laughed, tossing me into the pillows.

"Granny," I said, "I believe it's gotten bigger."

"The better to you-know-what you with, my dear," he told me, leaping on top of me.

"Why—I do believe you're not my grandmother at all!" I cried in mock horror.

"If you do such things with your grandmother, my dear—it's no wonder you've been confused about your gender."

"I'm not confused—I know exactly which parts go where," I assured him.

"You certainly do," he agreed as I crawled beneath the covers. "What do you think you're doing there?"

"Exploring some other parts—to find out what to do with them." I was running my tongue across his flesh and he shuddered. "It tastes salty—like the sea," I told him.

"Is this a status report?"

"Yes—I'll send you updates from the field," I said, moving lower.

"My God—that feels wonderful . . . what are you . . ." but his voice trailed off.

I felt his hands moving over my hair. Then he grasped it and pulled me up, his mouth over mine, crushing me to him ferociously. When I pulled away, his eyes burned darkly as he lay among the pillows. He was very pale in the fog-filtered light from the windows.

"How can one want someone so much that it actually hurts?" he asked.

"Perhaps this will hurt me more than it hurts you," I said. "But that doesn't mean I'm going to stop."

I pressed my lips to his stomach, and he shuddered. And then I moved over him as if he were a piece of sculpture I was learning by rote. I felt him stir and move beneath my hands and my lips as I memorized the hard, taut muscles that lay beneath the sheets. And at last, he moaned and cried out, and clutched at me again as his body stiffened and trembled and convulsed, and he lay still.

I moved beside him and looked at him as he lay there with eyes closed, his strong, angular face, the ringlets of coppery hair on the pillow. He opened his eyes and looked at me.

"What on earth did you do? That was magnificent," he whispered, without moving.

"Nasturtiums," I said. When he looked confused, I added, "You taste like nasturtiums."

"A flower?" he smiled.

"In Monet's garden at Giverny," I agreed, with a laugh.

But he looked suddenly worried, and I wasn't sure why.

"What's wrong?" I asked.

"There's something I suppose I should tell you," he said, looking up at me and studying my face. "I'm afraid it's rather worse than the problem of Lelia and the bonds—certainly not part of my initial plan. Though I've known about it for quite some time, I wasn't sure how to tell you."

"Is it something potentially dangerous?" I asked, sitting up, somewhat alarmed.

"Very," he admitted. "My dear, I love you."

MOVING MONEY

No where so well developed as in the pants of the people, wealth ain't.

—*Ezra Pound,*
The Cantos

Friday, December 25

SAID AL-ARABI WAS NOT GOING TO MECCA THIS YEAR. He was the wire transfer operator for National Commercial Bank in Riyadh, Saudi Arabia. On the afternoon of December 25, he was locked alone in the telex room of the bank, sending wires to banks in the United States to settle mortgage payments on Saudi real estate holdings there.

Said al-Arabi sat before the telex machine and typed in the test key, which was masked—blacked out—by the machine as he entered it so no one looking over his shoulder might see the secret code.

Then he entered the rest of the information needed to send the wire:

From: National Commercial Bank, Riyadh, Saudi Arabia
Account Number: XXX
To: Bank of the World, San Francisco, California, USA
Pay To The Order Of: Escrow Account Number XXXX
Amount: $50,000 and no/100
Date: December 25, 19xx
Message: For payment of commercial property, Lake Tahoe California
End.

Said al-Arabi hit the "send" button on his telex, releasing the wire into the network. Then he picked up the next wire transfer to enter from his stack.

Monday, December 28

AT EIGHT-THIRTY MONDAY MORNING, SUSAN ALdridge arrived at the wire room of the Bank of the World. She was the first operator to come in after Christmas, and the room was still locked. Cursing her boss and colleagues for coming in late, and realizing that *she* would have to pick up the bulk of the heavy holiday volume, she went downstairs to the security desk and signed out for the key. They were probably recovering from too much Christmas cheer, she thought sullenly as she returned to open up the room for business.

Susan powered up her terminal and checked her lipstick in a pocket mirror as she waited for the signal that it was ready to go. In a few minutes, she was able to pull up the first wire of the day:

From: National Commercial Bank, Riyadh, Saudi Arabia
Account Number: XXXX
To: Bank of the World, San Francisco, California, USA
Pay To The Order Of: Frederick Fillmore, Account Number XXXX
Amount: $800 and no/100
Date: December 25, 19xx
Message: None
End.

That was strange, thought Susan. This was about the time of month the Saudi bank settled all its real estate mortgage payments in California, but they were for amounts far larger than eight hundred dollars. It hardly seemed worth sending a nine-dollar wire for so small an amount. But who knew with those Arabs? They were rolling in so much dough.

The test key had been approved by the system, so she knew the transfer was legit. Susan typed in the data to prepare the debit and credit tickets, printed out the tickets, stamped them approved, clipped them together, and put them in her security envelope for the ten o'clock pickup.

"Mine not to reason why," she said aloud as she pulled up the next wire on her screen.

■

BY TEN O'CLOCK, THE WIRE ROOM WAS ABOUT HALF-full of operators who'd straggled in. The messenger arrived with her cart at the Dutch door.

"Anything to pick up?" she asked.

Susan collected the packets of wire transfer slips, sealed and stamped the envelopes, and brought them to the door.

"Not many," she apologized. "It's hard getting folks in after Christmas."

"Yeah," the messenger agreed. "*We* have to work, but the supervisors can't get out of the sack."

She signed for the envelopes, tossed them in her basket, and pushed the cart to the elevator bays.

■

IN CASH CLEARINGS, JOHNNY HANKS, THE DEBIT CLERK, slashed open the envelopes containing the ten o'clock wire transfers. It took less than half an hour to post all the debits and credits on his proof-and-posting machine. He wore earphones connected to the Sony Walkman strapped at his waist, listening to Guns 'N Roses to shut out the noise of the heavy machine with its rows of stacker pockets.

He cleared the wire transfers from the pocket and slapped on a batch-total header, winding a rubber band around the stack. Then he dropped it into a nearby pickup cart.

Those girls up in the wire room must still be asleep,

he thought to himself. They should clear more in the first batch this morning than any other day of the year—but the total batch came in under $3 million, and a lot of the transfers seemed really small.

Shit, he thought, swaying to the rhythm of heavy metal, *we* have to come in at the crack of dawn and plug our ears against all this racket. While the wire operators sit at quiet keyboards, filing their nails and gossiping. It really pissed him off.

■

DEEP WITHIN THE BOWELS OF AN UNMARKED BUILDING on Market Street was a bombproof, fireproof, security-sealed, four-acre vault, packed wall to wall with millions of dollars of gleaming hardware and equipment. The sign on the door read WORLDWIDE ITEM PROCESSING. It was here that all the bank's cash clearings took place.

At three P.M. each day, when the branches closed, this floor would leap to life. By midnight the night of December 28, it was a madhouse of activity—a wild underground sea of churning bodies and flying paper—racing against the legal deadline that declared banks must post all transactions before they could open the next day at nine A.M..

Worldwide Item Processing never went down. No mistake, breakdown, fire, storm, or earthquake could be permitted to halt or even delay production. There were safeguards and ancillary systems and backup power supplies and—should anyone forget the well-rehearsed emergency priorities—there was a huge sign on the far wall that read THE PAPER COMES FIRST! After all—paper meant money.

At ten minutes past midnight, a batch header came through the massive sorter/collator, followed by a debit-and-credit ticket that posted the wire transfer received that morning from National Commercial Bank in Saudi Arabia. This wire had been reviewed and approved in at least four locations throughout the bank before arriving here.

The tickets fed into a reader and the wire information was written onto magnetic tape. When the tape was full, an operator pulled it off the drive, slapped on a sticky label, and placed it on a rack. A few minutes later, the dispatcher came along and picked it up in his cart.

"How much longer for this run?" the dispatcher asked the operator.

"A few more tapes. Fifteen, maybe twenty minutes," he was told.

The dispatcher, with his cart of wire transfer tapes, took the elevator to the next floor up, where men were stacking boxes of tapes and disks against the wall. Truckers, down by the steel doors at the far end, were checking boxes against their bills of lading, then wheeling them out, stacked four deep, on dollies, to be loaded on the truck.

"If you guys hold on," the dispatcher called up the ramp to them, "you can get the last of the debit/credit run before you split."

The truckers nodded, and went outside for a smoke while they waited.

■

AT ONE A.M., FAR ACROSS TOWN, THE DOCK CLERK who'd unloaded the truck was buzzed into the Bank of the World data center. He shoved his dolly stacked with boxes up the loading ramp; a security guard checked the delivery ticket on top of the box and motioned the dock clerk to the window. The clerk unloaded the boxes and waited as the tape librarian behind the window prepared a receipt.

"Christ," said the librarian, "it's about time—we been waiting hours for these."

He picked up a microphone, which broadcast his voice across the vast floor of the machine room inside.

"Set up for cash clearings. Thirty-seven files—should take all night, boys!"

A moan went up across the floor of the machine room, and a few seconds later the librarian's phone buzzed at the window—just as he'd finished writing up the receipt and handed it to the dock clerk. It was Martinelli—the graveyard-shift supervisor.

"Tell that asshole from the dock to try to impress upon his drivers they should *not* pause for coffee when they've got twelve hours of stuff in their truck and we've got six hours to run it in."

The phone crashed down in the librarian's ear, and he smiled wryly at the dock clerk. "I guess you heard that as well as I did," he told him. Then he put the boxes on the flat cart and wheeled them into the center.

Tuesday, December 29

AT NINE A.M., A BLOND, SHAGGY-HAIRED YOUNG PROgrammer sat before a terminal at the data center. The floor was nearly deserted, and the few people arriving and removing their coats seemed not to notice him as he powered up and logged on to the machine.

He pulled a crumpled list from his pocket, and checking the numbers, he keyed into the private customer accounts file and reviewed a few account balances. The first was a new account opened under the name of Frederick Fillmore, which displayed an eight-hundred-dollar opening balance.

Tavish smiled, and reviewed a number of other accounts in quick succession. The thousands of accounts he'd sliced wire transfers into, using the "salami technique," should add up—for today at least—to over a million dollars.

■

IT WAS THE MORNING OF DECEMBER 30 WHEN SAID AL-Arabi unlocked his telex room at National Commercial Bank in Saudi Arabia. He logged on to the terminal to see whether anything had come in during the night.

There was a message sitting out there, so he pulled it off on the printer and read it:

From: Bank of the World, San Francisco, California, USA
To: Wire Room, Nat'l Commercial Bank, Riyadh, Saudi Arabia
Message: Ref: Your wire to transfer USD dated 12-25-XX. No deposit was made. Stop. Wire was scrambled in transmission. Stop. Please retransmit. Stop. Repeat. No deposit was made. Stop. Could not read wire. Stop. Please retransmit.
End.

Said al-Arabi sighed.

The problem was that the bloody phone lines in Saudi were totally worthless. Half the time, the desert lines were buried in sandstorms. How did they expect the bank to do business all over the world, when they used bloody camel drivers to repair the equipment?

He went over to the file, unlocked the drawer, and pulled out the transfer he'd done to Bank of the World—a full four days ago now. Then he remembered that the American banks had likely been closed for the Christian holidays. He'd just have to retransmit the thing, and hope there would be no penalties for being late with the mortgage payment.

He sat down again to send the wire. It was unlikely the money would be posted for another forty-eight hours now, he thought. At nine in the morning, Saudi time, it was seven P.M. yesterday—in San Francisco. The Bank of the World had already been closed four hours.

THE AUCTION

Gold is a wonderful thing! Whoever possesses it is master of everything he desires. With gold one can even get souls into heaven.

—*Christopher Columbus*

When I came into the office on Monday morning, Pearl was sitting on my desk with her legs crossed, looking out at the dazzling turquoise bay, the slim, silvery bridge sliding off into the distance.

"Well, well, well," she said slyly as I dropped my things and went around the desk to go though the mail. "Ten-thirty's a bit tardy even for you, isn't it? You were not at home this weekend—I called."

"Isn't that dress a bit low cut—'even for you'?" I asked. "Or are you trying a new approach to career advancement?"

"If anyone's broken new trails this weekend, it seems to be you." She laughed. "Romance improves the complexion, sweetheart, and you look as though you've just had the seven-day makeover at La Costa!"

"I find this conversation totally inappropriate to the setting in which we find ourselves," I told her as I slashed open an envelope.

"I'll bet. What setting *was* more appropriate? Satin sheets? Body oils? Hot tubs?"

"I spent the weekend deep in meditation," I assured her.

"Of course he *is* totally gorgeous," Pearl ran on. "And here I was, giving you advice about how to while away your hours in New York! But Tavish tells me you did make a trip to the data center the other night when you left us. Those programs were up and running just fine this morning. I suppose you were just too preoccupied to phone and let us know."

"Would you like to hear what I really did this weekend?" I asked, going over to shut the door. "You ought to—since the news may affect your entire career."

"What career?" Pearl said bitterly. "After your little tête-à-tête with Karp last week, my career has descended into the twilight of the toilet. My darling boss seems to think it's all wrapped up—that you'll find me another job on an instant's notice, and I'll waltz away from the bank without a blink."

"It is, I have, and you will," I told her, taking a seat across from where she perched on my desk. "It's no joke, Pearl. Besides, we're all leaving the bank sooner or later. It's simply a question of when."

"Right. 'Is there life beyond banking?' and all that," she said. "But I'm not quite ready to break camp yet. What are you—my career counselor or something?"

"I made a deal this weekend—with Tor, as a matter of fact. It turns out his side of the wager is a bit more complex than I thought."

"I'll bet," said Pearl, smiling slyly.

"To make it short and sweet," I cut in, "he has the perfect job for you: something that calls for someone with just your skills."

"I'll show him *my* skills if he shows me *his*," she said with a grin. When she saw I wasn't biting, she added, "Just what skills did you have in mind?"

"Two things. The first is foreign exchange. You know as much about that, I believe, as anyone in the business."

"And the second?" asked Pearl.

"Spending money," I told her.

■

It was strange. I'd known Tor for twelve years—known him as well as anyone could know a man like that. But after one weekend together, I realized I didn't really know him at all.

Like me, he kept a part of himself secret—contained—

veiled from the curiosity of others, just like that womblike office of his so many years ago. What was he hiding? His passion, he'd called it. But I knew by that, that he didn't mean simply making love.

Something had changed—not only between us, but within us—in the three days Tor and I spent on that island. It felt as if we'd been whirled together in a cyclotron, rearranging our molecules, so we each contained a share of each other's being. You didn't have to get to *know* someone when you'd already become part of them. But there was this unbearable craving for the other half. Wasn't that how Plato had defined love? The longing of the soul for its missing part, which it had lost somewhere in the primordial mists of time.

This feeling made it pretty tough to get back to work.

I was gazing out at the bay, trying to sort through these strange emotions, when Peter-Paul Karp came strolling into my office.

"Banks—you're staring through the window! Has something happened to you?" he said in surprise.

"Not to me. But something *has* happened," I told him, pulling myself together and rearranging the things on my desk. All I needed was to have my mind get mushier than Karp's.

"You know that problem of yours we discussed the other day?" I asked. "I think I've got the solution."

"Not really!" he said, pulling up a chair.

"I've recommended Pearl for the Forex seminar—the Foreign Exchange Traders' Consortium," I told him. "It's held every spring—it goes on for three months. You'd have to give her a leave of absence to attend it, and pay her way."

"A leave of absence," he said. "That means the bank would have to give her a job when she returns—but not necessarily in my department, right?"

"Right. The symposium begins next Sunday in New York." I pushed the papers across the desk for him to sign.

"Banks, I'll get this paperwork going at once," he said, scribbling his name across the approval forms.

"And my warmest thanks. I think Willingly's completely wrong in everything he's said about you."

Though I longed to learn exactly what that might be, I bit my tongue. I had more important fish to fry—and Karp was hardly the last one in the pond.

"I may have another surprise for you," I told him, "if you can keep it to yourself. I'm nearly through with my project. I could transfer Tavish back to you in a few weeks." A little more soap, and he'd land right in the tub.

"But this is more than I'd hoped for . . ." Karp began.

"I owe you," I assured him. "After all, you gave me that inside information. And with Kiwi trying to steal Tavish from both of us—"

"What are you talking about?" said Karp, his face darkening.

"Good heavens—I was sure you knew," I told him. "Kiwi took Tavish to lunch last week—and said he'd be coming to work for *him*, not for you."

Karp had turned a lovely shade of red.

"So Willingly's trying to play both ends against the center," he hissed. "I really can't thank you enough for sharing this with me."

He was halfway to the door when I added, "You can't say I didn't warn you about Kiwi, Peter-Paul. But I do suggest that you let everyone think this assignment for Pearl was *your* idea. We wouldn't want it said that we were plotting behind anyone's back—even if that's what was done to us."

"She'll be gone by the end of this week," he assured me, at the door.

I could see from his stormy expression that the seed of doubt I'd planted would not take much water to flourish into a healthy mistrust of everyone around him—most especially Kiwi. But of course, that suited me just fine.

I was singing the Valkyries' battle cry as I went down to the garage that night, where Pearl was to meet me.

"What the hell does *'ho-yo-to-ho'* mean?" she asked

as she got in the car. "Sounds like some kind of voodoo chant."

"A mantra for good luck on your trip," I told her. "I made a deal with your boss, Karp, this afternoon."

"More the fool you," she said as she got into my car. "That creep's so two-faced, he could pass for Siamese twins. I should have guessed that something was up—he's been grinning at me all day. I'd like to wipe that leer off his face with a Brillo pad. Just what kind of deal did you cut?"

"Financing," I told her as I pulled up the ramp. "He's going to foot the bill for your new job. But I think he'll be surprised to learn that someone else has a tongue as forked as his."

"You lied to him?"

"I'm afraid so. I gave him some authorization forms for the Foreign Exchange Traders' Consortium. He was so excited to unload you for the next three months, he'd have signed anything. He has just approved spending the bank's money to send some cocaine dealers on a boondoggle to Hong Kong—at least, that's what the paperwork says. I thought there should be something interesting in his file—in case he keeps leaning on me as he has been."

Pearl put her hand to her mouth and laughed as I came over the rise on California Street and headed for Russian Hill.

"So if you're not sending me off to Forex for three months—what are we discussing tonight at dinner?" she asked.

"I wanted to tell you what your new job's really about," I said, smiling privately at what Tor and I had worked out. "I think you're going to like this—staying with some friends of mine in a Park Avenue penthouse."

"Gray flannel types—or are you upgrading after all these years?"

"European nobility—of the slightly French variety. You can speak your native tongue to your heart's content while you're learning all about the family business."

"Which is?"

"I understand they attend a lot of auctions," I told her.

Sunday, January 10

AT ONE IN THE AFTERNOON, A LARGE BLACK LIMOUSINE pulled out of the underground garage of an apartment house on upper Park Avenue.

In the backseat were two women, so overdressed and bejeweled they might have been pricey courtesans. They were headed toward the Westerby-Lawne auction galleries on Madison Avenue.

"So tell me about your daughter, Georgian," Pearl asked Lelia. "Where is she now?"

"Ah, Zhorzhione, she is in France. We are making the plans to go to Greece for the *printemps*—what you call the springtime."

"You know, you may speak with me in French if it's easier for you," said Pearl.

"*Non*, I feel myself more comfortable in the *anglais* now," said Leila. "It is the best tongue I am speaking—I am what you say extremely fluid in English."

"I see," said Pearl, who was having trouble making sense of Lelia in any language. "And what's she doing in France, other than making your travel arrangements?"

"She visits the *banques*: the Banque Agricole, the Banque Nationale de Paris, Crédit Lyonnais . . . she makes the little investments, you see, to prepare for our trip abroad. *Tout droit!*" Leila tapped on the driver's shoulder. "Just ahead—it is just over there."

"Are we there already? I'm so excited about this," said Pearl.

"*Moi aussi*. It is very long since I am going to the auction *galeries*."

The chauffeur pulled up before the galleries and

handed Lelia and Pearl out of the limousine. Passersby turned to stare at them—both carrying fur muffs and dressed in fitted and flared, heavily embroidered Russian coats, which Lelia had taken from mothballs for the occasion.

"Now you will see, *chérie*, how the rich are bending *le genou* to the *pauvres*." Lelia said as they passed through the oversized doors of the galleries.

The doorman bowed, and people in the corridor ceased their conversation. Lelia took Pearl's arm as they strolled.

"But you're hardly poor, Lelia," Pearl pointed out. "You have that magnificent apartment, a chauffeured limousine, expensive furniture and clothes. Your jewels are magnificent."

"*Loués*—leased, *chérie*. And what can be sold has been solded. The jewels—all paste. Their little brothers and sisters are gone years ago. And the chauffeur, he comes to fetch me for two hundred francs an hour—that is the limit of his service. Money is all—money is power—no one respects you if you haven't got. Now you know my grand secret—which even Zhorzhione does not know."

"But how can you bid at an auction if you haven't any money?" asked Pearl.

"It's like magic," said Lelia with a smile. "We buy this piece of property with borrowed moneys—and after that, we all become rich."

"We're buying a piece of property? Like an apartment building or ranch or something?"

"*Non*," said Leila, putting her finger to her lips. "It is a *belle île* that we buy—and then we go to live there, in the *pays des merveilles*."

"We're buying an island in wonderland?" Pearl said in disbelief.

"*Oui*," said Lelia. "You are fond of the Aegean, I hope?"

■

LIONEL BREAM COULD NOT BELIEVE HIS EYES WHEN HE looked out across the room and saw Lelia von Daimlisch sitting in the audience. He'd seen the name Daimlisch on the attendance list, of course, but never imagined it would be Lelia. He hadn't seen her in years.

When he was a young man, she'd made his reputation in the auction business, though no one knew it. She'd come to him in confidence with her massive collection of jewels and asked how they might be disposed of. She didn't want to deal with anyone, she told him, who wasn't "*sympathique.*"

Though Lionel never learned how it was that Lelia had fallen upon such hard times, even his young and untrained eye had recognized at once the value of the jewels. Some were recorded in the Romanoff inventories—believed lost forever after the revolution. Though he knew little of Lelia's past, he certainly knew the heritage of the jewels in her possession. And that was all that mattered.

It had taken years to auction off the jewels with any sort of discretion. Leila hadn't wanted it known that she was the source of that incredible flow of gems. Above all, she'd desired to keep knowledge of it from her husband, who was quite ill at the time. Undoubtedly she needed the money and hadn't wanted him to know its source, but Lionel hadn't felt it his business to pry into personal matters, when so great a gift had been laid at his feet. To auction off the Daimlisch bequest was more than any auctioneer might hope for in a lifetime—and Lionel had been still a young man, a junior in the firm.

Shortly after her husband's death, Leila had disappeared from view. Perhaps this, too, was for financial reasons. Lionel heard her name spoken from time to time, but had never again called upon her. He felt it inappropriate to remind her of their former connection, and the situation that apparently had driven her to sell the jewels.

Now that he recognized her in the audience, his mind raced back to the time when he'd first met her. She'd been the great beauty of her day—and he, a young boy really, had fallen in love with her. She'd possessed such an air of tragedy, yet with humor underneath. He remembered the way her eyes twinkled when she looked at him, as if only they two shared a secret both magical and special. She had everything that young men, in those romantic days, believed women should have: *tristesse*, drama, and enormous beauty.

Lionel saw Lelia looking at him from the audience. In her eyes was the same secret twinkle, and he felt sure she remembered him—though he'd grown older than she in the interim, and his hair was thin and gray. Suddenly, as he looked down from the platform, he was overcome with a sense of his own past. He longed to sit at tea in the Plum Room of her exotic flat, and hear her play Scriabin on the old Bösendorfer, as she once did. His eyes became misty thinking about it and—in an unprecedented gesture—he stepped from the auction platform and strode into the audience where she sat.

"Lelia," he said softly, taking her hands in his.

On her right hand she wore a paste copy of the Falconer ruby, surrounded by black sapphires and diamonds, the original of which he'd sold to William Randolph Hearst in 1949.

"I can't believe you're here again at last," he told her. "How we've missed you."

"Ah, *mon cher Lionel*," she said, pronouncing it "Leo-nail," "I too am so happy, happy, happy. I have come to see you do the beautiful auction—which I have never seen before."

It was true, thought Lionel. She'd never attended a single auction where her jewels had been sold. She'd asked only that the checks be deposited to her account so she might not have to know the price for which she'd exchanged each of the "little brothers and sisters."

"But what are you doing here, my dear?" he asked her in an undertone. "You know this is a very strange auction today."

People had been turning in their seats to catch glimpses of the woman that the famous Lionel Bream had delayed the start of the auction to greet personally.

Though Lionel was certain no one here today would recognize or remember Lelia, he saw them all ogling the knockoff of the Fabergé emeralds she wore about her neck—copies of the ones he'd sold to King Farouk in 1947.

"I wish you to make the *connaissance* of my very dear *amie*—Mademoiselle Lorraine," said Leila as Lionel formally kissed Pearl's outstretched hand.

"I'm honored," he said, "and Mademoiselle Lorraine has the honor to be a friend of one of the truly great ladies of our century. I hope you cherish her friendship—as we all must who've known her."

Pearl nodded and smiled; she knew that something was going on in the room around her—the way people looked at them—but she wasn't sure what.

Just then, Lelia rose and wrapped her arms around Lionel, giving him a big bear hug. People murmured in the row behind them. Pearl wasn't sure—but she thought she saw Lelia whisper something in the auctioneer's ear.

"You know I'd do anything for you," Lionel said. "I hope you'll not make such a stranger of yourself—now that you're here in our lives once again."

Giving her hand a small squeeze, he returned to the platform and opened the auction. From time to time, he looked down at Lelia and smiled, as if they still shared a deep secret apart from the rest of the world.

The auction continued for nearly five hours. As the evening drew on, the crowd thinned somewhat. Lelia sat, as straight and motionless as an icon. Pearl was surprised that a woman of her age had so much stamina. Pearl herself was drowsy from the heat of the room and the drone of the auctioneer's voice. But suddenly she, too, was at attention—she sensed that something in the room had changed. When Pearl turned to Lelia, something in her appearance had altered—or did it only seem that way? Lelia's eyes were riveted on the auctioneer.

Lionel Bream's eyes drifted back and forth across the room, noting when someone raised a finger or scratched an ear, and mentioning the higher price. But after each bid, his eyes came at once back to Lelia. Each time, the twinkle in her eyes seemed to grow brighter. Pearl understood that Lelia was bidding on this property, though she couldn't decipher the code that was being used. Pearl paid attention to the property being bid upon.

In her program, it was property number seventeen, one of twenty tiny islands off the coast of Turkey. It was thirty square kilometers, and composed nearly all of stone: a cone-shaped mountain flattened at the top, with a deep circular bowl at center.

The auctioneer assured them the volcano had been extinct for thousands of years. Pearl didn't care whether it was extinct or not. From the program photo of this sparsely vegetated rock, she began to question Lelia's judgment.

It was called by the name Omphalos Apollonius—Apollo's navel. As Bream explained to the tittering audience, this was also the name of the hollow stone bowl at Delphi—or any such natural depression from which the oracle prophesied. It had to have been named for the hollow center of the volcanic cone, the most prominent feature of the island.

Pearl thought Lelia must have been possessed by oracular vision to bid on this horrid chunk of stone. Even as she sat there Lelia seemed to be in a mystical trance—and the bidding had already reached $5 million!

Pearl touched Lelia's arm and looked at her questioningly. Lelia smiled her assurance and looked again to the front. So Pearl returned to her program to hunt for further clues to this odd selection.

The island, it seemed, had a resident population of one hundred seventy people, engaged primarily in the fishing and sail-making industries. The only town—also called Omphalos—was on the western side of the island facing toward the Greek coastline; the deserted eastern coast had nothing but a few Venetian ruins.

She read further that the whole block of islands was being sold by an expatriate Yugoslav shipping magnate who'd acquired them shortly after World War II. It seemed that during the confusion of the partition of Europe, the Greek and Albanian governments had both claimed the islands; and since they lay between Greek and Turkish coastal waters, Turkey might have claimed them as well. But from a strategic, or even touristic standpoint, they were worthless. Their volcanic, irregular terrain made a landing strip impossible; the rugged coastlines offered harbors for only the smallest of vessels. Even now they all had few or no services—phone lines, plumbing, lights, or heat—not even coal or wood to burn, or grazing land for animals. Most foods, including essential dairy products, had to be brought in from the mainland.

The dispute over nationality quickly cooled when the limited value of the islands was recognized. And all interest completely dissipated when the shipping magnate lavishly bribed the right officials in all three countries with some claim to those islands to look the other way.

He'd been one smart Slav, thought Pearl. He'd built a vacation residence on one of the more charming islands, and would pay the cost by auctioning off the others to a market of rich New Yorkers, who'd pay for any worthless piece of rock that had a wraparound view of the Aegean.

The bidding on this particular rock had fallen off faster than on the others, for it seemed the least attractive of the lot. Only two competitors stayed in the bidding with Lelia. Pearl was becoming a bit alarmed whenever she glanced at Lelia's flushed and feverish face. It seemed she'd been transported—illuminated by some inner light Pearl couldn't fathom.

To make matters worse, the bidding was now above $10 million. Though this was less than the earlier-offered islands had gone for, it was still a hefty chunk—and Pearl hadn't a clue where the money was coming from. She noticed that the auctioneer, Lionel Bream, never took his eyes from Lelia's face. He, too, seemed concerned.

In fact, Lionel was more than concerned—and had

been, from the moment he'd seen Lelia sitting there in the room. No security or financial statement had been required in advance of the auction, for the guest list had been chosen and prepared by the owners themselves. Lelia's name had not been on the invitation list, but she'd managed to get in nonetheless. He hoped she would be able to pay for this property she was bidding on. No one here knew the former state of Lelia's fortunes but Lionel except Claude Westerby.

It was young Westerby who'd taken the risk to handle those jewels she'd brought to Lionel Bream so many years before. Though Lionel had agreed never to reveal their source, he had to show such a collection to one of the owners before accepting it for auction. He'd hit upon young Claude as being the most (Lionel smiled to himself) *sympathique*. And Claude knew a thing or two about jewels.

Not only were the stones magnificent, he assured Lionel, but the pieces themselves were often the rarer, more obscure examples of once-famous collections. Though the matter was never openly discussed, Lionel felt certain that Claude Westerby, through his research, had learned who the seller must be.

Lionel saw Claude Westerby seated at the rear of the paneled room, arms folded and observing the bidding. Lionel let his eyes rest briefly upon the director's son—long enough to convey the message that there was something wrong, and to ask for direction. Claude's shrug said that he, too, was concerned over Lelia's feverish bidding, but felt little could be done about it now. Short of stopping the auction, Lionel thought; that surely would be unprecedented.

But as the bidding continued a slight change in pace told him, through years of experience, that the property was about to close—and that Leila would take the bid. A peaceful sense of completion filled him, as if a weight had been lifted.

He tapped his gavel gently on the brass mount and said quietly, "Sold to Madame von Daimlisch for thirteen million dollars. Congratulations, Mrs. von Daimlisch—you've purchased a very fine piece of property."

Lelia nodded and, with Pearl's assistance, rose to leave the room. Among the several people who turned to watch her depart was Claude Westerby. Though it was irregular, when she'd first entered the auction gallery, he'd nodded to the guards to let her pass without seeing her invitation. He knew she had not received one, for he'd prepared the list himself. Now he rose to follow her.

"Where do we go from here?" Pearl was whispering as they went along the hallways.

"*La caisse*—the cashier," Lelia replied. "When we finish the meal, we must pay *l'addition.*"

"This is the fun part," Pearl said grimly. "How in hell do you plan to pick up this tab?"

"With a *chèque*, naturally!" Lelia laughed.

Nonetheless, she looked, at long last, really drained with exhaustion. Pearl was worried. After all, Lelia was no spring chicken.

"My congratulations, madame," Claude Westerby said, coming up behind them in the hall.

He took her free arm and joined them in their progress to the cashier. If something went wrong, he wanted to handle it himself.

"Monsieur, we have never made the acquaintance formally," Lelia began. "I am—"

"I know who you are, my dear—you're Lelia von Daimlisch. Though I'm sure I've changed since you saw me last, you're still the woman who was once considered the loveliest in New York."

Lelia dazzled him with a smile.

"I'm Claude Westerby," he went on. "You've received good value for your money today. I'm afraid the previous owner will be angry with me—we'd estimated that island to go for half again as much. Let's hope all the rest fare better, for my sake! I'm pleased that it should have been you who bought it."

And even more pleased, he thought, if you can pay

for it. What a nightmare it would be for all, if she could not!

"Here is the cashier," he said. "I shall leave you to do the unpleasant part alone, though I'll be nearby if you should need help. May I say it's been a great pleasure to have met you formally, after all these years."

"*Merci, monsieur,*" said Lelia. Then she reached out and took his hand. Her voice trembled in what he found an alarmingly feminine way for a woman of her age. "And thank you for . . . in the past, you were very discreet about my *bijoux*—my jewels. I know it was you who made the little inquisitions for me. I am like the elephant; I have a long memory for my good fortunes. Again, *merci, mon ami Claude.*"

He looked at her in surprise, and felt a sudden clutching at his heart. She had such beauty still, the sort of beauty that was magnified from within. She was, he thought, even lovelier than he remembered her forty years ago. He was so pleased she'd bought the island that for the moment, he didn't give a damn whether she could pay for it or not. He rather longed to buy it as a gift for her, himself.

Pressing her hand tightly, he took his leave abruptly, and walked briskly down the hall, back to the auction.

PART 3

Frankfurt, Germany
January 1810

IT WAS EARLY IN THE YEAR 1810, AND MEYER AMSCHEL Rothschild was still living in Frankfurt, though his children were grown and his favorite son, Nathan, had moved abroad.

"I had a dream last night," Meyer Amschel told his wife, Gutle, as they sat eating a breakfast of dried bread soaked in milk.

"A dream?" inquired Gutle, her tone seeming to suggest she'd never before heard of such a thing.

Her hair, cut short in the Orthodox tradition, was covered with a thick unpowdered wig, which in turn was covered with an enormous headpiece made of stiff cotton, Dutch lace, and taffeta ribbons.

"And what was this dream?" she asked her husband, spooning some more milk over his bread. "A dream of more fortune? I think we have more fortune already than is good for us. Sometimes I think so much fortune will one day bring us bad luck." She rapped on the table with her spoon to drive away the devils that might be listening.

"It was a strange dream," said Meyer Amschel pensively. "I saw our house tested in fire and water, as the old book says mankind will one day be tested before

God. Our sons fought together for a common cause, like Judas Maccabaeus, standing together like a force that defies nature—"

"We are all aware of your thoughts on this subject," Gutle told him, "how one twig may be easily snapped between two hands—but a bunch of twigs standing together may not be broken."

"I know from this dream that something great and magnificent is about to happen," Meyer Amschel told his wife. "And because of it, the house of Rothschild will stand for a hundred, hundred years. You will see, my dear—it will begin quite soon."

■

IN THE YEAR 1810, AS MEYER AMSCHEL'S DREAM HAD predicted, his son Nathan was devising a plan so daring and fraught with risk that it might well cost the family not only its fortune, but its freedom, too.

Nathan had been in England for over twelve years, and he'd done well there. Starting in Manchester in the year 1798, he'd exported English cottons to the continent, where his father and brothers sold the goods. By 1809, Nathan had become a naturalized Englishman, and in the following year he had opened his own bank. He was the middle son of the Rothschilds' five, but by far the most aggressive.

Early in March of 1810, Nathan wrote to his father in Frankfurt that he wished the youngest brother, James, to be sent to Paris with the freedom to move about elsewhere in France—as well as in Spain, Italy, and Germany. Meyer Amschel was perplexed. How might a Jew be granted such a privilege? It was particularly difficult to secure the ability to live in Paris—for the Rothschilds were not only Jewish but Prussian, too.

But believing that the premonition of his dream was about to flower, Meyer Amschel put on his silk hat, his lace jabot, and his finest black suit, and went to pay a call upon his friend the Prince of Thurn und Taxis, to whose family the Rothschilds had lent large sums of money in the past. Perhaps it was time to call in the debt—in another fashion.

"Ah, Rothschild, you are looking very dapper today," said the prince. "I can see in your countenance you've come for more than a social call. God willing, I shall find it within my power to grant whatever you wish."

"Your Highness is very astute, as always," said Meyer Amschel. "It's rather difficult; I wish my son James to be granted permission to establish residence in Paris."

"Ah, that indeed does pose a problem," agreed the prince. "Even I cannot gain this permission, being a Prussian."

"I know my request is difficult," said Meyer Amschel. "But it is necessary that I accomplish it, for personal family reasons."

"Since your 'personal family reasons' often have to do with the acquisition of more wealth, I suppose it's in my own best interest to help you as much as possible. Have you any ideas on the subject? You rarely seem short of those!" The prince laughed.

"In fact, I've thought of a possible solution," Rothschild modestly admitted. "If my son could travel in the equipage of a member of the nobility—someone whom Your Highness might be aware was planning a trip to France for some purpose—then the individual in question might be persuaded—"

"In fact, there's such an event about to transpire in Paris, to which all of Europe may be traveling quite soon, as I'm sure you are aware," said the prince, frowning slightly.

"You refer, perhaps, to the royal wedding?" suggested Meyer Amschel.

"If you can grace the marriage of that heathen Corsican upstart with such a kind description," growled the prince. "Good Lord, he puts his wife away in the eyes of God and espouses another before the first is forgotten. It chills the blood, I say! Even the cardinals are not attending, but the European nobility scramble to such an event as if it were a cockfight. Well, Rothschild, if it would make you glad to have your son in such company . . . but I confess, I cannot think of any among my acquaintance—if you'll excuse my saying so—who'd welcome the son of a mercantile Jew in his retinue on this sort of occasion. We'll have to think hard to solve that one, for I myself will not attend the debacle."

"Yes, Your Highness. We should have to find someone who wishes very badly to attend the wedding of Napoleon and the Archduchess Marie-Louise, but for some reason finds—perhaps through lack of funds . . ."

"Aha! Rothschild, I knew you'd not come to me without a plan! So it is my teakettle you want, and not my advice—is that it?" He chuckled.

This was a candid thing for the Prince of Thurn und Taxis to say—for in his role as chief postmaster of Central Europe, he'd often in the past been in a position to steam open official-looking letters and share their contents with Rothschild, to the benefit of both.

The prince clapped his hands twice, and an aide rushed to his side. The prince scribbled several names on a piece of paper and handed them to the aide.

"Go to the post and collect whatever you see pertaining to these," he said. "And Rothschild, perhaps we'll have your solution before the sun sets on another day."

"Your Highness is most gracious and, if I may say so, a clever solver of problems," said Meyer Amschel with a twinkle in his eye.

The Grand Duke von Dalberg had not wished to include young James Rothschild in his equipage to the royal wedding. Aware of the grand duke's financial situation, the prince had proposed other terms to him. Rothschild would compeletely finance all the carriages, elaborate clothing, and travel expenses for the duke's entourage to pass a lavish and lengthy stay in Paris—should the duke favor him by securing not one, but three open passports for Rothschild sons' prolonged stay in France. With this, the duke enthusiastically complied.

By March of 1811, Carl and Solomon Rothschild were firmly planted in France, and James—the youngest of the brothers—was having pastries with Monsieur Mollien, the French minister of finance, in the minister's study; it was filled with sunlight and with hyacinths gathered from the snowy gardens of the Tuileries.

"M. Rothschild," said M. Mollien, wiping at the bit of thick pastry cream that clung to his upper lip, "I have just written to the emperor, advising him of what you've told me. But even now I can scarcely believe that such good fortune could be true."

"Now you are making a jest with me," said James. "Surely the French minister of finance does not expect me to believe that he considers the British to be cleverer at financial matters than the French."

"Oh no! Surely not! They are fools, the British! All the world regards them so. I only mean to say it's hard for anyone to imagine that the ministers in London—unless they are the basest of traitors—would seriously devalue the pound by ten percent and the guinea by more than thirty! How can they reduce their own paper in wartime?"

"But you yourself, Monsieur Mollien, have seen the letters," James said calmly.

"Yes, yes, of course. And even if it were not so, it is the emperor's policy to drain England of her gold and silver reserves, a policy only aided by this measure. We know that an army cannot fight on an empty stomach, or without shoes. And we know how hard-pressed is their General Wellesley in the peninsula. The war will soon be over, I assure you—we've intercepted letters from Wellesley to his ministers in London, asking that his troops be recalled since their own government cannot provide these things. The English may control the seas, as they are so fond of saying, but we French control the land! So long as we keep them short of gold, they'll be unable to send large shipments to Wellesley—they cannot risk that we may cut their supply lines."

The French minister finished this lecture on warfare and economics with a flourish, and stuffed another pastry into his mouth.

"It's fortunate that the emperor has taken this position, M. Mollien," said James politely, "for I'd be most uncomfortably strained to slip this British gold into Germany. To do so, I'd have to pass through the lowlands, and so many bribes would be required it would hardly be worth the effort. Since you permit me to move it through Dunkerque, the French government will be the one to profit. I compliment you on your foresight."

"I pride myself," said Mollien, his mouth full of pastry, "on being an excellent judge of character. It's well understood here in France that you Jews are more interested in turning a profit for yourselves than in any national affiliations—in some way, you are men without a country. It may be costly to extract this gold from the crumbling British Empire, but any loss from your pocket will be France's gain, and when the Napoleonic Code is in effect in Germany, the Jews of Frankfurt will conduct business freely and own property for the first time in perhaps a thousand years."

"It's indeed fortunate for us that Monsieur Mollien perceives matters in his own light," said James. "And history will remember you for that."

■

FOR TWO YEARS, NATHAN HAD BEEN IN LONDON, BUYing gold bullion from the East India Company. He was able to acquire a large quantity, for while the British government was waiting for the price to drop, Nathan was willing to pay the full price.

But the price did not drop, and by the spring of 1811, when the British treasury was desperate for enough gold to finance its armies, Nathan was able to sell it to them below the market price, though still at a profit to himself. Nathan believed in performance—not in promises—and England was the only European country in which all citizens, regardless of their religion, had property rights. He intended to see that it continued that way.

"Mr. Herries," said Nathan to the commissary-in-chief, "now that we have concluded our transaction to your satisfaction, may I make so bold as to ask what you intend to do with all this gold?"

"That's a very forward question, Mr. Rothschild," said Herries, "but as anyone must have concluded by now, we are in dire straits because of that damned Corsican who's running all over Europe, marrying our allies and putting his relatives on the throne of every country in sight."

"And so you plan to use the money to expand your naval prowess, in order to further protect England's coastline from her neighbors?" asked Nathan.

"Rothschild, you're not a fool," said Herries abruptly. "You're the cleverest man I know—and surely the one with the greatest foresight. You know that Lord Wellington is in distress at this very moment. His army in the Iberian peninsula has received no gold in months, for we've had none to send him. Our economies are of the very worst sort just now, the American colonies are acting up again, and I openly admit there may be war with them soon, now that they feel bold enough to challenge our supremacy at sea. The king—let us be frank—is too ill to be of any use. The prime minister makes a different decision every day, and has angered the people thereby. I shall tell you confidentially that the state of our nation is one of utter confusion, that if Wellington fails to win this peninsular war, quickly and cleanly, he will be recalled from Spain."

"Indeed," said Nathan, who knew the state of the British treasury better than Herries himself.

Only last winter, Nathan had bought up the drastically discounted drafts that Herries's predecessor in office had advised Lord Wellington to draw on British treasury bills to help finance the war. Those drafts had passed into Nathan's hands through the ruthless and treacherous Sicilian financial bloc—whose ill-gotten wealth was earned solely through speculation on countries whose stars were waning. The Sicilians were the vultures of the European financial community, never buying anything at more than a quarter of face value. If England's paper were in their hands, they must have been the only ones Wellington could sell it to, in order to raise the essential funds. This alone revealed the position to Nathan, more starkly than a detailed financial statement from the treasury.

"So you plan to send this gold to Lord Wellington, to keep him alive in the peninsula?" said Nathan.

"That's what the gold's intended for—but I fear there's no way to do it," Herries admitted sadly. "Sending it by ship is out of the question; three ships have been sunk off the coast in as many months. And to send it through allied territory would take too long and pose too great a danger. The entire war may be concluded, in fact, before we can find a way to deliver this gold to Wellington."

"Perhaps I may make a suggestion, then," said Nathan.

"Any suggestion is welcome at this point," said Herries, "though I fear we've exhausted all solutions."

"Not quite," said Nathan. "There is one you haven't mentioned. If you choose, I'd be willing to convey the gold to Wellington myself—naturally, for a fee. I am prepared to guarantee its safe delivery."

"Yourself?" said Herries, a smile hovering about his lips. "My dear Rothschild, you're a brilliant financier, but I scarcely believe you can walk on water—the sort of miracle called for just now. And what would be our guarantee?"

"That any gold I cannot deliver will be replaced from my own pocket," said Nathan calmly.

"But how do you plan to get it there?"

"Let that be my concern," he said.

■

WHILE MOLLIEN CONGRATULATED HIMSELF IN LETTERS to his emperor upon the great success he was having in looting British coffers of their gold, James Rothschild was at the money markets in Paris, trading the steady flow of gold he received from Nathan into bills of exchange drawn on Spanish banks.

His brothers Carl and Solomon moved back and forth in relays across the Pyrenees from Paris into Spain, disappearing into the mountains with their bills of exchange, then returning with receipts from the Duke of Wellington. And the French never realized that the gold they'd permitted the Rothschild brothers to smuggle from England into France was being fed through legitimate channels into Spain and used by Wellington to feed his armies.

With his coffers replenished, Wellington soon achieved victory against the French in the peninsular war—and entered Madrid.

Nathan's father, Meyer Amschel, remained in Frankfurt with his eldest son, Amschel, carefully monitoring news of the war through the central post office, and feeding that news to the others. Now that he was an old man, he had little else to occupy himself—except for the daily care and feeding of the new dovecote, full of doves, that Nathan had sent him from London as a gift.

In September of 1812, when Napoleon was fighting at Borodino, en route to Moscow, Meyer Amschel passed away into his last dream. Three days later, the Russian general Count Rostopchin put the torch to Moscow, leaving Napoleon's armies to march back through Russia in winter, in final defeat. It was the end of an era.

THE FED

Under the Constitution, it is the right and duty of Congress to create money. It is left entirely to Congress. Congress has farmed out this power—has let it out to the banking system.

Constitutionally, the Federal Reserve is a pretty queer duck.

—*Wright Patman*

WHEN THE DUST HAD SETTLED AFTER THE FIRST OF THE year, Tavish took a look at the programs we'd installed at midnight Christmas Eve, and polished them up a bit.

We were grabbing a big percent of the money transfers that came in each day, slicing them up like a salami and dropping them into the fake bank accounts we had set up under all those ritzy names on the Bobbsey Twins' list. We hung on to each money wire like that for only about twenty-four hours so no one would get suspicious. We picked up the interest on it, then gave it back. But since our "borrowing" was now running in the hundreds of millions, the income from it was growing by leaps and bounds even though we rotated our pot each day.

Tor and his team—now including Pearl—had headed off to Europe. It seemed things were running smoothly at both ends. At least, so I thought until Tavish came in one Friday morning just after New Year's.

"There's good news and bad news," he said.

"Let's hear the good first," I told him.

"I've been tracking Dr. Tor's bonds from that list you gave me—following them in the newspapers. Nobody's trying to pay them off or redeem them, at least not yet, so we needn't be concerned about those loans in Europe you told me they're securing. Furthermore, I've tuned up our systems so we can take bigger slices of the salami. That's boosted our average pot to around three hundred million we can now invest."

"Terrific," I congratulated him. "Now what's the bad news?"

"I've redone those figures you got from Charles Babbage, about how much money you need to steal and invest in order to earn that thirty million by April first—that's forty-four banking days from now. Your numbers are wrong; you can't do it. And that's a really serious problem, not only because of winning your bet. If something did happen to those loans of Dr. Tor's, and we had to cover for him, I doubt we could wring out enough just from our profits. And you know we can never hold the actual wire transfers themselves for more than forty-eight hours at best."

How could it be that we wouldn't be making enough in profits? I'd run those figures a dozen times and they always came up the same. Tavish interrupted my thoughts to explain.

"You took into account *all* the wire transfers passing through the bank," he said. "Your plan was to slice off as much as we could from whatever action might pass through the door—without drawing undue attention."

"Right," I agreed. "So what's the problem?"

"One of the biggest volumes of wires is one we can't get our hands on—Fedwire. It's used to transfer, adjust, or fiddle with our reserve at the Fed. But the money's in *their* pocket—not ours. You shouldn't have counted the Fed activity in."

Blast. He was right, of course—but the problem this raised was even worse than the idea of knocking over a bank. Fedwire was a wire transfer network owned by the U.S. government; you could go to federal prison just for getting a parking ticket on U.S. government property—I didn't like to think what they'd do if they caught you mucking about with their loot.

"But here comes the worst part," Tavish added. "I saw Lawrence in the elevator a moment ago. He's sent you a memo. It seems he somehow learned that we've successfully broken through security. We couldn't have hoped to keep it a secret forever, but now even the auditors know—and they're all expecting some sort of statement from us. Lawrence says he's off on a business trip tonight, and he wants our project wrapped up, our report submitted, our hands off, and an impeccably restored system by the time he gets back. If we need to increase any activity on that system, we've got less than two weeks in which to do so. What should we do?''

I sighed and folded my hands on the desk. Then I gave Tavish a resigned smile.

''Looks like we're going to have to knock over the Fed,'' I said.

■

THE FEDERAL RESERVE SITS AT THE BOTTOM OF MARket Street, a forest of pink granite pillars supporting the trellised granite arches that conceal its blocklong façade. The Fed hasn't changed its architectural preferences, its operations, or its concept of technology in the more than seventy-five years since its inception. It still seems ossified in the traditions of the Parthenon.

All federally chartered banks must be members of the Fed, and are required to maintain insurance deposits there. Each type of business the Bank of the World conducted required a different type of account with the Fed, with different reserve requirements. Each Wednesday, those reserve amounts were tallied for the week before, to be sure our deposits stayed within the variance permitted by law. Banks that ran negative for two weeks in a row had their wrists slapped rather sharply by the Fed. But neither did bankers like to leave excess funds lying in there, since the deposits earn no interest or income. So the activity required to stay within the letter of the law was both continuous and frenetic—and generated tons of paper.

All the better for *moi*, I thought.

When a bank like ours increased or reduced the balance in our Fed accounts, we could move the money back and forth from the Fed itself—*or* we could buy or sell our reserves to another bank, in the appropriately named Fed Funds Market. All these types of transactions were handled through Fedwire, which meant cash rolling in and out the door like hotcakes—and to many, many locations. When I was through with *this* caper, I'd be an expert in federal banking security, par excellence.

■

"It seems to be a question of degree," Tavish commented as we sat locked in my glass-walled office that afternoon, studying the Fedwire interfaces—those systems I'd formerly managed along with the rest. "I mean, this business of stealing," he clarified. "A slip and you're in the quagmire up to your nose. But it's clear that if we *can* knock over the Fed, their security's just as poor as ours."

"One small step for the criminal—one large step for crime," I agreed. "But of course, we're criminals only if we get caught. If we make it through to the end of the theft, we'll yank all our code from the system, erasing our trail. They'll never be able to prove *we* did anything, but no one will be able to argue with the results—hundreds of millions sitting in accounts where it doesn't belong!"

I was so deeply embedded myself, I could no longer remember the time when I felt I could bail out. But Tor would be proud of me—and Bibi too, I thought—for taking the leap this time without a shove. I now knew beyond doubt that what we were doing was right.

I showed Tavish my plan, designed for maximum complexity to slow the auditors down as long as possible. He looked up, scratching his shaggy blond head.

"You want to grab a billion or more in under two weeks?" he said. "Don't you think the Fed might notice if that much of their money's missing all at once?"

"It's not their money—it's our money—the bank's," I explained. "And there's more than eight billion dollars of it sitting out there right now. We're required to keep an average percent of our assets there, by law.

That doesn't mean the Fed knows where it came from or what it's for. Even if they notice a discrepancy, it will take them months, the way I've set this up, to trace more than a few of these myriad transactions."

"You've improved on our former technique," Tavish agreed. "This is now like the salami from outer space—let's give her a whirl."

■

"WELL, BANKS," SAID LAWRENCE AS HE ENTERED MY office late that day, coat and carryall in hand, "isn't it a bit late for calling impromptu meetings? I have a flight to catch."

"I got your memo," I told him. "I understand I'm to shut down my project before your return. I think that might be jumping the gun a bit. I'd planned to prepare another proposal, about how to fix some of the problems we've—"

"I believe we've had enough proposals, Banks," he cut in abruptly. "Just write up what you've found and I'll see that it gets into the right hands. You won't be needed for the follow-up work, so far as I can see. I'm sending you back to Willingly's department in two weeks. Good man, Willingly—too bad you didn't see eye to eye, but you both have strong personalities. You're a protagonist, and he's—"

"An antagonist?" I suggested sweetly. This bastard was signing my death warrant. I had to play for time.

"In that case," I informed him, "before you leave, I'd like you to approve these transfer papers for me. I'm sending Bobby Tavish back to his old boss, Karp's department. It seems there's some debate about whom he must work for—but I agreed to this with Karp some time ago."

"You must learn to handle these teckies, Banks," Lawrence said as he scribbled his name across the forms. "You won't get far by coddling them and listening to their complaints, believe me. If you clean up this project—get rid of your group—these efforts won't go unrewarded. You have my word on that."

"Yes, sir," I said politely. "And you know how much I value your word."

Lawrence glanced at me briefly, then wished me good evening, and left.

I picked up the phone and booked the flight to New York. Then I called the personnel director and told him Tavish's transfer to Karp had been approved—they could cut the paperwork. I phoned Karp, who was effusive with thanks, lies, and bullshit at the other end.

Then I called Tavish.

"Did they take the bait?" he asked.

"Hook, line, sinker, and part of the pole," I assured him. "No one will be the least surprised when you resign on Monday—except maybe Karp, who's a bit slow on the uptake."

"I wish you could join me," he said sadly, "but I understand someone's got to stay behind and mind the shop. I'll think of you in New York."

"Give my love to Charles and the Bobbseys," I said, for we'd agreed that Tavish could monitor our operation quite well by using Charles—and the Bobbseys were grateful to hire someone who could help with their operation, even though on a temporary basis, and give them a long-needed break. "If you happen to hear from Pearl or Tor," I added, "give them my best—but tell them we're still going to beat them!"

When we hung up, I felt a terrible cold chill move through me. I was alone now—surrounded by villains—and who knew for how long? I hadn't heard from Tor in weeks, not since they'd left for Europe.

I glanced at the calendar on the wall—February 1—just over two months since my night at the opera. In the seventy-two days that had passed, I'd knocked over two of the largest financial institutions in the world (if you counted Tor's theft, it was three), and everything in my life had been turned upside down. Though I knew it, I couldn't really feel it; I just felt numb inside.

I was thirty-two years old, and by most standards, a success. All the achievements in my life had been won by beating the System. But soon there wasn't going to be a system to beat anymore. I was destroying it, wasn't I?

Tor had known this all along, of course. With one swift kick, he'd knocked away my supports, so the only thing I could cling to was reality—actual reality, not the kind found in systems and structures and other people's rules. He wanted me to take a good, hard look at my life, stop playing the games we all invent to pretend to ourselves that what we're living out isn't real. And if what I saw stretching behind me was a crumbling, rotten bridge of my own making—a wasted ruin—I knew what he'd tell me to do.

I sat in my office surrounded by glass, and looked at the fading orchid in the vase before me. A few brown blossoms had fallen, scattered across the desk. I heard Tor's voice whispering, ever so softly, in my ear. His voice said, "Light the match."

■

BY THE MONDAY OF LAWRENCE'S RETURN—WHEN I was expected to shut down my project and get off the system—I still had no solution to the dilemma.

By then, Tavish and I had finished transferring the monitoring of our crime to Charles Babbage's full-time diligence, though it meant the little computer would have to stay up around the clock for a while in New York. Someone still had to keep an eye on the systems here, just to see who might be snooping around. But if I got transferred back to Kiwi, as Lawrence had threatened, I'd be occupied full-time cleaning the lavatories with my toothbrush.

As I passed through the fairyland of glass walls to Lawrence's office, I was pretty glum. Though Tor had always said the best defense was a good offense, I wasn't sure what I could do that would be offensive enough to stop the wheels that were already set in motion. The least I could do was to give it my best shot.

Lawrence greeted me without rising; he was dug in behind the entrenchment of his desk and unwilling to part with ground. It hardly mattered—the ammo I had this time would melt under a small blowtorch, and I knew he could do better than that with his breath.

"Let's have a look—this is the wrap-up report?" he said, extending his hand.

He skimmed the first few pages, then read the rest more closely than I'd hoped for, considering that my hours on earth were numbered. I sat there swinging my legs, looking out at the fog-bound view. I knew I might get one shot if I were lucky. I closed my eyes and tried to visualize the terrain in the dark.

"Banks," he said, looking up with patience, "this study seems unnecessarily alarmist to me. You suggest our security can be violated—"

"*Has* been violated," I corrected.

"But I shouldn't describe our systems as 'lax in security.' It might be misunderstood. I realize these systems aren't exactly state-of-the-art—"

"Unless the art is Renaissance fresco painting," I agreed.

"But frankly I'm losing patience with all these studies, and I no longer plan to finance them. I'll be responsible for making sure that your concerns are addressed. Your request for follow-up work is denied."

"I'm not requesting that *you* finance any improvements to security," I assured him, "or that the Managing Committee should be involved either."

I stood up and took a deep breath—it was now or never. "That's why I'm turning my findings over to the audit department," I said. "It's really their job to ensure the appropriate safeguards are put into our systems, and now that Tavish has left, I'm the only one who can advise them about where to look for holes in security."

I surely didn't want the auditors inspecting the system just now, but since it seemed they already knew that we'd violated security (hopefully, not *why*!) they'd be expecting to see my report—that was the reason Lawrence had used for wrapping things up on my project. On the other hand, if I could work along *with* them, it would serve the double job of keeping me informed of their activities—and out of Kiwi's hands.

But Lawrence's response was something I hadn't bargained for, and it threw me for a loop. I assumed he'd either send me packing back to Kiwi or agree to my suggestion. Instead, he sat there with my report in his hands and said nothing. And then—after something more than a mere pause—he actually smiled!

"The auditors?" he said, raising a brow as if he found the idea a novelty. "I really can't see why they should be involved at all."

Wrong answer, my dear. And that will cost you queen and castle.

The *right* answer—as director of the largest division of the bank—was that we should call in the auditors at once. It was he who should stress that our lingerie was lily white—not I. It was he who should insist we had nothing to hide—not I. It was he who should pick up the phone at once and refer the whole matter to the boys in blue—not I.

The fact that he did none of the above meant we most assuredly *did* have something to hide. I wondered what in hell it could be.

Now he was standing up behind his desk, smiling and extending his hand for a shake as he slipped my report surreptitiously into his drawer. I hadn't a clue what was happening, but I got to my feet as well.

"I don't like to haul in the auditors to solve our problems, Banks," he told me. "Not until we've a solution of our own to propose. I'll tell you what—take a little time, a month or so, perhaps—and have a really good look at those security systems of ours. Be ruthless, if you like. Who knows? Maybe we need to start from scratch and design some brand-*new* security, even if it means a little extra spending. And let me know if you need any staff to help."

"Okay," I told him, totally confused. "I'll write up a schedule and plan and leave them for you tomorrow."

"No rush," he assured me, seeing me to the door. "We want to do this thing right."

I made my way down the glassed-in corridor in a daze. This was the man who'd told me—only week before last—to wrap up my project and put my staff in the pasture, who'd told me two minutes ago he was sick of proposals and studies. Suddenly he'd stopped the clocks, halted time, told me money was no object. My head was spinning as I approached my own office.

"Are you still employed?" asked Pavel. "You seem to have come out intact; have you counted your fingers and toes?"

"My fingers and toes are all there—but something's definitely missing. You can unpack the boxes while I try to figure it out. Looks like we're staying awhile."

I went into my office, closed the door, and looked out at the layer of fog sitting on the bay. A cabin cruiser broke through the mist. I watched it until it passed under the Bay Bridge. It reminded me of the one Tor and I had taken to the island. That seemed a hundred years ago. Where was he, and why hadn't he called? I needed to talk to someone who was a master at analyzing people and their motivations—and that certainly wasn't me.

I knew, as I sat there alone in the fog, that Lawrence had no interest in our security at the bank. He was even less interested in what the auditors thought of that security. This had nothing to do with security or the auditors; it had nothing to do with *me.* What it had to do with was Lawrence himself.

■

I REVIEWED LAWRENCE'S ACCOUNTS FOR WEEKS, UNTIL nearly the end of February, but could find nothing amiss. It was driving me crazy. He seemed clean as a whistle. Why would a guy like Lawrence, who got half a million in preferred stock in his Christmas sock each year, do anything to rock the sleigh?

Perhaps he wasn't *doing* anything—maybe it was something he was *about* to do. But how could I figure out what was on the agenda? I considered sending Pavel into his office for a peek at the calendar—but recalled that Lawrence kept everything in his mind and nothing on his desk.

But there *was* a correspondence file that wasn't in any drawer—and I had the key. It was the mail message file, used by every officer at the bank to send electronic memos via computer. If Lawrence was as nervous as his behavior had suggested, it must be something he was planning to do quite soon. I read two hundred boring memos before I found it.

It was just a half-page memo to the Managing Committee, entitled: "Shelter of Investable Funds." The subject was parking—of a kind that had nothing to do with cars. It had to do with money, and it was illegal. Nevertheless, nearly all banks did it, and camouflaged it as something else until they got caught.

At the end of each banking day, they moved their offshore profits to a tax haven, like the Bahamas, by having their branches there "buy up" those profits. That way, everything was transferred off the books before it was taxed. Was it mere coincidence that this memo pertained to exactly the sort of investment scheme being set up right now by my mentor—Dr. Zoltan Tor?

I was about to delve into the subject further, when I received an unannounced visit to my office by Lee Jay Strauss—director of internal audit.

■

LEE JAY STRAUSS WAS MORE THAN AN AUDIT MANAGER. His key job was to resolve unusual discrepancies in our Federal Reserve deposits. The accounting department handled the *usual* ones; that Lee was in my office meant some hanky-panky was suspected.

"Verity—may I call you Verity?" he asked, looking at me with droopy, sad-dog eyes though his horn-rim glasses. I told him that would be fine.

"This is just an informal visit—off the record," he assured me. "It seems we've a small glitch in our reserve position for last month. I'm sure it can be easily explained. Probably just a ripple in the system."

He laughed at his own witticism.

"I'm afraid I don't know much about the Federal Reserve," I told him. "I don't even know how much we send them each month."

"Actually, it's each day," he told me, checking his notes as if he had our conversation all outlined there on crib sheets.

"So they sock it to us every day, do they?"

"We probably shouldn't scoff," Lee told me seriously. "After all, the Federal Reserve provides many services and protective features that banks would otherwise have to provide on their own. Remember how difficult banking was before the system was established!"

"I'm afraid that was before my time," I said. "But I understand it was pretty rocky turf. Now, what can I do for you today?"

"Probably very little. It's just that we're missing some of our reserve for the end of January, and we're not sure where it went."

"Well, I haven't got it," I said, looking up my sleeve with a laugh.

"No, I'm sure not. The thing is, we *do* know where it went, but we can't explain it. It seems it went right into our own bank—here in San Francisco."

"Then what's the problem? Can't you just put it back where it belongs?"

"It isn't as simple as all that," he said—though he hardly needed to explain all this to me, since I was the one who'd cooked it up. "You see, the money we should have sent to the Federal Reserve seems to have been sold off to other banks, which we frequently do when we need to reduce our reserve and another bank needs to increase their own. In this case, however, that wasn't the situation—so it's quite unclear how the money ended up moving around that way."

He pushed a paper across the desk showing multiple transactions that had posted in various banks: Chase Manhattan, Banque Agricole, Crédit Suisse, First of Tulsa, and a few random money market accounts. I looked up from the paper and smiled.

"That's just *one* Fed deposit transaction," said Lee. "It took me a week to run it to earth, and when I did, it was back in the Fed. We believe there are many more such discrepancies—and it seems they're being caused by one of our systems here."

"Which one?" I asked, as if I didn't know.

"The interface to the Fedwire system—a part of wire transfers."

"I see. Unfortunately, I'm no longer in charge of those systems, Lee," I told him. "I left that department months ago."

"Yes, we know," he said, then looked at his hands in his lap. "But we understand you've just completed a study of security on all major systems. I thought . . . we thought you might have some findings that could help us out."

I'll just bet the subject of my study had been bandied about in the audit department. Not to mention the fact that the report had been suppressed.

"I'm afraid I'm not yet empowered to release that information, Lee," I told him. "Have you a clue how much money we're talking about?"

"For the last week of January alone, about sixty million so far. Of course, that's peanuts compared with our reserve balance, but there may be even more. Those correspondent accounts through which the money was moved have thousands of transactions a day, and we have to go through all that by hand."

"Wow, I had no idea! No computer aids for audit," I said. Better and better. "My sympathies are really with you. I'll tell you what—though I'm not supposed to share my findings with anyone yet, no one said I couldn't personally look over those findings myself, in private, with your specific problem in mind. After all, it might be the *Fedwire* system that screwed up, and not our interface—then we wouldn't be involved at all."

"Gee, that would be great," Lee assured me. "It would save us loads of time in audit, if we could just pinpoint *how* the money could get scattered like that." He stood up and gave me his hand.

"Oh—and Lee," I said when he reached the door, "you haven't discussed this problem with Kislick Willingly—have you?"

"Not yet," he said, looking wary. "You were the first one we've come to."

"That's okay. I know they're his systems now, so he should be informed—but perhaps it's best not to alarm anyone just yet, until we've learned what the problem is."

This tiny seed of doubt about Kiwi would surely grow like wildfire in the fertile neuroses of the audit department. Auditors were by nature suspicious—or they wouldn't be auditors.

I had a lot to tell Lee Jay Strauss when I was ready. But auditors always worked best when you gave their natural mistrust of humanity time to propagate on its own—like mushrooms—in the dark.

FOREIGN EXCHANGE

A dime for the bank, a penny to spend.

—John D. Rockefeller

Wednesday, March 3

PEARL WAS GOING FOR HER MORNING CONSTITUTIONAL along the quay at Omphalos. Across the sea lay the sunny coast of Turkey. She was glad this island they'd bought looked better than it had in the catalog photo. The sea glittered turquoise in the sun, little brightly colored caïques bobbed in the water, and healthy-looking young Greek boys cleaned their nets over big wooden racks down at the wharves.

Until six weeks ago, when she arrived here with Lelia, Pearl hadn't been involved in this caper at all—not really—except to give moral support and warn her friends of impending trouble. But now that she'd let herself be bulldozed into coming to the island—now that she was a full participant—she saw things differently. And what she saw, amazingly enough, was that most of this so-called caper *wasn't* even *illegal*!

Okay, it *was* against the law to counterfeit securities. But neither those counterfeits nor the real securities they'd exchanged them for had ever been turned into cash! In essence, using them as collateral was no different from using the title of your car to secure a loan—when you knew you'd driven it off a cliff the night before! You still had a valid piece of paper that *said* you owned the car. And if you paid off the loan with interest, no one would be the wiser and everyone might benefit.

So they bought a piece of rock to which no country had laid claim in fifty years; they declared sovereignty (though—as Tor had learned—there was no international court to which one must petition for the sovereignty of a piece of unclaimed land!); and they turned it into an international tax haven.

Pearl herself had done the econometrics and the setup single-handedly, requiring that any business done here on the island—if they wanted to receive the tax-free seal from her—must be conducted in the "local currency," and *she* would decide the rate of that currency against the others, taking her profit margin against the market. It was just like the retail FX business, where you changed money at an airport and *their* fee was built into the exchange rate—something Pearl did every day for the bank. Then, with those profits from her fees, she "took positions" in the world currency market each day, to increase her earnings—wholesale FX trading—the other side of the same coin.

But *none* of this was illegal, except the initial counterfeits they'd made. Even so, as long as those fake securities in the vault were believed by everybody to be real, the rightful owners still derived full benefit of their use as well!

The advantage to Pearl of joining this caper was that it was worth more than ten lifetime careers at any financial institution. Now she'd set up an economic system for an entire country—and a profitable one, at that. She was the Fed and the SEC, the treasury, Fort Knox, and all the mints and banks and brokers rolled into one! She wouldn't have to look hard for a job, with references like those—but perhaps she wouldn't need one. If they kept this island business going long enough to pay back all those loans with interest, she didn't see why they couldn't stay on an extra month or two and rake in a few more millions for themselves—and at no cost to anyone at all!

Pearl paused to survey the scene as she did every

morning, took a deep breath of sea air, and descended the stone steps to the harbor. The young Greek fishermen stopped working and waved gaily as she passed. She headed down to the dock. The morning boat had just arrived from the mainland, and she picked up her usual batch of newspapers, which she threw into a big woven basket over her shoulder. Then she went along the quay to the sailors' pub for a cup of coffee.

She was on her second cup and third newspaper when she found it. She sat there a moment without breathing, then took a red pencil from her bag and circled the ad. Cursing softly to herself, she gathered the scattered newspapers, threw some money on the table, and hurried out of the restaurant.

She climbed the hill and went along the cobbled street to the sail makers'—a barnlike structure that Tor had purchased as their headquarters. Entering the dark main floor, she nodded to the Greek boy who served as receptionist, handyman, and guard. Then she climbed the rickety stairs to the next floor. Without knocking, she threw open the door of the first room on the left.

"Read it and weep," she told a surprised Tor, tossing the tattered, two-day-old copy of *The Wall Street Journal* on the desk before him. It was folded open to the notice she'd circled in red.

He glanced at it quickly; his face became grave.

"So they've exercised their call option to pay off these bonds," he said. "What's the face value of what we hold of this issue—and how many banks is it scattered in?"

"Hang on to your hat," Pearl told him. "We have to come up with twenty million—right now—to cover these bonds. These that have been called are securing our loans in half a dozen French banks, and one in Italy. That's the money you used to buy this lovely island. If we can't cover those loans, and they find out about the fake duplicates in the vault, we're going to have plenty of time in prison to remember how charming—but brief—a time we spent here."

"I'm surprised you haven't earned that much in profit

already," said Tor with a smile. "You've been trading currency for six weeks, here in a tax-free haven. And you *are*, after all, one of the top FX traders in the world."

"Who told you that?" snapped Pearl.

"Why, *you* did, my dear. But I've anticipated this, and I know how to raise the money quickly without jeopardizing our freedom or asking our California friends to bail us out. If we handle it right, I might even wind up with enough cash left over to win my bet!"

"If you think I can pick up that kind of cash by peddling my body to those boy sailors down there—it won't even get us bus fare home," said Pearl. "What did you have in mind?"

"Something more pragmatic—though perhaps less interesting, from your viewpoint," he told her with a smile. "In fact, it's been part of my plan from the very beginning—we just need to change the schedule by a week or two. My dear, I think it's time to sell our little country."

Friday, March 12

THE VAGABOND CLUB SAT, DRIPPING IN IVY AND NOSTALGIA, on the steep-curved lip of Nob Hill in San Francisco. Just off the harlequin-marbled entrance hall lay the vast reading room, its beveled windows overlooking Taylor Street's hurtling descent to the Tenderloin. Here in the silence of the reading room—with its Prussian-blue-and-peach carpets, massive library tables, dark wood wainscoting, and French oils from various Paris exhibitions—the warm aura of nineteenth-century San Francisco still existed.

Downstairs in the Red Room, place settings for one hundred had been laid; the Waterford candlesticks sparkled, the bone china shone in the dim romantic light, and dark red roses, the color of blood, were thickly clustered in crystal bowls at the center of each round table.

In the adjoining room, behind heavy double doors, the gentlemen, dressed in black tie, were having cocktails and waiting for the announcement of dinner. They were men of every profession, from countries all over the world, but they all had two things in common: They were members of the Vagabond Club; and they had earned it. Whether through family connections, great wealth, or the prestige of personal power, each man in this room had paid his dues.

When at last the massive doors were thrown open, they filed into the dining hall and found their places. Seating arrangements had been prepared with customary discretion: those with the most lavish titles, positions, or bankrolls sat at the main table, with pecking order defined by relative proximity to them. A podium stood near the front, for the after-dinner speeches.

A light course of Scottish salmon—preferred by club members to the less costly Nova Scotia—was followed by the chef's famous roast duck. The salad was served after the entrée, in club tradition, and the cheeses were followed by a course of sweets.

When at last the coffee arrived, the first speaker, a British banker, took the podium. He waited until the room had quieted, then tapped his microphone a few times to be sure it was adjusted properly.

"Gentlemen, this is indeed a momentous occasion," he began. "As you know, it is the tradition—the unbroken rule—of this club never to mention world affairs, politics, or business here within the hallowed walls. We are Vagabonds, and proud of it—despite the fact that our membership rolls have listed more ambassadors, royalty, U.S. presidents, board chairmen, corporate founders—in short, more blue-chip and blue-blood men—than any private association in the world!

"So, in keeping with that one inviolable club rule never to discuss the sordid daily traffic that greets us outside these walls—I suggest instead we raise our glasses simply to *toast* the launching of the new and exciting venture we in this room are all aware of—the eve of whose inauguration we're foregathered here to celebrate—the dawn of whose—"

"What are you trying to say, Paul?" someone from a nearby table said as everyone laughed.

"Let's toast our new enterprise," said the banker, laughing as well.

A tinkling of wineglasses was heard. The waiters replenished the wine, then discreetly left the room.

The British banker was replaced at the podium by Livingston—speaker of the evening, and head of a worldwide petroleum conglomerate.

"Good evening, good friends. I believe you all know me—I've been a member of this club since I was twenty-five, and I'm a few years older than that now!" Light laughter. "My father and grandfather were also Vagabonds; the men of our family have considered the club a second home—often more friendly and familiar than the first!" Throaty chuckles and nudges in the crowd as Livingston continued.

"But in all my decades of membership, I've never felt the pride I feel at this moment, standing before you. For gentlemen, tonight we christen not only a new enterprise, but a new way of doing business—a bold venture into the future.

"When we set forth upon this sea, we lift our chains and leave the past in our wake. Should we fail, perhaps history will malign us. But if we succeed—yes, if we succeed—she'll crown us with the laurels that are our due. Therefore, it's not just a business venture—but an *adventure*. Our fraternity pitches its fortunes together and casts the lot—leaving a proud legacy to posterity, opening a new book in the history of money, and inscribing our names on a fresh new page of history!"

The members were on their feet at once in a storm of applause, crying "Hear, hear!" as they rang their glasses and pounded the tables. When the storm died down, Livingston continued.

"The members who set up this venture—who put the financial deck together and raised funds from those in this room—are sitting here among us. But if I started thanking everyone, we'd never get out of here sober!" Huzzahs and whistles. "So stand up, gentlemen—you know who you are—and take a bow."

A dozen men stood beside their chairs. They were greeted with thunderous applause. When they resumed their seats, Livingston added, "I hope you got a good look at them—so if this deal goes sour, you'll know who to blame!"

Much laughter and slaps on the back to the bankers.

"Tomorrow our representative leaves for Paris to conclude the last stage of negotiation. If all goes well, he'll be unloading a lot of your hard-earned cash. Once this negotiation is complete, our larger management team can head to Greece to assume control from the European consortium who set the business up. So by next week, gentlemen—with the help of God and a little money—we should be the owners of our own private country!"

The room was again pandemonium—men on their feet cheering, glasses raised aloft. As they started to file from the room to the lounge upstairs for after-dinner cognacs, a member caught up to one of the bankers Livingston had singled out earlier for praise.

"Well, Lawrence," he said warmly, "you boys have certainly put this together cleanly and quickly. If you swing this Paris negotiation, we'll all be a whole lot richer than today."

"Profit is the name of the game," said Lawrence as the two stepped onto the elevator.

"Yes—that's what I wanted to ask you. Livingston told me it was *your* clever idea to force out these Europeans—whoever they are—the ones who own the island now. Something about a leveraged takeover?"

"It's pretty much done, though they don't know it yet," Lawrence said. "They were asking a thirty-million-dollar fee over and above the asset value of their business. Our research revealed they had financed the entire operation—island and all—through loans drawn on numerous European banks. Yesterday, we bought up those loans."

"You mean we—the club—are now their creditor?"

"By holding this paper," said Lawrence, "we technically own their business. All they have to do is fail to meet one single payment, and we can pull the rug from beneath them completely. Under those circumstances, our spending an extra thirty million seems completely unnecessary to me."

"Brilliant," said his companion. "So your Paris negotiation will just involve their turning over the keys to you. By the way, where's your new candidate to the club this evening? Kislick Willingly. I somehow expected he might be here tonight."

"I've withdrawn his name from membership," said Lawrence. The other glanced at him quickly, in surprise, for such a thing was never done. "After all, anyone might blackball him when it came to the vote. He needn't know it was I."

The dim elevator light glinted on his gold-rimmed glasses. His companion thought with a sudden chill that he'd never seen eyes quite so cold. The elevator stopped, and they moved to the lounge with the others.

"Why the sudden change of heart?" he asked Lawrence.

"He really isn't one of us," Lawrence said.

Wednesday, March 17

THE RUE DE BERRI ANGLED LIKE A NARROW ALLEY OFF the Champs-Elysées, only a short distance from the Arc de Triomphe.

On the top floor of a three-story building, about a block down the street, was nestled the exclusive private watering hole La Banque—the bankers' club. In the corner of the main club room, across a sea of faded green carpeting, sat Tor, sipping a fizzy reddish drink and gazing out the window.

Across the street were the chestnut trees, unthawing after their long winter sleep. The stiff branches packed with tight red buds tapped gently against the boatlike windows of le bateau—Picasso's old Paris studio. The late-afternoon sun coated its dingy windows in gold.

Tor glanced at his watch, had another sip, and looked at the door. A man in a dove-gray suit entered, glanced once about the room, and sighting Tor, crossed to his table.

"Sorry I'm late—don't bother," he said as Tor was about to rise. "What's that you're drinking?"

"Cassis and soda," Tor replied.

"I'll have scotch on the rocks," he told the waiter who'd come up. As soon as the waiter had left he added, "Everything's nearly wrapped up. We just need your signature on these papers, and the transfer's complete."

"Not quite," said Tor, watching the cubes of sunlight reflect on the surface of the other's gold-rimmed glasses. "There's the little matter of payment, I believe."

"I'm afraid not," said Lawrence coldly. "You see, we've acquired your paper: all your loans are now in our hands. Technically, we own the island—the entire operation—already. You may repossess your collateral when you sign these papers."

"I see," said Tor, squinting a bit from the glitter of the spectacles. He paused as the waiter arrived with the scotch and departed. "And the thirty million you committed to? After all, you're buying a successful business, not just a chunk of rock with a view."

"We've reconsidered," said Lawrence. "After all, you operate under a shady legality—any country nearby might claim that rock—now that it's got some measure of value—to cut in on the action. We know they did in the past, though perhaps not with the same tenacity as was done with Cyprus. We've no assurance that what we're buying will continue to thrive. But to expedite things, as your creditors, we'll give you *one* million in cash to keep us from making a public display in court—and as well, we're willing to waive those prepayment penalties you seem to have gotten yourself into on those loans."

"One million instead of thirty—that's far from the

bargain you struck," said Tor in cold anger. "Your proposal is unacceptable."

"It's not a proposal," Lawrence told him, washing down his scotch. "It's final. One million is plenty; we're asking nothing of you but a smooth transition—your name on the dotted line."

"I'm sorry," said Tor with a bitter smile. "I'm not the right chap for you, under these revised circumstances. You should have let me know. I came here with power of attorney, thinking you planned to honor your commitments. But the key investors whom I represent couldn't guess you would break your word."

"This has nothing to do with honor—it's simply business," said Lawrence. "My colleagues expect to assume control of your operation in roughly a week. You must bring your investors around by then, or we'll attach your property in court the first time you make a wrong move on any loan in any country."

Tor knew there was little advantage in pointing out that their loans weren't secured by the island or the business. Lawrence wasn't a fool—he'd have noticed the callable bonds by now, and the fact there'd been no move yet to redeem them. Coupled with Tor's request to accelerate this deal, even a blind man could see that they couldn't cover those loans without selling out. He had to do something to play for time and cover himself.

"There's only one investor that counts—the principal and genius behind our whole enterprise," he told Lawrence with a smile. "If you can defer your trip by a week—say March thirty-first—perhaps I'll have time to discuss and gain consensus on these new terms of yours."

"Very well," Lawrence agreed, standing up to depart. "But not a moment longer. Who is this principal, anyway? It's the first I've heard mention of him."

"It's the Baroness von Daimlisch," said Tor. "I think you might find her quite a challenge—but then, who knows?"

LIQUIDATING ASSETS

Money is like a reputation for ability—more easily made than kept.

—*Samuel Butler,*
The Way of All Flesh

I WAS AT HOME, CHANGING FROM MY WORK CLOTHES, when I got the call from Tavish in New York.

"Hi there, my former boss," he greeted me. "How's things around the bank—same old bloodbaths and political assassinations?"

"Count yourself fortunate you're in nirvana," I told him. "How's Charles Babbage doing?"

"Keeping track of all our investments very well, thank you," he said. "I didn't tell you—but some of those bonds of Dr. Tor's were on the call list last week. They never asked for our help, though. And now it seems they've other plans altogether."

"How do you know?" I asked, excited. It was nearly ten weeks since I'd heard a word from any of them. They might have dropped off the earth.

"They're operating in a veil of mystery, as usual," he told me. "But I just got this cryptic communiqué from Pearl—no way to reply yes or no—just a one-way plane ticket to Greece. For you."

"I beg your pardon?" I said.

"Pearl has wired a whole packet of info to Charles here," Tavish was saying. "Times, schedules, money, tickets, instructions—I'll overnight-express them to you. You're to leave next Friday. Don't pretend you haven't enough vacation accrued—I've accessed your personnel files! Nor do Charles and the Bobbseys and I need you to carry on *our* end of things. Though Charles Babbage gets nothing out of all this, I've already won more than I could ever have hoped! You see, Dr. Tor's wired me the offer of a job with his own firm! He claims that my brilliant programs saved his life that night at the data center—though I hardly believe that. You understand, Mademoiselle Banks, that this is the fantasy of my life come true—and I know I owe it all to you."

"Oh, Bobby—many thanks. I'm thrilled for you, of course. But Tor would never have offered to hire you if he didn't mean everything he said. The credit's yours—not mine—and congratulations! But why have they suddenly sent for me?" I asked. "They've waited *months* to phone—you'd think they'd wait another few weeks until Tor could say he'd won the wager." Though, much as I'd wanted to beat Tor, the wager seemed a moot point now, compared with what we were up against.

"Who knows why they called?" said Tavish cheerfully. "Perhaps they've already won!"

I hadn't thought of that. And as Tavish said, I was totally useless here. I'd racked my brains and rifled every system to try to get the goods on Lawrence, but apart from that one memo, I had nothing. Though parking might be illegal, I couldn't prove he was pushing the bank to do it, based on that one scrap—nor could I ask Tor what *he* knew about it, if anything, since I didn't know how to reach him! So I thanked Tavish for sending the stuff ahead, hung up, and stared at the walls awhile. Then I turned out all the lights and sat in darkness.

I knew what was troubling me, of course. Less than four months after my night at the opera, I found myself alone—looking not at blank walls, but at a demolished life. I'd robbed two banks, abetted setting up a possibly illegal country—not to mention knocking over the entire securities industry—destroyed my career, *and* slept with my best friend, mentor, and competitor, who—for the three months immediately thereafter—had been listed among the missing. I felt I'd been socked in the gut by life. If this was the excitement Georgian was always touting, I confess I longed to return to the white womb of my former existence—the one Tor had called a mausoleum—the one that *I'd* thought was safe.

But it was too late to turn back now, I knew, though I hadn't a clue how to deal with Tor when I finally got to Greece. I'd lost the wager, it seemed—despite all his help—and I'd never been asked for the aid I'd expected to donate in return. Tavish said those bonds had been called—but no one had called *me*. Clearly, Tor didn't need to stoop to conquer.

But the worst part of all was the feeling of having lost everything because of this bet. My life had been sucked away—there was nothing left but Tor and a ticket to Greece. I sat there in darkness a very long time. Then I opened the small crystal box on the table, pulled out a match, and lit it. As I watched it slowly burn down in the dark, I imagined the bridge. And I smiled.

■

THE BOAT CHUGGED WITH EFFORT THROUGH THE CRYStalline waters that looped like scattered ribbons through the dotted chain of isles. Silhouetted against the sea was the black cone of Omphalos, its rugged lava crust glittering like black diamonds where the waves struck, drenching the cliffs with spray.

The shore was lined with a stately procession of cypresses, etched in charcoal against the chalk-white houses that clustered near the port. A small stone jetty curved into the sea. Within lay a few little fishing boats in red and blue. Waves silently lapped the quay.

As my boat pulled into berth I saw Lelia seated on a stone wall beside the quay, waving to me, her parasol fluttering in the breeze. Her flowered muslin dress with billowing sleeves, the tawny hair tumbling in ringlets at her brow, the basket of flowers beside her on the wall—it was all so lovely, it made me want to weep.

"Darlink," she cried, rushing to me breathlessly when the gate was down and I could step on land, "I was so worrying you would not come!"

"Of course I've come," I told her.

I inhaled the dark aroma of her flowers. I wanted to see Tor.

"Where is everyone?" I asked.

"All working—*tout le monde*. Zhorzhione, she takes pictures of the island here, she find it so beautiful she cannot resist. Pearl is making the moneys for us, as always. And the lovely Zoltan—he is in France."

"In France?" I said, amazed that Tor would bring me all this way, and then be absent himself. "Well—let's drop my bags at the hotel and see what the girls are doing."

"No hotel," said Lelia, beaming in a very possessive fashion as she took my arm. The heels of my shoes kept getting stuck between the picturesque cobbles on the quay. "We have a château—a castle," she was saying, "and I decorate it all myself. It is unique."

■

IT WAS UNIQUE. BUT REACHING IT WAS AN EVEN MORE fascinating experience.

We left the little village of whitewashed houses, red-tiled roofs, and fragrant lemon trees hugging the bay, and climbed the circuitous dirt path that crossed the mountain. Our rickety horse—something of a national treasure, according to Lelia—seemed to know the way himself, as he dragged our pony cart at his own leisurely pace, through silvery olive groves dotted with small, trickling streams. These fed the vegetation, which sprang everywhere: wild iris, periwinkle, blue, purple, and yellow, scattered through the dark green foliage. Good thing none of this was revealed on the auction gallery's photo, or Omphalos wouldn't have gone for the measly $13 million that was Lelia's winning bid.

Atop the cliff, at the brink of the volcano—at twelve hundred feet or more—we could see down the entire sharp face of black rock to the clear glassy water below, so transparent it seemed to be cut of aquamarine. Even at this distance I could make out schools of colorful fish moving among the shallow shoals. And at the edge of the farther point, there lay the castle.

Lelia wasn't exaggerating when she called it that. Made of ocher stone, it was encircled by crenellated walls enclosing the interior courtyard. Lelia said it was built by Venetians in the 1500s to defend the channel between the Turkish mainland and the more populous Greek isles. Though its past life was now a mystery, buried in the dust of centuries, she believed that Grimani—the powerful doge of Venice—might have spent his earlier years of exile in a place like this.

When at last we embarked at the sea, I saw the sturdy base of the castle nearly submerged in water, and the tower looming above, its one narrow window facing out to sea.

The moment we'd unloaded my things, I saw our horse swerve sharply away and trot off up the embankment.

"Our transportation is getting away!" I cried, starting to hoof it after him.

"Oh, he will come back," Lelia told me with a laugh. "He go to the *quai* for the tourists when he is done—he is trained like a pigeon that always is going home."

Home? I suddenly felt alone—abandoned—as if I were at the very brink of the earth, about to step off.

■

LELIA GLOWED WITH PLEASURE AS SHE SET THE LARGE platters of lamb and pilaf on the massive stone table. Pearl was helping her while Georgian sat on the parapet wall, her back to us, photographing the sea at sunset.

Lelia had filled the stone urns with flowers and stuffed wax candles into every crack of the crumbling stone walls. Though the castle had no electricity, thanks to her efforts the parapet glittered extravagantly.

Before us lay the sea, shaded from hot pink to dark vermilion in the waning light. The bloodred sun dropped below the cone of Omphalos, and the sea darkened to purple. A light dampness rose along the coast, but the candles contained us in their circle of warmth. I wrapped myself in the heavy uncombed-wool sweater

Lelia gave me, and went to the wall where Georgian sat.

"It's so lovely," I told her. "I feel I'd like to stay here forever and leave everything far behind."

"You'll get over that," Pearl said from behind me, "when you try to take your first bath with no plumbing."

"Or your first shit," agreed Georgian. "After a while, you get tired of hanging your ass out over the seawall. . . ."

"Please!" cried Lelia. "This is not the discussion *romantique!* Enough, *Madame la Photographe.* We must eat these dinners I am making here, no?"

Georgian clambered down from the wall in her heavy mirror-embroidered caftan—Lelia was wearing one in peacock blue, and Pearl was splendid in, of course, emerald green—and we all drew together around the stone slab that served as our table as Lelia poured the wine into hobnailed glasses. I spooned some vegetables over my lamb as Pearl spoke.

"Tomorrow I'll take you to see what we've set up," she said. "Tor should be back by then—we expected him today. But he phoned the offi^e—the only switchboard on the island, I believe—and said there had been a slight glitch he needed to take care of."

"In Paris?" I asked.

I was more than a little resentful that I'd come eight thousand miles at a snap of his fingers—just as I'd always suspected he expected of me—and he couldn't be bothered to be here, too. But Pearl misunderstood my tone.

"I'm sure there's nothing serious detaining him," she said. "He's very thorough, as I've learned while working with him all these months. In fact, I must thank you for sending me on this boondoggle. It's the best experience I've ever had—all packed into a few short months. It's changed my life. When we go back, I'll be able to do whatever I like. Not many people get that sort of chance."

"So you plan to go back, then?" I said a bit sarcastically. "I thought it might be so idyllic here, you'd all want to stay forever!"

"Not quite," said Pearl, exchanging mischievous looks with Lelia. "We may all have to confront reality a bit sooner than we wish."

■

GEORGIAN WOKE ME AT DAWN—HER FAVORITE HOUR—so I could watch the sunrise. Not among my favorite sights.

She was jostling me in the straw mattress that served as my bed on the floor of the tower. She threw a long, flowing caftan over my head and dragged me downstairs before my eyes were open.

"Coffee," I mumbled incoherently, groping for the railing.

"You won't need it," she assured me, dragging me into the aching light of day. "*Look* at this magnificent day! Doesn't it make your heart beat quicker to see nature in all its splendor like this? Doesn't it thrill you just to be alive?"

"Coffee would make me happy," I managed to stammer. "My eyes hurt. I don't think people were meant to see all this magnificence before breakfast."

"I'm taking you somewhere, and you're not wriggling out of it," she told me bossily. "After Tor returns from the mainland, we'll all have lots of work to do. I may not get you to myself for some time."

She took me by the arm and led me along a footpath that traversed the slope and then dropped toward the sea. At the base, a hot spring gurgled from the rock into a small dark pool in the lava rock—an oval basin suspended between sea and sky—then overflowed and tumbled in a waterfall into the sea. Wildflowers and succulents clambered over the surrounding cliffs in brilliant colors and diverse shapes reminiscent of a tropical jungle, though this was a dry Aegean rock.

Georgian, discarding her purple-and-yellow-striped caftan, had slipped into the black pool. The water churned foamy about her, and beads of water sparkled in her silvery hair. With the brilliant sapphire sea and darkly purpled Turkish cliffs in the distance behind her, she looked like a siren luring sailors to these rocks.

As I stood there on the path above I suddenly had an awful flash of reality. I saw the bank—the fluorescent lights, forced air, controlled humidity, security passes, mantraps, and bullet-proof glass walls—in short, all the makings of a model prison environment. How had I spent ten years of my life that way, when this existed, too?

"Stop daydreaming, lazybones, and get in," Georgian was calling up to me. "This water comes from the volcano. When we got here, it was still winter—I bathed in the steamy hot water as cold rains pounded on my head—yin-yang."

"I hope you took pictures," I told her, coming down to dabble my toe in the water.

"You can't photograph magic, as I learned long ago," she told me. "That's your problem—you want everything white and flawless and perfect. And frozen in aspic. Thor and I have agreed the time has come to rattle your chain a bit."

"Oh really?" I said, yanking off my own robe and slipping into the bubbling pool. "Just what have you two cooked up?"

"Why don't you ask *him*? He's stumbling down the hill just now."

I glanced up the slope, and sure enough, Tor was picking his way down the uneven terrain, looking out of place in a business suit and elegant Italian shoes that slipped on the rocky trail.

"I've come upon a couple of ondines," he called down to us, letting his eyes wander out over the vista. "I never knew this place existed! Lelia dropped me off from the boat and told me to go along this path. I must say—it was worth the hike. What a breathtaking sight!"

This last he directed to me—not just the landscape—and I flushed a bit. I had to admit he looked lovelier than I'd wanted to remember these past lonely months. And now he was tanned and golden, his coppery hair tumbling to the collar of his white silk shirt. He was loosening his tie as he spoke.

"I'll join you if you promise not to peek. I must confess, I'm modest to the extreme around pretty young girls. . . ."

Georgian, pleased at this description of herself, turned away with hands over her eyes as Tor undressed and slipped into the pool along with us. I wondered what she and Lelia had learned from Pearl about the change in Tor's and my relations. It seemed clear they'd spent plenty of time plotting behind my back.

"Look what I found coming along the trail," Tor was saying, moving to me through the hot steamy water. He held a small wild orchid in his hand, and twined it in my hair.

"How marvelous," I said. "Perhaps I could transplant a few to my place in San Francisco when I return."

Tor looked at Georgian in mock puzzlement and raised his brow. "She thinks she's going back there," he said, "and you've let her proceed with this fantasy? Doesn't she know she's been kidnapped to Treasure Island?"

"It's your turn to deal with the gray flannel mind," she told him. "And it's your turn not to peek—I'm getting out of this hot tub."

We turned away, and after a moment heard Georgian calling from the upper slope, turned to see her purple-and-yellow robes fluttering about her like a butterfly.

"Don't do anything I wouldn't do!" she called with a grin, and disappeared over the rim.

"What wouldn't Georgian do?" Tor asked with a smile.

"Very little that I can think of," I said.

"Perhaps then, we should try one of those things she *would* do," he suggested. "Hmm. I suppose we could float around here and talk about sex all day."

I laughed, but I was having trouble concealing the fact I was quite upset, seeing Tor suddenly like that on the trail—after my isolation all these months. My emotions were jumbled together and tangled like skeins of yarn, and I knew why.

For twelve years the two of us had had a mental rapport so powerful that, I had to agree with Tor, it often seemed like a psychic umbilical cord. Then two months of heady competition and danger, followed by a weekend of lovemaking so powerful—so magnificent—I could hardly bear even now to think of it.

And then nothing. No phone call—no letter—no cheery card: "Having a swell time in Bora-Bora; wish you were here." He'd abandoned me to a plot of my own devising, and gone about living his own adventure as if I'd never existed. Now all at once, I thought furiously, with one third-person phone call, he'd expected me to come running back into his arms. I was even angrier with myself, that I'd done as instructed.

"I'm sorry I wasn't here when you arrived," he said, as if he'd read my mind. "There's no place I'd rather have been—but something urgent happened. . . ."

He came over to me, moving through the black waters, put his hands on my face, and bent to kiss me, pulling his wet fingers through my hair and sliding his hands down my back.

"Your skin is like silk—I can't bear not to touch you," he said softly. "You're like a slippery golden eel. . . ."

"An eel?" I laughed. "That's not very seductive."

"You'd be surprised what the thought does to *me*," he said with a smile.

"I can tell what it's doing to you," I assured him. "But you were going to tell me about something urgent in Paris."

"It's the hot water," he said, closing his eyes. "All thoughts have fled—strength is seeping from my mind."

"Yes, I can tell where it's marshaling its forces," I agreed. "But shouldn't we climb out of here and find some mossy spot to lie down? Or is that too pragmatic?"

"Have you never made love in a pool of water?" he asked, his lips on my throat and moving lower.

"No—and I don't plan to," I assured him, feeling weak despite all effort. "I think it would be difficult, complicated, and uncomfortable. I might drown trying to figure out how."

"You won't drown, my dear," he said. His hands and tongue were moving over me until I shuddered and grasped his hair with wet hands. "Believe me," he murmured, "you were designed for it."

■

AS WE WALKED BACK TO THE HOUSE, TOR'S SHIRT STILL unbuttoned and trouser legs rolled up, his coat tossed over a shoulder and his tie and socks stuffed in the pockets, he turned to me with a smile.

"Wet and disheveled and barefoot—who'd think a bank vice-president could look so ravishing?"

"Don't you mean ravished?" I smiled back. I had never felt so drained and warm and peaceful in my life.

As we came to the house we could see Georgian, Lelia, and Pearl, all below us on the parapet. They were in bathing attire, sunning themselves and sipping Chartreuse. They rose as we came down the trail.

"All my little *poulets* have arrived—time for the *déjeuner*," said Lelia, bringing out a big platter of sandwiches: long crusty baguettes stuffed with tuna, calamata olives, purple onions, sliced sweet and hot peppers. We helped ourselves to the sloppy fare, washed down with icy pitchers of beer.

"Lelia baked the bread herself," Pearl told me, "in a stone oven we rigged from an old fire stove downstairs. She can do my cooking any day. But I'll bet this little jaunt has already put ten pounds on me."

"We do not talk of this—we talk of *affaires* now," said Lelia, turning to Tor. "What of these men who are wishing to buy our business?"

Buy their business? So that was how they planned to win! They could pay off those loans and make a tidy profit—then return the stolen bonds with no one the wiser as to how they'd been used. In fact, they'd stolen *nothing*—just borrowed bank money and paid it back.

No one need ever know that the collateral had been "borrowed" for three months from the Depository Trust. Any profit they made in the interim was like having a loan without using collateral at all.

"Who are the buyers?" I asked, when I understood what was afoot.

"Mystery candidates," whispered Georgian. "No one but Thor knows who they are or where they've come from. Frankly—it's scary. After all, there are loads of unsavory types out there who'd love to get their hands on a business like this. We might even be in their way!"

"May I join in this chat?" Tor asked irritably. "After all, I conducted this deal—the results are hardly a mystery to *me*."

Georgian sat, duly chastened, as he went on: "I've been in negotiation with an international group of businessmen for quite some time," he informed us.

"How much time?" I asked.

"Since I attended that meeting at the SEC—where the bankers refused to take stock of their own stocks. That's when I started this plan—"

"But that was *before* you owned the island or even had the bonds," I pointed out. "It was before you met Lelia or Georgian or Pearl. . . . It was before we had our bet!" I cried.

"Quite so," he said with his dazzling smile. "But I believe in planning ahead, my dear—and I knew you'd come around."

I was so infuriated, I felt my fists clenching. That bastard had won unfairly. He'd planned the whole thing and found buyers for the sale, before we'd even loaded the starting gun. If he thought I'd put myself in bondage to him for a year after that, he had another think coming!

"Who are these guys—and how did you find them?" asked Pearl, interrupting my thoughts.

"They're well connected, with real estate holdings and plenty of financial clout. But that's not all they have in common," said Tor. "I found their names from the same place True found those on *your* list: Charles Babbage gave them to me!"

"Good Lord!" cried Pearl. I snapped around to stare at Tor as the realization struck me, too. "I know what those names have in common—not only their social rank. If I'm not mistaken, most were members of the Vagabond Club!"

"Bull's-eye," said Tor with a smile. "I thought you'd appreciate that."

"That means Lawrence is in on this, too?" I asked.

"I'm afraid so," Tor answered me. "And that's the problem I encountered in Paris. You see, after four months of negotiation, these charming gentlemen don't want to pay up."

So *that's* what that memo on parking was all about! That bastard Lawrence was getting the bank to park money—illegally—in a tax haven he planned to buy himself! Using the power of his position for personal financial gain was identical to insider trading! I had to laugh bitterly at the irony of it all. I'd chosen the sleaziest folks I knew—in a sort of private joke—as a place to tuck *my* illegally gotten cash. Now I learn they'd been plotting to do something even more nefarious themselves! What a thin line was walked by men of fine affairs, I thought.

But the worst irony of all was one that could be truly appreciated only by me: What Lawrence had done to Tor and the others was almost precisely what had happened to my grandfather nearly twenty years ago. Take someone's brilliant idea, nurtured with sweat and tears, and rip it from under him like a rug, milking it for all it's worth until you bleed it dry. There had to be a way to retaliate.

"That snake," said Pearl when Tor had finished explaining where he'd left things with Lawrence. "If we don't redeem those bonds within two weeks, he'll redeem them for us—as our creditor—and then we're really screwed."

"*Oui*," agreed Lelia, "they are making the screwings in us like a nail."

"I don't think that's what she meant, Mother," said Georgian.

"But it's close enough," Tor agreed.

"We've got to get those stolen bonds out of his hands, before he learns what they are," said Pearl, turning to me. "I've been giving this some thought. Have you and Tavish earned enough—if you transferred the money you're kiting—to pay off our loan?"

I knew what she was saying—I'd known from the first time Tor mentioned the idea—and it was more than dangerous. Stealing money from a bank to cover a personal debt in a foreign country wasn't the same as using "borrowed" bonds to secure a loan you were going to pay back. If I got caught before we could put the money back—it would be international fraud on a really major scale.

But Tor cut in—his voice strangely detached. "I can't accept that," he said. "After all, I'm the one she has a wager with—not the rest of you. We're still competing. If I accept money at this point, it's tantamount to losing the bet."

"But a moment ago, you told us you were about to lose your shirt anyway," I said, exasperated. "Why won't you admit it's done? This miserable bet has already cost me plenty—my job, my career, maybe my independence—everything I've worked for all my life—"

"Perhaps you'd care to hear what *I've* worked for?" he cut in with bitterness. "Honor and integrity, a fair day's wages for a fair day's work, justice in the marketplace so that people of honor and value are rewarded, and that those without honor are always, always punished." He paused and looked at me with a coldness I'd never seen. "What *you* work for is Lawrence." He turned away in anger.

"It's cruelly unfair of you to say that," I protested, in shock. But all at once, I knew he was totally right.

Why had I been so hung up about working for Tor? What sort of independence would I really be losing in that—the freedom to play cat and mouse with people like Lawrence and Karp and Kiwi—winning small triumphs while losing my life, my ability to produce, as Tor would say? What was I really, but the cleverest rat in the maze?

"I don't care about winning," I told him, pacing about, as my three friends sat riveted, looking at us helplessly. "I got into this bet for the same reasons you did—to show there were cheats and wastrels and liars rife through the whole financial industry. I'm not going back to the bank when it's through, regardless how the bet winds up. I want to stay here and help you beat them. But I don't know how—without giving you the money to cover those loans—"

"It's too late for that," said Tor. "Far, far too late."

"I don't want my friends to wind up in jail when I have the means to help," I said. "Besides—you helped *me* when I needed it."

"Indeed?" said Tor. "Is that what you think? Perhaps I did just the reverse."

He stood up unexpectedly and left the terrace as Pearl and I looked at each other in surprise.

"What was that all about?" asked Georgian. "*She* offers to save our asses and *he* declines because of a 'gentleman's wager.' Doesn't sound too damned gentlemanly to me!"

"This is because you have not the ears to hear inside the heart," Lelia pointed out calmly. "The divine Zoltan—he feels he does wrong when he brings Verity into this wager—when he helps her to continue onward in it, despite that she was losing at first. If not for that 'help,' she might be safely free from all which happens now. And we—we are *her* friends—he feels guilty because of us, too. We must make him to understand that we are all grown human beings. What we have done, we do freely of choice."

She was right, of course; that explained the frustration and anger he must feel—but it didn't solve the problem. I rose and went off to find Tor. It took half an hour or more of wandering through the woods and down to the stony shore before I saw him—still in his wrinkled city shirt and rolled trousers—sitting glumly on a rock beside the sea.

"So you just can't stop competing," I said. Coming

up with a smile, I took a seat on his knee. "Too proud to accept a nickel of my dough."

"If it were really 'your dough,' as you so charmingly put it, I couldn't be more delighted to be a kept man," he said, sounding less than convincing. "But when you offered to put yourself in federal penitentiary for twenty years to help me out—I really felt I should draw the line. Did you find that too harsh?"

"Okay, so it's war then," I said, still smiling. "What's your next step, if I may ask?"

"Damned if I know," he said, absently kissing my wrist as he gazed at the water. "I've been trying to come up with an idea ever since this happened. I was too clever by half, and it may cost us all our freedom. It's amazing that I, of all people, could be taken off guard by a double-cross such as this."

"How did you leave it?" I asked.

"I played for as much time as I could, claiming Lelia was in charge and must be consulted. But they're coming to the island in two weeks, and they'll expect us to sign on the dotted line then—or have our assets attached in court."

"Look, I already know Lawrence is a crook," I told him, "but I can't prove it with just one memo and circumstantial evidence—like the kind of clubs he belongs to. Not to mention that Lawrence covers his ass so well, he might hold a degree in paperhanging. But two weeks is better than nothing—and since it's all we've got—I hoped you might not disdain my aid, if it only involved investigative reporting?"

"If you honestly feel as you've just said up there," he told me, searching inside me with those incredible red-gold eyes, "then help me destroy them as they deserve. That's what it's all about."

up with a smile. I took a seat on his knee. "Too proud to accept a nickel of my dough?"

"If it were really 'your dough,' as you so charmingly put it, I couldn't be more delighted to be a kept man," he said, sounding less than convincing. "But when you offered to put yourself in federal penitentiary for twenty years to help me out—I really felt I should draw the line. Did you find that too harsh?"

"Okay, so it's war then," I said, still smiling. "What's your next step, if I may ask?"

"Damned if I know," he said, absently kissing my wrist as he gazed at the water. "I've been trying to come up with an idea ever since this happened. I was too clever by half, and it may cost us all our freedom. It's amazing that I, of all people, could be taken off guard by a double-cross such as this."

"How did you leave it?" I asked.

"I stayed for as much time as I could, [illegible]. Lelia was in charge and may be complicated. But they're coming to the island in two weeks, and they'll expect us to sign on the dotted line then—or have our assets attached in court."

"Look, I already know Lawrence is a crook," I told him, "but I can't prove it with just one memo and circumstantial evidence—like the kind of class he belongs to. Not to mention that Lawrence covers his ass so well, he might hold a degree in paperhanging. But two weeks is better than nothing—and since it's all we've got—I hoped you might not disdain my aid, if it only involved investigative reporting."

"If you honestly feel as you've just laid it out there," he told me, searching inside me with those incredible red-gold eyes, "then help me destroy them as they deserve. That's what it's all about."

PART 4

London
September 1814

TWO YEARS AFTER MEYER AMSCHEL ROTHSCHILD'S death, almost to the day, the united heads of Europe met at Vienna to decide how they would divide up the European continent, now that the tyrant Napoleon had been incarcerated on the island of Elba.

In London, Nathan Rothschild was receiving another luminary in his chambers—one who'd helped put Napoleon on the rock.

"Lord Wellington," said Nathan, "I understand that your wish has finally been granted, and that you are given permission to retire from the field of battle."

"Yes," said Wellington. "As I've often observed, anyone who's ever seen a battle, even for a day, would not willingly choose to see one again, even for an hour."

"And yet you do so well in a field for which you have no taste. Imagine, if you'd chosen something you'd loved, what you might have accomplished!"

"Yes, I can see that you are the living example of that, Rothschild. It's said of you always that you love money better than anyone else has ever loved it. And now you're wealthier than anyone—living or dead—has ever been—rich enough to have saved the British Empire from devastating ruin, and most of Europe as well."

"Money has bought freedom and a way of life that even my father could not have imagined when he began," agreed Nathan. "The power of wealth for good—or ill—should never be underestimated."

"I understand that with Europe now free, you and your brothers are beginning something new, something that will give you even more control."

"It's a simple idea, really, and a service that has been provided by financiers informally for centuries. We call it a clearinghouse."

"You're changing money for the crowned heads of Europe—is that it?"

"That and far more," said Nathan. "Until now banks have provided financing or interest on deposits. But henceforth, we'll be able to change coin as required—even during wartime—without depressing the value of any currency. In effect, we will control the stability of currencies in this fashion."

"It will be a great boon to the economy of Europe—a kind of common currency market," agreed Wellington. "I admit, I've never been so astonished as when I left Spain after defeating the French army there. We entered France to meet Napoleon's armies as they retreated from Russia—and the gold I received from *you* was sent through France—the country of the enemy—and in French coin! How did you work this miracle?"

"We persuaded the British government to spread the rumor that they were devaluing their own currency. As a result, the French permitted us to bring British gold into France, thinking that in doing so they were draining the enemy's gold supply. We used it to purchase letters of credit drawn on Spanish banks. In this manner, we moved the money across international borders, avoiding both suspicion and taxation. My dear Wellington, one day governments will understand, as bankers do, that the purse strings are the only strings worth pulling. And a just government is one that supports a free economy."

"Ah Rothschild, you're a man of genius and ambition. I am only a poor soldier, sick to death of war. For myself—now that I've an annuity and a title, I long only for peace. I leave tomorrow for my estate in Ireland, where I'll 'tend my own garden,' as Voltaire once advised us to do. And may there never be war again in our time. What has made you rich has made me weary."

"Do not take too keenly to planting, is my advice," said Nathan. "One never knows what the future may hold. My father was a chess player, you know. He always used to say that the best player was not the one who could see ahead; rather, he was the one who could adapt his strategy to the placement of the pieces at any given time. And that's true of many things besides chess."

"It's surely true in battle," agreed Wellington. "But I wanted to say good-bye before I went into retreat in Ireland. I even thought of bringing a gift in thanks for all that you've done for me—and for Britain—but I couldn't imagine what one might give a man of your wealth and position. You've already a title you do not choose to use. Is there something you've wanted that I might provide, in thanks for all your aid?"

"In fact, there is," said Rothschild. "I'd like you to accept a gift from me."

"From you? Impossible! You've done so much already. . . ."

"My dear Wellington, you must remember that the gifts a rich man bestows always have strings attached—that's how he becomes so rich."

"What is it then?" Wellington laughed. "You pique my curiosity."

"This small basket," said Nathan, "which I hope you will keep by your side at all times. No—don't open it now. Inside, you will find some small gray birds, and I will tell you what I want you to do with them. . . ."

THE PAYOFF

Money is the root of all civilization.

—*Will and Ariel Durant*

WE HIKED OVER THE HILL THAT NEXT MORNING, LELIA and Pearl riding in the cart behind like a small army preparing for battle.

When the Vagabond committee showed up two weeks hence as new proprietors, someone would have to show them the ropes of the business they'd bought. Since Lawrence might recognize Pearl and would surely know me, we two would have to remain in hiding at the castle during their stay.

Therefore, we hit upon Georgian to demonstrate the foreign exchange operation. Today was her first day of training and she was none too pleased.

"Camera F-stops are the only numbers I understand," she complained as we walked before the cart, kicking up dust. "They told me I have to explain this stuff as if I've been doing it all my life."

"How tough could it be?" I asked her. "After all, if Pearl's made millions at it in only a few short months, anyone can do it!"

I glanced over my shoulder at Pearl, who shot me a look from her perch in the cart. Georgian, Tor, and I stepped aside to let the horse and cart pass, jouncing Lelia and Pearl as they descended the mountain.

We went through the streets between rows of small stucco houses, their fronts stenciled in turquoise and gold, with little gold balconies and flower trellises. At the end of the street stood the two-story structure, long and thick, with a peaked roof like a granary.

"This used to be the sail makers' barn," Pearl explained. "It was the only industry in town before we arrived; but we needed shelter at once for our business. So we paid them enough to go build themselves another."

It was a big, dark building, smelling faintly of mildew and the sea, with high vaulted ceilings in front, and at center a stairway up to the loftlike second floor. At the front desk, I glanced at the sign-in sheet, which bore names of some pretty weighty international firms, presumably doing business there even now.

"European clients?" I asked Tor as our group headed upstairs.

"Middle Eastern . . . Oriental . . . you name it," he said with a smile. "Anyone who wants to avoid taxes and is willing to play by our rules is welcome."

Upstairs was a long, dark hallway with a small window at the far end. At either side was a row of doors; we entered the first room at left. Pearl went to the large desk across the floor, decorated only by a single lamp, and picked up some papers. Beside the desk was a tiny switchboard of vintage make, and a bank of phones on a table just behind it. Instead of the standard wire service "ticker tape" light panel, Pearl had a blackboard with a piece of chalk, where she'd already scratched up today's currency rates by the time we'd collected chairs from against the walls and taken our seats before the board.

"Okay, friends," she said, all business, "we're trading foreign currency here—'FX' to you—and this business has a lingo of its own, like any other. Georgian, when our buyers come in, you're our seasoned professional trader. The first thing you'll explain to them is how we make our money. Keep it simple. Show them the rates we use and give a few details. For instance, tell them that each morning you phone up the large money-center banks to check world rates, and then you set our rates against our vehicle currency, which happens to be the gold Krugerrand—''

''What's a 'vehicle currency'?'' Georgian asked.

''The one against which we compare the others, sweetie—the numeraire.''

''I will *explique*,'' offered Lelia, raising her hand. ''You see, *chérie*, you cannot change dollars against francs and francs against marks and marks for pounds sterling—it will all be too confusing. So you choose one kind of money to make value with, against all the others.''

''Okay,'' said Georgian, looking a bit dazed as Pearl began again.

''Once you've explained to them how we establish the vehicle rate, you'll tell them how we—''

''Wait,'' said Georgian. ''How *do* we establish the, um . . . vehicle rate?''

''We set it a few pips above market,'' said Pearl. ''I'll show you the formula when we've—''

''What are pips?'' asked Georgian, sounding slightly desperate.

''Percentage interest points,'' said Pearl with controlled patience. She glanced sideways at Tor and me with an arched brow, as if asking whether to continue.

''Why don't you start by defining all the terminology?'' I suggested to Pearl. ''That might make it simpler to follow.''

''Good idea,'' Pearl agreed. ''Now, for one thing, every currency has a nickname of its own. It's not in any book; it's just the slang we traders use with one another when making deals. For instance, Italian lira are called 'spaghetti' and British pounds sterling are 'cable' and French francs are called 'Paris' and Arabian riyals are called 'Saudi.' When you're doing a trade, you refer to the size of the deal as tiny or a yard—so one million lira, for example, would be 'a yard of spaghetti.' ''

''I can't believe I have to learn all this jargon in under two weeks,'' Georgian told me under her breath. ''I can't even remember what 'ropes' are—''

"Cable," corrected Pearl, squinting at her with thinly veiled irritation. "But that's hardly important—I'll give you a list. The critical thing is that you understand how deals are done. Now, there are two markets in the FX business: the spot, meaning now, and the forward, meaning then. Which leads us into the distinction between hedging and speculating." She picked up her chalk.

"You see, *chérie*," Lelia interjected calmly, "it is really quite simple when you think of this—that you may offer the price the money has today, or instead you may choose to guess the amount you hope the money will have tomorrow. But there are different ways to agree to buy the money, and—"

"I can't stand it!" cried Georgian, jumping to her feet. "It's clear that even *Mother* understands this better than I do!"

"It certainly is," said Pearl firmly. "Lelia—how would you like to replace your daughter on the trading floor?"

"Oh, I am happy, happy, happy for doing so very important a thing!" said Lelia, glowing with this recognition of her worth. "But one problem I fear—it is my speaking of English. I think it is sometimes too much suffer even for the ears of my friends."

"That's okay, sugar," said Pearl, coming up to put an arm around her. "When I'm through with you, you'll be such a hotshot, you could be speaking Russkie and no one would notice."

Pearl asked the rest of us to leave for the afternoon so she could begin Lelia's intense training alone. So Georgian headed off with relief to take more photos around the isle, and Tor and I headed back to the castle for lunch and a plotting session—until later that day when the time differential would permit us to phone Tavish in New York.

"I *know* Lawrence is a crook," I told Tor. "I found a memo from him about parking—he's planned this gig as long as you have yourself. If only I could prove it before he learns too much about *us*."

"I shouldn't be too concerned about all this," said Tor as we climbed the hill. "I don't think any of us shall go to prison or even be brought to court. These gentlemen are unlikely to draw attention to us, if it means drawing attention to *themselves*. I'd wager anything that they've *all* tried to coerce their own firms into parking money here—in a tax haven they themselves own. As you pointed out, that's not only illegal evasion of taxation, but using their positions for private financial gain. Furthermore—those who are bankers, like Lawrence himself, are prohibited by law from trading FX in direct competition with their own institutions! They're in double jeopardy. They'll surely want to conceal their involvement; and I doubt they can prove ours, in terms of implicating us in actual theft."

It was true. Though the Depository Trust might be filled with counterfeit bonds, it'd be awfully hard to trace how they got there, or where the real ones had gone. Although Lawrence had bought out Tor's loans—and taken over those callable bonds in the process—we couldn't be sure he suspected that duplicates existed somewhere (after all, ours were the *real* ones!)—and he'd agreed to turn them over to us as soon as we signed over the island to him. We still had time to do so before their due date for recall.

As for Tavish and me, we had only to self-destruct our programs in order to erase them in an instant. We'd never used any passwords—or put any money into accounts—in our own names. In point of fact, none of us could be proven to have benefited from crime. For the most part, it would be hard to prove we'd even engaged in one.

So it was still possible for us to wrap things up neatly without getting caught. But that wasn't enough for me. I'd progressed well beyond mere concern for saving my ass. I had wasted four months of my life—all without accomplishing one damned thing that Tor and I had initially set out to do. The picture seemed bleak, all right, but I was far from finished. That you've missed your goal doesn't mean you don't still have one.

Tor and I were passing through a grove where orange trees, heavy with blossom, scattered richly scented petals on the orchard floor. Tor snapped off a twig from a nearby tree, and twined it in my hair. Tossing his arm across my shoulders, he inhaled the aroma as we continued on our way.

We came upon a cluster of small boys, running down the rows of trees, carrying roughly cut wooden birds covered with spring flowers. Tor laughed, reached in his pocket, and scattered a handful of pennies among them. They scrambled to pick up the loot, chattered their thanks with merriment, and dashed away.

"It's a very ancient Mediterranean tradition," Tor explained. "Around Easter, young boys make hand-carved wooden swallows, paint them, deck them with flowers, and go about begging for coins. It's mentioned in the oldest of writings and legends."

"It's a very charming custom," I agreed.

"It reminds me of that children's fable of the bird in the gilded cage. A bird that—like you—had to be left free in order to sing. I've thought of it often these last months. It's been nearly impossible, staying away from you like this, after what's passed between us. I couldn't bear not to hear your voice—I wanted to phone you each night, and to wake with you each morning. But I knew any such gesture on my part—even if it were possible—would be construed by you as the worst form of—"

"What?" I said, halting in my tracks and staring at him. I couldn't believe my ears. Then I burst into startled laughter. He, too, had stopped in surprise to look at me. But I couldn't stop laughing; there were tears in my eyes. Tor watched me in stony silence.

"Perhaps you could share the joke, if it's not asking too much," he suggested with irritation. "It seems to amuse you that I should want you—and perhaps it is a bit odd, after all."

"That's not it." I choked down the laughter as I brushed back my tears. "You don't understand; I was furious with you for leaving like that. I'd have called *you*—if you'd only told me how! I was absolutely miserable, wondering why you didn't phone, why you didn't write, what had become of you. And all the while, you were only trying to make me happy by setting me free like that little bird!''

Tor looked at me with those strange flame-colored eyes as it dawned on us both precisely the sort of admission I'd at long last made. His stony expression faded into the familiar wry smile.

''It does seem odd,'' he admitted, ''that two people whose minds share a powerful wavelength—and whose bodies combine so beautifully, I might add—should require a translator to interpret such a simple thing as feeling.''

''Perhaps you can translate *this* simple feeling,'' I said, returning the smile: ''I love you.''

He paused a moment, as if he'd never before heard the word. Then he pulled me to him with one swift movement, embraced me, and buried his face in my hair.

''I believe we've arrived,'' he whispered.

■

BUT THOUGH TOR AND I MIGHT HAVE GOTTEN OUR ROmantic bearings at last, seas were still choppy when it came to more pragmatic ventures.

As the days trickled by, bringing closer the arrival date of the island's new owners, my mood progressed from real fury (the *vendetta impassionata*, as Lelia called it)—to intense determination—to righteous indignation—to helpless frustration—to miserable desperation—at last to hopeless exhaustion. And though I spoke to Tavish daily and racked my brains day and night, in the end I had no solution, nor a way to snatch us from the grasp of the nefarious Vagabond Club.

At the forefront of all our minds, of course, was that *these* were the very men against whom we'd made our wager! It was to expose men such as these that we'd risked and lost everything.

These were the sort of men who'd leveraged Bibi out

of his bank—a bank built by nickel-and-dime investors at the cost of their lifeblood. A bank built by people who believed that bankers would honor their word—protect deposits and increase assets—instead of slipping those assets under the counter in bad loans to their pals and bribes to indulgent senators. Men like these should be drawn and quartered in the old town square—not invited to the White House to dine. But that wasn't the way it worked.

But the cruelest cut of all from my perspective, strange as it might seem, was the club itself. Not only the Vagabond Club—which held no special carte blanche—but *all* such clubs.

These clubs did not exist in order to make the world a better place. They performed no service, delivered no product, provided no function—such as improving their members through learning or counsel to take productive and valued roles in society. Men like these joined clubs like these because they believed they already *were* the most valued members of society, and they wanted to shut everybody else out.

If the main purpose of the Vagabond Club had been only a little boyish camaraderie, who would care? But this so-called brotherhood was a license to unearned privilege *outside* club walls. The last three CEOs of the Bank of the World, for instance, had been chosen in the paneled rooms of private clubs like these. They were not selected for intelligence, competence, productivity, leadership, or value, nor were the handful of men who chose them necessarily qualified to judge such things. They were chosen *because they belonged to the Club*!

I felt it was time to end this ghost government of the American economy—but the task was daunting and time was running out. Inevitable as fate, the night came at last—the night before the arrival of the Vagabonds. I gave one last call to Tavish to see if he'd found a single trace of anything I might pin on Lawrence. I'd been so desperate in these last two weeks, I'd even asked him to phone his teckie pals around the bank to troll for gossip—but this, too, had proven fruitless.

Tonight he sounded as gloomy as I felt. We knew that by ten o'clock tomorrow, Aegean time—when the ship from the mainland arrived here on the isle—it would be the end. And there wasn't a damned thing that we could do.

"Though it's no help at all," said Tavish on the watery-sounding line, "there's one rather amusing thing I thought might cheer you. I spoke with your secretary; Pavel always has the juiciest gossip around the bank. Guess what the fates have brought your old boss, Kiwi? He's been blackballed from joining the Vagabond Club!"

"Not really?" I gasped. "How could something like that happen?"

"It seems it was during the secret vote to decide on his admission," Tavish explained. "But Pavel says that hearsay indicates it might have been Lawrence *himself* who cast the dissenting vote."

"Impossible," I assured him. "I have it from the horse's mouth—Lawrence was his only sponsor. You'd hardly peg him as a chap who'd change his mind at the finish line."

"Nevertheless, even Kiwi believes it," Tavish told me. "You can't imagine his behavior. Pavel says he's been locked up for days, wearing mirrored glasses and frothing at the mouth! No one seems to know, either, if he's still next in line to succeed Lawrence at the bank. The only thing that would cheer me more would be if Karp got deported to Germany!"

We hung up, laughing a lot and pretending we were more uplifted than we were. I told Tavish I'd phone the next day with a postmortem on our joint fate, once I knew what it was. But if Kiwi's blackball was the only news Tavish could dredge from the bank, I was afraid I knew our fate already.

■

THE SUN ROSE BRILLIANTLY ON THE DREADFUL DAY—casting its sparkling diamonds indifferently upon the sea beneath, like that old tale about pearls before swine.

The swine boat had not yet arrived, but those in our group looked as if *they* were the ones being taken to slaughter as they headed over the hill to town—leaving Pearl and me behind at the castle to hide our recognizable faces. I lay on the sun-splashed parapet in an absolute daze, mindlessly watching a butterfly moving like a silvery bit of paper among Lelia's many flowers.

I couldn't bring myself to believe that—right or wrong, success or failure—this was really the end. It didn't seem possible, after all our cleverness and hard work, that we could go down in a complete shutout, without scoring a single point.

Pearl went off to the hot pool to bathe alone, probably so that we didn't have to look at each other like miserable, helpless lumps while waiting for the knell of fate that might not come for hours.

I sat there alone and watched the butterfly; it was zipping around with no apparent goal, sometimes bouncing off the wall, riding an air current in an aimless circle, disinterestedly exploring a flower. How strange that an insect could survive without any goal, I thought, when people never could.

Lawrence, for example. I knew from the first that his every act was triggered by a motive, though I hadn't been able to prove any of them to be nefarious and illegal. His motive for keeping the auditors at bay was because he planned to buy this island and park money here. And his motive for sponsoring Kiwi to the Vagabond Club was—

I sat up in my deck chair and looked at the butterfly more closely. That flitting, aimless motion around one spot—could it be camouflage?—or an evasion tactic? What *was* Lawrence's motive for sponsoring Kiwi to the Vagabond Club? And if a guy like Lawrence did sponsor someone like Kiwi, surely he'd first make certain beyond a doubt that no one would blackball his handpicked candidate. It *must* have been Lawrence himself who'd put the kibosh on Kiwi—but why?

Then in a sudden flash, I understood. I had been

asking myself the wrong question, all along. The question I should have asked was not *why*—but *when.*

When did Lawrence propose Kiwi for membership in the Vagabond Club? Answer: The week my quality circle project started.

When did Lawrence move my project to report directly to him? Answer: When Pearl and Tavish suggested that it should be moved to the Managing Committee, or to the audit department, instead.

When did Lawrence decide my project should continue, instead of being canceled? Answer: When I threatened to turn it over to audit.

When did Kiwi get blackballed from club membership? Answer: The week my project ended and I left for vacation.

Last question: If Lawrence did all of the above because his goal was to get rid of *me* so he could do something crooked on the bank computer systems—*when* would be the perfect time to do it? Answer: Now! Now!! *Now!!!*

What an idiot I'd been not to see it. It must have been Lawrence all along! Lawrence who'd killed my very first proposal about security—Lawrence who'd arranged to bash any chance of that job with the Fed—Lawrence who'd tried to ship me to Frankfurt for the winter.

So understated was Lawrence's handling of others, that poor Kiwi might even think all those ideas were his own—even that someone other than Lawrence had dumped him from the club. But the fact that Kiwi *had* been dumped for outlasting his usefulness—that *I* was absent from the bank, and that Lawrence was about to arrive *here* on the island—assured me that the time was now.

I had to get to those phones and call Tavish at once. I leaped to my feet and raced for the house, cursing Pearl for leaving me in the lurch. I didn't have time to dash to the pool to get her help—but I hadn't a clue where things were kept here at the castle, or where to find something I might use as a disguise.

I went through three or four rooms, pawing through trunks and barrels and boxes until at last I found an old black burnoose with a hood to cover my hair. I threw it on quickly, then grabbed one of Tor's big silk hankies and fastened it over my lower face. Casting a quick glance in the rusty wall mirror, I seemed to resemble a Franciscan monk wearing a surgical mask—but it would have to serve. I threw on a pair of leather sandals, hitched up my skirts, and tore up the side of the rocky slope, without bothering to follow the switchback; it took too long.

It was half an hour, running at full clip, before I sighted the tiled roofs of the village. By the time I reached the waterfront, having scrambled the last hundred yards like a goat, my heart was beating like a caged bird, as much from fear as exertion. I was terrified I might be too late.

Coming up to the sail makers' building, I pulled up the hood closely about my already veiled face, with only one eye peeping out, as an Islamic hausfrau might do. As I reached the entrance a distinguished Middle Eastern chap in Western-style clothes stepped out the doors, and I winced at my luck—an authority who could unmask my unprofessional disguise.

"*Allah karim*," he said, brushing past me with some distaste. "God is beneficent"—in other words, ask Him, not me, for a handout. I'd have to speak with Georgian sometime about the state of her wardrobe. On the other hand, maybe it had made me safe—for the moment.

I raced up the stairs inside and, with skirts still hiked, dashed for the room with the phones. I threw the door wide with a bang, barged in—and froze.

Lelia was standing there at the blackboard, chalk poised in midair. Before her, sitting in neat little classroom rows, were Tor and Georgian—and the dozen or more members of the Vagabond Club!

Lelia stared, they all craned in their seats to check out this disruption, and Lawrence—in the last row, only inches from me—started to rise from his seat! Bowing and backing up as fast as I could, I retreated into the corridor and reached out to shut the door. But Tor was too fast for me. As soon as he saw me, in three swift strides he bounded across the room. He grabbed me by the arm, shoved me against the wall, and slammed the door behind us.

"What in hell are you doing here?" he whispered frantically. "Have you completely lost your mind? What if they'd recognized you?"

". . . desperate . . . telephone . . ." I muttered through the layers of veil and hood.

"What do you have stuffed in your mouth—an apple?" he said irritably, yanking open my hood. He stared at the handkerchief, then smiled as he put his hand beneath my chin, turning my veiled face to left and right for a better view. "How charming," he said, still smiling. "I rather like this new look of yours. Perhaps if you only wore the napkin and nothing else . . ."

Just then the door, not fully latched, swung open again, Lelia again frozen with chalk in her hand, Georgian wincing at my choice of attire, and the others continuing to stare. Tor remained, still grasping my arm, his other hand beneath my chin—smiling sheepishly at the group within.

"Forgive me," he said, recovering himself and clearing his throat. "Gentlemen—may I present Madame Rahadzi, the wife of one of our most important clients from Kuwait. She's asked to be shown to a private room where she waits until her husband has completed his business here. If you'll excuse me? . . ."

"Of course," Lelia replied for them, bowing to us. "And *saha*, Madame Rahadzi!" As Tor closed the door again, more firmly this time, I heard her say, "Now let us to continue, gentlemen."

Tor nearly dragged me along the hallway. At the far end, he shoved me into an empty room with hardwood floors, stepped in behind me, shut the door, and—leaning against it—pulled me to him, pulled down my veil, and kissed me so deeply I felt my knees go weak.

"Madame Rahadzi," he whispered when we surfaced for air, "would your husband mind it very much if I played around under your burnoose?"

"This is serious!" I said fiercely, trying to focus on what I'd come for.

"I should say it is," he agreed. "I can't keep my hands off of you—I can't keep my mind on track—that's more than serious!" He bent down and kissed me again, until I could feel it in my toes. "Madame Rahadzi, I'm going to have a *very* hard time returning you to your husband. Why don't we lock the door and pretend you aren't married?" he said.

I took a deep breath and held him away as he reached for me again.

"I must get to those phones and call Tavish," I managed to get out. "I've figured out what Lawrence is up to—but now I have to prove it."

"You mean, something more than what we already know?" said Tor, his eyes lightening.

"I think he's their banker," I told him. "Where else did they get all that money—hundreds of millions of dollars—to buy up those loans? I think he's done some creative financing in these last few weeks."

"Without passing through the loan department for approvals?" he suggested.

"He's the head of bank-wide data processing. If *we* could get into the system and grab that dough, why couldn't *he*?—he'd only need it for the short term—"

"Especially if he cut a few corners, like refusing to pay us," agreed Tor. "I think you're onto something. The only phones for international calls are right there in that room. Stay here. I'll get Lelia to wrap things up quickly, drag them off, and show them a bit of the island or something. Never fear—I'll get you in there."

■

"COULDN'T YOU HAVE FOUND A MORE REASONABLE hour to phone?" Tavish moaned, his voice gravelly with sleep. "Have you any idea what time it is here?"

"This is an emergency," I told him. "Get up, dunk your head in ice water, make a pot of coffee—anything.

I want you to get on-line to the bank in San Francisco and hit every file till you find what I'm looking for."

"What are you looking for?" he asked.

"Money. Lots and lots of money. About four hundred million dollars in short-term, low-interest, no-penalty loans."

"Anybody we know?" asked Tavish, his voice sounding considerably more cheerful.

"Only time will tell," I said.

■

BUT TWO HOURS LATER, I WAS A BIT LESS OPTIMISTIC. We were still on the phone, Tor and Lelia having left a note that they were taking the Vagabonds on a lengthy walking tour of the island, and would meet me for cocktails at the castle.

I was lying on the floor of the boardroom, the World War II telephone sitting on my chest, the receiver propped on the floor near my ear as Tavish and I pounded through our paces.

"I've tried every bloody loan in the system that's short-term and has low rates," he informed me. "I even checked those loans for automobile flooring, recreational vehicles, small boats, and student education! I'm afraid—rumors to the contrary—that there are no four-year-college degrees that cost over fifty million dollars!"

"There has to be *something* out there," I said, cursing under my breath. "There aren't that many of these Vagabonds. How many men would they trust in a deal this confidential—twenty-five—fifty—a hundred max? And these guys are all CEOs of major corporations—not idle heirs to a dimestore fortune. They may be well paid, but not *that* well. They don't have that kind of cash lying around their checking accounts. They got it from someone—and that someone was Lawrence. Why else was he so frantic to keep me and the auditors off that system?"

"Terrific theory—I'm in total awe," said Tavish. "But I've rather exhausted my supply of rocks under which to look. Any new ideas—so long as we're footing the global bill for satellite communications?''

''Try the password file,'' I said. ''Whatever Lawrence did, he must have done under his own password.''

''You can't be serious,'' said Tavish. ''There are fifty thousand IDs out there. He might have used anything—or two or three, or a dozen—or a hundred!''

''Try Lawrence,'' I suggested.

''Beg pardon?''

''Lawrence!'' I repeated. ''L-a-w-r-e-n-c-e. Or Larry—something like that.''

''Don't be absurd,'' said Tavish with disdain. ''No one would use his *own name* as a password—like a birth date or mother's maiden name—it's the very first thing a thief would think of trying.''

''We have nothing to lose at this point,'' I said. ''Humor me—give it a shot.''

Tavish went off mumbling, but a few moments later, I heard exclamations—then a shriek.

''There *is* a password of Lawrence!'' he cried. ''By God, this is the bloodiest, ugliest, most criminal thing I've ever witnessed in my life!''

''What is it?'' I cried, sitting up and clutching the phone to my ear.

''I'll print it all off on Charles Babbage so we'll have the hard copy later,'' he said, ''since I can't print on your line. But I'll read the basics off to you. I hope you've got a quill handy.''

''What is it?'' I repeated, clutching the pen and pad in my hands.

''It's stocks, ducky—three hundred million in bank stock—all of it transferred in the last two weeks.''

''Bank stock? You mean, shares in the Bank of the World?''

''Believe me, I haven't a clue where it came from,'' said Tavish, ''but I can quote you name, rank, and serial number for mucho millions of shares.''

Perhaps Tavish didn't know where it had come from—but I did. And I smiled. It wasn't too hard to figure out where there was a block of bank stock that size, and one that was really handy. In fact, it could be transferred without ever leaving the bank's computer system.

They'd ripped off the bank's own employee pension fund!

■

IT WAS LATE AFTERNOON—NEARLY EVENING—WHEN I cut through the woods and dropped down below the castle to enter from the small peninsula beneath. From there, cobwebbed internal stairwells led directly to the observation tower overlooking the parapet and the sea—without passing through the courtyard, where I might be seen.

I knew that sound traveled better uphill, and thought it might be to my advantage to learn first how things stood—down below on the parapet, where Lelia, Tor, and the Vagabonds would by now, presumably, be having cocktails.

But when I glanced through the slitlike window, I saw only three figures standing on the vast expanse of tile: Lawrence, and my two friends. Their voices reached me as clearly as if we were standing three feet apart.

"Baroness Daimlisch," Lawrence was saying as Tor poured the champagne, "Dr. Tor informs me that you are the key principal in this consortium. I hope you won't mind if I say I find it difficult to believe you've been in the world of high finance for long. Your expectation to receive an additional markup of thirty million for this business is quite untenable."

"Then why did you agree to it *initialement*, monsieur?" asked Lelia sweetly.

"Not only is this piece of rock nearly worthless as a property," he said, ignoring her, "but as purchasers we have no assurance we can continue forever to operate here as a tax haven. Geographically, we're between Greek and Turkish coastal waters. If those countries chose to dispute ownership—as they did with Cyprus—we'd find ourselves in a lot of trouble."

"And yet you wish so badly to purchase this valueless business of ours that you attempt to force us to give it to you. I hope that you do not mind, monsieur, if I tell you that you are not very *gentil*."

"In the real world, madame—the world of business and finance—being a gentleman is hardly a criterion. If you do not sign the contracts we've brought today—for the one million we've agreed to, and no more—I assure you that we shall take ungentlemanly measures to remove you and your colleagues from your positions with no further consideration. We all agreed to take a risk in this venture—but a calculated risk. And my calculations suggest we've risked enough by assuming those loans that financed you in the first place."

"It's hardly a risk," Tor chimed in, bringing the champagne glasses from the table where he'd poured them. "Not when you plan for your bank, and all the corporations of which you men are officers, to park their assets and execute taxable contracts here, as soon as you take over."

"It's illegal for banks and other corporations to park reserves in tax havens," Lawrence said coldly, "as surely you know."

"They all do it nevertheless—as surely *you* know," said Tor with a smile. "What would the board of your bank think if they knew you'd been pressing them to an illegal act from which you yourself would profit as a principal?"

"I don't know where your information comes from, but these unfounded allegations would hardly hold up in a court of law," snapped Lawrence.

"This isn't a court of law, and more than one brilliant reputation has foundered on the shore of innuendo," said Tor.

But he must have wondered—as I did—why Lawrence seemed so unconcerned about his reputation at the bank. After all, if they learned one of their key officers was a principal in a tax haven trading against the bank, wouldn't they take steps to protect themselves first? Unless Lawrence had far more influence at the bank than I had guessed.

And then, of course, I saw the picture in its entirety—and red blood rushed up behind my eyes. He hadn't *stolen* that stock from the pension fund—he owned it! This wasn't a short-term takeover of our little island business at all; that was only the tip of the iceberg. They didn't just want a tax haven to shelter other people's funds—they wanted their own country. And now I knew why!

"You clearly don't understand with whom you're dealing," Lawrence was saying to Tor.

"But I do!" I cried from my window in the tower, unable to control myself one second longer.

All three looked up and squinted into the sun—and I saw Tor smile.

"Ah," he said with casual grace, "it seems our silent partner has found a tongue at last."

"Silent partner?" said Lawrence, glancing at him.

I lifted my robes, dashed down the spiral stairs three at a time, and came out onto the parapet.

Lawrence looked at me coldly. I was certain I must be the very last person on earth he wished to see just now—but to do him credit, he didn't show it.

"Banks, perhaps you can explain just what you think you're doing here," he said.

"I'd rather explain what *you're* doing here, instead," I told him, trying to control the fury in my voice. "You sons of bitches are taking over the bank!"

Tor's head snapped around to stare at me, and Lelia put her hand to her breast. Lawrence stood there, his face an expressionless mask. His pupils were slits of icy self-containment. He set his champagne glass on the wall and pulled a packet of papers from his breast pocket.

"Indeed we are," he told me gravely. "There's little you can do about it at this late date—so I suggest you make the best of your situation, accept our million-dollar offer, and autograph these papers. That is—if you can figure out which among you might be empowered to sign."

"Perhaps someone can fill me in, first, on just what's happening?" suggested Tor.

"They must have been planning this deal for ages," I told him. "They own hundreds of millions in bank stock—maybe bought on margin at fifty cents on the dollar—but bought by them with their own money. As soon as they own this island—which we've conveniently provided for them—they can incorporate a parent company *here*, under their own laws, transfer that bank stock to this company—and have it take over the Bank of the World!"

"A fairly accurate summary," Lawrence agreed, still holding the contracts between his fingers. "We'd planned to incorporate in Liechtenstein or Luxembourg or Malta—or wherever—until *this* opportunity arose. But we've spent time and money enough; I believe it's time to wrap things up. You see, nothing you do can really stop us now. Essentially, we own this island and the bank as well."

He was right, and I knew exactly what they'd do as soon as they took command. They hadn't gone to all these lengths to install better management, improve services, or increase corporate assets for the other shareholders. When they got their hands on a business like that—they'd milk it dry, and not only of dividends. They'd do what had been done to Bibi's bank. But this time, on an inconceivable scale. What they were proposing might topple the entire U.S. economy. And thanks to the fact we'd handed a brand-new country over to them, everything they did would remain entirely within the parameters of the law—laws that they would clearly be able to write all by themselves!

The biggest mistake I had made in all of this was in failing to recognize genuine evil when it stared me in the face. I'd been pussyfooting around with Lawrence, trying to slip one over on him by proving the bank's security was no good. What a fool I'd been—when the corruption itself started at the top; not in a computer system or a steering committee, but in the black and power-hungry mind of a single man. I might not be able to stop him—but I certainly wasn't going to help him get away with this.

But suddenly Tor appeared at my elbow, handing me a glass of champagne with a smile. What came next was a real surprise.

"My dear Verity, let's have a toast to the better man, and try to assuage our failure with the million he's offered. After all, we put up a good fight, but even the cleverest among us can't always win."

I stared at him, but for the life of me couldn't imagine what he was doing. Tor never gave up without a fight. Indeed, I'd never seen him give up anything—including his courtship of me—until he won.

But he clinked his glass against mine and raised it aloft as Lelia, in confusion, did the same.

"To Lawrence, and his compatriots who are still off exploring the isle. Too bad they can't be here as well to witness our capitulation. But their celebration will surely be just as joyous when they return to see these contracts duly signed and witnessed." He took another sip of the wine and gripped my arm with unnecessary force. "And to Verity, our silent partner, whose cleverness put this deal together. Though it isn't the prize you'd hoped for, I'm certain the million you've earned will compensate somewhat for the billion or so you've invested these three or four months—"

"What did Banks have to do with that capital?" demanded Lawrence. "I thought that the baroness was the backer of this deal."

"Not in the back, but in the front," said Lelia, gracing me with a conspiratorial smile.

Obviously, everybody knew what was going on but me.

"What the baroness means," Tor explained, "is that *she* was the front for our whole investment—the purchase of the bonds we used as collateral, the acquisition of financing, as well as the island's purchase and creation of the business. But the mastermind—and financial angel, if you will—was Verity Banks."

"That's completely absurd," said Lawrence. "Where

could Banks raise capital of that magnitude? You're talking about a billion in securities!''

He looked more than a bit uneasy. It was clear even to him that things weren't as they should be. But I myself was still at sea.

''Perhaps you should tell him how you raised the funds,'' suggested Tor, with that ravishing smile. He pressed my arm more firmly, and added, ''*Exactly* how you raised a billion dollars—and on such short notice, too!''

And then, of course, I knew, and I smiled myself.

''I stole it,'' I said sweetly, polished off my champagne, and went to replenish my glass.

''I beg your pardon?'' said Lawrence. When I glanced up from pouring, his pupils had disappeared in tiny slits. He actually removed his glasses and polished them, as if that would help him hear better.

''Do I stammer?'' I asked politely with raised brow. ''I stole a billion dollars from the bank's wire services—oh, and a bit from the Fed Reserve as well, which I shouldn't forget to mention. We used it to buy securities—but we'd planned to return it all as soon as we made our thirty million. Of course now that you've reneged on your part, that won't be possible.''

Lawrence stood there silently, as we three beamed at him.

''Of course, it really won't matter—since I obviously didn't move the money through accounts in my own name. Those stolen funds will never be traced to *me*,'' I explained. Then I paused a beat. ''They'll be traced to you, of course—and your little friends.''

Everything was so silent there on the terrace, it seemed we'd been sucked away into a vacuum. Lawrence was deathly pale and he gripped his glass so tightly I thought he might crush it in his hand. Surely it had dawned on him that no court of law in the land would believe a man who could put together a leveraged buyout of a major bank and a country—but who tried to pretend he knew nothing about how a billion in stolen money had wound up in his own bank account.

Suddenly, Lawrence flung his glass across the terrace—directly at my head—and Tor shoved me out of the way as it struck the wall behind.

"You miserable goddamned bitch!" he screamed in a voice so shrill, for a moment I thought it was an animal.

I recovered from my shock, but Tor had raced to Lawrence's side and pinned his arms as he screamed and screamed. Then all at once, everything was pandemonium as Pearl and Georgian came rushing down the road to the parapet, the Vagabonds just behind. Everyone was shouting at once and trying to hear at the same time as Tor wrestled the shrieking Lawrence into a nearby chair.

Lelia banged a spoon on her champagne glass until we all came to order.

"Gentlemen," she said quietly, smiling at them, "I suggest you all are having some seats again. Our class is not yet finished—and we have something we wish for you to sign. It is not a contract, though."

"What's going on here, Baroness?" asked one of the bankers, his eyes riveted on the frothing Lawrence.

"We are just going to do the screwings in you like a nail," she said sweetly, and she poured some more champagne.

■

"DO YOU LIKE IT?" TOR ASKED, STUDYING ME IN THE candlelight.

"This is the most disgusting stuff I've ever tasted," I told him, spitting over the wall.

"One must acquire a taste for retsina," Pearl said.

"It tastes like chlorine from a swimming pool," I told her.

"It's pine resin," Tor explained. "The ancient Greeks used to seal their wine in pine barrels to discourage the Romans from stealing it."

"Right," said Georgian. "Give me a shooter of absinthe any day."

She was balanced on the seawall, wearing a dark red

caftan, the sky beyond a pearly orchid, the sea dipped in flamingo. The candles had melted down in the walls, the few remaining flames flickering and sputtering. The musicians sat around in a small circle, the soft tinkling of the santouri mingling with the sweetish strains of the bouzouki. Tor had been teaching Lelia the complex steps of a dance as the rest of us watched the candles burn out one by one.

"That little flute is a floghera, and the soft drum is a defi," said Georgian. "We listened to them every week down in the harbor before you arrived. I hate to think of leaving this place—it's lucky we could stay an extra week while Tor went up to Paris with the Vagabonds to get back our bonds."

"Do you think they'll ever let Lawrence out of that nuthouse in Lourdes?" asked Pearl. "I guess when you're that emotionally constipated, it just eats away your brain."

"He certainly did flip out," I agreed. "But his colleagues seemed to see the reasonableness of our case. They've returned our collateral, unloaded their 'takeover stock,' and signed those confessions of their intent to defraud—all without a glitch. Just so we'd put all the stolen money back where it belongs and take it out of their names. But even though they'll be hauled up on charges, they'll surely get off easily. And they're bound to blame it all on Lawrence, since he can hardly speak for himself."

"We gave them a little push in the right direction—just in case." Georgian laughed. "Pearl and I took them to the hot pool while you were here chatting. I've got some rather nice Polaroids to show you. . . ."

She handed over the glossy photos—there were the dozen Vagabonds, splashing about in the buff and pouring champagne on Pearl! They were having a hell of a time.

"We thought it best to have some insurance of blackmail, in the event things didn't work out with you," said Georgian, admiring her handiwork. "Look at that resolution! You can see every drop of champagne on her tits! I had to hide in the bushes to take these, too."

"You two are ruthless." I laughed.

"The deadlier of the species," agreed Pearl. "You taught me that."

At midnight, when the musicians had wrapped up to go, we sat in the cool, damp darkness and watched the first of the procession ascend the mountain. The candles were massed below us at the sea, and we could see against the plum-and-silvertinted waters the silhouettes of figures as they broke and moved single file slowly, singing, up the hill.

"It's called the Akathistos," Tor whispered as he sat with his arm around me. "One of the kontakion—the only one that's remained intact. It was written by Serge the Patriarch on the eve of the deliverance of Constantinople from the Persians—a hymn of thanksgiving. But they sing it at midnight here each Easter."

"It's beautiful," I murmured.

Lelia was rising from her seat.

"Now we will go to hear the Mass," she said. But as the others rose Tor restrained me with a hand.

"Not the two of us," he said, and turning to the others, he explained, "We've still some unfinished business."

So the others trooped down to the cart to follow the procession across the cone of Omphalos to the little church. When we could no longer see the lights of the procession, Tor turned to me.

"Today is the last day of our wager," he told me. "And I believe you've won. At least, I assume you came a bit closer than I in gathering the thirty million we'd agreed upon. I'd like to discuss our settlement. But first, I'd like to discuss us."

"I don't know if I can even think about this," I said. "It seems my life's been ripped away and a new one put in its place—one I'm hardly familiar with just yet. I want to be with you, but four months ago, I couldn't even imagine having a relationship."

"I don't want a relationship with a capital *R*," he

assured me, studying me carefully in the dim moonlight. "What about starting out with a small-*r* relationship?"

"How about no *r* at all?" I suggested with a smile. "Then it will be an elationship."

"Absolutely." He smiled. "But if I get you that job at the Fed, you'll be in Washington, and I'll still be in New York. Haven't we had enough years apart already? Tell me—exactly how old are you now?"

"I must confess that I *am* on the dark side of twenty. Why do you ask?"

"Old enough to know that very few people are graced—as we've been—with what we have. I'd like to shed some light on the matter. Just a moment; I'll be right back."

He went into the house, leaving me out on the parapet with the bottle of cognac and glasses. I poured myself a drink and watched the clouds scudding across the moon and listened to the waves softly lapping at the fortifications below. When Tor returned, he was carrying a large portfolio. He dumped the contents out on the tiles and lit a match. I saw his coppery hair illuminated in the glow, then glanced at the pile on the ground just as he picked up a sheet and lit it.

"What are you doing?" I cried in alarm. "Those are the bonds! The real ones! That's a billion dollars' worth of paper you're setting fire to! Are you mad?"

"Perhaps," he said with a smile, his flame-colored eyes turned golden in the firelight. "I've wired the Depository from Paris with the serial numbers of the counterfeits in their vaults. I thought it best to destroy all trace of how they might have arrived there—just in case the Vagabonds ever got wise and tried to do unto us as we've done unto them. Our point has been made nonetheless. Those brokers and bankers who refused a physical inventory will have trouble explaining how the securities *they* sent there are forgeries—though the clients they sold them to will be protected by their proof of purchase— Oh, do sit down, my dear—you're making me nervous, standing on one foot like that."

I was making *him* nervous! I sat on the edge of the table and watched as he lit one paper after another until the mass caught fire. At last, the flames died down to a mass of crumbling ash, and the wind lifted and moved it away in slow curls across the parapet. By morning, a billion dollars would have disappeared without a trace, along with our theft. Were the next thirty-two years of my life to be like that, too? Tor came to me and drew me into his arms as if he'd read my thoughts, and buried his face in my neck and inhaled my hair.

"I have to go home and water my orchids and think about this for a while," I told him, my arms around him. "When I got into this wager, I had no way of seeing I'd be a different person at the end. I'm not prescient like you."

"Clearly," he said as he kissed my throat and held me away to search my face. "But instead of worrying about yesterday or tomorrow, what of today? I have the feeling there's something we've left undone."

"Undone?" I said, surprised. "What does that mean?"

"Don't you see that—although we've stopped the Vagabonds in their progress—anyone choosing to try the same again could do so, with or without a country of his own, as *they* might have done? Furthermore, any bank can easily buy up another using overvalued stock as part of the purchase. There's simply no way, through the international economic system, to ensure that bank assets are properly valued or insured—or that any greedy bastard who comes along tomorrow can't pull the same caper as today."

"What does this have to do with us?" I asked.

"With you at the Fed—examining their reserves and asset liquidity," he said, smiling that strange and dangerous smile as he looked at me in the moonlight, "and me analyzing acquisition portfolios through the exchanges, we ought to do a rather thorough job of it, wouldn't you say? I'd wager that I could knock off more illicit mergers and corrupt takeovers than you could in, say, a one-year time frame. What do you think of that, my little competitor?''

I shot him a look of indignation—but I couldn't stay sober for long. I started to laugh.

''Okay—how much do you want to bet?'' I said.

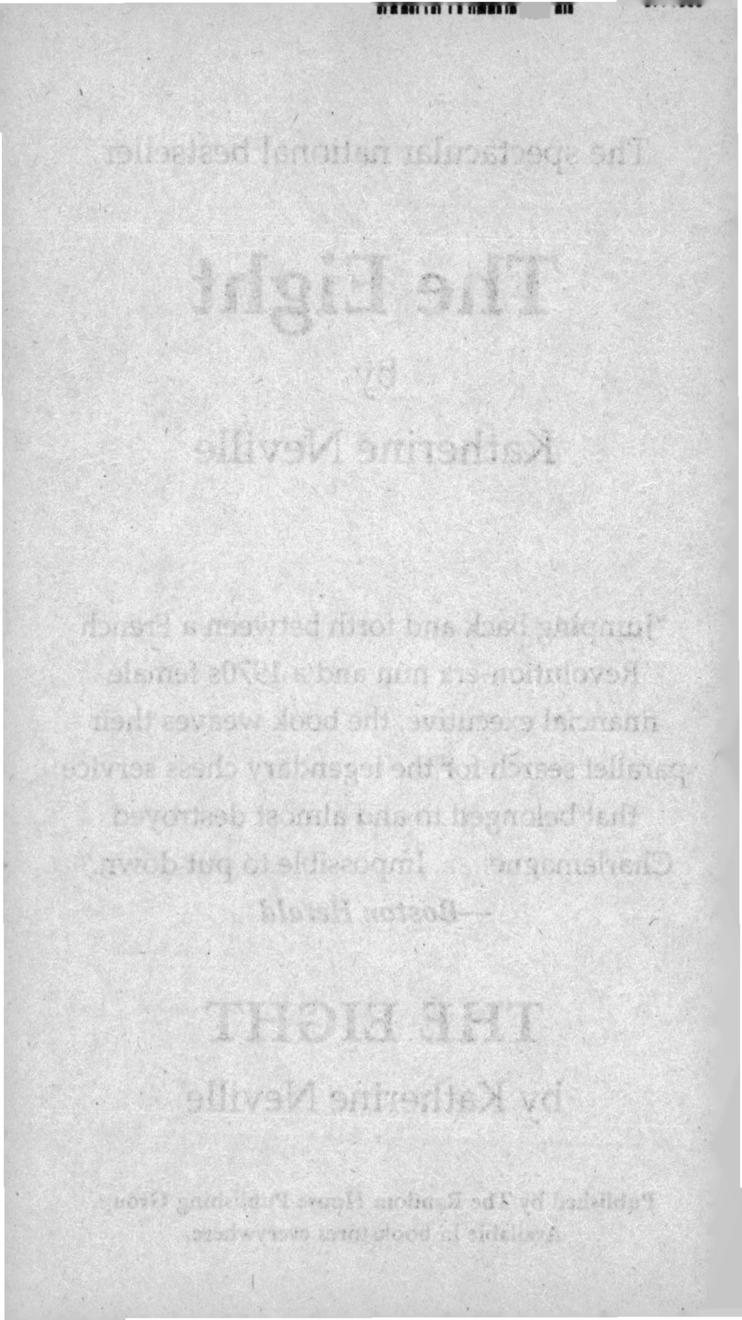